Bad Bachelor

STEFANIE LONDON

sourcebooks
casablanca

Originally published as *Bad Bachelor* in 2018 in the United States of
America by Sourcebooks Casablanca, an imprint of Sourcebooks.

Published by Sourcebooks Casablanca, an imprint of Sourcebooks.
P.O. Box 4410, Naperville, Illinois 60567-4410
(630) 961-3900
sourcebooks.com

Library of Congress Cataloging-in-Publication Data

Names: London, Stefanie, author.
Title: Bad bachelor / Stefanie London.
Description: Naperville, Illinois : Sourcebooks Casablanca, [2018] |
   Summary: "If one more person mentions the Bad Bachelors app to Reed McMahon,
   someone's gonna get hurt. A PR whiz, Reed is known as an 'image fixer' but
   his womanizing ways have caught up with him. What he needs is a PR miracle
   of his own. When Reed strolls into Darcy Greer's workplace offering to help save
   the struggling library, she isn't buying it. The prickly Brooklynite knows Reed is
   exactly the kind of guy she should avoid. But the library does need his help... As she
   reluctantly works with Reed, she realizes there's more to a man than his reputation.
   Maybe, just maybe Bad Bachelor #1 is THE one for her"-- Provided by publisher.
Identifiers: LCCN 2019050848
Subjects: GSAFD: Love stories.
Classification: LCC PR9199.4.L5948 B33 2018 | DDC 813/.6--dc23
LC record available at https://lccn.loc.gov/2019050848

Printed and bound in the United States of America.
SB 10 9 8 7 6 5 4 3 2 1

So bad it's good? Save that for your Liam Neeson movie marathon. Bad has no place in your love life.

With more ways than ever to meet your future Mr. Right, you'd think the women of New York would be at an advantage. But trying to find a soul mate in a world of Instagram filters and mobile dating apps is tough—expectations are high and attention spans are low.

It's all too easy for your date to check out potential matches while you're in the restroom. He could be swiping right on a dozen other ladies in the vicinity. Chances are he'll be out the door in less time than it took to read your bio.

So how can you sort the good guys from the serial bachelors? That's where the Bad Bachelors app comes to the rescue. Our app is designed for the women of New York to have their say. Going on a date? Simply search your bachelor's name to see what his previous dates have said about him.

How do reviews work? Well, it's no different from leaving a review for your favorite restaurant on Yelp. Bad Bachelors uses a five-star rating system and allows users to share more detail in the review section. We'll guide you through the process with review prompts—such as "Did he turn up on time?" and "Did he want to know more about you?"—to ensure that your review provides useful information.

We respect that our users may not feel comfortable posting reviews under their real names, so we do allow anonymous reviews. However, only verified users can add a bachelor to the Bad Bachelors database—your profile must be linked to identifying information such as a Facebook profile or phone number.

If your date moves to the bedroom, that's great! However, we ask that you keep reviews PG-13. We don't need to re-create Fifty Shades of Grey here.

User MidTownMolly had her best date in weeks thanks to reading a positive review of her workplace crush. "The review spurred me to ask him out, and he said yes! We went for dinner and talked nonstop until he dropped me off at home. I'm already excited for date number two."

If you date a stand-up guy and it doesn't work out, don't be afraid to let your fellow ladies know he's a potential catch. Remember, even if he didn't knock your socks off, that doesn't mean he's not happy-ever-after material for someone else.

We're in the business of helping you make informed choices and we rely on our users to get quality data. So, next time you date, don't forget to rate. Tomorrow, we'll be posting a profile spotlight on our "Bad Bachelor." This one should be avoided at all costs. I don't want to spoil anything before our post goes live, but let's just say he's our worst-rated bachelor yet!

With love,

Your Dating Information Warrior

Helping the single women of New York

since 2018

Chapter 1

"Reed McMahon is a master manipulator. He knows exactly what to say and how to say it. Don't believe a word he says."

—*MisguidedinManhattan*

S weat beaded along Darcy Greer's brow as she smoothed her shaking hands over the full skirt of her wedding gown, her fingertips catching on the subtle pattern embroidered into the silk. Long sleeves masked her tattoos, turning her into a picture-perfect bride. Her mother had been so pleased when she'd chosen this dress because the priest wasn't too thrilled with her ink. Truthfully, Darcy hadn't been thrilled with looking like a cake topper. But she also hadn't wanted any drama to mar her big day. Besides, it was only a dress.

I can't believe I'm doing this...

She sucked in a breath and surveyed the picturesque blue sky with clouds so white and fluffy they looked like globs of marshmallow. A flawless day, the photographer had assured her, all the better to capture this important moment.

Empty space stretched out from all sides, making her feel small, like a blip on the surface of the earth. A smile tugged at her lips and she tilted her face up, letting her eyes flutter shut as a cool breeze drifted past.

Just breathe...

Her best friends stood before her, looking immaculate in their bridesmaid gowns. They each wore a color that matched their personality—Remi, the ballerina, in soft pink and the ever-practical Annie in a classic royal blue. These women had gotten her through the toughest times in her life. They'd made sure she was here today in one piece, finally ready to release her old life.

"All right, ladies." The photographer raised his camera, the big lens pointing in Darcy's direction, unblinking like a Cyclops's eye. "Everyone get into position. I want this first shot to be perfect."

Darcy's heart skipped a beat. This was it, her last opportunity to put a stop to this madness.

You okay? Annie mouthed.

Darcy nodded. She would be okay, she would be okay, she *would* be okay.

Pop!

The first shot hit her straight in the ribs and stung like hell. She gasped, her hands clutching at the spot where crimson bled across the white silk. The camera clicked. A moment captured.

The pain was more than she'd expected, but there was something deeply satisfying about seeing the splash of color against the ugly, white silk.

Pop! Pop! Pop!

"Wow, guys, give me a minute." Darcy backed up, dodging a green balloon sailing through the air. "And don't look so happy about being able to throw stuff at me."

She reached for a water balloon of her own and took aim, Remi's soft-pink dress in her sights. Her throw was off and the balloon burst against the ground, splashing orange paint over Remi's feet and legs.

"Now you look like a beautiful sunset," Annie said, hiking up her long skirt in one hand and reaching for a ketchup bottle filled with red paint. She ran over to Darcy and squeezed a stream of it all over the sweetheart neckline of her wedding dress. "Ah, much better!"

"I look like I'm starring in a remake of *Psycho*." Darcy glanced down at herself. Red paint dripped along her body, running in rivulets across the silk. "I need more color."

"Coming right up." Remi grabbed a small paint can and a tiny brush. "Watch me unleash my artistic side."

She splashed purple paint in a flamboyant arc, turning Darcy from a horror movie extra into something out of a modern art exhibition.

"This is wonderful, ladies." The photographer clicked and clicked, capturing Darcy's shock as Annie paint bombed her out of nowhere. "These photos will be amazing."

A high-pitched shriek pierced the air as Annie turned on Remi and the two girls battled it out with their respective weapons. Soon, the elegant dresses looked like a finger-painting lesson gone horribly wrong. Splotches of orange and green peppered Remi's blond hair.

They'd decided against using the proper paintball guns on advisement of the venue owner—safety first and all that jazz. Getting shot at close range apparently stung like a bitch. So they'd spent a painstaking hour filling up water balloons and other containers before the shoot.

Darcy picked up another ketchup bottle filled with paint and used it to make a sad face on the bottom of her gown. "I hate this goddamn dress."

Annie covered her mouth in a failed attempt to stifle her laughter but instead smeared paint across her cheek. "Sorry, Darcy. I know you only picked it to keep your mom happy."

"You're right." She frowned. "The whole damn wedding was more about her than it was about me."

Annie slung an arm around Darcy's shoulder. "Come on, this is your anti-anniversary party. Your 'thank God I got out while I could' bash. It's time to celebrate, not mope about your family issues. That dress is ugly as hell anyway."

The beginnings of a smile tugged at Darcy's lips. "It *is* ugly, isn't it?"

"Fugly even. Seriously, I didn't have the heart to say anything because you know I love your mom"—Annie wrinkled her nose—"but I wouldn't even bury my cat in that thing."

Out of nowhere, a balloon burst between them. "Hey!"

"Two for the price of one," Remi crowed, her Australian accent amplified as she raised her voice and pumped her fist in the air. "You beauty!"

"We were having a moment," Darcy said in mock protest.

"Yeah, and now it's a rainbow moment." Remi toyed with two fresh water balloons, a cheeky grin on her face.

"Do it," Annie said. "I dare you."

"Do you double dare me?" Remi walked toward them, her arms swinging in that dainty, fluid way of hers.

Annie tried to make a break for it, but Darcy wrapped her arms around her waist and held on tight. "Get her, Remi."

The balloons exploded and both girls screamed.

By the time they'd run out of things to throw at one another, Darcy was famished. The owner of the venue—which was normally an outdoor paintball arena—had kindly allowed them space to conduct the photo shoot and let them make use of the open-air cafeteria as well.

She glanced at the picnic table full of cupcakes and let her eyes settle on the top tier of what would have been her wedding cake. Apparently, you were supposed to save it for the first anniversary.

But what if the wedding never happened? Surely that was an excuse not to keep it. Except her mother had; she'd saved it when the rest of the cake had been thrown into the trash. Now, a year after Darcy *should* have been married, her mother had foisted it on her like some kind of cruel joke.

It said a lot about their relationship.

The offending lump of cake—covered in thick, Italian-style marzipan icing—sat in the middle of the table. Poking at it with her forefinger as if it were an alien species, Darcy considered her options. Eat it or toss it?

"Let me show you how to deal with this." Remi picked up the cake and signaled for the photographer to follow her. She hurled it into the air and it landed with a satisfying splat on the ground a few feet away.

"See?" she said. "No more devil cake."

Annie clapped her hands together. "Now we can get this party started."

This "party" was something that had taken a lot of convincing. Darcy had wanted to let the day come and go without ceremony or recognition. She would have been perfectly happy to sit in her sweats and eat ice cream straight out of the tub like a Bridget Jones cliché. But she was the kind of woman who could admit when she was wrong—the trash-the-dress party had proved far more entertaining than she'd first anticipated. Plus, it made for an interesting catch-up rather than their usual wine-and-vent sessions.

Every week, the three friends got together to unload their latest funny stories and problems on one another. It'd been a tradition since high school, when Darcy and Annie would meet to do their homework together. Translation: talk about boys and update their Myspace profiles or whatever else sixteen-year-old girls did before smartphones.

Remi had completed their trio when she'd moved to New York from Australia a few years ago and ended up being Darcy's roommate. These women had glued her back together—and *kept* her that way—since her wedding had been canceled the previous year.

"These look delicious," Annie announced as she pored over the tiered cake stand filled with cupcakes supplied by Remi. "I wish I could bake like you."

"I wish I could bake something without setting the oven on fire," Darcy quipped as she washed her hands at the small outdoor sink, scrubbing at the green paint under her fingernails. "But we can't all be Martha Stewart, can we?"

"Just don't tell my family that I'm using sugar and wheat flour—they'll think I'm poisoning you." She cringed. "Everything in their house is hemp-infused, plant-based bullshit."

"Well, I can't cook *or* bake," Annie said. "According to my mother, that means I'll make a terrible wife."

"Ugh." Darcy forced down a wave of nausea. Nothing could recall her lunch faster than the thought of motherly expectations. "Please don't use the *W* word around me. Mom's been trying to set me up with her friends' sons. Literally any and all of them. I don't think she cares who it is so long as I get a ring on my finger."

"Did you remind her what happened the last time she set you up with someone?" Annie snorted. "Or won't she take any responsibility for that?"

"She dropped off the top layer of the wedding cake as a reminder that I should be trying to find 'the one.' *And* she had the audacity to tell me she hadn't given up on me, like I'm some hundred-year-old spinster who's about to be eaten by a houseful of cats."

Annie blinked. "Right."

"If only she could see you now." Remi grinned.

The photographer hovered around them, snapping pictures of what must have been a hilarious scene: three women in full hair and makeup, wearing paint-splattered dresses and eating cupcakes. What a sight.

"Maybe she meant it as an encouragement," Remi said.

"The message couldn't have been clearer. It's been one year and she wants to know why I'm not out there trying to find a man so I can fulfill my purpose as a woman and start making babies."

"Screw that." Remi wrinkled her nose.

Annie opened the champagne with a *pop* and poured the fizzing liquid into each of the three champagne flutes. She measured precisely, ensuring each glass was equal.

"Here's to you, Darcy. Happy anti-anniversary." She handed the glasses out and held up her own. "Congratulations on dodging a bullet."

"Still feels like I got shot." She shook her head as their flutes all met in a cacophony of clinks.

"Better to have loved and lost than to have gone down the aisle with the wrong guy," Remi said, sipping her drink. "Here's to moving on."

There was a chorus of "hear, hear" from the girls as they clinked their glasses again.

"Nothing like a new fling to take your mind off the old one," Remi added, gesturing with her champagne. "Forget about relationships and have a little fun. You've earned it."

It sounded so simple when she said it like that, but Darcy was out of practice. Besides, there was this little, tiny problem that had developed since the almost-wedding. The very few times she'd gotten close to getting physical with a guy, her nerves had kicked in and she'd lost all sense of excitement. Was *sex anxiety* a thing? Because that was probably what she had.

"I don't know…" Darcy sunk her teeth into the pile of frosting on her cupcake.

"Think about it. If you quit a bad job, you would start looking for another one, right?" Annie said. "You don't stop working because you had *one* bad job."

Remi snorted. "Only you would compare a relationship to a job."

"I'm serious. Getting a job and dating aren't all that different. You have to assess each other to see if you're a good fit and then you have a trial period to see if it's going to work out."

"Do you make your dates sign a contract too?" Darcy teased.

"I'll tell you when I have enough time to go on a date." Annie sighed. "Like in the year 2045."

Remi peeled back the brightly colored paper on another cupcake. "As ridiculous as that comparison is, she has a point. One bad experience doesn't mean a lifetime without sex. It's perfectly acceptable for men to enjoy casual sex, so why not us too?"

The group murmured their agreement. Even the photographer nodded emphatically.

"Have you been with *anyone* since Ben?" Annie asked.

The girls looked at her curiously. Darcy hadn't spoken much about the demise of her engagement or her failed attempts to put herself back into the dating scene. She'd always been the most private one of the group. Growing up with a mother who was emotional to the extreme had made her develop a natural resistance to showing her feelings.

Maybe that's why you never saw it coming. You didn't ask enough questions or pay attention to the right things.

"The only kind of sex I've had in the last year has been with me, myself, and I." Darcy sighed.

"Oh, a threesome." Remi winked. "Kinky."

"And even that hasn't been too spectacular," Darcy said. "Not for a lack of trying, mind you. I've had a few dates, but anytime the guy even tries to kiss me, I freeze up."

Annie reached out and patted her knee. "You're stressed. That's totally understandable."

"What do I have to be stressed about? I love my job, I'm healthy, I have a great family…"

Annie raised a brow.

"Okay, not *great* but they're decent human beings…most of the time." Well, barring the cake incident. "Finding your fiancé making out with someone the day before your wedding doesn't have to ruin everything. Single is the new black, right?"

"I love you, Darcy, but this #foreveralone thing is stopping right *now*." She set her drink and half-eaten dessert down on the table. "You need to break the dry spell."

After the split, getting back into the dating scene had gradually moved from the "too hard" basket to the "never, ever again" basket. Except there had been this little voice in the back of her mind lately, whispering dangerous thoughts to her, asking questions she wasn't sure how to answer, like whether she was happy being alone. Or if she'd be able to watch her beautiful friends walk down the aisle and be okay missing out on that experience herself.

Despite hating her mother's über-conservative ways, deep down, she still wanted the white-picket-fence dream—a wedding, a loving husband…even the babies.

But all that required her to date. And that meant facing up to the fact that she had no idea *how* to date. She'd given up her chance of learning those lessons when she'd fallen head over Dr. Martens at nineteen. Now, eight years later, she was starting from scratch with no skills and no real experience to draw on.

Casual sex might sound like a piece of cake to some people, but the idea of dating was terrifying enough. As for casual sex? Darcy had never had a one-night stand. Ever.

"I wouldn't even know where to go to meet someone," she muttered. "And I deleted Tinder the second I started getting dick pics. Not to mention that I'm so out of practice even if I *could* make it past a first date. I can't flirt. I can't do witty banter. I can't play the temptress. So how am I supposed to have casual sex?"

And that wasn't even the hard part. Being able to trust someone again and not be paranoid that they were secretly living a double life, now *that* was the real challenge.

"Being celibate is so much easier."

"Hey, if that's what you want, I support you one hundred percent." Annie reached out and squeezed her shoulder.

"Say the word and we won't mention the dating thing ever again," Remi chimed in.

Darcy scratched at a fleck of dried paint on her dress. "I *do* want to get back out there," she admitted. "But I'm scared I'll pick the wrong guy again."

"Then you need to find a guy who's trustworthy," Annie said, pausing to sip her drink. "Someone who wants the same things you do."

"And how would I find a guy like that? It's not like I can trust what they write in their dating profiles."

"You could try the Bad Bachelors app," the photographer piped up. All eyes turned to the young man in the vest and bow tie. A heavy-looking camera hung from a thick strap around his neck. "I read about it the other day."

Darcy shook her head. "What on earth is the Bad Bachelors app?"

"Oh!" Remi bounced up and down in her seat. "I heard about this. Apparently, someone started this app that has all the single guys in New York listed and you can rate and review them."

"You're kidding." Darcy blinked. "So it's Yelp...for guys?"

"Or Uber? You know, go for a ride and then rate your driver," Remi said and Annie choked on a mouthful of cupcake.

Darcy shook her head and downed the rest of her champagne, immediately reaching for the bottle to refill her glass. "You're making this up."

"I swear, I'm not. Does anyone have the app?" Remi asked, but the girls shook their heads. "Give me your phone."

Within minutes, they'd downloaded the app and were browsing through profile after profile of gorgeous, single New York men. Each profile had at least one photo, a brief description, and a star rating. It looked as though the app was fairly new, but there were already a ton of reviews posted.

"These are hilarious," Remi said, swiping across the screen. "Look at this one. 'Trenton Conner, thirty-eight. Doctor. The only thing that's large about this guy is his ego and his credit limit.'"

"Let me read." Annie grabbed the phone and swiped a few times. "'Jacob Morales, thirty-nine. Technology executive. Things were going well until he rolled over and fell asleep right after sex. Then his maid came into the bedroom to shoo me out of his apartment.'"

Darcy laughed. "Oh my God."

"This one's nice." Annie held the phone in one hand and her drink in the other. "'Darren Montgomery, thirty-one. IT manager and entrepreneur. Darren is a lovely guy, very sweet and kind. Romantic. But we didn't have much in common—I hope he finds the right woman for him.' I'm going to mark this one as a favorite for you."

"Gimme." Remi grabbed the phone back. "What about this guy? 'Alexei Petrov, thirty. Investor. This guy will take you on the ride of your life...' Oh no. Looks like he might've been dating a few women at once. Next!"

Darcy pressed her fingertips to her temples. "No cheaters, please."

"Oh dear." Remi turned the phone around to show a photo of the most beautiful man Darcy had ever seen. And yes, *beautiful* was the right way to describe him. He was so perfect looking, and yet there was a hardness to him, like a marble statue—beautiful and cold and unyielding. "'Reed McMahon, thirty-two. Marketing and PR executive. Reed McMahon is a master manipulator. He knows exactly what to say and how to say it. Don't believe a word he says. He goes through women like candy.'"

Darcy wrinkled her nose. "He sounds like one to stay away from."

"Look, you can sort by highest and lowest rated." She laughed. "This guy is the lowest rated—number one on the Bad Bachelors list. Fifty women have rated him already. Serial dater, not interested in commitment, colder than an iceberg…looks like he always has a different woman on his arm."

"What about the good guys? *Are* there any decent men on that thing?" Darcy sighed. "I feel like I'm searching for a unicorn."

"We'll find the right guy." Remi's eyes sparkled at the thought of playing virtual matchmaker. "Why don't we swipe through and put a list together?"

"A list will make it easier. I like that idea," Annie said.

Remi rolled her eyes. "Of course you do."

"Say I *hypothetically* agree this is a good idea," Darcy said, drumming her fingers on the edge of the table. "What am I supposed to do? Walk up to these guys and say, 'Hey, you've got a five-star rating. Let's date'?"

"It's called recon." Annie grinned and Darcy could already see the cogs turning in her mind. "We'll go through the top-rated list and help you narrow down some options. You never know, with six degrees of separation and all that, you might have a friend in common who can introduce you. But at least you know up front that the guy is a decent person…unlike if you met someone randomly at a bar."

Darcy rolled the idea around in her head.

Maybe this wasn't such a terrible idea: a lower-risk, research-led type of dating. As a librarian, that appealed to her. She could get all the information she needed up front and avoid the dangers associated with spontaneous dating.

Besides, what harm could a little research do?

Chapter 2

"When something seems too good to be true, it usually is.
Reed McMahon is not the guy you want him to be."

—*LittleMissMidTown*

Every muscle in Reed McMahon's body tensed, anticipating, assessing. He shifted his weight, moving his hips as he prepared to unleash all his frustration into a single powerful swing. He'd had the kind of week that made him want to pound something into oblivion.

With a white-knuckled grip, he pulled back and focused on his target until the rest of the world fell away. The baseball whizzed past him and his bat connected with air.

Reed swore under his breath and reset his position. His team, Smokin' Bases, was one run down in the final inning with two outs. Losing to a group of Columbia graduates who loved to fist-bump one another was *not* an option. The week from hell would not be made worse by a crushing ball game defeat.

Reed *had* to make this swing count.

The pitcher went through his routine of rubbing the ball in his gloveless hand and stretching his neck from side to side. He drew his arm back and sent the next ball sailing in Reed's direction. It was perfect—fast, but perfect. He swung and the bat made a satisfying crack as it sent the ball flying through the air, eventually bouncing in the empty pocket between right and center field.

He took off, pumping his legs as fast as he could toward first base. An outfielder scooped the ball up and threw it hard, but he overthrew it and it grazed the top of the first baseman's glove, giving Smokin' Bases enough time to get a runner across home plate.

That tied them. "Keep going!" the third base coach shouted as their captain, Gabriel, legged it down the home stretch.

Reed ran for second, but the other team recovered and their second baseman landed the tag perfectly across Reed's midsection.

"Out!" the pitcher called. But Gabriel had already made it home and the run counted.

Reed's hit had given them a one-run victory. The rest of his team whooped and jogged onto the field to shake hands with the opposition.

"I knew you'd save us." His teammate and friend, Emil Resnik, slapped a hand on his back as they walked off the field.

Reed grabbed his workout bag and fished around for a bottle of water. "Just waiting for the right moment to attack."

"Like a snake." Emil flattened his fingers against his thumb and made a striking motion. "I think we've earned a beer or three."

"God yes."

Reed brought the water bottle to his lips and tossed his head back, relishing the slide of the cool liquid down his throat. After a game, his body felt looser. The tension he carried with him Monday through Friday eased out of his muscles. This was the thing he looked forward to each week.

He pulled his phone out of the small pocket on the side of the sports bag and turned it on. Multiple alerts made the device buzz in some kind of digital battle cry.

One hundred notifications. That *couldn't* be good.

He scrolled through the list and sure enough, the majority had "Bad Bachelors" in the title. "God fucking damn it," he muttered. "Not this shit again."

"That was a killer hit you had there, man." Gabriel came over to where Reed stood, ready to congratulate him on locking in the win. "What's going on?"

A new message appeared in his inbox from a colleague titled *I knew you got around but daaamn.*

"There's some bullshit new app that rates New York 'bachelors.'" He made air quotes with his fingers. "And apparently I'm top of the bad guys list. I've been getting emails about it since Friday."

"Have you checked it out?" Gabriel asked as he whipped off his T-shirt and changed into a fresh one.

Reed glanced at a woman leaning against the black railing that sectioned off the North Meadow diamond from the rest of Central

Park. She was dressed in a suit, which was an odd choice given it was the weekend. "Hell no. I couldn't care less what these women are saying about me. Probably that I'm some heartless brute who only cares about sex."

"Accurate," Emil said with a grin. "And it's nothing you haven't heard before."

"Except now it's out there for the whole world to see and the guys in the office are having a field day." He shook his head. "They think it's hilarious."

He'd come back to his desk after a meeting on Friday afternoon to find some cheap plastic trophy with Reed's picture affixed to it, along with the words *#1 Lady Killer* in bright-red letters. This person had also taken the liberty of "enhancing" the little gold man's appendage with putty.

Classy.

But Reed wasn't worried. Gossip like that tended to fizzle quickly, in his experience. There was *always* something more scandalous to worry about than a man having sex.

"What's wrong with loving women so much you can't have just one?" Gabriel chuckled when his pregnant wife, Sofia, whacked him in the arm with the scoring clipboard. "What? I'm talking about Reed."

Reed stuffed his phone into the pocket of his sweatpants. "They know what they're getting into, but then they cry foul when I don't want to see them again."

"Because they all think they could be the one to change you." Emil dug his elbow into Reed's rib cage. "They think they can tame the beast."

"There's nothing to tame." He picked up his gym bag and slung it over one shoulder.

The sun hung low in the sky. Central Park was busy as always, full of tourists and locals out soaking up the rays now that the cold weather had finally started to disappear. Everything was green again, and that usually put a smile on his face. But Reed's frustration settled like a weight on his chest.

"I'm sure it'll blow over." Emil slung an arm around Reed's neck and pulled him away from the field. "I'll buy you a beer. That should cheer you up."

They made their way to the edge of the field, heading in the direction of the path that would lead them out to West Ninety-Sixth Street. It was Reed's Sunday ritual: baseball in Central Park, beers at his favorite sports bar in Brooklyn Heights so they could watch a game—preferably the Mets—and then he'd head over to Red Hook to check on his dad before going home. Nothing messed with his Sunday routine, not even a shitty mood.

"Doesn't matter anyway," Sofia said with a cheeky wink. "He's got enough money for a therapist. Isn't that how rich people handle their problems?"

Gabriel and Emil, along with a few other guys and girls on the team, were mechanics, and they loved to rib Reed about his white-collar job. Sofia joined in the fun, even though she had a degree and worked in an office just like Reed.

"None of you seem to have an issue with my money when I'm paying for drinks," he responded dryly.

"Yeah, that's right. Maybe we won't buy you a beer after all,"

Gabriel quipped. "Although we did get a new client at the shop. Some trust-fund baby with a hard-on for Audis. God knows why he'd spend so much money on them when he could have something better."

Gabriel and Emil dissolved into their long-running argument about the best luxury car manufacturers and Sofia pretended to stick her fingers in her ears. Reed tuned out the familiar banter. Despite having a salary with enough zeros to make most people's eyes bulge, he didn't live in Manhattan or drive a sports car. A huge chunk of his money went to paying for health care and a near full-time caregiver for his father. The leftover cash was funneled into conservative investments.

Beyond keeping up appearances at work—which required a wardrobe fit for dealing with upper-crust Manhattanites—his home life was fuss free. He'd paid off his DUMBO apartment a year ago when he'd made partner and received a generous signing bonus, and had turned that place into his personal sanctuary.

"Reed?" The woman who'd been watching their game waved to catch his attention. She wore a light-gray suit and her eyes squinted behind a pair of black glasses. "Are you Reed McMahon?"

"Who's asking?" Emil piped up.

"I'm Diana Lay with *Scion* magazine. I was hoping to grab a few moments of your time, Mr. McMahon." She looked directly at him but he could see the hesitation in her face.

In his sweats and a red baseball cap, he looked totally different from the photos floating around online, which were mostly corporate headshots and a few professional photos from galas he'd attended for work. But they all showed the same image—a polished, curated, and tailored level of perfection he prided himself on. A fake version of him that didn't exist at a weekend ball game. Or any other time when he wasn't at work.

Ugh, he should have guessed she worked for *Scion*. They'd been trying since the previous Wednesday to get ahold of him. The "society journal," which could only be referred to as such in the loosest of terms, was now mostly online. But it continued to boast a half-million readership of gossip-hungry people with no lives of their own. *Scion* wrote about the upper echelons of the "socially prominent" in New York, Greenwich, and the Hamptons. Surrounding the articles was extensive advertising for boat shoes and diving watches.

"You missed him," Reed said without breaking his stride.

"I don't think I did." The woman hurried after him, her sensible, low-heeled shoes no match for his well-loved sneakers. "How do you feel about being rated New York's Most Notorious Bachelor?"

"You'll have to ask the man himself."

"So you're denying you're Reed McMahon who works at Bath and Weston?" she asked, out of breath as she tried to keep up with his long strides. "And that you're the son of Adam McMahon?"

At the sound of his father's name, Reed stopped dead in his tracks and the woman almost slammed into him. "Leave him out of this."

She smiled like a cat who'd gotten the cream. "Were you aware of the Bad Bachelors app before today?"

He was tempted to keep walking, but the last thing he needed was for her to think there was a story here. "No comment."

"Come on, you must have something to say about it." She used a cajoling tone that made his blood boil.

He knew her type—parasitic gossip columnists who called themselves journalists but were more likely to talk about a sex tape than anything of substance. However, he wasn't about to let his anger show. That would only make her dig deeper.

He gave her a cool, well-practiced smile and shrugged. "I'm afraid I don't have anything for you."

"Does it bother you that all these women are airing your dirty laundry to the world? Or does part of you believe you're getting what you deserve?"

He kept his gaze steady. "No comment."

"What does your father think about all this?" She looked at him with a bland expression, although he had no doubt bringing up his father was intended to incite an ugly emotional reaction in him. "Do you think you've disappointed him?"

Hell would freeze over before he gave this woman—or anyone—an ounce of satisfaction in seeing him break over this nonstory. "You mentioned you worked for *Scion*, correct?"

"That's right." She held her phone out, the recording app on, ready for a juicy quote he'd never give her.

He'd had dealings with *Scion* in the past, namely when he'd needed to help a wealthy businessman get his family-friendly image back on track after photos leaked of him and his wife engaging in some more unique BDSM activities. As much as he wasn't a fan of *Scion*'s work, he'd never done anything to piss them off.

"So you work for Craig Peterson?" He kept his tone even.

Her tongue darted out to moisten her lips. "I do."

"Craig's a close personal friend of mine." It was a total lie, but he'd met the guy on a few occasions at work functions. He allowed the awkward silence to stretch long enough to make the woman shift on her heels. "In fact, Bath and Weston does good business with *Scion*. I'm not sure he'd appreciate you harassing the source of some important advertising money. Money that, if I'm not mistaken, is quite critical to keeping the company afloat, given how your CFO has been suspected of embezzling company funds."

Thank God he had *that* little tidbit up his sleeve. Rule number one of working in PR: always keep your ear to the ground.

Her face paled. "I'm just doing my job."

"I understand. I'm also doing mine." He paused. "If I find out that you or anyone from your establishment has gone near my father, I will make sure more people know why *Scion* is in such bad shape."

"You'd do that to your close personal friend?" Her lip curled.

"To protect my family? Sure." He leaned in closer to her. "And if I'd do that to Craig, imagine what I'd do to someone I don't care about." Reed didn't wait for a response. Instead, he turned and stalked to where Emil, Gabriel, and Sofia waited for him. "Come on, let's get out of here."

A few hours later, Reed parked in the street outside his father's house. He'd been jittery all evening, unable to sit still and concentrate on watching the game. Eventually, he'd slipped out of the bar while the others were mid-discussion about a fielding error. They didn't need him bringing down the mood.

And he had this horrible, niggling suspicion it wouldn't be long before the reporters went after his father.

The temperature had dropped, and Reed shoved his hands

into the pockets of his sweats as he walked up the steps leading to the front door. The stairs were effectively his father's prison guard, because he could no longer walk up or down them unassisted. But Reed's offers to buy his father a new place—or at the very least have some kind of ramp or elevator installed—had fallen on deaf ears.

The house itself was in serious need of a makeover. The old clapboards were cracked and peeling. At some point they'd been a light blue, but now they looked like flaking reptile skin. Spider webs decorated the corner of the screen door with thin, silvery strands. Reed brushed them away with his hand and wiped his palm down the front of his thigh.

"You know you don't have to come around every weekend." Adam McMahon's raspy voice sounded as he opened the door. Light spilled onto the small landing where a few long-dead potted plants sat.

"I'm hoping one weekend you might let me do some work around his place." Reed walked into the house and embraced his father, careful not to knock the oxygen tank that was his constant companion.

"I'm hoping one weekend you might come here and not give me a hard time." His father paused to catch his breath before they made their way slowly to the living room.

"If it were anyone else, I would show up and do it without asking permission."

"If it were anyone else, you wouldn't care."

Reed grunted his agreement. "Did Donna come by today?"

"Yes." His father frowned. "She gave me a hard time…on your orders apparently."

"She's a caregiver, Dad. That's her job." Reed sunk down into the old green sofa his father refused to replace, sitting in the exact spot required to avoid having a spring poking into his ass. "That's what I pay her for."

"Yeah, yeah." His father ambled over to the leather recliner Reed had purchased a few months back as a surprise gift. One that hadn't been well received at the time—earning a muttered "waste of money" comment from his father—but now bore a nicely worn groove from daily use. "You want a drink?"

"Nah, I'm good. I had a beer with the guys before I came over." His phone vibrated, but he didn't recognize the number flashing up on the screen. Probably someone else poking their nose into his business. He ignored the call and shoved the phone back into his pocket.

Bracing a bony hand against the recliner's armrest, his father lowered himself slowly into a sitting position. Even the simplest of actions left him breathless these days, but God forbid anyone try to help him. Adam McMahon might not be in the best of health, but he'd swat a hand in your direction that would still sting like hell if it connected.

"So tell me about this phone dating thing," his father said. "Bad Bastards something or other."

Ice ran through Reed's veins. "How do you know about that?"

"A lovely young lady came by the house today." His father's lips lifted into a wry smile. "She had a lot of questions about you."

"What was her name?" His fingers dug into the couch cushion.

"I don't know. I didn't write it down." His father rubbed a hand along the whiskery, gray stubble that coated his jaw. "But I told her I wasn't going to talk about my son behind his back no matter how much he needs a clip over the ears."

Of course the old man would turn it on him. "For what?"

"For being a shortsighted idiot. You're telling me you date all these women and not one of them is worth more than a single meal?"

It probably wouldn't help to admit that a good portion of his dates never even made it to dinner—not that the women seemed to mind too much when they were legs up, screaming his name. "I don't have time for a relationship."

"Bullshit. You don't want to end up like me."

Reed's chest squeezed and that made him want to punch something. He hated feeling like he couldn't help his father. And this was the one problem that couldn't be fixed by whipping out his credit card or arguing the old man into submission.

"That's not it, Dad."

"Sure it is." A rattling cough broke the quiet, the ugly sound echoing in Reed's ears.

The muscles in his jaw twitched as he tried to think of a response. He was a master talker, always quick with the right thing to say. But his father's honesty never ceased to render him speechless.

"You should find a nice girl, Reed." His father grunted as he struggled to shift in the recliner. The chair seemed to swallow the old man's deteriorating frame. "You should settle down, get married, have a family…before it's too late."

No way. Fate had stopped him from getting into a sham marriage once before, and he couldn't be happier that he'd dodged that bullet. He was perfectly happy being single and playing the field. And no amount of judgment from his father or some pushy reporter would change that.

Chapter 3

The Bad Bachelors' Club: Nice Guys Need Not Apply!

I know the women of New York are busy being successful and chasing their dreams, so I've rounded up the men you should stay away from. These are the bachelors our users have rated as the worst in the city. We'll start with…

Reed McMahon.

If you've checked out our app, you may have stumbled across him. Don't be fooled by the gorgeous profile picture and endless list of social engagements. He's bad news, ladies.

Reed is a notorious bachelor, known for his smooth moves, career pedigree, and rubbing elbows with the rich. Mr. Image Fixer has spent years practicing his morning-after escape on the women of New York by luring them into his bed (well, not his bed—rumor has it he only has visitors to his hotel room) with empty promises and a talented mouth.

User BroadwayBelle was kind enough to give us the inside scoop.

He'll stomp on your heart without thinking twice, she told us. He's the worst kind of man because he makes you think the world revolves around you…and then he'll have someone drag you out of his office.

Ouch! If you're a dating daredevil, then be our guest, but make sure you take your parachute with you.

Stay tuned for tomorrow's blog post, where we give you tips on how to overcome first-date jitters and make sure he's thinking about you the next morning for all the right reasons. Have your notebooks ready.

With love,

Your Dating Information Warrior

Helping the single women of New York

since 2018

*W*hen Reed walked into his office building the following morning, it was to the sound of whispers. Two junior consultants exchanged looks as they held the elevator door for him. As it slid shut, the shiny reflection showed one of the women digging her phone out of her bag and turning the screen toward her colleague.

"Good morning, ladies," he said, watching them in the reflection.

Their heads snapped up, eyes wide. A chorused "good morning, Mr. McMahon" made him feel way too much like a school principal. But it had the intended effect. The woman put her phone away and the whispering ceased.

The elevator stopped a few ear-popping seconds later on level thirty-six. As Reed exited, he could have sworn one of the women had said, "See, I told you."

Aaron waved and fell into step with Reed, his laptop tucked under one arm. "Hey, man. How was the weekend?"

Never before had such an obligatory office greeting been accompanied by such genuine interest. "Fine," Reed replied carefully. "How was yours?"

"Good." Aaron continued to walk beside him even though his office was in the opposite direction. "Get up to anything interesting?"

"Nope."

"Oh, come on." Aaron nudged him with an elbow. "Cat's out of the bag now. Surely you've got something juicy for me."

Reed stifled the urge to tell the guy to leave him the fuck alone. "What do you want, Aaron?"

"A tidbit. A story to keep me going. I've been married for ten years. I need to live vicariously. If I were your age and single, I'd be all over this Bad Bachelors thing."

"It's not a thing."

"Sure it is. You've been Tiger Woods-ing all over Manhattan and now everybody knows it."

"Firstly, I'm not married, so your Tiger Woods comparison doesn't really work. Secondly…" Reed stopped in front of his assistant's desk. "If your wife is that much of a noose around your neck, perhaps you should look into getting a marriage counselor."

"Wow, for a guy who's getting laid as much as you are, you sure are a cranky fucker," Aaron grumbled as he turned tail and headed toward his office.

Reed sucked in a breath and counted to ten. If he got through the day without actually murdering someone, then he would count it as a win.

Way to set the bar low. Any closer to the ground and you'd trip over it.

"Good morning, Reed." His assistant, Kerrie, smiled. She was the only person at Bath and Weston who seemed to know when not to poke the bear, which made her a rarity.

He'd joked once about marrying her because she was the only woman who would put up with him. But Kerrie, while dedicated and organized, was old enough to be his mother.

"Morning, Kerrie." He nodded. "Should I expect any surprises on my desk today?"

"No." She pressed her lips together. "And I *am* sorry about the trophy. Aaron told me he'd borrowed one of the files from your office. If I'd known—"

"It's fine." He held up a hand. "Honestly. You shouldn't have to question partners about their behavior."

"Clearly I do," she replied with a sigh. "You had an 8:00 a.m. call scheduled with Chrissy Stardust, but her agent canceled a few minutes ago."

He grunted. "Shocker."

"That means you're free until ten." She inclined her head toward his office door. "And I picked up an Americano for you on the way in—peace offering for messing up on Friday."

"It's absolutely not required." He placed a hand on her shoulder. "But I am going to enjoy the hell out of it."

"Good." Her brows knitted together. "How's your dad doing?"

"Frustrating, but no more than normal. Well…" It wasn't like him to air his personal business. Kerrie only knew about the issues with his dad because she'd fielded calls from his father's caretaker, Donna, on a few occasions. But what he considered personal was suddenly open for public consumption. "The woman who kept calling from *Scion* last week got ahold of him. At least, I think it was the same person. She turned up at his house."

"That's despicable." Kerrie shook her head, her lips pursed. "Honestly, turning up at a sick man's home like that…" She broke off with an annoyed huff. "Have they no shame?"

"Apparently not," he said dryly. "They'll probably call again."

"I'll deal with it."

"Thank you."

He headed into his office feeling like he'd already worked a whole day. Perhaps it was time to have a closer look at Bad Bachelors. It pained him to assign energy to such a stupid thing, but if people were sniffing around his father, then he should at least know what was being said about him.

Reed picked up the coffee cup from his desk and dropped into his office chair. A quick search took him to a website with a bright-pink banner, which had a set of glossy lips parted seductively while a manicured finger hovered over them in a *shh* motion.

The website advertised a free download of their mobile app, but it appeared everything could be accessed on desktop as well. His slick corporate headshot looked back at him. It was the same one they'd used for the Bath and Weston website. Underneath that was a little red banner that said "bad bachelor" and another with "most reviewed." Such accolades.

He scanned the reviews, and one immediately jumped out.

"He'll stomp on your heart without thinking twice. He's the worst kind of man because he makes you think the world revolves around you. He'll take you out and treat you like a princess. But don't you dare encroach on his space. Get too close and he'll have someone drag you out of his office."

—*BroadwayBelle*

Ah, Karlie.

The Broadway-show enthusiast with a crazy streak wider than the Hudson.

They'd dated over two years ago, *well* before the app was created. Obviously she still held a grudge. And the only reason she'd been "dragged out of his office" was because she'd breached security and threatened Kerrie after he forgot to call her back after a date. Never mind that his father had been rushed to the hospital with severe dehydration. Reed hadn't even been *in* the office when security had escorted her out. But the facts didn't matter, clearly.

He scrolled farther down the page. Since the site allowed women to review with anonymity, the usernames didn't really tell him much. He could pick a few of them out, but mostly it was nonsense. A good portion of the reviews didn't even say anything specific.

But one made him pause.

"He took me on the most romantic date. Like, Hollywood romantic. We went to the top of Rockefeller Center and looked out at the view. I thought everything was going well. But when we went to a bar, he got really drunk and started talking about all his clients at work. It was totally weird and unprofessional, and I don't know how anyone could trust him."

—*RedheadForNow*

Reed frowned. He had a running joke with Kerrie about how much he hated Rockefeller Center—he'd never been to the top of the tourist trap to see the view. Not once. And since one of the guys at work had proposed to his fiancée there, like something out of a sappy Hallmark movie, Reed had dubbed it off-limits. He loathed clichés, and so he refused to take part in that piece of New York City.

So why the hell was there a review citing a date in a place he'd never been? And the comment about him getting drunk and talking about clients was totally off too. For one, Reed could hold his liquor. He came from good Irish stock and knew how to put his drinks away. For two, building trust with his clients was the only thing that would keep him in business. So why would he break that trust?

It didn't add up.

Was it possible that this person had him mixed up with someone else? Or was it something more sinister?

Whatever the reason, it just proved that Bad Bachelors was as full of shit as he'd assumed. No better than a tabloid magazine. He'd have bet his last dollar that by the end of the week, everyone would have forgotten about this joke of a website. He wasn't going to waste any more precious time on it.

A knock at his office door pulled him out of his thoughts and he closed the Bad Bachelors website. Good riddance. "Yes?"

Kerrie came into his office. "I know this probably isn't the best time to ask a favor…"

"I'm willing to forget last week happened if you are." He gave her a pointed look. One tiny mistake that wasn't even a mistake was nothing compared to her years of hard work for the company and the fact that she'd had his back since the day she'd been assigned to him. "What do you need?"

"Well, the Pro Bono Drive is happening this week and I know you've gotten a ton of submissions."

"But you're coming to plead your case anyway?"

The Pro Bono Drive was one of Edward Weston's initiatives. Every year, employees of Bath and Weston put forward suggestions for charities or companies in underprivileged areas to receive a free PR consultancy from a partner. Ed was a soft touch like that, always trying to help the underdogs of the world.

This was Reed's first year participating. He was happy to be involved, since he'd been on the receiving end of Edward's generosity a long time ago.

"I am." Kerrie nodded. "My grandson's library is in dire need of support."

He had to fight back the automatic curl of his lip—of all the goddamn things, why did it have to be a library? It'd been a long time since he'd set foot in one. Over a decade.

"They've had funding cuts, and they tried to run a GoFundMe campaign recently, but it didn't get much traction. I donated, of course. But they need more than what one person can provide." She sucked in a breath. "I go there every week with Finn, because he loves to read. I even started him in a creative writing program for elementary school kids, and he was having so much fun. But they had to cut a lot of their programs."

Kerrie's eyes glistened behind her thick-rimmed, blue glasses. Her grandson was the light of her life, and her desk was dotted with photos of him. Her daughter-in-law had passed away two years ago with an unusually aggressive form of breast cancer. Since then, Kerrie had moved in with her son and Finn, playing the role of mother and grandmother as best she could. It always made Reed a little guilty when they had to work long hours, because he knew it meant he was stealing her time from Finn. He would have given anything to have a person like Kerrie in his life when he was a kid.

But a library... Fuck.

"I know you can't pick favorites, but I've made a compelling argument in the submission. The people who run the library are always going above and beyond to help people." She paused. "They do good things for the community. I was talking with one of the librarians there and I know they're looking at running some kind of fundraising event. They could really use your help."

"Where's the library?"

"Flatbush."

He nodded. "Ah, so you thought you'd appeal to my Brooklyn roots, did you?"

"You're exactly what they need. Finn and I would be forever grateful." She smiled.

"I have to look at all the submissions and give them equal consideration," he said. "But I appreciate you giving me the personal explanation."

"Of course, I understand."

She retreated from his office and Reed rubbed his hands over his face. Kerrie wasn't aware of his history with libraries. If she had been, she probably wouldn't have asked. Which was why he knew that he'd end up choosing her entry.

Good people were hard to find in this city. He spent most of his time covering up the bad behavior and wrongdoings of his paying clients, so he owed it to her to help out the people who actually gave a shit about their community.

Even if it meant facing his past.

Chapter 4

"He'll keep you on your toes and on your knees. I'm not sure which is worse."

—LucyinLoubs

By Thursday, Annie had presented Darcy with a short list of suitable dating candidates. The list had been checked by Remi, who'd vetoed two guys based on reviews that they were nice but boring in bed. That left four men: an accountant who loved museums, an IT manager of some big bank who built furniture in his spare time (according to Remi, that indicated he was good with his hands), a journalist/Oxford-comma enthusiast, and an Italian chef.

All four men appeared to be good looking, successful, and, if the reviews could be believed, were decent human beings who would screw her but wouldn't screw her *over*. Well, at least not immediately.

Yet Darcy didn't experience a single spark of excitement when she thought about dating any of these men.

She leaned against the checkout counter of the Hawthorne Public Library and tapped her nails against the countertop. It wasn't her style to get all swoony over celebrities or good-looking men on the street. And she knew better than anyone that one's outside didn't always reflect their inside.

After all, the conservative branch manager had deliberated about hiring her, thinking Darcy's tattoos and piercings wouldn't suit their library's community-friendly vibe. But Darcy had proven herself, as she'd done many times over, to be hardworking, diligent, and passionate about her job—even with her ink.

"Are you sure you don't need me to hang around tonight?"

Darcy turned toward the voice. Lily, one of the library assistants, hovered next to the counter.

"No, that's fine. I'm meeting with the consultant who's going to help us with the fundraiser. That shouldn't require both of us to stay." Truthfully, she thought having a PR consultant for a library fundraiser was over the top. But apparently the services of some corporate bigwig were being offered for free.

Hopefully this wouldn't mean Darcy's idea for a nice, family-friendly event was twisted into some fancy, bigger than *Ben-Hur* gala. Because that was so *not* her style. In fact, she would have been perfectly happy to organize the fundraiser herself.

You're such an introvert.

"I'm hoping this means we can start the after-school creative writing program back up," Lily said. "I was really sad to see it go."

"Me too. But I think equipment upgrades will be first on the list." Darcy looked at the row of chunky computer monitors that had seen better days. "At this point, they're practically a museum exhibition."

"Maybe we should pitch it as a 'vintage experience' and then the hipsters will flock to us. We'll call our coffee 'small batch' and charge five bucks a pop." Lily laughed. "All right. I'll round up the stragglers and get going."

The library was still occupied by a few people—students, a grandmother with two young children, and a woman carrying some rather precariously stacked romance novels. They teetered as she placed them on the counter.

"I'm a fast reader," the woman said with a sheepish smile.

"You're a regular here, aren't you?" Darcy asked. "I'm sure I've seen your face before."

"I am." She dug into her expensive-looking purse, pulled her library card out, and handed it over. "You guys have a really great romance collection."

"Do you read a lot of romance?" Darcy dragged the books over the scanning plate.

"I devour them. Guess I'm addicted to the happy ending." She grinned. "That's all any of us want, right? Or maybe that's me being a hopeless romantic."

I'd be happy to go on a date without feeling like I'm going to have a panic attack, happy ending or not.

"You should come along to our book club," Darcy said, shoving aside the negative thoughts and grabbing a brochure for the

Literature Loving Ladies. "We try to switch up our genres, but we do have a romance novel every couple of months. It's a small group and everyone is really friendly."

"That sounds great." The woman tucked the brochure into her bag. "Thanks."

The book club had been Darcy's idea. She'd hoped it would be a way to get more people coming into the library—they put out a spread of cakes that Remi helped her bake each month and offered coffee and good company. The club ran on next to nothing, other than a little electricity to keep the library open for an extra few hours. But book clubs weren't enough, and they certainly didn't make up for dwindling community support and cuts to government funding.

Which was precisely why Darcy had brought up the idea of the fundraising event to her boss. Parties weren't normally her thing—she was a paperbacks-and-wine rather than a canapés-and-conversation kind of gal—but the library was her second home. Her happy place.

And desperate times called for desperate party planning.

Lily rounded up the remaining patrons of the library and gave them a five-minute warning. Thankfully, Darcy had done the closing procedure so many times she could practically do it blindfolded. That meant her mind was free to wander through all the bits of information she'd gathered through the week.

At first she'd felt a little strange, researching these guys who had no idea she was looking into them, like she was invading their privacy. But it wasn't any different from her helping a student with a school project, right? The information was already there; all she did was search and gather.

The last few patrons cleared out and Lily waved, leaving Darcy alone. The air-conditioning hummed, its noise amplified in the quiet space. The second this meeting was over, Darcy would be heading back to her Park Slope apartment. And, since Remi had a date tonight, Darcy would round off the week in peace and quiet, with a new book.

"I'm hoping the library is usually more populated than this."

Darcy snapped her head up at the masculine voice shattering her concentration.

"I take it you're…" The words died on her lips as she stuck her hand out and found herself staring at a man with a sharp jaw and deep brown eyes. A man that looked entirely familiar, though she knew for a fact they'd never met. "Reed McMahon," she finished.

Bad bachelor numero uno. Notorious womanizer. Top dog of the New York dating food chain, according to the Bad Bachelors blog.

They'd done a piece on him yesterday, which Darcy had gobbled up with an unusual amount of interest. She'd never been into gossip rags or reading the society pages, but for some reason, she'd been unable to turn her attention away from Reed's picture. He hadn't been smiling—there was just a slight lift of his full lips, a cross between a smirk and a grimace. She supposed men as good looking as him didn't need to bother with niceties such as smiles.

"The one and only," he quipped, accepting her proffered hand. The second a tingle of awareness sped through her body she wished she could take the polite gesture back. "I'm sorry, my assistant didn't pass on your name."

Darcy was certain Reed's name had also been left off the email from her boss detailing this meeting, because she would definitely have noticed it.

"It's Darcy." She drew her hand back and tried to ignore the buzz setting off butterflies in her stomach.

"Darcy." The smooth way he said her name sent a tremor through her.

Which annoyed her to no end. He was a coldhearted rake. No thought spared for anyone but himself, if the reviews could be trusted. But when it came to guys like him, better safe than sorry in her book. That meant his irritatingly charming personality was most likely a front and she'd do well to remember that.

"No last name?" He raised a brow. "That puts you in good company."

"Yeah. Me and Sophocles," she said dryly. "We're quite the pair."

"I was going to say Madonna, but I guess that's why you're the librarian and I'm not." On the surface it appeared to be a compliment, but something in his tone told her it wasn't.

Not that she should have been surprised—guys like him probably didn't place much value on literature.

Darcy stepped out from behind the counter, motioning for him to follow her to one of the activity rooms. "Right. And you're the person who's going to help us drum up interest in the library."

"I'm going to help you improve the library's reputation," he corrected.

The man exuded confidence. It wasn't simply the way he dressed in a suit that fitted like a dream, or the way his crisp, white shirt contrasted with his lightly tanned skin. It wasn't even the imposing height or the masculine breadth of his shoulders. It was the way he looked at her—direct without being confrontational, as though he knew he didn't need to intimidate to get what he wanted. One glance and the other person would hand their soul over without protest.

No doubt that glance made women melt into a puddle at his feet.

As much as her insides were reacting to his magnetic energy on some basic level, she was determined *not* to be one of those puddles. "Improve our reputation?"

"Yes. People in the community don't see libraries being worthy of taxpayer dollars. They think they're old fashioned and a waste of money."

While part of her knew he must be right—why else would they be struggling for funding and donations?—she couldn't help bristling at the statement. It sounded a hell of a lot like *he* thought they were a waste of money.

"Libraries aren't old fashioned."

"Yes, they are. With the internet, who needs books?"

"I have one on etiquette and manners that you might benefit from," she said archly.

A sly smile quirked his mouth, making her blood boil—fast. "Manners are overrated and etiquette...well, you're not exactly convincing me this place isn't old fashioned."

Who did he think he was, insulting her passion? "Tell me then: If our reputation is so bad, how are *you* the right person to help us?"

She'd been hoping for some reaction—a tensing of his jaw, a

blaze in those bottomless, brown eyes. Something to show she'd hit her mark. Instead, he looked at her with utter nothingness.

"What do you mean by that?" he asked, his voice as neutral as his expression.

"Well, from everything I've read, you haven't been able to keep your own reputation in check. Why should I trust you with ours?"

....

Frustration ripped through him like a freight train. Did every single person in New York think he was a social delinquent?

Somehow, by not offering women anything more than sex—which they readily agreed to at the time—he was a horrible human being. And now this prickly little librarian was giving him attitude. As if coming to this blasted place for a meeting wasn't bad enough.

Darcy cocked her head, as if challenging him to bite back. Over his dead body. Reed McMahon was not a loose cannon; everything he did was calculated, strategic—purposeful.

"And how do you know about that?" he asked.

Her hands knotted in front of her. Each finger was long and slender, graceful. She wore no rings, no nail polish. No adornments—anywhere. Her face was bare of makeup and she wore no other jewelry. And despite that spare styling, there was something unabashedly feminine about her long, dark lashes and full, pillowy lips.

"I've been following the articles about you," she said.

"You and every other woman in New York. And they're blog posts, *big* difference."

She shrugged a shoulder.

"Everyone in this city knows my name. They may not appreciate how I go about my life, but, if you haven't noticed, I draw attention," he said smoothly. He resisted a smile when dots of pink colored her cheeks. "You need that attention."

"We need *money*." She folded her arms across her chest. "Attention won't pay for our programs or new computers."

"Money won't come without attention."

"So I guess you're of the belief that all publicity is good publicity then?"

That wasn't necessarily true, especially given his current situation. He'd have much preferred to get on with his job without the constant ribbing from his colleagues. The little trophy wasn't the only surprise he'd found in his office. He'd walked in after lunch one day to find a vibrator hidden under a stack of papers with a bow tied around it. No doubt Aaron or one of his cronies had snuck in the second Kerrie had stepped away from her desk.

Reed wasn't the kind of guy to go running to HR over a practical joke, but he *was* over being the center of attention.

"People won't support what doesn't interest them." He looked around at the walls decorated with colored-paper shapes and posters illustrated crudely with markers, and had to force himself not to shudder.

God, he hated libraries. All that false cheer and insincere kindness felt like an overdose of candy—it made him jittery, uncomfortable.

"We need to make this place interesting," he added.

"I have to say 'interesting' hasn't really been at the top of our priority list, what with all the focus being on education and community enrichment," she said sharply. The girl had an acid tongue and a defensive shield that would be harder to scale than a forty-story building. Not that he was the kind of guy to back down from a challenge, mind you.

"No matter. That's why I'm here." He fought back a laugh as she rolled her eyes.

"Glad we've got someone to show us where the real priorities are." Her tongue darted out to lick her lips and he caught a flash of silver. A tongue piercing.

Christ. The unexpected detail stopped him in his tracks. She'd hit the On switch to his nervous system and a low hum started up like the first twig lighting up in a bonfire. His eyes skated over her lithe figure, over the almost-masculine jeans and combat boots, over the black shirt where the cuffs stopped just shy of her wrists, allowing some elaborate ink to peek out. He wondered how much of her body was covered with it.

So much darkness, and yet there was a light and earnestness in her face that struck him deep in the chest. Curiosity skittered through his brain. He wondered what the piercing would feel like running over his skin.

Stop that right fucking now.

"I'm not the enemy, Darcy. I'm here to help you. But I'm also not going to give you some rose-colored-glasses bullshit."

"Why *are* you helping us?" she asked. "Apparently, you're offering your services for free. We don't exactly seem like your regular kind of client."

"How would you know that?" he asked, enjoying the narrowing of her eyes.

"I can tell from all this"—she waved her hand in his general direction—"that you're not in your comfort zone."

He looked down at his custom suit, a purchase made from one of his favorite tailors, and stifled a grin. The number of zeroes on that bill had made his eyes water, but it was all a necessary part of the Reed McMahon image. The real him—the boy who'd come from nothing—wouldn't appear until he was home and hanging up his public identity in his modest bedroom.

Not that people like Darcy would ever assume there was more beneath the surface.

"Is this your way of telling me I'm not in Kansas anymore?" he drawled.

"Correct. And don't go thinking I'm Glinda the Good Witch or some pushover munchkin." She walked past him with her nose in the air. "If I think you're going to do anything to make our situation worse, I'll get all Wicked Witch of the West on your ass."

....

After Reed listened to Darcy talk for an hour about all the things that needed fixing in the library, two things were clear. One, she was incredibly passionate about her job. Two, he would need to end this conversation now; otherwise, he'd be here all night. The sexy little librarian had written her own version of *War and Peace* in the form of a detailed spending plan for the funds raised.

"This is all very interesting, but I honestly don't care how you spend the money." Reed checked his watch. "The public doesn't care either."

Darcy narrowed her eyes. "Why would they donate money if they don't know how it will be spent?"

"Because computers and curriculum aren't interesting."

"There's that word again," she muttered.

"Why are you so afraid to be interesting, Darcy? You should try it some time. It's so much fun." Lord help him, he couldn't resist tugging on the strings of someone as prickly as her. His reward was an irritated huffing noise. "People care about feelings."

"That's an *interesting* assessment coming from a guy who doesn't seem to *have* any."

"You shouldn't believe everything you read on the internet," he said. "And computers don't make people feel anything. They want to know that their money means a brighter future for little Jimmy down the road."

"Did I not just talk about the after-school program?" She folded her arms across her chest and the action made the buttons strain on her black shirt.

Focus, McMahon.

"That's exactly what's going to help the kids in our community," she added.

"But we're not selling them on the program. We're selling them on little Jimmy. We're going to appeal to what they care about, which is themselves."

"You think people only care about themselves?" she scoffed. "Not that I should be entirely surprised by that..."

"I never said they *only* care about themselves. But they do care about themselves first." In all his years dealing with people's image problems, he knew one thing for certain: people were a hell of a lot more selfish than they wanted to admit.

"That's incredibly cynical."

"Maybe. But it's accurate." He sucked in a breath. For a situation where he was offering his expertise for free, he was certainly having to explain himself a hell of a lot. "Think about it this way. It's a caveman thing, self-preservation. We all take an interest in what's best for ourselves and, therefore, so long as our needs aren't in direct competition, we're all better off."

"What does this have to do with asking people for money?" she asked.

"Because helping little Jimmy have a brighter future means an improvement to the community. Educated kids means less crime and better job prospects. They'll grow up, have educated kids of their own, and give back to the community. Success begets success."

"So we appeal to people by showing them how improving the library will benefit the community—a.k.a. them—in the long term?"

"See, I knew you'd be a good student." He grinned when she shot him a murderous look. "Now, let's talk about a possible venue for the fundraiser."

"I thought we would have it here."

"No."

He looked around the library and tried to resist the automatic lip curl. This was one area where he *wouldn't* be budging.

Fundraisers weren't meant to depress people, and that meant the venue couldn't be in some run-down building painted entirely in baby-puke beige.

"What do you mean, no?" Darcy looked at him incredulously. "Do you think we've got spare cash lying around to pay for some fancy function room?"

"You don't need to pay for a venue—that's Fundraising 101. I'll use my contacts to secure us an appropriate place willing to donate the space in exchange for some good press."

"I still don't see what's wrong with having it here."

He resisted the urge to ask her if she'd prefer to run the event on her own without his help, because he suspected he knew what her answer would be. But he wasn't going to let Kerrie down just because some snippy librarian wanted to question his approach. He *knew* what worked best to get the dollars rolling in, and therefore, he knew what was best for this library.

"I get that you're really passionate about this place," he said, using the sincerest tone he could muster. "I really do. But this is what I do for a living. I promise if you trust me to take care of the library, you'll be able to get *everything* you need to keep this place running the way you want."

Darcy's tongue darted out to moisten her lips and he caught that sinful flash of silver again. Her vivid-blue eyes watched him, assessing and cool. Her distrust was palpable.

"I'm no saint," he added. "But you don't need a saint right now. You need someone who can convince the world to eat out of the palm of his hand."

"And you think you can do that?" She cocked her head. "Even when the whole city thinks you're an asshole?"

"I'm good at my job, Darcy. And the fact is, I don't see anyone else lining up to help you out."

"Maybe I don't need help," she said stubbornly, but the hardness had leached out of her voice.

"If you truly care about this place, you won't take that chance. But I'll put the ball in your court. If you want me out, I'm gone."

It was ballsy. She was about as warm and fuzzy as a porcupine and he hadn't exactly started out on a positive note. But he knew the best way to reel someone in was to show you were confident enough to walk away.

"Fine," she said after a painfully long pause. "I'm willing to hear your approach. But I don't want this to be some flashy, grand event. That might be how you do things in your world, but that's not how we operate here."

"Got it." He stuck out his hand. "So we're working together now?"

She hesitated for a moment, and when she slipped her small hand into his, a little thrill of accomplishment ran through him. The buzz of convincing someone to do what he wanted never faded. If he were a more philosophical guy, he might have contemplated what that said about him.

"I guess we are," Darcy said. "I hope you don't make me regret it."

"Regret is for chumps." He flashed her his most winning smile. "We, Darcy, are most certainly not chumps."

Chapter 5

"Don't go there with Reed. Just don't."

—*TheOtherMonica*

*D*arcy hated herself for the prickle of attraction she felt toward Reed since she knew what kind of guy he was. Okay, so the attraction was more like being struck with defibrillator pads. But still, the guy was cocky beyond belief.

Cocky and pushy and utterly gorgeous.

He had the kind of charisma that an awkward turtle like her would never embody. A confidence and comfort in his own skin that she would kill for.

Ever since their meeting, she'd been distracted by the fact that they would be working together. The weekend had ticked past slower than usual, and she'd found herself unable to concentrate. Even her favorite comfort read hadn't been able to get her in the zone. Then she'd awoken to an email on Monday morning requesting she meet him that evening at a potential venue for their fundraiser. Some place with a difficult to pronounce name. Some place that was exactly *not* what she'd wanted.

Now she was being forced to spend another evening with him. A dinner, no less.

"Do my eyes deceive me?" Remi poked her head into Darcy's bedroom. "Are you wearing…a color?"

"Very funny, Rem." She smoothed her hands down the front of the deep indigo blouse.

"Clearly I'm mistaken." Remi leaned against the doorframe. Her long legs were encased in a pair of lilac leggings and pink legwarmers. "It must be some new shade of black I don't know about yet."

"We can't all dress like a My Little Pony."

"It's the parents-and-kids class today. The little ones get pissed if I don't wear pink." A dainty hand patted the edge of her plump ballerina bun. "Where are you off to? That doesn't look like your usual attire for a night on the couch. Have you got a date already?"

"No." The word shot out of her like a missile. Dinner with Reed was strictly business. "It's, uh…a work thing."

She hadn't been able to bring herself to tell the girls about Reed. Her poker face was shitty at the best of times, let alone when talking about someone who'd made a surprise appearance in the form of an unusually sexy dream. *Highly* unusually sexy. To make matters worse, Annie had sent a screenshot of one of his latest reviews to her yesterday with a string of laughing-crying emojis. Needless to say, that had sealed Darcy's decision to keep her new colleague's identity a secret.

"I'm looking at a potential venue for the fundraiser. I can't turn up in my old jeans and T-shirt, you know." God, could she sound any more nervous? Clearly a career in acting wasn't in her future. Hopefully she could keep it together in front of Reed.

"Right." Remi nodded, a curious twinkle in her eye.

"Do you think I look…" Her eyes flicked to the mirror. "Appropriately dressed?"

The blouse was old, but it hadn't been worn. Darcy had originally purchased it for her honeymoon, thinking it looked like something a wife should wear. She realized now that was a stupid concept, and she shouldn't have been planning to change herself simply because she'd gotten married. So she'd ripped the tags off and now it was just a blouse.

The silky fabric was sheer on the arms, enough that a faint glimpse of her tattoos could be seen through it. A single gold button dotted each cuff.

"For a work function? Sure. It's gorgeous." Remi's gaze drifted down to Darcy's feet, but she didn't say anything.

Dark jeans and black, lace-up combat boots probably weren't the best accompaniment to a silk blouse. But high heels were Darcy's sworn enemy. At five feet nine inches, she didn't need them anyway.

"I don't want to wear heels, so don't even suggest it."

Remi's eyes lit up as she raised a finger to signal Darcy should wait a moment. If she were a cartoon, a big lightbulb would have appeared above her head. A few seconds later, she returned with a pair of pointy-toed black flats, the edges decorated with gold studs.

"What about these?" She held them out as if offering a sacred gift. "I thought they might be a nice compromise…and they're Valentino."

"I'm going to assume that's a good thing." Darcy reached down and unlaced her boots.

"They're very *work* appropriate." Remi bit back a smile.

"Good, because that's what I'm doing tonight." She concentrated on peeling off her stripy socks so Remi wouldn't see the warmth in her cheeks. "Work."

"Yes, you mentioned that."

Slipping the shoes on, she stood and checked out her reflection. "You know what? I kind of like them."

Remi shook her head. "Only you could sound so surprised that an eight-hundred-dollar pair of shoes looks good."

"Eight hundred dollars?" She froze on the spot. "Why the hell would you spend so much money on something that goes on your feet?"

"I'm a ballerina, Darcy. My feet are important." She grinned. "Besides, they were a gift from my ex. I can't blame the shoes because they were purchased by an evil wanker. That would be unfair."

"Yes, we must consider the feelings of the shoes at all times." She rolled her eyes.

Joking aside, Darcy could see why Remi had kept them. They managed to look dainty and tough at the same time. They also made her legs look longer, leaner. And they were sexy without looking as though they tried.

Not that you're trying to look sexy for tonight. You're trying to look professional, *remember? Confident. In control.*

"Maybe you could wear a necklace," Remi suggested. "I have one that—"

"That's my limit for girlie stuff." Darcy grinned. "But thanks for letting me wear a chunk of your rent on my feet."

"Try not to scuff them. Please."

"Don't worry. I don't expect to be doing anything strenuous tonight."

"Why would you?" Remi said with a grin. "It's just work, right?"

"Right."

Forty-five minutes later, Darcy stepped out of a cab at the address that Reed had emailed her. The borrowed shoes were already starting to pinch her feet and Darcy cursed herself for not sticking with her boots. Who cared what Reed thought of the way she looked anyway?

Anticipation fluttered low in her belly, her insides tickled by the gossamer wings of anxious butterflies. It was different to how she'd felt on her last date a few months ago. Different, good. Different, scary.

Repeat after me: this is not a date.

"You scrub up well." Reed came up beside her out of nowhere. Like a ninja, but better dressed.

"Don't sound so surprised." Darcy flicked her gaze over his ink-black suit and tried not to let any appreciation show.

But it was tough to ignore the zing of excitement that shot through her, stirring up the butterflies once more. She liked him in black. It made him look dangerous. Beautiful dangerous.

"I'm not surprised at all." He gestured to the heavy wooden doors. "Shall we?"

As they walked, Darcy almost expected his hand to find the small of her back in that awful, clichéd way often seen in movies. Her skin anticipated the touch. But it never came. He did, however, hold the door for her.

"Can I help you?" A woman in a sleek, gray dress stood with her hands clasped in front of her.

"Uh…" Darcy faltered, feeling instantly out of place next to the chic marble-and-brushed-silver decor. She looked to Reed for a cue. "I believe we have a reservation."

"Mr. McMahon," the woman said as a knowing smile spread across her lips. "You must be here for the tasting."

"Yes. This is my companion, Darcy Greer. We'll be doing the tasting together."

As they followed the woman through the restaurant, Darcy fought back a smile. "Your companion?"

"Would you have preferred client?" He was close behind her as they wove through the tables covered in white linen. "But you're not paying me. Associate then?"

"Why do we need to label it?"

"Ah, commitment issues. You're a woman after my own heart."

"I *don't* have commitment issues. I think that's what psychologists call 'projecting.'"

She turned to retort further, but the pointed toe of her shoe clipped a wayward chair and she stumbled. Reed's hand shot out and steadied her, his grip sure and strong. Confident. His touch burned through the thin silk of her top.

"One foot in front of the other," he said. "Haven't you made it around to the biomechanics section of the library yet? You must be too busy reading books on manners and etiquette."

Flames licked at the inside of her cheeks. She'd give anything to have a book on hand now. A nice hefty hardback she could whack over his head.

"Actually, I've been spending most of my time in the hand-to-hand-combat section. So don't try me." She glared at him over her shoulder. "Or I'll put you in a sleeper hold."

Reed cleared his throat. Was it her imagination or was it covering up a laugh?

"Our event coordinator will be over shortly to run you through our function menu." The maître d' stopped in front of an empty booth. "The chef has selected the most popular options for you to taste, but we can certainly bring out more if you'd like. And if there's anything else I can do for you, please don't hesitate to let me know."

The comment was obviously directed at Reed. The woman spoke with a clipped, professional tone, but her tongue darted out to moisten her lips in a way that said she'd very much like to be of service to him.

"Do you ever get sick of women fawning over you?" Darcy asked once the woman was out of earshot. She slid into the booth.

"No." He appeared totally unapologetic. "Why would I get sick of it?"

"I don't know. Don't men live for the thrill of the chase?"

"Some men do." He popped the button of his suit jacket as he sat. "I find women who need to be chased are usually more trouble than suits my needs."

"You mean they don't want to be chewed up and spat out?"

"You say that like it's a bad thing. Most of the women who encounter my 'chewing' leave without any complaints."

Darcy picked up the drinks menu and pretended to study the options. It was clear she should shut her mouth around Reed. The man had a comeback for everything. And the more they bantered, the more she was tempted to inflict bodily harm.

Besides, if they were going to be working together, she should try to be professional. Even if it was proving difficult.

....

It wasn't that Reed tried to make himself sound like an asshole. But winding up Darcy was fast becoming his new favorite sport. Anything to make her purse those pouty lips and narrow her electric-blue eyes at him.

The women he dated were smooth. Confident in their ability to seduce. They were all soft tones and suggestive eyes. Fluttering lashes.

Darcy was as smooth as a cactus.

But despite her thorny disposition, she'd dressed up tonight by ditching the semi-Goth tones for something softer. Her tattoos played peekaboo with the fabric of her top.

"Why did you pick this venue?" she asked, cutting into his thoughts. "I thought we'd agreed nothing too flashy."

"It's classy."

"It's over the top." She reached for the bottle of sparkling water and inspected the gold label with a smirk before pouring them both a glass. How considerate—the girl had manners even when she disliked her dinner guest. "It's not the sort of environment that I can see our members feeling comfortable in."

"That's because your members aren't necessarily going to be on the guest list. And they aren't the ones who'll be donating money. Not the kind of money you need anyway."

"Okay." She stretched the word out like toffee. "But I was thinking the fundraiser could be a community-engagement thing as well. We could advertise some of the programs we'd start up with the funding, get their feedback—"

"No."

She sucked in a breath. "You say no a lot."

"This is a fundraiser." He sipped his water. "The key to a successful event is simplicity. If you crowd the agenda with too many things, people will become confused. And confused people don't part with their money." And besides, he wanted to avoid setting foot in that library again unless absolutely necessary.

"Okay, fine. So we're inviting people who expect to be wined and dined in some fancy-pants restaurant." Her hand fluttered in the air.

"Yes. There's a function room on the other side of the foyer that will be perfect. We'll do a short sit-down portion, nothing too formal but still elegant. Then we'll follow it up with a cocktail portion while we run a silent auction." A smirk tugged at his lips. "You might even be able to wear a dress."

She narrowed her eyes. "Figures you'd give me style advice. Looks like you spent more time on your hair this morning than I did."

Darcy's dark-chocolate hair was pulled back into a ponytail.

He was tempted to point out that most preschoolers probably spent more time on their hair than she did, but he held back. The fact was Darcy didn't need any bells and whistles to look hot as hell. An image of tugging on that thick ribbon of hair played across his mind.

"Are you calling me high maintenance?" he asked, shrugging off the dirty little flicker in his imagination.

"I could call you a lot of things, Reed. High maintenance is low on the list."

He wanted to ask her what she *would* call him, but he knew better than to court a woman's derision. Especially when they were supposed to be working together. He really *should* rein in his teasing.

Before the silence could stretch on too long, the first round of tasting plates arrived. Darcy's brows rose as she picked up a small hors d'oeuvre with cheese, blackberry, and fresh dill on a skewer and popped it into her mouth. She twirled the empty stick.

"Do people really eat like this?" she asked, shaking her head. "God, no wonder all these rich women are so skinny. Give me a cheeseburger any day of the week."

"You don't pull any punches, do you?" Reed asked with a smirk, taking an hors d'oeuvre for himself. Truth be told, he'd have preferred a cheeseburger too.

"I don't care for BS." She reached for another item from the tasting plate and instead of taking a delicate bite like most people would have, she shoved the whole thing into her mouth. "That's just how I roll."

She was guarded, that was for damn sure, and it only served to stir his curiosity. Most women he dined with were all too happy to talk about themselves—he assumed because they'd all suffered through many a bad date where that wasn't the case. But Darcy played her cards close to her chest.

"You're a bundle of contradictions," he said. The corner of his lips lifted. "You like manners and etiquette, but you hate BS. I've always thought those two went hand in hand."

"It's possible to be honest *and* nice." She smirked. "You should try it sometime."

"No, I don't think I will."

"There's that word again." She scrunched up her nose. "I really hate being told no."

Too bad. There's plenty more where that came from.

"Doesn't everyone?" he asked.

"I guess so." She inclined her head. "Or maybe I hear it too much and it makes me want to do the opposite."

Ah, *that* was something real. A hint of rebellion under the surface, just like the tattoos peeking through her top. Her right arm was covered entirely—a full sleeve. He hadn't expected that. The design featured some books, birds, and flowers. Some words too, but he couldn't read them through the sheer fabric covering her arms.

"Who told you not to get the tats, then?"

"My mother." Her eyes met his, hard and direct. "She said she didn't go through indescribable pain to bring me into the world only for me to graffiti my body. Apparently, if I treat myself like public property, others will too."

To her credit, she didn't flinch as she said the words. Old wounds, he suspected. He had a few of those himself.

"Harsh."

She lifted a delicate shoulder in a half-hearted shrug. "Sticks and stones. What about you, any ink?"

"No ink. But I got drunk at a frat party once and had my belly button pierced."

"Really?" Her eyes lit up.

"No."

The smile fell from her lips and she turned her attention back to the tasting plate. "Boring."

He stifled a laugh. "Gullible."

Darkness flickered over her face, uninhibited. She was easy to read—too easy. That quality would hurt her if it hadn't already.

"What can I say?" Her fingers hovered over the tasting plate as she decided on another bite-size appetizer. "It's been a while since I had to deal with such an accomplished bullshit artist. You'll have to forgive me. I'm a bit rusty."

"I'm more than happy to help you sharpen your skills, Darcy. Bullshit is my specialty." A chuckle forced its way up his throat when she folded her arms across her chest indignantly. If looks could kill… "Did you expect me to be insulted? Sorry, I'm not that easily rattled."

"I'd like to rattle you right now," she muttered, picking up the drink menu.

"I wish you would. We could go back to my place once we're done."

Ignoring him, Darcy signaled to the waiter. "I'm going to need some alcohol. Now."

Chapter 6

"If you're looking for a good time, Reed is totally your man. He's incredible in bed. But don't expect him to recognize you if you bump into each other on the street."

—JadedLady89

*D*arcy steeled herself as she stood outside in the dying light. The door in front of her had been recently painted pistachio green. Retro cheerful. It made her sick to her stomach.

"Come on, you've done worse things in your life."

She shut her eyes and tried to remember getting her last tattoo. The blinding pain had stolen her breath as the needle etched words into her skin, spelling out her personal message in permanent ink.

The quote "In the end, we'll all become stories" by Margaret Atwood was curled around the underside of her right breast. Each letter had been a reminder that she would never let other people make her feel less than, that she would never let other people make her feel unworthy. No one had seen it except Darcy and the artist.

In other words, no one had seen her naked in a year.

"You can do this." She sucked in a breath and shook off the unsettling thoughts. "Three, two…one."

She brought her knuckles down on the door, and a moment later, it swung open. Her mother, Marietta, stood there with arms outstretched, her round figure illuminated by the warm light within the house. It could have been a perfect picture of familial love. But she wasn't fooled. Her family might have looked perfect on the outside, but it wouldn't take long for them to start chipping away at her. Like always.

"Hey, Ma," she said, leaning in for the requisite kiss on each cheek. Her mother's chubby hands clutched at her shoulders. "The house smells wonderful."

"We're having lasagna." Marietta held the door open. "Come on. Dinner is ready. We've been waiting for you."

Darcy was no more than three minutes late, but she'd hear about it at least twice more before the night was over. She started a mental bingo sheet of all the things her family would criticize. She'd even switched her tongue ring out with a clear retainer for the night to avoid her mother commenting on it. Sure, she hated skulking around like a teenager when she was a grown woman, but it was easier than dealing with the guilt trip.

"You look lovely. I can't even see that awful piercing." Her mother beamed as if she'd said something nice.

Backhanded compliment. Check.

Her mother ushered her into the dining room where her stepfather and half sister were already seated. Genio muttered something about punctuality under his breath and took the foil off the lasagna tray without waiting for Darcy to sit.

Given some of the things he'd said upon her arrival previously, this didn't even warrant a response.

"Hey, Big Sis," Cynthia said cheerfully as she stood, oblivious to the tension crackling in the air. As usual.

Blissful ignorance was practically Cynthia's middle name.

Darcy wrapped her arms around her sister and squeezed. Seeing her was the only reason she bothered to turn up to their monthly family dinners anymore. "Hmm, you smell good."

"I've been doing some recruitment for Bergdorf Goodman and they sent me a little gift basket. It's Chanel." She gave a little shimmy before taking her seat again. "I feel super fancy."

"Cynthia gave me a bottle of perfume too," her mother said, as she started dishing up the dinner. "So thoughtful of her."

Subtle comparison between the good child and the bad child. Check.

"I would have given you one, Darcy"—Cynthia looked guilty—"but they're all so expensive and I know you don't bother with that stuff."

"All good. I prefer going au naturel."

Genio grunted from his position at the head of the table. "Maybe if you made more of an effort you'd be able to find a man to marry."

Not so subtle dig at marital status. Check.

"Dad!" Cynthia frowned and patted Darcy's arm. "That's really rude. Besides, you were complaining to me before that most boys these days are disgusting."

"That's because you're not old enough to date," he grumbled.

Apparently, there was a big difference between being twenty-two and twenty-seven. At what point had Darcy veered into left-on-the-shelf territory? Or perhaps Genio just wanted Darcy to be someone else's problem.

"Speaking of which," her mother said as she handed over a plate with a piece of lasagna bigger than Darcy's head. "How was the cake? Did you share it with the girls?"

Mention the devil cake. Ding, ding, ding! Congratulations, you've won a lifetime supply of familial guilt and a fast track to mental fragility.

"In a manner of speaking," Darcy said, digging into her dinner. "Let's say the cake disappeared very quickly."

Marietta clapped her hands together. "Oh, I am so pleased. We paid so much for that wedding. It would have been a shame for everything to go to waste."

Darcy cursed her ex, for what must have been the millionth time, for lying to her right up until the wedding. If he was going to ruin her life, couldn't he have done it before the venue's no-refund cutoff date?

"But it doesn't matter," Marietta continued with her best cheerful martyr expression. "We know you'll find the right man. Someday."

The rebellious side of her wanted to declare that she'd sworn off the opposite sex and decided to embrace celibacy, that her lady parts had shut up shop for good—to show her the pictures from the trash-the-dress shoot and watch the shock on her mother's face.

Okay, that made her sound like a bitch…but doing the opposite of what her mother wanted was the one way she could gain control. To take back the ground she'd lost by being a yes-woman for too long.

They got through the rest of dinner without too much drama, and then Cynthia tugged Darcy toward her bedroom to show her some new, shiny thing she'd purchased.

"You're never going to believe what I did," Cynthia said as she closed the door behind them with a soft *snick*. She grinned and jumped up and down on the spot.

"If you spent a stupid amount of money on shoes, I *would* believe it." Darcy glanced around her sister's room.

It looked more like the kind of bedroom suited to a twelve-year-old girl than a young woman. A pink-and-white bedspread was topped with enough lace-trimmed pillows that Darcy wondered how her sister wasn't smothered in the middle of the night. A porcelain figurine of a girl with a large sun hat sat on her bedside table, next to a vanilla-scented candle and an old picture of the two of them. The frame was encrusted with rhinestones.

"Look." Cynthia's high-pitched squeal dragged Darcy's gaze to where she'd pulled up the hem of her skirt to reveal a tattoo.

A *fresh* tattoo. The skin around the scrolling ink was still a little red and the letters etched into her sister's upper thigh spelled out a name—*Brad*. The location was designed for easy cover-up. It was parent proof so long as they didn't go to the beach.

"What the hell were you thinking?" Darcy pressed her finger-tips to her forehead.

"What? Are you the only one who's allowed to have tattoos in this family?" Cynthia pouted, her glossy, pink lips turned down. "I thought you'd be happy for me."

"You *never* get a boyfriend's name tattooed on your body. That's, like, rule number one." Her mind reeled. Darcy knew exactly how this would go down if her parents ever found out—they'd blame her, thinking poor, little Cynthia had been led astray by the big, bad family failure.

"We're in *love*," Cynthia said, dropping her skirt and folding her arms across her chest. "I thought you of all people would understand."

"If you wanted to get a piece of art created, then I *would* understand. But that"—she pointed to her sister's leg—"is not art. It's a mistake."

"Gee, tell me how you really feel."

"I just... It's a shock. I can't believe you didn't come to me to talk about this first. I could have shown you some reputable studios, helped you pick a design..."

"Brad helped me. He has three tattoos," her sister huffed. "But that's it, isn't it? It's nothing to do with the ink—it's that I went to him instead of you."

Darcy forced herself to swallow the frustration rising up her throat. If she'd learned one thing about her sister over the years, it was that she didn't respond well to conflict. They *were* related after all. "That's not it at all. Who is this guy? You haven't even mentioned him before."

"Not that I should even be telling you," she said trying to maintain her annoyance, "but he's a mechanic. He lives in

Williamsburg and he's so romantic. He bought me flowers on our first date and he's the sweetest guy."

"How old is he?" She cringed at how much she sounded like their mother.

"He's a little older."

Darcy speared her sister with a look. "Don't be vague."

"He's thirty-two. But age doesn't matter. What matters is that I'm totally in love with him."

In love enough to get some guy's name—a guy who was a decade older than her, no less—tattooed on her thigh. Darcy knew how this would go. She'd heard about it a dozen times from the artist at the studio where she had most of her work done.

Lovesick couple comes in for matching tattoos, and then six months later, they were back for a cover-up job after the relationship had gone south. Every. Damn. Time.

"I'm not going to talk to you if you keep giving me the judgment face." Cynthia waved her hand in front of Darcy's eyes. "I thought we were supposed to be able to tell each other anything?"

"We are. I'm sorry I reacted like that. I was surprised." She pulled her sister in for a hug and grappled for the right thing to say. "I'm happy you're happy."

Cynthia leaned back and narrowed her expertly made-up eyes. "That sounds a hell of a lot like 'I think you're making poor life decisions, but I'm not going to say it.'"

"Who's got the judgment face now?"

A smile twitched on her sister's lips. "I want you to meet him."

Darcy fought back a groan. The chance of her meeting this

douche canoe without putting him in a headlock was slim. But Cynthia would continue to see him with or without her blessing, which meant it was better if Darcy stayed involved…just in case.

"Anything for you," she said.

"Don't worry, you'll love him as much as I do." A grin lit Cynthia's face. "He's wonderful."

"I'm sure he is, Cyn. If you're dating him, he must be pretty amazing."

....

Darcy rolled the empty coffee cup between her palms and watched as the dregs swished around. She never finished the last bit. There would always be one mouthful at the bottom like a sacrifice to the coffee gods. It was a weird quirk that had developed over the years, but she couldn't seem to break it.

She glanced up and looked around the small café where she was supposed to be meeting Reed to discuss the guest list and venue for the fundraiser. The place he'd taken her to on Monday was all kinds of wrong—too posh, too…fussy. She wanted somewhere with character. Hopefully he had other options up his sleeve.

Except that Reed was supposed to meet her half an hour ago and he hadn't contacted her with an excuse for his tardiness. Why would he? He'd probably stroll in here like he owned the place, without a hint of apology.

Just the way he did everything else.

Wednesdays were her sacred days. Since she didn't get a typical weekend, like people who worked in an office, she relished having a free day midweek. She'd often spend it alone, taking her bike to Prospect Park to enjoy the scenery. Or she'd curl up on the couch with a book. She'd brought one with her today in anticipation of getting some reading done, but her concentration had waned. The words seemed to move about on the page, and eventually, she'd shoved the book back into her bag.

Ever since she'd seen Cynthia last night, Darcy had struggled not to worry about her little sister. What kind of thirtysomething guy dated a girl barely old enough to drink and let her get a tattoo of his name on her thigh? It'd taken all her willpower not to tell her sister to dump this Brad guy. Warning flags had popped up all over the place. But she, unlike her parents, could accept that Cynthia *was* a grown woman capable of making her own decisions. However bad they may be…

But Darcy would check in more often out of sisterly concern. Like, every couple of hours.

Her phone vibrated against the café's table and a number flashed up on screen. She swallowed. She might have deleted Ben's contact information, but she would recognize his number anywhere.

After she'd canceled the wedding, he'd called a lot. Left messages on her phone and with her mother, claiming that he wanted to make amends. That he wanted to apologize for how he'd handled things. Not once had she answered him. It'd been a year and he still called every other month, still left a voice message. And she *still* deleted it the second she heard his familiar, "Hi, Darcy."

She rejected the call and rubbed her hands over her eyes. If she ever figured out what to say to him, then maybe she'd pick up his call. But until then, she was going to play the avoidance game. Thankfully, he hadn't decided to push the issue by turning up at her house or her work. For all his faults, he knew her well enough not to do that.

Maybe this would be a good time to check out one of the men Annie and Remi had suggested—distract herself with thinking about the future instead of the past. She brought up the Bad Bachelors app and looked at her favorites list. The profile for Darren Montgomery sat at the top, his picture smiling up at her.

Darren was the IT manager who built furniture in his spare time. He had a solidly positive rating corroborated by several reviews…but not *too* many reviews. There was a fine line between the two, she'd discovered. Too many reviews could mean commitment issues, higher potential for crazy exes, or some other reason why things continually didn't work out.

But Darren could be an option. He was kind and funny, according to one reviewer. A true gentleman, said another. The only negative thing was that apparently he worked a lot. That wasn't so bad.

"Not you too," a deep male voice came from close behind her. Reed. "Is everyone using that goddamn app?"

His voice was like liquid sex. Hot, deep, smooth.

Get ahold of yourself, Darcy. Remember the thing about not *becoming a puddle?*

"Research is important. If women read reviews online before they buy a book, why wouldn't they read reviews before they go on a date?"

"Maybe I'm old fashioned, but I thought dating was about getting to know someone without any preconceived judgments." No apology for his tardiness…as she'd expected.

"If you'd actually taken the time to get to know more women, you wouldn't be in such a bind."

To her surprise, he laughed. "You know what? I like you, Darcy."

The words bounced around in her brain, colliding with the questions she would never dare ask—like whether her attraction was reciprocated.

Today, he looked less done than he had on their previous meetings. His dark hair was rumpled, like he'd run his fingers through it one too many times. He didn't wear a tie, and his open collar revealed a sliver of tanned skin. Reed certainly wasn't the stereotypical pasty office worker, that was for damn sure.

"Close your mouth, darlin'. You're staring." His lips quirked.

And just like that, her buzzing anticipation was replaced by the resounding urge to toss a drink in his face. "You wish, Reed. You're not my type."

"Oh no? You'd prefer Five-Star Darren, would you?" He inclined his head toward her phone and she snatched it out of his line of sight. "Nice guys aren't good in bed."

Her face was so hot she had serious concerns about spontaneous combustion. "And I suppose you're the authority on what constitutes being good in bed."

"I see my reputation precedes me." The smirk bloomed into a full-blown wolfish grin. "My offer still stands, by the way. If you want to throttle me, I'm definitely up for it."

"You…just.…" The words stuttered out of her mouth like a toddler had taken over her brain and was mashing the controls with its fist. "You're a jerk."

He shrugged and signaled for her to follow him. "I've been called worse."

"I thought we were going to discuss the guest list," she said, annoyed that he was getting under her skin so quickly.

"We are. But I've got an appointment in the financial district, so we're going to conduct our meeting on the way."

"And what exactly am I going to do down there?" Her protest might have had more weight if she hadn't immediately followed him out of the café like a devoted puppy.

"Whatever you like. The company driver will bring you back whenever you're ready. Don't worry. I wouldn't leave you stranded."

"How do you know I don't have somewhere to be?"

"Do you?" His gaze swept over her. "I can tell you're not going to work."

Damn it. She should have worn something other than a pair of tattered denim shorts, a black House Stark T-shirt, and Dr. Martens. "Okay fine, I don't have anywhere to be. I'm just pointing it out so you know how rude you sound."

He blinked. "So we're still having the meeting?"

"Yes," she huffed.

They stopped beside a black car with tinted windows. Out of nowhere, a driver appeared and opened the door for them. Darcy suddenly felt underdressed, which was stupid since they were only going for a ride.

"So tell me: What's so appealing about Five-Star Darren?" Reed asked as they slid into the back seat. A glass partition separated them from the driver.

"None of your business." Oh God, they were *not* having this conversation. Not while a billion dirty thoughts were driving her to distraction. Damn him, why did he have to mention sex?

Her hormones hadn't been this rowdy since high school. But the second he got close and his clean, warm scent invaded her nostrils, it was like the sexy bits of her body started doing tequila shots.

"Oh come on, you can trust me. I might even be able to give you some advice." His brown eyes twinkled. They were framed by full, thick lashes—the kind of lashes that had no business being on a man.

God, they were far too close in the back seat of the car. Her bare leg was mere inches from his, and the scent of his aftershave invaded her nostrils. It was crisp, clean, with a hint of citrus.

Damn delectable.

"You were late today," she blurted out, hoping the abrupt change in conversation might steer him away from delving into her nonexistent dating life—and perhaps jolt her brain into *not* focusing on how good he smelled. "Half an hour late and I was sitting there, waiting."

"My meeting ran over and my phone died. I could have gone back to the office to email you, but that would have meant being later than I already was." He reached for a bottle of water that sat in a compartment in the door. When he offered her one, she shook her head. "I apologize for keeping you waiting."

"Thank you. I appreciate it."

"Now, back to your dating life—"

"No. We're not having this conversation." She held up a hand. "Besides, why do you care?"

"Because, after careful deliberation, I've decided that you *are* interesting."

"Gee, thanks." Darcy snorted. "I'll pass on that so-called compliment."

"So-called?"

"You do know 'interesting' is usually a code word for 'weird,' right? It's not much better than telling a girl she has a great personality."

"What's that a code for?"

"Ugly."

He brought the water bottle to his mouth and sipped. Full lips hinted at sinful activities and Darcy tried to quash the flutter low in her belly. He probably knew *exactly* what to do with his lips too.

Stop it.

"You are interesting…in the non-code word sense. Even if you do think I'm a jerk. And Five-Star Darren would be a terrible match, for what it's worth."

Curiosity tugged at her. She knew nothing about the dating world, and it was clear he was well experienced. Surely there wouldn't be any harm in gleaning some information from him…for research purposes, of course.

"Why's that?" she asked.

"All these women have rated him highly, yet they haven't stayed with him. Why would that be?"

"I don't know." She frowned. "Maybe it just wasn't the right time."

"For *all* those women?"

Okay, so that did sound a bit suspicious when he put it like that. "But the reviews—"

"What do the reviews say?"

She pulled up Darren's profile on the app and scanned down the page. "'Great guy but the timing wasn't right.'" She shot him a smug look. "See? Told you."

"Keep reading."

"He's a total gentleman, but they didn't have many common interests. Uh, another one says their jobs made dating too hard but that he was a nice person. Apparently, he's romantic, but there wasn't enough spark." Darcy kept scrolling. "He's kind and funny, a great conversationalist. I can't see any red flags here."

"He's got a small dick."

Darcy almost choked. "Excuse me?"

Reed shrugged. "Or he doesn't know how to make a woman come."

"Stop," she hissed, the heat flushing through her body in a way that was entirely too pleasurable. Totally, *totally* inappropriate. "You can't say that."

"Why not? It's just sex. And sometimes you have to look at what people aren't saying to understand what they are." He nodded. "Words can be unreliable like that."

Darcy shook her head and stuffed her phone into her bag. This conversation had shot out of her comfort zone. Like a whole solar system out of her comfort zone. Listening to Reed talk about sex was… God, she didn't even know. Her imagination was serving up all kinds of dirty scenarios, but she tamped them down.

Reed was off-limits. Not only because of the bad reviews, but also because it was clear he could run circles around her verbally. There wasn't a doubt in her mind that he would do the same thing in the bedroom.

Maybe that's what you need. Someone to show you the ropes…with his rope.

No. Stop. Right now.

"You're staring again," he said. "You got a crush on me or something?"

"I'm trying to see if telekinesis is a real thing so I can pop your head like a grape."

He barked a laugh. "Right, well, at least you're honest. Shall we get on with the work?"

"Yes, please."

Chuckling, Reed reached for his laptop, which was jutting out of the pocket behind the driver's seat when the driver lowered the glass partition.

"Sorry to interrupt. There's an urgent call for you, sir." The driver took his earpiece out and handed a cell phone back to Reed. "Someone's been trying to get ahold of you."

"Hello?" A moment later, the color drained from Reed's face. "Of course. I'll be right there."

Chapter 7

"Reed McMahon doesn't give a crap about anyone but himself."

—ILoveBagels88

R eed kept the phone to his ear a moment longer than necessary so he could put reality off for as long as possible. There weren't a lot of things that could throw him off balance. But this... this was his Achilles' heel.

Your father's been admitted to the emergency room. He had a fall...

His chest clenched. They'd admitted him over an hour ago. He fought the urge to pound his fist into something. Why today of all days did his phone have to flake out? Donna had likely tried the office first. But it probably took them a while to figure out which driver he'd gone with, since he didn't use the booking system like he was supposed to.

The thought of the old man lying there while Reed had no idea anything was going on made him want to scream.

He's okay, but they're keeping him overnight for observation. It was lucky I was there with him...

What if she hadn't been? What if he'd been alone like he always wanted to be? Reed's breath came short and choppy. What if he'd hit his head?

You don't have to come now. I know you're busy...

Is that what they thought of him? That he would leave his father to suffer alone while he took care of more important things? He wasn't his mother, for crying out loud.

"Reed?" Darcy touched him tentatively on his arm. "Is everything okay?"

She snatched her hand back when he sucked in a breath, his fist curling around the phone tight enough that the screen was close to cracking. He would not lose his shit now, not while someone might see. Not while *she* might see.

"We have to postpone this meeting." He ground the words out, packing down the worry and concern until it was nothing more than a little lump behind his breastbone. He'd deal with it later. "I have something to attend to."

Darcy's gaze tracked his face, her concern a foreign expression to him. It wasn't the kind of look people aimed in his direction too often. Since he'd met her, she'd looked at him as one might an intimidating dog. But now her brows were crinkled and her blue eyes were unusually soft. It made the vicious churn in his stomach even worse.

Reed directed the driver to take them to the Brooklyn Hospital

Center. Luckily, they were headed in the right direction. "We can let you out here, if you like," he said, turning back to Darcy.

"It's okay." She toyed with the hem of her shorts. "I'm in Park Slope, so the hospital isn't too far from me. I only came into the city to meet with you."

He nodded stiffly. "I'll get Phil to give you a lift home after he drops me off."

During the week, the roads were like a clogged artery. As much as he wanted to be at the hospital right this second, there was no rushing the lumbering beast that was Manhattan traffic.

He stole a glance at Darcy and her eyes were still on him. But this time he couldn't bring himself to tease her for staring. Usually women's appreciative gazes slid over his skin, stroking his ego but otherwise having little impact. Darcy didn't stare so much as study. Her eyes picked him apart, peeling back the layers until he was nothing but bone.

"Why do you look at me like that?" he asked.

She blinked. "Like what?"

"Like you're trying to figure me out." He ran a hand over his jaw, his finger feeling for the little nick he'd made when shaving that morning. "You look at me like I'm a hieroglyph."

"You know, that's very poetic." Her lips twisted into a smirk. "You might be a frustrated writer."

"Is this the point where you tell me I should spend more time in your library?" He looked out the window and willed the traffic to move faster.

"You never know, you might enjoy it." She wrinkled her nose. "*Do* you enjoy things?"

The question—along with her exaggeratedly inquisitive expression—caught him by surprise and a hearty laugh erupted from deep inside him. "Do I enjoy things? What kind of a question is that?"

She sat up straighter, clearly pleased by his reaction. "A genuine one. All I've seen so far is your ability to talk circles around me, but it's mostly insubstantial fluff. I wondered if you ever take the time to enjoy things…like, having a hobby or something."

"That's a little insulting," he said. "I'm a regular guy, and I take pleasure in regular things."

"You're not a regular guy."

"No, I suppose not. I'm the *bad* guy." He stifled the flash of resentment as he thought of the review he read earlier that morning.

Reed doesn't give a crap about anyone but himself.

That was it. No mention of the date, nothing to be gleaned from the username. He'd started to check in on the reviews more regularly, because something was sitting funny. His intuition told him that perhaps the whole Bad Bachelors thing wasn't going to blow over like he'd hoped.

He shook the niggling thought away. "Even villains need hobbies, I suppose. I play baseball."

"Beer league?"

"Yeah, for shits and giggles."

"I doubt you do anything for shits and giggles." She folded her arms across her chest and studied him openly. Her tongue darted out and she captured the ball of her stud between her teeth, playing with it in a way that captivated his attention. "I bet you're super competitive."

His eyes tracked the flash of silver as she spoke. "So are most people." He shrugged. "Difference is I have no problem admitting it."

"Fair." She bobbed her head.

What Darcy didn't know was that she'd zeroed in on a messy bundle of memories from his past. Memories that had no place streaking across his mind like they were fresh and vivid when they should have stayed in the neat, little box where they belonged. But these memories were superstrength—no matter how many years passed, they had the ability to hit him with the force of a sucker punch.

He remembered the air ruffling his hair as he looked up to the stands, pretending to smile at his folks. But really he was taking note of the scouts who'd come to watch him and another Little Leaguer. The men who sat and stared and took notes. They made him nervous, but in a good way. It filled him with extra-special energy that made his throws faster and his swings harder.

"What do you do for fun?" He raked a hand through his hair. "I suppose you read."

"I do. I'm an unrepentant book nerd." She pointed to the satchel by her feet. "I always have a book or my e-reader with me in case I have a few minutes to spare."

"And yet you were busy looking up Five-Star Darren while you waited for me."

She pursed her lips. "I know you think the app is evil because of the stuff they posted about you, but some women might find it helpful."

"Women like you?"

"Yeah. Like me." She narrowed her eyes defiantly. "You probably have no idea what it's like, but I'm new to this dating thing and it's a little daunting."

"And you think the app is going to be your safety net," he scoffed. "Oh, Darcy, tell me you're not that naive. You can't believe everything you read."

"Says the guy with the bad score." She looked him up and down. "I'm sure you'll understand why I take your opinion with a grain of salt."

He opened his mouth to retort, but for once he had nothing to say. Nor any energy to think up a quip. As much as he enjoyed to-ing and fro-ing with Darcy, his mind was occupied with other things.

You don't have to come right now. I know you're busy…

They spent the rest of the journey in relative silence, with Reed staring out the window as the city slowly rolled by.

Darcy's expression sobered as they pulled up in front of the hospital. "I hope they're okay…whoever it is."

His dad would be fine. He *had* to be.

. . . .

Darcy watched the emotion disappear from Reed's face as they pulled into the circular driveway in front of the Brooklyn Hospital Center. He looked as though he might be about to step into a meeting. Gone was the deep furrow between his brows; gone was the haunted look in his eyes. Even as they'd joked—something Darcy often did when she wasn't sure how to deal with a situation—there'd been an undercurrent of tension in his voice. For a guy who was on the ball, he'd seemed distracted.

Whoever was in that hospital meant a great deal to him.

"I trust you'll keep this detour to yourself," he said, unbuckling his belt.

"You really think you need to say that?" She frowned. "Who the hell would I tell?"

"Forgive me for being overly cautious, but my life has moved into the spotlight recently." He shoved the door open and the noise of the outside world filtered in. "A lot of people seem quite happy to share the nitty-gritty details of my life with the whole world."

Maybe Reed was more hurt by his Bad Bachelor reviews than he let on. For the first time since she'd downloaded the app's little, pink icon onto her phone, she thought about what it meant beyond her. All these men were being rated like they were products for people to dump into a shopping cart. How would she feel if someone did that to her? What if her ex-fiancé had decided to spill the beans on their failed relationship to the whole world?

Darcy Greer is a sweet, loyal girl, but she's totally oblivious to the outside world. She didn't even realize I was gay until she walked in on me kissing another man...

"I won't say anything," she said. "I promise."

He paused for a moment, his eyes burning into her with a fierce intensity. "Thank you."

He shut the door and the sound ping-ponged through her head as she watched him walk up to the hospital's large entrance. People streamed in and out, like ants running up and down a hill. But her eyes were stuck on Reed—on his smooth gait and the way he held himself like a king.

"Miss?"

Darcy jumped. She'd totally forgotten Reed's driver was waiting for her to hand over an address…and that the partition was down, meaning he would've had full view of her staring after his client.

"Do you know who's in there?" she asked as Reed disappeared into the building.

"No, I don't." The driver met her eyes in the rearview mirror, his expression cool and professional. Even if he did know, he didn't seem the type to gossip. Probably a good thing, considering Reed's current issues. "Now, where can I take you?"

She was about to hand over her address when her gaze snagged on something resting on Reed's seat. His wallet. Her hand smoothed over the buttery soft leather, her thumb brushing the subtle *RM* stitched into one corner.

"I think I'll walk." She scooted along the back seat and cupped Reed's wallet in her hand. If the driver noticed, he didn't say anything. "Thanks anyway."

"You sure?" The driver asked and she nodded. "All right."

Darcy stepped out into the mild air and looked up. The sky was bright and sunny, creating a vivid backdrop for the behemoth building in front of her. It was ugly and brown, and had the strange, unintentional shape of a building that'd grown out of necessity, with more thought to function than form.

What the hell was she doing here?

Reed's haunted expression stuck in her head. For a guy who

was, from all accounts, a selfish, manipulative, say-anything-to-get-what-he-wants bastard…it didn't fit. Darcy looked back to the curb. The black car had already taken off into the steady stream of traffic, leaving her alone. Maybe she should walk home and then call Reed later to let him know about the wallet, rather than intruding.

She flipped it open. An old photo stared back at her—a young Reed with the man who presumably was his father. They both wore baseball gloves and identical crooked smiles.

"Why are you getting involved?" she muttered to herself.

She should have handed the wallet over to the driver and gone on her way. It would have been the smart thing to do. Perhaps it was curiosity—she'd discovered a little imperfection in the fabric of Reed McMahon's image and now she was pulling at that rogue thread so she could see what unraveled.

He's not a mystery for you to uncover. He's a real person, a work associate. *It's none of your business.*

Her mouth twitched. No, not associate. What had he called her? His companion? That slick wordsmith wasn't the same man she'd seen a moment ago, the one who was worried about what people thought and who was concerned for someone else's well-being. The one-two slap of her Docs against concrete rang in her ears.

The closer she got the hospital, the faster her heart beat. There was something about the smell of hospitals that unsettled her—that unique mix of antiseptic and sickness that curdled in her nostrils.

"Just hand over the wallet and get the hell out of here," she said under her breath.

She had no business butting into Reed's personal life. But, from the glimpse he'd given her a moment ago, it didn't sound like he had many friends on speed dial. She spotted him standing at the reception desk, in a heated discussion with an older woman. Were they arguing? No, she was trying to calm him down. A nurse behind the desk intervened, pushing some papers toward Reed.

Reed had shucked his jacket and rolled up his shirtsleeves, exposing strong forearms smattered with hair. A heavy watch glinted at his wrist. Even amid the worst lighting in the world, he looked as though he'd stepped out of a photo shoot for a men's fashion magazine. But his hair was even more roughed up than before and his brows were creased in unconcealed worry. Somehow, he managed to look furious and despondent all at once.

This is crossing a line. You don't know him and his personal issues are none of your business.

Reed turned and headed for the elevators, shoulders squared and jaw set. People moved out of his way, as Darcy imagined they did most of the time. He had the kind of presence that caused others to change their course, to accommodate him without even realizing what they were doing.

"Reed," she called out, waving his wallet.

The crowd didn't part for her the way it did for him. She shoved her way past a large group gathered by the reception desk.

"Reed!" Her voice was lost in the din of wailing babies and hospital chatter.

He stepped into the elevator before she could catch his attention and the doors slid shut. *Shit.* Now what was she supposed to do? Darcy spotted the woman who'd been speaking to Reed a moment ago. She had a bag slung over one arm and a weary expression that deepened the wrinkles around her eyes.

"Excuse me," Darcy said, approaching her. "I need to find Reed McMahon. Do you know what room he's going to?"

The older woman narrowed her eyes, her gaze sweeping up and down Darcy, lingering on the tattoos decorating her arm. Darcy was used to it; she called it the *I'm glad you're not dating my son* look. It was usually encountered whenever she bumped into one of her mother's friends or if she got stuck waiting in line at the drugstore.

"Why would I tell you that?" She pursed her lips.

"I'm guessing he'd like this back." Darcy held the wallet up. "He dropped it."

"Is this a trick?" She held her hand out. "How do I even know it's his?"

Darcy flipped the wallet open and handed it over. "We were supposed to have a meeting when he got the call to come here. He rushed out of the car and I found this on the back seat."

The woman's expression softened. "I'm sorry. I didn't mean to insinuate that you were being dishonest. We've had a few reporters lurking around and they're not above using those kinds of tricks."

"Oh." Darcy blinked. "Sorry to hear that."

She handed the wallet back. "I'm Donna, by the way. I take care of Reed's father."

"Darcy Greer. I'm a client...sort of." She thought about elaborating but decided against it. "So, do you know where I can find him?"

"They've just transferred Adam to a single room." She rattled off the number and some vague directions. "I'd offer to take it up for you, but I'm running late for an appointment."

"That's okay. I'll manage."

"I really am sorry about before. There's a reporter who's been bothering Adam and I'm at my wit's end about it all." She sighed. "They're painting that poor boy as a devil all because of some stupid website. Imagine hounding a sickly man for gossip about his only son."

"That's terrible."

Darcy bid Donna goodbye and headed toward the elevators, her mind whirring with questions. Reed's father must have been ill if he had someone looking after him even before he went into hospital. She flipped the wallet open and looked at the picture again, her heart squeezing at the love shining out of young Reed's face. What must it be like to have that kind of a bond with a parent?

She honestly didn't know. If she'd known her father, her life might've been different. She could have become a person who carried a treasured memory in her back pocket at all times. But her mother had never even given her the chance.

Maybe, might have, could have.

Dangerous words that led to dangerous thoughts. She stepped into the elevator and jabbed at the fourth-floor button. All she had to do was get in, give him the wallet, and then get the hell out of there before she made any more stupid decisions.

Chapter 8

"I 'dated' Reed for three weeks. In that time, I didn't learn a thing about him—nothing about where he came from, nothing about his family or his personal life. Nada. The man is locked up tighter than Fort Knox."

—*IDreamofGeniality*

"Jesus, Dad." Reed walked into the small single hospital room where his father lay in bed, machines beeping softly in the background. "Do I need to start padding the house with Bubble-Wrap?"

His father scowled. "Enjoy this while it lasts. The second they haven't got me hooked up to these blasted tubes, I'll swat you with the back of my hand."

"I saw Donna downstairs." He glanced at the table containing Adam's barely touched lunch. In keeping with his last few hospital visits, he'd only eaten the pudding.

"Did you fire her? I told her I didn't need no ambulance." He grunted. "That woman is always making a mountain out of a mole hill."

Reed didn't bother to mention that Donna had been well and truly spooked by Adam's fall. Apparently, he'd hit the coffee table so hard on the way down that the glass had shattered, and all she'd been able to focus on was the splatter of blood on his white undershirt. It was a miracle Adam hadn't put his hand straight through it and severed a major artery. As it was, his right hand and wrist were badly scratched up, but the damage was mostly superficial.

The real issue, however, was whether he had a concussion. Signs appeared negative, but they were keeping him overnight just in case.

"I told her not to call you," Adam added. He tried to lift his injured hand to reach for the glass of water but winced when he flexed his muscles against the bandages. "You shouldn't be worrying yourself with such trivial crap."

"In what universe is your health 'trivial crap'? Give me some credit."

The words stung more than Reed would ever let on, but he knew his father was only trying to minimize the situation. At some point, however, Adam would have to face up to his declining health. Unfortunately, no matter how much Donna and Reed tried to discuss it with him, the denial still had him in an iron grip.

"I'm just saying, maybe it's time for Donna to go." Adam brought the water glass to his lips, his hand shaking so much he almost spilled it on himself.

Reed reached out. "Here, let me—"

"I'm not a child," he snapped. "I can hold my own goddamn glass."

Don't poke the bear. "Okay, okay."

Every time Adam ended up in the hospital, they played this game. Reed would pay the bills, and Adam would get cranky about the littlest things because he hated accepting help but knew he had no choice where the finances were concerned. So he'd take back his power by complaining about everything in an effort to forget what he was really upset about.

And around and around and around they went. Every. Fucking. Time.

"I don't want you hanging around here all night either." Adam set the glass down. "So don't even think about staying."

"I'll run back to your place and bring you a change of clothes for tomorrow."

"Don't worry about—"

"Wasn't a suggestion." He stared the older man down for a moment until he saw a flash of reluctant resignation.

"You're a stubborn bastard, Reed." His father laughed, a cough abruptly cutting off the rare sound.

"I learned from the best," he said dryly. His eyes skated over the room, taking in the generic setup—one bed, one visitor chair, one bland print on the wall. White on white. The constant hum of machinery. Every time he got a call from Donna or the hospital, Reed wondered if his father might let him help this time. If he might *want* him there.

As yet, no such luck.

"Did you bring a visitor?" Adam interrupted Reed's thoughts with a raised, bushy brow and a nod to the door.

"What? No." He turned, wondering what the hell kind of drugs they'd given the old man, when he caught a familiar face staring at him from the doorway.

Darcy. What was she doing here?

"Uh, hi." She raised her hand in a tentative greeting.

Her teeny tiny denim shorts and chunky, black boots looked wildly out of place against the sterile backdrop of the hospital hallway. Her blue eyes were vibrant and so full of personality that everything else faded around her.

"Did you follow me up here?" He cringed internally at how harsh he sounded. But dealing with his dad never failed to give his worry a jagged edge.

"You dropped this." She held up his wallet, but she still hadn't ventured into the room.

Her gaze darted back and forth between him and his father, her curiosity unconcealed. Instinct roared at him to push her away, to close the door so she couldn't see the real him—the raw and unedited and unfiltered him.

"Who's this lovely young woman?" Suddenly Adam's voice was smooth as butter. "Is she a friend of yours, Reed?"

"Don't even think about it," he muttered in his father's direction. "This is Darcy. She's a client and I was with her when I got the call to come see you."

He walked over, hand outstretched. Her eyes widened and it struck him that she looked…nervous. No wonder. He probably had the fire of hell in his eyes right now. But in the two long-legged strides it took him to cross the room, all the fight left him. He spent so much of his time battling people—arguing with his dad about what care he needed, arguing with the people at work who wanted to see him topple, arguing with his clients who thought they knew better. Arguing with himself when he looked at his reflection in the mornings.

Lately he'd stopped looking.

"Here." She handed the wallet over. "I didn't mean to intrude."

"You saved me a call to the bank." He tried to smile but it probably looked more like a grimace. "I appreciate it."

Christ. If only the vultures behind Bad Bachelors could see him now. He wasn't smooth talking the pants off anyone.

"Bring her here, Reed," his father demanded.

Oh God, this was the last thing he needed. "Darcy came to drop this off. Let's not waste her time."

"Nonsense. With what's going on at the moment, the fact that she didn't rifle through it and call the newspaper is saying something."

Reed sighed, but Darcy laid a hand on his arm. "It's fine," she said. "It would be rude not to say hello."

He stepped aside so she could enter the room. "Have at it."

In the next five minutes, Reed watched, awestruck, as Darcy charmed his notoriously difficult to impress father. Turned out they had a shared love of Jules Verne. It was the most animated Reed had seen his father in…well, years.

"How come you're never that nice to *me*?" he quipped as they hovered at the door.

Her lips twitched. "Maybe it's because I don't like you."

"And you like him? Well, no accounting for taste I guess."

"I heard that!" Adam said with a gravelly laugh. "Can't handle the fact that your old man's still got it, can you?"

He leaned down to Darcy's ear. "You've created a monster. I'm going to hear about this for weeks."

"Good. You could learn a thing or two." She shifted on the spot, her hand braced against the doorframe as though she wasn't quite ready to leave. "It's nice that you're so close."

"We have something, all right." He glanced back at his father, whose head was now resting against the pillows, eyes closed. The sound of his labored breathing filled the room. "How about I walk you out? I need to get going anyway."

"Wow. I didn't expect my comments to have such an immediate reaction." Her eyes glinted. "Since when are you a gentleman?"

Shaking his head, he closed the door behind them. "Come on. The offer expires in two seconds."

"Fine." Darcy fell into step beside him as they wound their way through the maze-like halls of the hospital. "Is he going to be okay?"

"I think so. They're keeping him as a precaution."

Normally, he would have felt Darcy's presence invaded on what was a very private—very precious—part of his life. For some reason, the normal resentment wasn't there. Instead, he found words stumbling off his tongue as he filled her in on his father's accident.

"Lucky someone was there," she said, her eyes wide.

"It's part of the reason I get Donna to check on him daily. The last time he hurt himself she was only working a few days a week and

Dad didn't bother to call anyone." His jaw clenched at the memory. "He got his oxygen tank caught on a piece of furniture and broke his wrist when he fell. Took two days before either Donna or I checked in on him, and he'd just been popping painkillers like they were fucking breath mints instead of telling someone about it."

"You worry about him."

"Hard not to when he seems hell-bent on ignoring his health." He let out a bitter laugh. "Not that it gets me anything but a string of obscenities."

"When was the last time *you* accepted someone's help?" she asked.

His mind flickered back to the past weekend, when Gabriel had offered to come to his dad's so they could clean up the front yard together. Reed had brushed him off, making the job sound smaller than it really was.

"I'll take that silence as your admission of guilt," she said. "You're two peas in a pod."

"That's a worry," he muttered.

They walked through the hospital's reception area and out into the late-afternoon sunshine. His assistant had canceled his meetings for the rest of the day. Usually, Reed would have headed back to the office regardless. But today he couldn't seem to muster the energy. That was happening more and more lately. Trying to keep up the Reed McMahon persona at work was tiring him out.

"Thanks for not going on a spending spree with my credit card," he said.

"Damn. Why didn't I think of that?" Darcy grinned. "I could be rampaging through Saks right now, buying myself a new wardrobe."

She shoved her hands into her pockets and rocked back on her heels. This was the part where he should offer to reschedule their meeting and bid her a good day. The part where he should walk away unaffected by her on any level.

But he couldn't.

It's not her. You're just being sentimental because of everything that's going on. Say goodbye, go home, and get your head back in the game.

"Are you okay?" She cocked her head, the sun glinting off her tongue stud as she spoke. "You look a little pale."

A group of three women walked past, their conversation halting abruptly as they stared. One of them immediately pulled out her phone, but the other two laughed and hurried her along.

Now he was second-guessing his decision not to worry about Bad Bachelors. Perhaps it was time to do some digging.

"Never better, sweetheart." The old defensive walls slid back into place. Muscle memory kicked in, pulling his lips up into a charming smile. Out here, he could wear it like armor. Out here, he could be the Reed he wanted people to see. "Never better."

....

Score one for the girls!

Today I'm thrilled to be able to share a success story from user IDreamofGeniality. In the big, bad world of dating, nothing pleases me more than knowing that Bad Bachelors is able to help women find the relationships they deserve.

Before the Bad Bachelors app, I was in a really bad place. I'd come out of a long-term relationship that broke down rather suddenly and unexpectedly. I'd gone from planning a wedding to being totally adrift. I had no idea how to date, no idea where to even start.

I met a wonderful guy at an industry event and was totally swept off my feet...or so I thought. Turns out this guy was used to dealing with women like me. He knew exactly what to say and how to act. But after a while, I started to feel like something wasn't right. Boy, do I wish I had the Bad Bachelors app back then. At least I would have known I was dealing with the number one guy on the bad list!

I "dated" Reed for three weeks. In that time, I didn't learn a thing about him—nothing about where he came from, nothing about his family or his personal life. Nada. The man is locked up tighter than Fort Knox.

Luckily, I kept at it. Once I'd found out about the Bad Bachelors app, I felt confident to reenter the dating arena. I happened to recognize one of my neighbors on the site and saw all the wonderful things people were saying about him. I even plucked up the courage to stop and talk to him at work one day. Then he asked me out.

Thank you, Bad Bachelors team. You've helped make this woman very happy indeed.

I bet you can hear me applauding all around New York City right now. This is exactly why I created the Bad Bachelors app—to hand the power back to you. Now, with all the information you need at the swipe of a finger, you can make informed, smart decisions about your dating life just like you do with everything else.

Stay tuned for tomorrow's post on a new feature we're going to launch for beta testing. This new functionality will help you prioritize and keep track of the bachelors on your favorites list. You'll even be able to add private notes only you can see. We're excited and hope you are too!

With love,
Your Dating Information Warrior
Helping the single women of New York
since 2018

Chapter 9

"When I'm with a guy, I don't want to feel like everything is an experiment in power plays. Reed pushes people's buttons for sport."

—*MadMelissa*

R eed rolled his shoulders, trying to ease the tension there. He'd come into the office late this morning, since his father had been discharged and he'd wanted to be there to take him home. They'd kept Adam at the hospital for two nights and the doctor had pulled Reed aside that morning to inform him that Adam had refused treatment from the nurses.

So his dad was being a difficult bastard. What else was new?

Yawning, Reed opened his laptop to answer a few emails before heading off to his first meeting of the day. The Bad Bachelors website was still open from yesterday. The colorful banner with the glossy, pink lips and single, manicured finger raised in a *shh* motion mocked him.

Doubt didn't rear its ugly head often anymore, but the negative voices clawed their way back in.

Several new reviews had been added overnight. Well, wasn't he Mr. Popular?

> "When I'm with a guy, I don't want to feel like everything is an experiment in power plays. Reed pushes people's buttons for sport."
>
> —MadMelissa

For some reason, his mind immediately jumped to the Melissa who worked at Bath and Weston. She'd said something similar after he was made partner, beating her out for a position she'd been coveting.

You push people's buttons, Reed. You're a bully and you're not right for this job.

He sucked in a deep breath and clicked the *X* in the corner of the browser window. Was it possible that this review wasn't about dating, but rather a bumpy work relationship?

But before he could ponder the review further, his office door swung open and in marched Donald Bath—one of the firm's founding partners, the last living dinosaur and asshole extraordinaire.

"Mr. Bath is here to see you." Kerrie came in behind him, scowling. Donald Bath waited for no one. No doubt he would have marched right past her desk in that pompous way of his.

"That will be all, Kelly," Donald said.

She shot Reed a look before closing the door. "It's *Kerrie*, Don. If you're going to address someone by name, it pays to get it right. She's worked here for over ten years."

The older man took a seat without invitation. His white hair was combed over an ever-increasing bald patch on the top of his head. But there was nothing about him that looked frail. Donald could issue a withering stare that was rumored to reduce a grown man to a pile of bones in seconds.

"I won't be taking advice on how to treat women from the likes of you," he replied. "Seems our resident bachelor has made quite a name for himself."

"It's a nonissue, Don. The only people who seem interested are gossip columns."

"You're wrong about that," Donald said. "Clients are worried."

Reed had to stop himself from rolling his eyes. So far, the only thing that had caused concern was the idea of reporters hassling his dad. *One* client—the CEO of a family company that owned several prestigious Manhattan restaurants—had called with concerns over the app. But Reed had assured them it wasn't a big deal and that it would be over quicker than it started.

That was hardly cause for alarm.

"I always knew you were trouble." The founding partner leaned forward and narrowed his eyes. "And as far as I'm concerned, Edward should have dealt with this already. But we all know he's a soft touch where you're concerned."

Edward Weston was more than a boss; he'd been Reed's mentor for years now.

"He's not a soft touch, but compared to you…" Reed shrugged. "I guess the idea for the Grinch had to come from somewhere."

Donald's expression was ice-cold. "I don't have time for children's books and neither should you."

Reed shrugged. "I watched the movie. You know books aren't my thing."

"You've got big problems, you know. We lost Chrissy Stardust."

Reed stifled a groan. The twentysomething pop singer was such a strong repeat customer that he had two of his consultants working with her at all times. Her unapologetic interviews and predilection for drunken Twitter rants had brought Bath and Weston considerable income. And Reed had signed her personally. She'd been his stepping-stone to a partner position.

And she'd canceled her meeting last week. Kerrie hadn't been able to get ahold of her agent to reschedule, which wasn't entirely unusual. But now it looked as though he should have been more concerned.

"She's gone to Morgan, Stanley, and Archer." In any other situation, Donald wouldn't have looked so smug that they'd lost a huge client to their biggest competitor. But this would be the stake on which Donald planned to mount Reed's head. "More will follow, I assure you."

"I'll fix it."

"You'd better." Donald pushed up from his chair and braced his hands on Reed's desk, leaning over so he cast an imposing shadow. "Or I will personally see that you don't work here or anywhere else. You might have fooled Weston, but I will not stand by while you ruin everything we built because you can't keep your dick in your pants."

A tight ache spread through Reed's jaw and he realized he'd been grinding his teeth. He needed to get Chrissy back.

And it looked like it was time to squash Bad Bachelors like the cockroach it was. He'd been prepared to wait for it to blow over, but not now. Not when Ed might bend to his partner's will and then Reed would be out of both a job *and* an important relationship. And he would *not* let this affect his ability to support his father.

Whoever had set up the Bad Bachelors app was going down. Internet anonymity was a false security. Reed *would* find the person causing him trouble and make them pay.

....

Darcy rolled her head from side to side, stretching out the tight muscles in her neck. She'd been hard at work designing a flyer for the next Literature Loving Ladies book club event when a new email had popped into her inbox.

She was still subscribed to the Bad Bachelors newsletter even though she'd done nothing about following up on the short list of men Annie and Remi had put together. Reed's words still rang in her ears from yesterday: *Maybe he doesn't know how to make a woman come.*

Five-Star Darren. She pulled up his profile to see he still maintained a high average rating, even with a new review.

"Darren is a wonderful guy. It was too bad I've decided to move away for work—I hope he finds the right girl to love and cherish." Darcy screwed up her nose. She could already hear Reed's mocking voice.

Nice guys are boring in bed.

Maybe that wasn't the worst thing in the world. Hell, it wasn't like she would know any better. She and Ben had never had a scintillating sex life, and now she knew it was possibly because Ben had been wishing she were someone else…namely, a *male* someone else. So she reasoned that boring sex was better than no sex.

It certainly seemed safer than sleeping with someone like Reed.

But ever since she'd walked away from the hospital two days ago, with his gaze burning into her back, her mind had been stuck on him. Last night, she'd woken up around 2:00 a.m. with her hand down her panties and a film of perspiration on her forehead. That wasn't the worst bit. The disappointment that'd stabbed through her chest when she realized it was her own hand and not Reed's head between her legs had been particularly humiliating.

"Hey." Remi poked her head out of her bedroom. "Get dressed. We're going for drinks."

"I thought you had class tonight." Darcy swiveled around on the chair that sat in the makeshift office space they'd jammed into one corner of the living room. The desk was littered with lengths of ribbon that Remi had been sewing onto a pair of ballet shoes.

"Nope. They refreshed the schedule and I switched nights with one of the other instructors." She bounced on the spot. "Which means it's time for cocktails. There's this cute place right near Annie's work, which is perfect because we can swing past and pry her away from her desk."

"Should I pack my crowbar?" Darcy asked dryly. "You know she doesn't leave the office before pumpkin hour."

"Tough." Remi grinned, retreating to her room. "I got a tip that one of the guys on your list is going to be there tonight. So we're doing this thing."

"Wait, what?" Darcy looked up, Remi's evil cackling sounding from the bedroom. "Doing what thing?"

"Getting you some man candy." Remi reappeared and tossed a black silk top at Darcy's head. "Wear this. And no ripped jeans and combat boots either."

She inspected the scrap of fabric and could already envisage the amount of cleavage that would be on display, and shook her head. "Uh-uh. No way."

"I'm not taking no for an answer." Remi tapped her foot. "And would you hurry up already? We need to leave."

An hour later, they were standing in the reception area of Annie's office and Darcy couldn't stop tugging at the neckline of her top. The damn thing was short and clingy—two things she avoided at all costs. But apparently, a button-down shirt was not an appropriate man-candy-acquiring outfit. That hadn't stopped Darcy from throwing a light cardigan over it, though she'd had to bargain with Remi. The trade-off was wearing a pair of dangly earrings, which were already driving her insane.

How the hell did women wear those jangly things without feeling like a freaking house cat?

"Just give me another half hour or so," Annie said. "I have a report to—"

"No. Now." Remi stopped short of stamping her foot. "What if he's gone by the time we get there?"

"How the hell do you know he's going to be there anyway?" Darcy crossed her arms. "Have you got an army of spies out there tracking all my potential dates?"

"Darren Montgomery happens to live next door to one of the barre instructors at the Lexington studio. She invited us to come for a drink." Remi winked. "She said she's more than happy to introduce you if you like what you see."

"No. No introductions." Darcy shook her head. "Not yet."

"Good men are hard to find. Do you want to watch the Darrens of the world get snapped up by women who are willing to put themselves out there?" She folded her arms across her chest with the pinched expression of a disapproving schoolteacher. "Sitting around doing nothing hasn't worked so far, has it?"

"No," Darcy admitted.

Annie threw her hands up in the air. "Fine, I'll leave the damn report. I don't know whether you two coordinated this guilt trip, but I'll remember it next time I need something from either one of you."

Remi clapped her hands together. "Excellent. Let's get our manhunt on."

The cute place Remi had described wasn't so much cute as it was all-out glamorous—funky chandeliers, plush seating, and a smooth bar that curved in waves along the length of the room, mimicking the dip at a woman's waist. It was dimly lit, designed for intimate conversation and suggestive touches.

The girls had snagged a spot at the end of the bar that gave them enough privacy to talk, but also a good vantage point from which to scope out the room. The bar was busy. They were in the financial district and the crowd was of the suited variety—bankers, management consultants, bean counters. In other words, not Darcy's type. She preferred the eclectic bars in the Village—but in order to find herself a decent guy, she needed to not only get out of her comfort zone but also out of her preferred zip code.

Darcy reached for her old-fashioned and sipped. "So what, exactly, is your colleague going to say? 'Hey, this chick likes your reviews. Want to date her?' Not sure how well that will go down."

"I'm sure she knows how to frame an introduction." Remi chuckled and toyed with the straw in her drink. "Or you could go over and introduce yourself."

"Oh yeah, no problem. Maybe I should bust out my wings and fly over there while I'm at it," Darcy scoffed. "I need a *reason* to speak to him. You can't send me in cold."

Annie and Remi debated the best methods for striking up a conversation, but Darcy tuned out. This whole thing made her want to puke up her cocktail all over the expensive, shiny bar. Her people skills had never earned her any gold stars growing up, and not much had changed. Hadn't she already learned that from her interactions with Reed?

That's different. He eats girls like you for breakfast.

The dirty thought that zinged through her brain almost made her choke on her drink. God, she needed to stop thinking about that. About *him*. But yesterday had done something to her opinion of him. Seeing him with his father—stressed and worried and all the things one should be when their loved one was in the hospital—made him seem a little more human.

A little more…entry level.

There is nothing entry level about Reed McMahon. He's for experienced players only.

Even if he wasn't as bad as Bad Bachelors made out, he was still a shameless playboy with far too many skills when it came to seducing women into bed. The last thing her confidence needed was to be shattered by someone who could write the book on sex and seduction while she was still sweating bullets about striking up a conversation in a bar. But Remi had a point—doing nothing had gotten her exactly that.

"I'm going to the restroom," she said, in need of a moment to herself. "I'll see if I can get a vibe from him as I walk past."

"That's code for stalling," Remi grumbled, but she didn't say anything further when Annie shot her a look. Darcy slid off her stool and let out a relieved breath.

Baby steps.

Tugging down the hem of her top, she shuffled through the crowd, edging closer to Five-Star Darren. From a distance, she could see he was thinning on top, his blond-brown hair looking a little dull even in the flattering bar lighting. He was cute…kind of. Darcy looked on as he laughed with his friends, hoping even the tiniest flame of attraction might flicker in her belly.

Nada. She could have been staring at her aunt's collection of vintage porcelain dogs for all the excitement she felt. Darren didn't do it for her, that much was crystal clear.

Shoulders slumping, she continued pushing through the crowd until she reached the hallway that led to the restrooms. She leaned against the wall, letting her head roll back so she could suck in a breath and wait an appropriate amount of time before returning. Not that anyone would have noticed her coming or going—none of the men in the bar had looked twice at her.

"What are you doing here?"

Reed's wolfish smile engulfed her whole body in heat. If the man were any hotter, a single glance would have set her hair on fire. He leaned his shoulder against the wall, his large frame blocking the entry to the hallway. Crowding her. Hiding her.

The deep, rich, and all-too-familiar scent made Darcy's heart start to gallop. "Enjoying the booze, like everyone else."

"I'm not here to enjoy the booze," he said.

For a brief second, her stupid heart wondered if he was here for her. But that was just the late-onset horniness doing terrible things to her brain, like destroying whichever section was responsible for logic and reasoning.

"Got your eye on someone?" She ran her tongue across her lower lip. His eyes tracked the movement, intently following the half-moon swipe as if his life depended on it. "Chasing a little skirt?"

He smirked. "I'm pretty sure people don't say that anymore."

Darcy's cheeks burned, but she tried to hide it with a haughty flick of her ponytail over one shoulder. "Dodging the question, I see. Nice move, but it won't work on me."

"What would work on you?" He leaned a little closer and

Darcy's brain short-circuited. It would be a goddamn miracle if sparks weren't flying out of her ears.

Mayday, mayday. Brain is down. I repeat: Brain is down.

"Respect. A little courtesy."

He frowned. "You think I don't respect you?"

"I don't know if you respect any of the women you pursue. How can you when all you want is sex?" The second the words were out of her mouth, she wanted to take them back.

Reed wasn't the kind of guy with whom she should engage in verbal sparring. Not only that, but she was also starting to wonder exactly how much her opinion of him was based on what had been spoon-fed to her. It was easy to see him as the villain with his hypnotic good looks and commanding charm.

"Why do you think wanting sex and being respectful are mutually exclusive?"

The question halted her internal parade of confusion. "I don't know, actually."

"Because you've been conditioned to think that once you hand over the keys to the kingdom, you've lost all bargaining power." His tilted his chin up ever so slightly. "Women are taught to believe that once men get sex, they won't want anything else."

"Isn't it true?" She folded her arms across her chest. The moment Reed's eyes eased down to where her breasts pressed against the low neckline of her borrowed top, she dropped her hands again. "Do you want anything else from a woman after you've slept with her?"

"Why don't you find out?"

He inched closer, his head dipping to hers. The air in Darcy's lungs stilled, an indignant squeak clogging the back of her throat as her lips parted. A protest should have shot out of her, a "no fucking way" aimed squarely in his direction. But her dignity melted under the fire crackling between them, causing her body to prepare itself for his kiss. A dull ache pulsed between her legs, and she squeezed her thighs together—but it didn't quash the knowledge that should he slip a hand down her pants, he'd find her ready and willing.

"You're not my type," she gritted out.

Instead of looking affronted, Reed threw his head back and laughed. The booming sound cut the tension like a knife through butter.

"What?" she huffed. "Is it really so hard to believe I don't find you attractive?"

"Sweetheart, most women find me attractive. Some just hide it better than others." His hand came up to brush a strand of hair that had fallen across her forehead. "For the record, you *don't* hide it. At all."

"Screw you." She planted a hand against his chest and gave him a warning shove.

Mistake. The hard muscle beneath his crisp, white shirt felt even better than it looked. Her imagination was already having a field day filling in the blanks—the smooth skin, the little trail of hair that would guide her hand down below the waistband of his pants. The hefty weight she'd feel in her palm.

She resolutely kept her eyes forward. No way was she going to get caught checking out his crotch, regardless of how much her eyes wanted to pull downward.

"I'll have you know I'm here for someone else."

"Yes, Five-Star Darren." Reed smirked. "I saw him at the bar. You know he's balding on top, right?"

"I hadn't noticed," she lied. "How about you make yourself useful and give me some tips? What should I say when I walk up to him?"

To her delight, Reed's expression darkened. He looked... jealous. "You can do better, Darcy."

"What, like with you?" She wrinkled her nose. "No thanks."

....

There was something about Darcy that caused Reed's competitive streak to flare up. It prickled under his skin, turning a fleeting thought into a persistent drone. It was the exact reason he'd come into this bar when he'd spotted Darcy by chance. She'd walked in with two friends, laughing and smiling in a way she didn't around him. Before he'd even given it a second thought, he'd headed into the bar after her, desperate to see more of Darcy in her natural state.

Then he'd seen Five-Star Darren too. He didn't know the guy personally, but he'd trawled through Bad Bachelors looking at the guys they'd deemed better than him.

So that's why she was here? To chase some guy who'd likely leave her wanting and unfulfilled?

It was obvious she was attracted to Reed—and not because he believed the drivel he spouted about women wanting him, but because he could see it plain as day. Yet she fought it at every turn.

Her chest rose and fell in uneven bursts, as though she had to remind herself to continue breathing. Then there was the fidgeting, the hair flipping, and the tightening of that perfect, pouty mouth.

Unfortunately for him, the game wasn't one-sided. Because every time that delicate pink tongue darted out to moisten her lips, he got a flash of silver that had made him hard as a fucking rock.

This is a dangerous game. Do you want to piss off anyone else right now?

"I bet if I kissed you, that sweet, little mouth would part like the Red Sea." Satisfaction coursed through him when her nostrils flared. He dipped his head lower, so he could whisper right into her ear. "And I bet your hands would curl into my shirt, so you could hang on for dear life."

Her breath stuttered in and out. "You don't affect me, Reed."

"Bullshit."

Defiance rolled off her in waves, but there was a flicker of uncertainty in her eyes. She was torn between wanting to prove him wrong and the fear that she wouldn't be able to. The music from the bar had gotten louder; a thumping bass rolled through his bloodstream and urged him on. He wanted nothing more than to press her up against this wall and kiss her until all that resistance blew away in the wind.

"Kiss me then," she taunted. "You'll be disappointed with my reaction."

"I doubt that very much."

Her eyes widened when she realized he fully intended to prove her wrong. Shifting, he moved his body over hers, trapping her by planting his palms against the wall, one on either side of her. Caging her in. Sealing off the exits.

"Reed…" Her breath came in ragged bursts, but she didn't tell him to stop. Instead, she flattened her hands behind her and blinked her long, sooty lashes up at him.

"Darcy." His lips hovered over hers, their breath mingling in that delicious pre-kiss limbo.

Just as he predicted, her lips parted in that final second, inviting him in. He pressed against her, locking her down with his hips and his mouth. She didn't kiss like a woman who wasn't interested. Hell no. She kissed like a woman starved. Any pretense of tenderness was crushed when her tongue slid along his, her piercing bumping him in a way that was foreign and exciting. He stifled a moan—the combination of metal with the sweet taste of bourbon winding through his system like a drug.

She ground her hips against him and his cock pulsed. The thought of unzipping her pants so he could slide a hand into her panties rocketed through him. It would be oh so easy to glide that little bit of metal down and feel her hot and ready. To find that tight bundle of nerves and toy with her until she came against his hand. Until she begged for him to be inside her.

But this was about proving a point…wasn't it?

Teeth nipped at his lower lip and he growled, returning the action as one hand came to her ponytail. He had to force himself not to wind the silken length around his fist, so he could yank her head back and plunder that pouty, little mouth further. Christ, what was she doing to him? He *never* lost his head.

When he moved against her, she shifted, opening her legs to accommodate the press of his thigh. Her hips rolled with the rhythm of their kiss, with the thrust of his tongue. Her body was already so in tune with his. His hand dropped to her leg and she gasped, a shudder rippling through her as he felt for her inner thigh.

She pulled back, eyes wide. "I think I've proved my point," she said shakily.

"That I'm not pleased with your reaction? Think again." He grinned. The second he got home he was going to need the mother of all cold showers. "Or are you going to tell me it was all an act?"

"It was practice," she ground out, glaring at him. "For when I get Darren to buy me a drink."

Liar. He'd seen her walk straight past the guy before, a perplexed expression on her delicate features. It wasn't the same wide-eyed, flushed-cheek look she'd given Reed, that was for damn sure. But the thought of her doing this with Darren—grinding those hips and letting that damn piercing tease someone else's mouth...

It's none of your business.

Maybe so, but that didn't stop him wanting to go all caveman and kiss the hell out of her in the middle of the bar and wipe all thought of Five-Star fucking Darren from her mind forever.

"Make it a strong drink, then. You'll need more than a Shirley Temple to forget you're with him instead of me."

She opened her mouth to retort, but they were interrupted when a group of girls teetering in tall heels stumbled past, giggling and whispering as they looked Reed up and down. That was happening far too much lately.

"I won't need a drink to forget," Darcy said, using the distraction to step around him. "By the time I set foot outside, this will be a distant memory."

"Bullshit again," he said, but she was already fading into the crowd.

Damn her. Since when did he give a shit about women who thought they were above him? Normally he'd get a whiff of that superiority and be outta there faster than a single guy at a garter toss. But Darcy was messing with his head. Normal reactions didn't seem to apply to her, and unless he wanted another person siding against him, he was *really* going to have to stop tugging on her pigtails.

Too bad it was the only shred of enjoyment in his life right now.

Chapter 10

"The guy makes a living helping bad people look good. What makes you think you could trust someone like that?"

—*NotCarrie*

Reed made it out of his apartment before six the following Monday morning. He was used to getting up at the ass crack of dawn, but he *wasn't* used to doing it on minimal sleep, which he was now, thanks to a certain prickly woman who'd burrowed her way into his brain.

Friday night had been hell. He'd tossed and turned, restless and dissatisfied, until well into the night. Darcy and her impossibly sexy piercing. Darcy and her judging, pouty lips. Darcy and her undisguised loathing of him.

And that damned kiss…

The power struggle turned him on, as did the memory of

Darcy's lithe body pinned between him and a hard surface. But right now, Reed had bigger things to worry about than an epic case of blue balls. After hounding Chrissy Stardust's agent all weekend for a meeting, giving up his precious personal time to fix something that shouldn't need fixing, the guy had eventually relented. Reed had half an hour of her time. But she sat like a sullen teenager, eyes glued to her phone and bleach-blond hair hanging like a curtain in front of her face. Not that it hid last night's makeup or what looked to be a nasty hangover.

It was impossible to know exactly what to expect from a meeting with Chrissy Stardust. The pop starlet, whose real name was Eloise Christine Johnson, had a predilection for drinking heavily at breakfast and popping Xanax like they were M&M's. Which meant her temperament varied from barely coherent to Charlie Sheen on a thirty-six-hour bender.

"I told you," she said without looking up. "The move wasn't personal."

"No?" Reed reached for his coffee and sipped the steaming black liquid. "It just so happened to coincide with me having some image problems of my own?"

No response. Gritting his teeth, he scanned the room. They were in the restaurant at the hotel Chrissy was currently staying in. A view of Manhattan bathed in early-summer sunlight wrapped around them. But it was hard to enjoy the view with Chrissy's team of beefcakes hovering around them like a bad smell. One of the guys looked at Reed with his lip curled.

"Your muscle got a problem with me?" he asked.

Chrissy finally looked up, her pale-green eyes darting to her team and back. "Drako? Ah, don't mind him."

Drako continued to stare at Reed as though he was a piece of dog crap scraped from the bottom of someone's shoe. The guy was built like a brick wall and looked twice as thick. But Reed guessed Chrissy's team wasn't employed for witty banter and intellectual discussions.

"He's just…" She waved a hand in the air, her rhinestone-covered nails flashing like disco lights. "He's a feminist."

"Excuse me?" Reed blinked. "What the hell has that got to do with anything?"

Chrissy signaled to the waiter to top up her orange juice. She commanded people as though she'd been doing it her whole life and not like she'd been discovered in some dingy, two-bit mall talent contest down in Florida. "He doesn't agree with the way you treat women."

"Your G.I. Joe Ken doll has a problem with how I treat women?" He stopped short of saying *What the actual fuck?*

"Women deserve to be treated with respect," Drako said in what sounded like a heavy Ukrainian accent.

Chrissy held up a hand. "Drako's right. We're not, like, second-class citizens, you know."

This from the woman whose lyrics included such literary gems as "boom boom lock that bitch down…ho." Reed gritted his teeth. He was here to convince Chrissy to come back to Bath and Weston, questioning her loyalty to her gender would not help achieve that.

"Chrissy, you of all people should know you can't believe

everything you read." He raised a brow. "Otherwise, you've had three marriages, four divorces, and at least as many accidental pregnancies."

"Are you telling me it's bullshit?" She rubbed at her eyes and spread the black mess further. "You don't trick women into bed?"

Chrissy Stardust and her band of merry beefcakes were judging him? What alternate universe had he slipped into? His first instinct was to correct her. There was no trickery, since he was always up front about how he operated.

But he had to get control of this situation, and that meant not allowing her to derail the conversation. Because without Chrissy, he was at serious risk of being under his projected targets for the first time *ever* since he'd started at Bath and Weston. And that would not look good when he had to go to Edward for a lifeline. If he was going to save his job, he needed to keep the dollars rolling in.

"How about you remind your team that they're meant to be seen, not heard"—Reed drained the rest of his coffee, wishing he'd thought to ask the waiter to slip in a shot of something stronger—"and let the grown-ups talk?"

Chrissy waved her hand and Drako motioned for the team to fall back a few steps.

"Look, I understand this is an awkward situation," Reed said. "But can we cut the bullshit? We've worked together long enough not to need pretenses."

"Fine. Whatever." Chrissy raked a hand through her hair, bangles jangling at her wrist.

"I know you leaving Bath and Weston wasn't about needing a change. It was about what's happening with me."

Her lips were painted in something that looked sticky enough to put a china bowl back together. "Okay."

"Can you at least admit it?"

"Yes, I left Bath and Weston because of what I read about you." She huffed and slunk farther down into her seat. "Does that make you feel better?"

"No. But I want everything on the table." He forced himself to keep a soft expression despite wanting to spit out the bitter taste in his mouth. His team had worked like dogs on so many occasions to make Chrissy look good. Where was the loyalty? "And my team was very disappointed to see you go, Chrissy. We've done some great work together over the years. We know what works with your audience. We know what works with the media who follow you. Why throw away all that knowledge for something that won't even be an issue a week from now?"

"I don't think this is going away."

The words sent a chill through him. It *would* go away because it had to. He'd already scheduled a meeting with a PI for that afternoon to make sure this bullshit didn't continue.

"It is going away because it's not a real issue to begin with." He curled and uncurled his fists under the pristine white tablecloth. "You know what the media is like. This week Bad Bachelors is big news, and then next week someone will get divorced or go swimming topless and people will move on. That's how it works."

Chrissy sighed. "The thing is, Reed, I have to think about my audience. They're young girls. I want to be a role model."

The day Chrissy Stardust was a role model for young women

was the day he was officially going to tap out of life. The woman had good intentions, but he'd pulled her reputation out of the gutter enough times to seriously doubt Chrissy would be changing her ways anytime soon.

"It doesn't matter where the rumors came from." Chrissy shoved her orange juice away and reached into her purse for a silver flask. Christ, and she'd been admonishing him a moment ago. "What matters is my message. I don't want my fans seeing me work with a womanizer. They're better than that. *I'm* better than that." She took a swig of the flask and the scent of vodka hit Reed's nose like a punch. "We're done here."

He stayed rooted to his chair as she sauntered off, wobbling on her thigh-high stiletto boots until Drako steadied her. The bastard winked over his shoulder before they exited the restaurant, leaving Reed to seethe alone.

....

Later that day, he walked into the Brooklyn diner where he was due to have his first meeting with a PI named Peter Law. The place was kitsch. Clichéd '50s style and signs proclaiming their onion rings to be the best in the state. It was the kind of place he wouldn't have been caught dead in usually. Which was exactly why he'd picked it for this meeting.

Darcy had been stuck in his head all day, their kiss playing on repeat in his mind. It was a distraction. One he could do without. "It's sad that you're turned on by a woman who so clearly hates you,"

Reed muttered as he drummed his fingers against the Formica table-top in front of him.

Perhaps it was a survival mechanism. Given the pool of women who didn't hate him was drastically shrinking in the wake of Bad Bachelors' "exposé" on him, his options for a date were reduced to women looking for a story to share. Or worse, the deluded types who thought they could change him. But Darcy was neither of those things.

"Mr. McMahon, good to see you again." The PI stopped at his table, almost cutting off Reed's circulation as he grasped Reed's outstretched hand. He was old-school, the kind of guy who knew the importance of a strong handshake. "What can I do for you this time?"

He'd worked with Peter before. The guy was a former NYPD cop and had proved to be both reliable and discreet—two qualities Reed admired greatly, especially since he was keeping this meeting off the books. Having a meeting scheduled with a private investigator wasn't exactly uncommon in his world—he'd used them plenty of times to discredit people speaking out against his clients. But this was different.

This was personal.

"I'm hoping it will be a simple job. I want to know who created this website and the corresponding app." Reed handed over a piece of paper with the Bad Bachelors URL written on it.

"Okay." Peter took the piece of paper and studied the address for a moment before folding it up and tucking it into a worn leather notebook. "Just a name?"

"And personal contact information."

"Right." Peter's lip twitched and a surge of annoyance ran

through Reed's veins. "I can imagine you'd be interested in speaking to this person."

Damn it, had *everyone* read the post about him?

"This is a sensitive matter, as I'm sure you can understand. So we're clear, *I'm* employing you, not Bath and Weston." He paused as the server came over to offer them coffee. "You report to me and only me."

"Of course," he said. "Confidentiality is always my top priority."

Trust wasn't something he had in reserve, let alone for an issue that impacted both his career and his personal life.

"You must have pissed off one hell of a woman," Peter said, his bushy mustache brushing the top of his cup as he took a sip of his coffee. "We've all been there."

Reed swallowed back a bitter taste in his mouth. He wasn't looking for camaraderie right now. Not from Peter, not from his friends. Not from anyone.

He was far too practical for that; all he wanted was a solution. Because his job—and the care it afforded his father—was all he cared about in this fucked-up world. People could say whatever the hell they liked behind his back. He couldn't give two shits if they labeled him a player, a womanizer.

But the second it impacted Adam, he was going to bring out the big guns and put it to an end.

Peter nodded when it was clear he wasn't going to get a response. "I'll come back to you as soon as I have something."

....

Darcy had been in a daze all day. Ever since Reed had kissed her on Friday night, it had felt as though she were floating on a cloud…a cloud that was lumpy and uncomfortable and possibly stuffed with cacti. The memory was like a splinter; it'd burrowed too far under her skin, and all she could do was wait for her body to reject it.

She'd assigned herself to shelving the returned books today because the thought of having to be perky with the library's patrons was too damned much. Even her favorite library assistant, Lily, had steered clear, and that girl was practically immune to bad moods. Not that Darcy was in a bad mood per se… The feeling wasn't something she could so easily categorize in binary terms. It was kind of like the love child of confusion, horniness, and shame. Not a great combo by anyone's standards.

Sighing, she looked at the cart in front of her. The books felt like they were multiplying rather than diminishing. Someone had decided to leave a bunch in the wrong areas. There'd been religious books in the language section, philosophy books in the arts section, and a book about sexual reproduction shelved next to a self-help book about why people make bad decisions.

Perhaps the universe was trying to tell her something.

"There you are." Lily tentatively approached. "You have a visitor."

"I wasn't expecting anyone today." She turned over a book titled *The Art of Getting What You Want* and frowned. "Did they leave a name?"

"I didn't ask. He's waiting by the front desk." Lily leaned in conspiratorially. "Are you seeing someone?"

"No." Darcy pushed the cart against the shelves to keep it out of the way. "I'm not."

After she'd returned to Remi and Annie on Friday night, all hot under the collar, she'd wheeled out excuse after excuse not to approach Five-Star Darren. Reed's kiss had flipped some switch in her brain that made every other person appear in black and white, while he was in full HD color.

"Well, it didn't sound like a business call and he's *very* cute." Lily clapped her hands together. "Like Chris Pine levels of cute."

A "very cute" male visitor? Surely it wasn't Reed. But Lily was happily married to her high school sweetheart and one of those disgustingly smitten people Darcy avoided at weddings and family functions. She didn't make a fuss about any men who came into the library. Ever.

Which meant this was no ordinary man.

The second Darcy scanned the area near the front desk, her stomach flipped. Reed was here…without warning. Cursing under her breath, she smoothed her hands down the front of her T-shirt that said *Book boyfriends do it better*. Of *course* he was here on the day when she'd slept through her alarm and had barely enough time to run a brush through her hair, let alone spare a moment to make her skin look like a regular human pallor with concealer and blush. She caught a glimpse of herself in the reflection of a mirrored display case and cringed. Gollum chic wasn't a thing, was it?

"Who *is* he?" Lily whispered, as though it wasn't totally obvious they were both talking about him.

Reed tilted his chin in acknowledgment as Darcy headed

toward him, Lily following close behind. "That's the PR person who's helping us with our fundraiser."

"And you were saying getting in a pro would be overkill," she scoffed. "Maybe we should hire him full-time."

"Oh yeah, with all the extra money we have floating around." Darcy rolled her eyes and signaled for Reed to meet her in one of the empty reading rooms. If she was going to make a fool of herself, better that she limit the opportunity for witnesses. "Great idea."

Reed looked like he'd had a rough day, although he wore it with a little more panache than she did. His dark hair was unusually messy and his tie sat off center. Kind of how he'd looked after he kissed her on Friday night...

Stop it. It was a dare, nothing more. You didn't feel anything.

Oh boy, was that ever a lie. Reed's kiss had been a jolt of electricity straight to her lady parts. She'd woken up in a tangle of sheets at 3:00 a.m. and had thrown them off in a huff so she could have a cold shower. Not that shivering under the spray had worked. She'd fallen asleep sometime around six and had woken feeling just as tingly and the sensation had stayed with her over the weekend.

"Why are you here?" she asked as they entered the reading room. It felt strange to talk to Reed in a place where he looked so incredibly out of place, even if he was a little less polished than usual.

"We missed our meeting last week, remember?" His eyes flickered over her, a slight smirk tugging on his lips as his gaze came to rest on her T-shirt. "Book boyfriends do it better, huh? Either you've got some really good books, or your boyfriends are setting a low bar."

Heat snaked up her neck. "I know we missed our meeting," she said, ignoring the taunt. "Didn't you think to check in with me to see whether I was free before you wasted your time coming over?"

"I called ahead to make sure you were here and I was told you were." He poked his head out of the room and looked around. "Anyway, doesn't seem like you're that busy."

She sucked in a calming breath and busied her hands with straightening a piece of artwork. "And you know enough about my job to determine that?"

"I wanted to get away from the office, so I thought I would drop by and see if you were free," he said with a sigh. "Is that okay with you, Your Highness?"

Don't punch the guy who's supposed to be helping you, even if you want to really, really badly...

"I might be able to sit with you for a bit," she conceded.

Reed looked around the room with unconcealed disdain. "I was thinking we could grab a coffee...somewhere that doesn't smell like glue sticks and baby food."

Darcy resisted the urge to sniff the wall next to her. Was that really how it smelled? Tempting as it was to force Reed to stay, the lure of a real coffee—not that cheap crap they stocked the staff room with—was strong. "Fine. I'll see if Lily can cover for me. I'm due to have a lunch break anyway." She paused in the doorway. "Though I'm not sure how you're supposed to generate sympathy for a place you can't stand to be in for more than three seconds."

He shrugged and a funny expression settled onto his face. "What can I say? I have unusual talents."

Ten minutes later, they were seated in a coffee shop down the road from the library. It was one of Darcy's personal favorites because they had a mouthwatering pastry selection, including the almond-flavored *sfogliatella* she favored, and their coffee was smooth and strong.

"This is more like it," Reed said as they grabbed a table by the window.

The place was small and would probably only seat ten to twelve people, max. She hadn't realized until now how intimate the tables were, and her knees knocked against Reed's annoyingly long legs as they sat. The man took up more than his fair share of space in the world.

Don't you mean he's taking up more than his share of space in your head?

To her surprise, he'd opted for a pastry as well. He seemed like the type that would only see food as fuel. "So," she said, "why don't you want to be in the office?"

"I needed fresh air." He brought the pastry up to his mouth and took a bite.

A dusting of powdered sugar coated his top lip and Darcy's tongue darted out as if in response. Damn it, she was practically salivating. She needed to get a grip and stop acting so…Pavlovian.

"You're avoiding people?" she guessed.

"Something like that." He dusted his hands off on a napkin and then worked his tie loose. "It's been a rough day."

"Everything okay with your dad?" The question popped out before she could stop it. The last thing she needed was a reminder of Reed at his most vulnerable and raw. It was easier to keep her distance when she thought of him as Reed the womanizing douche canoe, rather than Reed the caring son.

And you need to keep your distance why?

Because he would chew her up and spit her out like he did with every other woman he dated. Though for some reason that didn't sound so unappealing now. Perhaps she was putting too much pressure on herself by trying to walk up to a guy that had potential. Someone who was allergic to commitment might be exactly what she needed...kind of like a dry run.

Or a wet run, as the case would most definitely be.

Oh my God, put a lid on it.

"He's doing all right. They discharged him and there was no concussion, thankfully." He stuffed his tie into the inside pocket of his jacket. "Too bad they couldn't give him something for his mood."

Darcy stifled a grin. "Grumpy?"

"Yeah, he gives Donna a hard time. That woman is pretty much a saint." He grunted. "Some days I just wish he'd lighten up a little."

"Hmm, grumpy guy giving grief to those around him...sound like anyone you know?" She sipped her coffee.

"Don't you start. I need to talk to someone who isn't ready to crucify me today." He smirked. "Probably wasn't the best move coming to see *you*."

Darcy stared into her coffee. Was Reed trying to say he'd chosen to come and see her because he thought she would treat him better than everyone else? Because he could relax around her? Absurd. They had a prickly relationship at best, antagonistic at worst. But there was the confusing element of that kiss...

"If you're looking for someone to stroke your ego, I am *not* your woman."

"No, you aren't my woman."

Something about the way he said it shot tiny arrows of anticipation through her. "I'm probably not even your type."

"What's my type?"

Oh boy, here they went. "I'm not sure I feel like completely decimating this relationship today."

His interested expression morphed into a wide *I'm going to blow your house down* grin. Wolfish, indeed. "You think we have a relationship?"

"A *business* relationship. And as much as I'm perfectly capable of running a fundraiser on my own, my boss has told me I have to play nice." She took a bite out of her pastry and chewed. "Which means curbing my honesty."

"Come on, I know you hate following the rules." He rolled his hand around. "Enlighten me, oh wise one. What is my type?"

"I was tempted to say anything that walks and is female." She cocked her head. "But I figure you're a little more discerning than that."

"You give me too much credit," he said dryly.

"I would say…" She tapped her finger to her chin. "You like women who are a little on the quiet side but not too introverted. Women who come from money or make a lot of it, so you know they're not after yours. You also want women who aren't looking for commitment but also aren't going to be a liability—so I'd say recent divorcées or those just out of a long-term relationship."

He stared at her for a moment, his expression neutral. "You've given that a lot of thought."

She couldn't argue there. There may have been one or two nights where she'd pored over Reed's reviews on the Bad Bachelors app, trying to glean whatever information she could. "I read people."

"It sounds more like you read bullshit websites." His eyes darkened.

She shrugged. "You asked."

"How about I return the favor?" He leaned back in his chair, his coffee and snack abandoned as his eyes raked over her.

It was like being scanned by a machine—all that was missing was the red laser running up and down her body. Reed seemed like the kind of guy who didn't miss a trick, though she wasn't sure she wanted him to be too accurate in his assessment of her. Or rather, she didn't want the full extent of her pathetic-ness showing through.

"You don't know what you want," he said eventually.

"That's cheating." Not that it wasn't accurate…

"Okay. You want something that doesn't exist." He rubbed a hand along his jaw, eyes boring into her as though he could read her soul like the Sunday paper. "You want a man who'll take charge but leave you to be free to make your own decisions. You want a guy who's romantic but not cheesy, someone who'll be attentive but not stifling. He needs to be good looking but not so good looking that you feel intimidated. And he needs to be a little alternative but still have traditional ideals."

She blinked. "Right."

"Basically you want the Goldilocks of men." He bobbed his

head, a self-satisfied smile prickling at Darcy's resolve to be professional. "Unfortunately for you, fairy tales don't exist."

"You're wrong." She frowned, indignation raising her hackles. "I don't want a guy like that at all."

"My mistake. You want the prematurely balding, small-dicked Darren." He let out a disbelieving little puff of air. "The unsalted cracker of men."

"This is a real person you're speaking about." She put her mug down a little harder than necessary and the liquid sloshed up the side, a small dribble going over the edge. Out of habit, she grabbed a napkin and wiped it up before it left a ring under the mug.

"A real person, right. Tell me, what's the difference between me saying those things about him and all the women who've gone on to that godforsaken app to rate him like he's a prize fucking pony?"

"But he has good reviews." A flimsy excuse at best.

"So it's fine if the reviews are good, but what if they're bad? Or is that fine too, because men like me deserve to be called out?"

Reed was rattled. His tone had changed from his usual superior teasing to something that was far more hard-edged. Far more…real.

"Do the reviews bother you?" she asked.

"People can say what they like," he said. But the muscles working in his jaw belied his words. "However, when it comes to people harassing my father over what some keyboard warriors have to say on the internet…"

"Donna mentioned that," she said. "That's wrong. They shouldn't bring your father into this."

"Doesn't matter though, does it? I'm just getting what I deserve."

"I never said that." But she'd thought it, hadn't she?

"You don't need to. Everyone else is saying it for you." He grimaced. "Doesn't matter. The people who run Bad Bachelors won't be hiding behind their keyboards forever." He pushed back from his chair and tossed a few bills onto the table. "I'll have my assistant call you to reschedule our meeting."

Darcy watched him stride out of the café, guilt twinging in her gut. He'd admitted to having a rough day and all she'd done was pour salt in the wound. Based on what? Her decision to blindly believe what people said about him. Sure, he was cocky and pushy and a little too confident for her tastes. But jumping to Darren's defense while still labeling Reed was hypocritical. He wasn't an evil person. He was just…a guy.

An insanely hot, talented with his mouth, too far under your skin guy.

Chapter 11

"I wish Bad Bachelors had been around when I dated Reed. I'm not saying I would have done things differently, but at least I would've had my eyes open."

—RobynHood

Remi, you have outdone yourself." Darcy planted her hands on her hips and surveyed the snack table for the Literature Loving Ladies book club. "Seriously, you could give up teaching barre and get a job as a pastry chef."

The trestle table was covered in a pink-and-white-checkered tablecloth. A three-tiered cake stand housed an array of mini cupcakes with icing in every color of the rainbow. They made Darcy's store-bought cookies look kind of sad, but she wasn't about to complain. The book club was her baby, and Remi supported her every month with sweet treats that looked good enough to have come from Magnolia Bakery.

"I may have to if I keep eating the test batches." She patted her washboard-flat stomach. "Won't be able to fit into my tutu much longer."

"You have a tutu?" Lily asked as she leaned over the table and plugged in the coffee machine. She'd brought her Keurig from home and had kindly donated a stack of pods for the meeting.

"Several. Although they live at my parents' place now. We don't really have the space for them in that crack in the wall they call a wardrobe in this damned city." She sniffed. "I can barely fit my regular clothes in there, let alone my dance stuff. That's two things I miss about home—wardrobe space and Tim Tams."

Darcy tried not to laugh. She'd seen Remi's wardrobe; the problem was not so much a lack of space but a shoe collection large enough to support an army of supermodels. It was certainly in stark contrast to Darcy's own modest collection.

"Just be thankful you have something with a door. In my first apartment, I had a single clothing rack and everything was crammed onto it. I couldn't hide it away anywhere." Annie shook her head. "I used to throw a sheet over it, but then I'd wake up in the middle of the night thinking there was a ghost in my room."

"At least you have the closet to yourself," Lily said. "I have to share with Jim, and I swear his stuff takes up more room than mine."

"Perks of being single." Darcy grinned.

"One of many." Annie picked up a paper cup and shoved it under the Keurig's spout. "In fact, I'm starting to wonder if the pros outweigh the cons."

"You two make me sad," Remi said with a shake of her head.

"There's a whole wide world of men out there and you're not even having a nibble. There's a bloody app to help you for crying out loud. When is dating going to get easier than that?"

"Ooh, are you talking about Bad Bachelors?" Lily swiped an Oreo from the packet on the table. "I read an article the other day that said some guy found out his colleague had set up a bunch of fake profiles to bring his rating down after they had a falling-out at work."

Darcy wrinkled her nose. "That's low."

What if that was going on with Reed? He'd said not to believe everything she read. But so many of the reviews had pointed out that he was amazing in bed, surely *that* wasn't a lie. A warm feeling unfurled in her belly. If his kiss was the hottest thing she'd ever experienced in her life, then he'd *have* to be good in bed.

Doesn't mean anything. Even a plain, old cracker would taste gourmet after months of starvation.

Who the hell was she kidding? Reed wasn't plain, old anything.

"It's really unfair actually," Darcy said. The three women turned to her with unconcealed surprise. "To lie and ruin someone's reputation like that."

She wasn't about to draw attention to the fact that her "PR savior," as her boss had taken to calling Reed, was sitting pretty on the top of the Bad Bachelors hit list. No doubt Remi and Annie would wonder why she hadn't clued them in on what should be prime gossip fodder, but the truth was Darcy wasn't sure how she felt about it. Her resistance to Reed had thawed, and yet he still unapologetically poked at her. Teased her.

She *shouldn't* find it appealing.

"It's very easy to call something fake just because you don't want to hear it," Annie said, tearing open a packet of napkins and laying them out next to the food. "I doubt people would go to such lengths."

"Really?" Darcy scoffed. "Look at how people behave online. There's a sense of entitlement that comes with anonymity, it makes people…mean."

"It makes them honest," Remi corrected. "Besides, since when are you team Douchebags R Us?"

"I'm not."

"Maybe it's because she was getting all cozy with some hottie that came into the library on Thursday." Libby dug her elbow into Darcy's ribs. "He was *divine*."

"You didn't tell me about this." Remi folded her arms across her chest. "Who is he? Are you seeing him? Is that the reason you were so funny at the bar the other night?"

The questions were fired in rapid succession. How the hell did she find time to breathe between all those words?

"He's the PR guy helping us out with the fundraiser." Darcy shot Lily a dagger-sharp look. "Nothing to report."

Nope definitely nothing at all. Zilch, zero, and zip.

"Then why do you look guilty as sin, Miss Darcy Lucia Greer?" Annie's eagle eyes could have burned a hole through her head.

"I'm not guilty. And can we please finish getting ready?" She busied herself with putting the rest of the snacks out—Cheetos, Pringles, and some kind of weird-looking blue corn chips. Organic. *Ew.* "It's almost time for people to arrive."

"Nuh-uh." Remi shook her head, a devious grin on her pale-pink lips. "We've got half an hour before showtime. So you're going to spill, missy."

"There's nothing to spill."

"Only that he was six feet plus of pure Manhattan sex-god goodness." Lily cackled as Darcy rolled her eyes. "Judging by the suit he was wearing, he wasn't from the burbs. That's for damn sure."

"What's his name? Maybe we can find him on the app." Annie pulled her cell from the inside pocket of her blazer. She looked *way* too dressed up for book club.

Stop stalling and figure out what you're going to say.

"We're not doing this. It's work and it's inappropriate."

"Darcy," Remi said in a singsong voice that said she'd well and truly been caught. "What are you hiding?"

Panic settled in; the girls had her backed into a corner like a pack of hungry hyenas. There was no way they'd let it go now, not when they'd caught the scent of a secret. She had three options. One, fess up about Reed. Two, lie and give another name, which was problematic, because if she accidentally gave the name of someone who *was* on the app, Lily would call her on it. Or three, go for pure and utter denial Sergeant Schultz style.

I see nothing. I was not here. I did not even get up this morning!

"You've got an active imagination, Rem." She swallowed. "You should write these things down. Might make a good book."

"What did you say his name was again?" Lily clucked her tongue.

"I don't think I did."

"Yes, you said, 'I'm going to get coffee with...' Ugh, what *was* it? Something short. Very manly." Lily pressed her lips together and stared into space. "Rich or Rick or something? Gosh, why can't I remember?"

"Too busy being moonstruck," Darcy muttered.

"Come on. You've got us all curious now." Annie slung an arm around her shoulder. "And don't give me this BS about it being unprofessional. It's not like we're going to contact the guy."

"Reed!" Lily shouted with her fist pumped in the air. "His name is Reed."

Annie's eyes narrowed as she swiped Remi's phone. This was about to go downhill. Fast. "Is this the guy?"

Lily peered at the screen and nodded. "Yes, that's him. Wow. Are you like some kind of hot-guy psychic?"

"No. But I *do* know my best friend," Annie said. "And I know that she only ever hides something when she's ashamed."

"I have nothing to be ashamed about," Darcy said, throwing up her hands. "I didn't say anything because I knew you would make a big deal out of it, and it's totally pointless because it's just business and there's nothing going on."

"Want to take a breath in there?" Remi teased.

"I wouldn't be so defensive if you crazies didn't make me feel like I was about to get burned at the stake for keeping work business to myself." She huffed. "Seriously. It's feeling like a witch hunt in here."

For the first time since they'd entered the library, the room was quiet. Lily was scrolling through Remi's phone, a curious expression on her face. She was tempted to remind the assistant librarian that raking her colleague over the coals was not a cool way to act. But she knew Lily wanted to fit in with the girls. She hadn't been in Brooklyn that long and the book club was her way of meeting people.

You're too damn soft. You know that, right? Such a freaking bleeding heart.

"What do you want me to say? We're working together. End. Of. Story." She grabbed a handful of M&M's and stuffed them into her mouth.

Don't mention the kiss. Don't mention the kiss. Don't mention the kiss.

"What's he like? Have you talked about the app? Does he know that you know who he is?" Remi's head looked like it was about to explode. "I have so many questions!"

Darcy chewed through the crunchy shells of the candy, wondering how the hell she managed to end up with such a nosy bunch of friends. "Yes, we've talked about the app, and yes, he knows I'm aware of his reputation." Darcy fiddled with the end of her braid. "And he's…nice."

"Nice?" Annie scoffed.

"Sometimes." It was an inadequate descriptor for a guy like Reed, but she feared anything more accurate might get her into trouble. Because the next few words that sprang to mind were *delectable*, *infuriatingly sexy*, and *world's best kisser*.

"You've really got nothing more to say than the fact that he's 'nice sometimes'? Come *on*." Remi shook her head in a perfect imitation of motherly disappointment. "What did he say about the reviews?"

"He doesn't like them." She felt strange discussing what was clearly a raw topic for Reed behind his back, but the floodgates had been opened and the gossip monsters would not be sated until they'd had their fill. "In fact, I would say he finds the whole thing embarrassing. People are harassing his sick father for an interview. It's...wrong."

"Right." Annie snorted as she unstacked the chairs, arranging them in a circle in the middle of the room. "Excuse me if I can't feel sorry for the guy. Sounds like it's a little *what goes around comes around* kind of thing."

"How can you say that? You don't even know him."

My, my, my. How the tables have turned.

Darcy pushed down the guilt at how she'd treated Reed on their first meeting. Admonishing Annie was a hypocritical move.

"I know his type." Annie pushed a strand of dark hair out of her eyes and straightened the chairs until they were perfectly spaced. "Believe me."

"You're just saying that because of what happened with..." Darcy trailed off when Annie's head snapped up, her mouth pulled into a grim line.

The subject of Annie's ex was TOL. Totally Off-Limits. Like friendship-ending level off-limits. The guy was basically Voldemort. Darcy suspected that kind of repression wasn't entirely healthy, but for the girl who was currently inhaling M&M's by the handful, she probably didn't have a leg to stand on where health was concerned.

"I'm saying that because of what happened to all of us." Annie curled and uncurled her fists. "You were cheated on the day before your wedding. You"—she pointed to Remi—"sent your career down the toilet because you slept with the wrong guy. And I was a damned fool to fall for a man whose family hated me." Her gaze skated over to Lily. "I'm sorry I don't have anything to say for you, but I'm sure you were wronged in the past as well."

"So all men are evil, is that it?" Darcy shook her head.

"No, not all men. But the ones who treat women like crap don't get to be crybabies because someone called them on their bad behavior."

This was *exactly* why she'd planned to keep Reed as her dirty little secret until the end of time. Because if by some chance they did have chemistry, she'd never be able to go out in public with him… not unless she wanted the wrath of her overprotective friends.

Moot point. Reed isn't into women like you—that was well established during your last conversation.

"I don't think he's going to cry about it. He's a man of action, it would seem." She made her way around the circle of chairs, laying down hot-pink flyers advertising their upcoming donation drive on each one.

"What do you mean by that?" Lily asked.

"He said something about the people who created Bad Bachelors not being able to hide behind their keyboards forever. Maybe he's planning to out them."

"Typical." Annie rolled her eyes. "The asshole can't take responsibility for his actions so he's going to lash out."

"Surely people who created an app like that would keep their identities well hidden," Lily said, nibbling on her lower lip. "I mean, they've pissed a lot of people off."

For once, Remi didn't have any questions to ask. "They sure have."

Chapter 12

"Reed is upfront about who he is. I know this will put me in the minority, but I'm not sure people have the right to complain when they try to change someone and aren't successful."

—HonestyHurts

*D*arcy hurried up Sixth Avenue, hoping that a brisk pace would distract her from the fact that she was about to have a meeting with Reed. And not just any old meeting. They were meeting in his office, a.k.a. his natural habitat.

For some reason, that had roused the kaleidoscope of butterflies in her stomach.

To make matters worse, one of the kids she'd been reading to at work had decided to puke his lunch all over her black pants. And of course it was laundry day. Well, technically, it was laundry day two weeks ago, and now it bordered on literally-wear-anything-that-is-clean day. So there were no clean replacement pants. No jeans. Not even a pair of shorts that might pass as partway decent for an office meeting.

Her only option had been a pair of black, studded cutoffs with a rip in the behind that would show either panties or bare ass, depending on what underwear she'd chosen. Not. Going. To. Happen.

She'd been forced to borrow something from Remi, which was how Darcy had come to be wearing a dress. She shrieked as a gust of wind blew the flimsy skirt around her legs, threatening to reveal the fact that she had on her Thursday panties even though it was Monday. Which wouldn't have been an issue if it hadn't been for Pukey McDemon Child.

Just concentrate on what matters—not letting Reed rattle you.

She came to a stop in front of a tall building that screamed *you don't belong here* and sighed. Of course the door was trimmed in gold and it looked as though everyone entering had stepped off the cover of *Boring Expensive Suits* monthly. Should she have expected any less?

Smoothing her hands down the front of her dress, she cursed Remi. Her friend had not only laughed her ass off at Darcy's misfortune, but also had been predictably annoying about what clothes she would and wouldn't hand over. Remi had been trying to force her to wear a dress for months. But it wasn't Darcy's style—too many opportunities to have your ass on display…among other things.

And Remi was a good size smaller than Darcy, and so she claimed her jeans would be too tight. A likely story.

"Come on," she said to herself as she stared into the gaudy gold mouth of Reed's building. "It's just a meeting."

She hitched her bag higher up on her shoulder and filed into the turnstile behind a man in a navy pinstripe suit. The foyer of the building was grand looking and a board hung on the wall with all the tenants and their floors listed in alphabetical order. She scanned down the first column. Bath and Weston, floor thirty-six.

The elevator was crammed with people, and Darcy huddled into the corner, keeping her bag in front of her to preserve what was left of her personal space. Nothing worse than some stranger getting all up in your grill.

You didn't seem to mind when Reed invaded your personal space.

Ugh. Why did her brain have to keep flashing up that little memory at the most inopportune moments? One kiss and she'd been stuck on it like a needle catching a scratch in a record. It interrupted her flow with frustrating regularity.

The elevator pinged and Darcy excused herself, trying to get past a man blocking the door. He didn't move, even on her polite request, so she had to push her way out, using her bag as a shield.

"Inconsiderate jerk," she muttered as she stepped into the Bath and Weston reception area.

The space was decorated in cool tones. A white reception desk was flanked by a chrome floor lamp and a bunch of white flowers sat in a clear vase. It was a little more minimalist than Darcy had expected. But then again, what the hell did she know about PR firms?

"Can I help you?" The receptionist smiled and cocked her head, her gaze skating over Darcy in an assessing but not intrusive way.

"I'm here to see Reed McMahon."

Surprise streaked across the receptionist's face, but she covered it quickly. "Do you have an appointment?"

"Yeah. Six o'clock." She checked her watch: 6:32. "I'm a little late."

"Yes, you are." Reed's voice sounded behind her and Darcy resisted the shiver of anticipation that crawled down her spine as she turned.

There was something about his voice that curled around her. It was rich, smooth. A voice designed with husky-toned demands in mind.

"Consider it payback for last time." She smiled sweetly and the receptionist bit down on her lip, clearly stifling a smirk of her own.

"Come on. My office is this way." He gestured for her to follow him. "Let's get you into a room before you can shoot me down in front of anyone else."

"That wasn't shooting you down." She fell into step beside him. "If I shot you down, you'd be bleeding on the floor. Trust me, that was nothing."

His lips quirked. "And here I was thinking I'd get lucky because you're wearing a dress."

"Not by choice," she huffed. "And certainly not for you."

"You got a date then?"

She could tell he'd meant it as a quip, but his lip was stiff, his expression hard around the edges. "What if I did?"

He chuckled. "That's a no."

"If I meant no, I would have said it. Am I not speaking English?"

"I'd say it's more like an ancient dialect of bullshit." His hand came to the small of her back and he leaned in closer. "You forget, I'm familiar with liars."

"And *you* forget, I'm immune to your tricks."

Darcy felt eyes burning into her back and she risked a glance over her shoulder. People milled around the office, several of them shooting curious glances her way. She tugged on the hem of her dress. It was short, but it wasn't *that* short.

"Why are people staring at me?"

"I don't usually have clients in the office." Reed pulled his office door open and held it for her. "They're probably trying to figure out if you're a celebrity."

"Oh." She set her bag down on one of two plush chairs facing his desk, and sunk into the other. "Why don't you usually have clients in the office?"

"Famous people like their privacy. Wouldn't be a great idea to have the paparazzi catch a client coming into the office." He dropped down into his chair. "My services work best behind the scenes. It's hard to get the public to buy into someone's rehabilitated image if they know it's been engineered."

"Surely the public aren't stupid enough to think the stuff you set up is being done out of the goodness of your clients' hearts?" She screwed up her nose. "How gullible are they?"

"Very." Reed pulled a folder from a stack on the side of his desk and flipped it open. "You'd be surprised what people believe, even when there's tons of evidence to the contrary."

For some reason, Darcy's mind drifted to the day she'd walked in on her fiancé, Ben, kissing their best man. Instead of anger, she'd only felt confusion—had there been signs all along? Had she known deep down that Ben had a secret life? Or had she really been so gullible to believe he'd loved her?

Most of all, why didn't she feel as devastated as she knew she should have been?

"Which brings me to the purpose of this meeting." He leaned back in his chair and popped the cuff link at one wrist. The silver knot glinted in the office lighting. "I've got a guest in mind that will be a huge draw for the fundraiser. A famous author."

"Did you manage to get J. K. Rowling?" Darcy clapped her hands together. "A girl can hope, right?"

"Sure, you can hope. Won't do you much good." He rolled the cuffs back on his shirt. "I was thinking someone a little more...local. Dave Bretton, to be precise."

"Don't you mean 'a little more controversial,' then?"

"Ah, so you do know him." Reed set the cuff links down with a clink on his desk.

"I know *of* him," she said. "Enough to say that I'm nervous about him representing my library."

"He's a *New York Times* bestseller. He's wildly successful."

She ignored the cajoling tone. "He's also wildly inappropriate and a drunk. Why would we want a loose cannon at our fundraiser?"

"He's spent the last couple of months at a rehab facility upstate. His agent says he's dried out. Turned a corner even." Reed leaned forward and the scent of his aftershave drifted over the desk to taunt Darcy's nostrils. Damn him. How did he smell like fresh-cut pine and the great outdoors in the middle of a concrete jungle? "*And* he's got a new book coming out. They've been keeping it hush-hush."

"But I suppose you have all the gossip." She tried to act uninterested. Dave Bretton was a bad idea, but Darcy had been reading his books for years. The last in his series—which was Jack Reacher meets *Stargate*—had ended on quite the cliffhanger three years ago. "It wouldn't happen to be the next book in the Martin Pollinger Chronicles, would it?"

Reed's smile broadened. "It might be."

"Don't toy with me, McMahon. Not when it comes to books."

He opened his desk drawer and reached inside, fishing out what appeared to be a book without a proper cover. "I wouldn't dream of it."

"Is that what I think it is?" She squinted. Yep, it was an advanced reader copy of book eight in the Martin Pollinger Chronicles. The holy freaking grail of books…well, until J. K. Rowling wrote another Harry Potter book, that was.

"I'll happily hand this over," he said, holding it out of her reach. "*If* you agree to have Mr. Bretton at the fundraiser."

"Bold move." She folded her arms across her chest, but her eyes were trained on the unfinished cover. "How did you even know I liked his books? A lucky guess?"

"I don't believe in luck." When she raised a brow, he continued. "I looked up your Goodreads profile. You've read every one of his books and rated them all five stars. I have to say, I found your reading list quite telling."

"What's that supposed to mean?"

She frantically scanned her memory for anything embarrassing that might have made it onto the list. Being a stickler for detail, Darcy recorded *all* her reading activities and didn't generally care what people thought of her taste in books.

But there *had* been a phase when she'd read some monster erotica books for fun. Bigfoot's virgin mistress…or something. Her tummy fluttered at the thought of Reed thinking about her reading something smutty like that. Had he guessed that it'd sent her to bed with an ache between her thighs? *Shit.*

"How did you find *Claimed by Cthulhu*? It had mixed reviews." His eyes danced with unconcealed amusement. "Are you well-versed in tentacle porn?"

"It's not porn," she said with a sniff. "Giant squid monsters deserve love too, you know. It was quite an endearing romance."

He chuckled. "If you say so."

"Fine," she said, holding out her hand. "Mr. Bretton can come to the fundraiser if you think it will draw bigger donations."

"It will. I'm planning to ask him to donate something to the silent auction."

"But he needs a handler or something. What do alcoholics have, a sponsor? Whoever it is, I want someone there to keep an eye on him." She narrowed her eyes. "While I appreciate his art, I won't appreciate a repeat of what happened at Book Expo America."

Reed nodded and slid the book across his desk. "Deal."

Darcy snatched it up before she could change her mind. "I know what I'll be doing tonight," she said gleefully.

"After dinner," he said, pushing back on his chair.

"Excuse me?"

"Dinner. It's that meal at the end of the day that usually happens somewhere between seven and nine." He slipped his suit jacket off the back of his desk chair and slung it over one arm.

"I know *what* it is, but I don't understand why you think our dinners have anything to do with each other."

"We have more to discuss, and I'm hungry." He came around the side of the desk and leaned against it.

The pose reminded her of the way he'd crowded her at that bar. The way he'd leaned in, backing her up against the wall and pressing into her so she could feel the hard length of him rubbing against her thigh. Desperate need flashed through her as she remembered how much she'd wanted to reach down and wrap her hand around him to see if his moans would sound as good in real life as they did in her fantasies.

The kiss had been a power play. A negotiation tactic. He wanted her off balance so she'd let him run the show. And it appeared to be working, since all she could do was come up with reasons why she should allow herself to be tempted.

One, take-charge guys didn't rely on the woman to make the moves. Which was good, because Darcy had no moves. Two, a little practice before she started dating for real might take the pressure off. Three…well, he was damn hot. And infamous. Lord help her, she was curious to see how their antagonistic chemistry would translate into the bedroom.

Bad idea, Darcy. Colossally bad idea. You have to work together until the fundraiser.

She could almost hear her mother's voice scolding her: *He's not the kind of man who respects women.* No doubt Remi and Annie would agree. For some reason that only made Darcy find the whole thing *more* appealing.

She never had been good at doing what she was told.

"And you were late," he added. "It messed up my schedule."

"So order in." She swallowed. The rebellious side of her was gaining strength, whispering in her ear that maybe Reed was exactly what she needed right now.

"I missed lunch and I make it a point to eat one decent meal a day." He picked up her bag from the chair and handed it to her. "You, me, dinner, business. Nothing to be scared of."

"I'm not scared," she said, smoothing her hands over her dress. His eyes tracked her every movement. "But I do understand why so many women are angry at you. If this is how you ask them to dinner, I can see why your reviews are up and down."

"They're not up and down." He held out his arm. "They're consistently bad."

"I was trying to be polite," she huffed. When her stomach grumbled loudly, he raised a brow.

"Can we go now?"

"Okay fine." She slipped her bag over her shoulder and allowed him to help her up. The strong, warm grip of his hand did nothing to quiet her inner rebel. "Where are we going?"

"Never you mind, Darcy Greer. Let me handle that."

I wish you would.

....

Reed hadn't intended on taking Darcy to dinner and the excuse that they had more business to discuss was flimsy. About as flimsy as that tease of a dress she was wearing. The second they'd stepped outside into the evening air, the fabric around her thighs had swirled, revealing a flash of ink high up on her thigh.

It was a dress made to be pushed up and bunched in a fist.

"Guess I was right about you not having a date then," he said. Better to keep focused on teasing her than drooling over her. Not that the two were mutually exclusive.

"You're an ass," she said with a dramatic sigh. "You'd better not be taking me to some fancy-pants place where they serve entrees the size of my pinkie."

He stifled a grin. "Big appetite?"

"Yeah and you won't like me when I'm hangry."

"Who says I like you now?" He stuck his hand out and hailed a cab.

"You said I was interesting." She slid across the back seat and her hem rode up her legs.

God, she was hot. Miles of porcelain-white skin, all that long, dark hair. The tattoos, the piercings, and the chunky, black boots. It was everything he shouldn't want. She looked like a throwback to the nineties, a Goth girl who'd been told to tone it down for a Sunday family dinner. Restraint mixed with rebelliousness. A potent combination if the blood flooding to the southern parts of his body was anything to go on.

He wanted to blame this ludicrous crush on the fact that he was in the longest dry spell of his life. Ever since the Bad Bachelor bombshell had dropped, he hadn't slept with anyone. Too risky. He couldn't add any more fuel to the fire until he'd smoothed things over at work. Which would get a whole lot easier now that he had this fundraising opportunity to present to Dave Bretton's agent.

Realistically, he could have gone ahead without Darcy's permission. After all, he was there for his expertise, not to play Mr. Nice Guy, though he couldn't deny it'd made him pretty fucking happy to see the smile lighting her face when he'd handed over that book. Something had him wanting to keep her on his side...and take her out to dinner.

Yeah...dinner. That's really *what you want.*

Okay fine, so his desires were a little along the lines of hauling her up to a hotel room and burying himself in her over and over until she'd gone hoarse from screaming his name. But that was a bad idea. A *very* bad idea.

He slid into the seat beside her and gave the address to the driver. "You are interesting."

"Interesting enough for dinner but not for anything else."

He shot her a sidelong glance. Those startling, blue eyes were trained on him and if he didn't know any better, he'd say that she wanted him. But Darcy had made her disdain clear before. "You don't want anything else. Not from me anyway."

"Why's that?"

"I'm not the guy who calls the morning after." He raked a hand through his hair. "Or ever."

"Not all girls want to be called the next morning."

"Yes they do, even if they don't admit it. My reviews are testament to that." He rubbed his hands up and down his thighs to keep them busy. "And you definitely do."

"You think you know a lot about me and what I want." She picked at the hem of her dress, her short, unpolished nails working at a thread that threatened to come loose. "Maybe I'm tired of looking for nice guys." Her full lips twisted. "Maybe you were right and I *don't* want a guy like Five-Star Darren."

Well, fuck. He wouldn't have persisted with teasing her if he'd thought she would come around to his way of thinking. Not that he could deny she deserved fireworks in bed. But she also deserved the guy who'd get up and make her pancakes in the morning. And that guy was not him.

"That's a big range you're talking about."

"What's wrong with jumping in the deep end?" Her voice had grown a little breathy, and it took everything in him not to unclick her seat belt and yank her into his lap.

"You'll wake up in the morning and regret it, that's why." He was hard as a rock and quickly losing his grip on control. "There's a reason I've pissed a lot of people off. I'm not a nice guy."

She frowned. "Sure you are. You got me an ARC of my favorite author."

"Because I *wanted* something." Self-loathing flowed through him, thick and fast. This was the guy he'd become, the one would use people any way he could to get what he wanted. The one who would manipulate a situation to his advantage without a worry in the world. "I got you that book because I wanted you to say yes to having

Dave at the fundraiser. He's not my client and I know I can use this event to sign him to Bath and Weston. I did it for me."

"I'm not an idiot," she said softly. "But I also know that your job is important to you because you support your father."

"I like shiny things," he lied through gritted teeth. "I like money because it means people say yes to me."

"Why are you trying to convince me you're a bad guy?" She placed her hand on his thigh, the gentle touch slaying him. He was used to grabbing, pulling—the passionate touches of people driving toward a pleasurable goal—but not this. "You got pissy the last time we spoke because I called you out."

"And now you're Team Reed all of a sudden?" He grabbed her hand and meant to push her away, but instead he held on to her. "What's changed?"

"I…I don't know." Her eyes were wild—scared and excited. The blacks of her pupils grew. God, she was gorgeous. "I've just been thinking…"

"About?"

She squared her shoulders. "I'm sick of going to bed alone."

"And you think a wild night with Manhattan's biggest bastard is a good way to indulge yourself?" He all but snarled the words.

Damn her. He was tangled up in knots and that *never* happened. She'd crawled under his skin when he wasn't looking. When he was too busy taunting her because he thought he had the upper hand.

Big fucking mistake.

"Yes." She nodded as though convincing herself. "I do."

"Don't go thinking I'll act like it means something. I don't pretend, Darcy." He reached across the spare space between them and pushed down on the seat belt lock. The click sounded like a gun being cocked. "I don't act."

"So when you kissed me it wasn't an act?"

"I kissed you because I'd been thinking about that goddamn mouth for days." He pulled her closer, still gripping her wrist in one hand. She didn't fight him. "I wanted to know whether you were as prim as you acted or if all that ink was a sign of a tiger in sheep's clothing."

"And?"

"You were lucky you weren't wearing a dress that night." His lips were at her ear now, the last vestige of his restraint hanging by a thread.

The second she tilted her face to his it would all be over. The waiting now was just drawing out the inevitable. His palm came to her knee, slipping up and in, so he could feel the tightening of her muscles as she pressed her legs together—though whether that was to stop him or to trap him, he had no idea.

"What would you have done to me?" she whispered.

"Let me show you." He gently parted her legs, giving himself room to skate his fingertips higher. She placed her bag over her lap, to hide what they were doing.

His touch barely created friction on her skin. It was a tease. A promise. When he grazed the soft cotton of her panties, he twisted his hand, brushing his knuckles over her sex. Darcy stifled a moan by sinking her teeth into her lower lip, that sexy, little action hardening him beyond belief.

"I would have warmed you up," he whispered, stroking her

gently. The material grew damp against his hand, but he took it slow, stringing her anticipation out. "Then I would have slipped my finger inside your underwear, like this."

He almost groaned aloud at how wet she was. How ready. They needed to take this somewhere private. Now. Because Reed had crossed the line and there was no way he'd be going back until he got his fill.

"Yes." The word hissed out between her teeth. "More."

He sucked her earlobe between his lips as he pushed a finger inside her. Christ, she was even tighter than he'd fantasized. Her hips rolled against his hand as he thrust in and out with slow deliberation.

"I would have fucked you with my finger until you were shaking and dripping all over my hand." He kissed the sensitive spot behind her ear and she shivered. "I wouldn't have stopped even if people could see me sliding my fingers in and out of your wet pussy. Not until you came so hard your knees gave out."

Her muscles fluttered around his finger. God, he wanted to slip another one in, to stretch her in preparation for him. But not yet. If Darcy wanted a walk on the wild side, then he was going to give it to her—but he would make her wait. He wouldn't call tomorrow, but he'd send her home aching so much she'd think of nothing but his cock inside her for weeks.

He pulled his hand away and stifled her frustrated moan by pressing a finger to her lips. Her eyes widened. No doubt she could smell herself on him. When he was confident she wouldn't say anything, he leaned forward.

"Change of plans," he said to the cab driver. "Turn us around."

Chapter 13

"I knew what I was getting into when I dated Reed. The guy doesn't have what it takes to be in a relationship. It's sad, really, how broken he is."

—*NotYourGirl*

D arcy felt as though she'd been holding her breath ever since the driver had swung the car around and headed back uptown, toward some hotel. Reed had carefully buckled her back into her seat belt with hot and dirty words whispered into her ear about how he wanted her in one piece for all the things he had planned.

Planned, like he'd thought about it before. That must be how he knew exactly where to take her. He hadn't even hesitated when reciting the address to the driver. Was this usually where he brought women?

They certainly hadn't struggled to get a room despite the lobby being full to the brim with people—some in suits, some in tourist getups with chunky cameras hanging from their neck like Olympic medals. Darcy wondered if it was obvious what she and Reed had come for, that they were about to embark on a debauched night of no-strings, carnal pleasure. But with nothing more than a swift "of course, Mr. McMahon" from the concierge desk, he had a key card in his hand and she didn't have time to ponder the potential consequences of her actions—or if anyone was judging her.

Does it matter? You said you were sick of all the rules and bullshit. You know he's going to make you feel good. Who cares if there's nothing more than that?

She was a modern woman who'd been determined to do her own thing, despite growing up with a strong sense of guilt instilled in her by her parents. Sex was something to be enjoyed, so why should she feel bad for wanting it with a partner who was likely to be very skilled?

"Stop thinking so loud." Reed pulled her against him as they waited for an elevator. "You're disturbing the peace."

It was a strange feeling to suddenly have a barrier removed. His hands were splayed over her hips as he hugged her from behind, his breath warm against her ear. It was intimate.

No shit. You just agreed to a one-night stand and now you think it's strange he's being intimate?

"I'm not thinking," she said.

"So many lies, Darcy. Be careful or else you'll start to believe your own bullshit." He pressed her harder against him, the curve of her ass fitting squarely against his crotch. Even after they'd kept their hands to themselves while checking in, he was still hard.

"More chance of that than me believing yours." She shot him a look over her shoulder, but he just smirked.

The hotel was sleek. They had a fancy setup for the bay of elevators, where you had to punch your floor into a PIN pad and it would tell you exactly which elevator to stand in front of. When another couple walked up beside them, Darcy stepped out of Reed's grasp and smoothed her hands over her skirt.

"So we're clear, I don't expect anything out of this," she said quietly. Her eyes darted to the other couple, but they seemed caught up in one another.

"You should expect *something*." The elevator pinged and Reed held the door for everyone before taking his place next to Darcy. He draped an arm around her shoulder in a way that felt far too casual for what they were about to do.

She swallowed down the rising tide of anticipation in her throat. Her whole body buzzed with energy—some good, excited… some worrisome. The negative, little voice in her head was never far away, no matter how much she rationalized her decision.

I want this. End of story.

When the other couple exited on the third floor, Reed jabbed at the button to close the doors. Then he pinned her against the wall, his thigh nudging her legs apart. "You should expect me to make you come so many times you forget how to say your own name."

Her breath hitched when his mouth came down to hers, hovering so close that his lips brushed hers in a series of microkisses as he spoke.

"You should also expect me to make you so wet and so hungry that you'll be begging me to stick my cock in you."

Oh dear. "Well, uh…."

Really, what *could* she say to that? Her brain had decided to pack up shop for the night and had officially handed over the keys to her lady parts. Words were not required—her words anyway.

"You should expect me to make you feel like a fucking goddess all night." He nipped at her lower lip, only pulling back when the elevator dinged, signaling their arrival.

This was it. Welcome to the sex zone.

"A goddess, huh?" She stepped into the hallway and headed in the direction of their room. "I like the sound of that."

Nerves bundled tightly in her belly as they walked. The opportunity for her to turn and flee was closing fast. She could walk away now, forget that she ever started down this path, and go back to being the old Darcy.

Why? So you can continue to not *do anything about your sorry excuse for a love life? Not. Happening.*

But what had Reed said about her earlier? He wanted to know if she was a tiger in sheep's clothing?

"What are your expectations?" she asked as Reed swiped the key card. A click sounded and he pushed the door open.

"That we keep this night to ourselves." He held out his hand. "Other than that, we just enjoy the hell out of it."

"Right." She hovered at the door.

"Do you need a formal invitation?" he asked, a dark brow raised.

She gazed past him into the plush suite. It was light and airy, certainly no seedy, pay-by-the-hour motel vibes here. "Does a goddess need an invitation?"

He chuckled and pulled her to him, crushing her body against his with one arm around her waist. He moved them into the room, letting the door swing shut so he could back her up against it.

"Are you nervous?" He hoisted her thigh over his hip, his hand sliding along her bare leg until he cupped her ass.

In this open, vulnerable position, she could feel everything—the hard length of his cock rubbing at the sensitive spot between her legs, the sharp press of his belt buckle into her lower belly. The bite of his fingers into her flesh.

She let her head drop back against the door. "A little. I've only ever been with one man."

That was her way of telling him not to quiz her on the Kama Sutra. Because her experience with Ben had been about as spicy as baby food—missionary or doggy. Never with her on top. Oral sex had been an annual birthday treat, but Ben had made it clear he didn't enjoy it, so she'd never asked. Had she been satisfied? She'd thought so, but now that illusion was about to be shattered.

"You're not going to make me do any weird shit, are you?" She wrinkled her nose.

Reed dropped his forehead to hers, his warm, dark eyes crinkling at their corners. For once, he looked totally at ease...like maybe this was who he really was. "Weird shit? What *have* you read about me?"

His hands continued to massage her ass cheeks, the lazy rhythm making her hum in enjoyment. He was taking it slow, giving her time to ease into the idea of a one-night stand. Something told her this wasn't how he usually operated.

"That you're a wicked rake no girl in her right mind would

get involved with." She grinned. "That you're a master manipulator who's so good in bed you turn women into quivering messes."

"And you wanted to be my next quivering mess?" One hand skated up her back, his fingers feeling for the long zipper that ran the length of her spine.

"Yes," she breathed. "Very much."

He drew the zipper down while his lips feasted on her neck. She sighed, but nothing would quell the cavernous ache until he threw her down on the bed and had his way with her. The thought of him pressing her into the soft-looking duvet while he plunged deep inside her sex sent Darcy's temperature skyrocketing. Her nipples beaded against the fabric of her dress, and that's when she remembered it was laundry day.

No bra. Thursday panties on Monday. *Shit.*

"I should freshen up," she said breathlessly.

"I'll be the judge of that." He slipped the shoulder of her dress down, kissing the exposed skin in a way that would have been sweet if he wasn't pinning her to the door with his erection. "You taste pretty damn fresh to me."

"I don't know if that's a compliment."

The other shoulder followed and soon she was bare-chested, the cool air making her nipples achingly hard. "Oh it is, Darcy." He kissed his way down her chest until he was at eye level with her breasts. "In the end, we all become stories."

She stiffened when he ran a finger along where the tattoo curved underneath her right breast. It was like he was branding her, the touch hot against her already-flushed skin. This wasn't the intimacy she'd imagined—in her head, it had been quick. Shades drawn and lights off, furious and fast and over before she had time to think. Not this gentle exploration.

"Tonight you're going to become a dirty story, Darcy." His smile was wicked. "Maybe not quite as dirty as the monster erotica you so favor, but I'll do my best."

She swatted at him. "Just get on with it, will you?"

"Get on with it?" He chuckled. "There's no rush at all." He sucked one nipple into his mouth and she gasped. The way he rolled it around over his tongue, using his teeth with a pressure so perfect it would have made Goldilocks weep—damn, he was good.

....

There was nothing more satisfying than a woman's excited moans. The pleasure sounds emanating from Darcy were particularly enjoyable, however, because until today she'd held him at arm's length. She teased and bantered with him; occasionally she barbed him. But there was always an invisible—and yet very real—barrier between them.

Now, with her splayed against the door, her fingers in his hair—tugging, pulling—she was utterly and perfectly undone. And goddamn if she didn't taste as sweet as a ripe peach. He was aching to drop to his knees and push his face between her legs. He knew some guys loathed the act of going down on a woman, but Reed considered it his specialty. He loved the way a woman moved when he put his mouth on her, the way her hips would buck and roll. The desperate gasps and pleas that would fill his ears…if her thighs hadn't clamped around his head hard enough to block his hearing, that was.

"Reeeeed," she groaned as he gently tugged on her nipple. "I don't know if I can stand much longer."

"But I haven't gotten started on the other side yet." He raked his teeth over her left nipple, and her body jerked against him. "I can't leave you uneven."

"You're a real Prince Charming, you know that." She shook her head, laughing. "Let me get onto the bed. The last thing you want to do is scrape me off the floor when I fall."

Right then and there, he couldn't think of a single thing he didn't want to do with her. Darcy's fair skin was flushed with pink, matching the beautiful rosy tips of her breasts. They were some fucking perfect breasts too—round and no bigger than a handful, perky. And that damn scrolling text etched into her skin…

"Why did you get those words?"

Her blue eyes avoided his gaze, and she tugged the top of the dress back up over her breasts. "It's a Margaret Atwood quote… I admire her work."

More lies. Darcy didn't seem to lie about anything of significance. Just lots and lots of little white lies designed to hide the real her from the world. Bricks in her protective wall. Perhaps they were more alike than he'd first thought. He straightened up and cupped her face with his hands.

"Such a pretty mouth you have." He plunged his tongue between her lips, automatically feeling for the hardness of her piercing. He was growing fond of the sensation of that little metal ball on his tongue, and he groaned at the realization that he might get to feel it bump against his cock tonight.

She planted her hands against his chest. "Bed. Now."

"So impatient." He wrapped his arms around her waist and stumbled them backward into the room, not even knowing if he was headed for the bed or the desk. When he knocked into something hard, glass and metal rattling, he changed course. They were in the living area.

"You're a terrible driver." She laughed against his chest as he walked them to the bedroom sectioned off by a sliding door. "You know, I thought you were going to be smoother than this."

"You got a problem with my moves?" he asked in mock offense. "Guess I'll have to step up my game then."

This wasn't normally how he acted when he took a woman too bed—his usual MO was slick. Champagne ordered to the room, a steamy shower to start. Women *loved* that. He'd always take them once in the shower, without finishing. Just enough to get them off. Then it was to the bed, low lighting. Up against the glass overlooking the city.

But running through the routine with Darcy felt...wrong. Dirty. Not in the good, smutty-monster erotica way either. For some reason, he doubted he could pull off his usual persona with her. Reed the Lady Slayer, as Gabriel had once called him. But tonight he was improvising, making shit up on the fly.

And that unnerved the hell out of him.

He grabbed Darcy by the shoulders and walked her to the edge of the bed. She was still clutching her dress over her breasts, a nervous energy zipping around her like fireflies. She wanted him to be smooth, to put on the moves like she'd read about. Fine.

Your wish is my command, sweetheart.

"Lose the dress," he said, shoving his hands into the pockets of his suit pants. It was necessary because the second he saw those nipples again, he'd want to devour her.

"I could change in the bathroom." Her voice was ragged, rough around the edges. "I—"

"I said, lose the dress." His command bounced off the walls of the bedroom.

Darcy sucked in a breath and slipped the floral fabric down her body, wriggling when it got stuck on her hips. She was trying to take her underwear down as well.

"Did I say you could take off your panties?" He stalked forward and put his hands over hers. "If you can't do this properly, I'll have to take over."

Bright spots of pink dotted her cheeks. "It's laundry day," she mumbled.

"What?"

She squeezed her eyes shut and sucked on her lower lip. "Laundry day. This was all that was clean."

She let the dress slide over her hips, leaving her standing there in only a pair of cotton briefs with *Thursday* stamped across the front. It looked as though they might have had flowers printed on them at one point, but they'd faded terribly. There was a hole in the elastic above her right hip.

Normally the women he brought to this hotel would turn

their nose up at anything that wasn't La Perla or Agent Provocateur. Sometimes they wore lacy thongs; sometimes they had those horribly strappy contraptions that held up stockings. Sexy? Yeah. Pain in the ass? Absolutely. But here was Darcy in her falling-apart panties, complaining that it was laundry day, and yet he was harder than he'd ever been. *What the fuck?* Reed chuckled.

"Stop laughing!" She bent down to reach for the puddle of fabric at her feet but Reed's hand shot out.

"It's not you," he said.

She tried to shake him off. "You don't have to be such an asshole about it."

"I'm sorry." He cleared his throat. "You're just so different and it took me by surprise. Stand up. Come on." He sucked in a breath. "It's refreshing."

"Tell me something, Reed." She yanked her wrist free and crossed her arms over her chest. "Are you agreeing to sleep with me as some kind of consolation prize?"

Her words stung harder than a slap across the face. "Excuse me?"

"Is this a consolation fuck because the women you'd usually bring here hate you now?" Her lower lip trembled, but she forced it into submission. "Are you lowering your standards because there's no one else?"

"No. God, Darcy. Is that what you think of me?" Anger flared in his chest like a struck match. "You think I'd stick my dick in anyone just to get laid?"

"Why else would I be here? I'm not your type. You've made that *very* clear."

He fought against the swell of resentment stampeding up his throat and locked his jaw firmly so he didn't say anything out of spite. This wasn't about him. It was about her. *Her* insecurities. *Her* doubts and fears.

"I'm going to put a stop to this right now." He scanned the room until he found what he was looking for. "Come out here."

Darcy's eyes dropped down to the dress at her feet, but she didn't make a move to pick it up. Instead, she followed him, naked except for her Thursday panties and a pair of chunky black boots that looked way hotter than they should have. He stopped in front of the full-length mirror inside the entrance to the hotel suite.

"Stand here." He pointed to the space in front of him and she complied, her brows drawn together. "What do you see?"

She kept her arms covering her chest. "Me standing in front of a bossy asshole. It's quite the picture."

"Cute." He swept her hair behind her so that her shoulders and chest were uncovered, and then he reached around and pulled her hands gently down by her sides. "Want to know what I see?"

Vulnerability flickered across her face, but she hid it with her usual snark. "Are you going to tell me I'm beautiful?" Her voice dripped with sarcasm. "Are you going to tell me you brought me here because the thought of not having me breaks your heart?"

"Sweetheart, there's a lump of coal where my heart should be. So shut your smart mouth and let me speak."

Her electric eyes snapped up to his in the mirror. "Please, go right ahead, Mr. McMahon. I can't wait to hear it."

"I see a woman who lashes out at other people to cover up her own insecurities." He smoothed his hands up and down her arms, ready to hold her tight if she dared to storm away. "She's different, which she thinks is bad. But it's not bad. It's sexy. She thinks she *should* be someone else…but she can't."

"Nice story," Darcy quipped, but the sting had gone out of her tone.

Her muscles were thawing under his touch, her back pressing to his chest. It was hard not to notice how different they looked—him in his expensive Italian suit and her in combat boots and not much else. His fingertips traced the swirl of flowers etched into the skin above her elbow. She had a full sleeve—from shoulder to wrist—birds and books and words and leaves, all expertly executed in black and gray. A small black cat and a moon decorated her right thigh.

"She wants desperately to feel comfortable in her body." He moved his hands to her rib cage, soothing her with a gentle up and down motion. The words under her breast called to his fingertips and he traced the curved design. "To regain something she lost a long time ago."

Darcy's chest moved up and down with each breath. The tension had leached out of her body now and she watched him with a mix of wonderment and anticipation. His hands continued to move steady and slowly, one closing in on her nipple and the other smoothing down over her stomach toward the edge of the Thursday panties.

"What else do you see?" she asked, this time without any sarcasm.

He dipped a finger under the elastic. "A woman who's going to look incredible when I make her come."

"Who says you're good enough to do that?" She chuckled as her head lolled back against his chest.

"Did you read all the reviews?" he said dryly. "I might be a monster, but I'm good in bed. That's the assessment."

"But we're not in bed."

Her ass wriggled back and forth as he dipped his hand lower, seeking out her sensitive spot. "There's a bed in the vicinity. Good enough for me."

A strangled *unghh* shot out of her lips when he curled his fingers against her sex, brushing her clit back and forth. She was wet, hot. Reed ground his erection against her backside, needing to relieve the pressure building there.

Not yet. Wait for her.

"Oh God." Her hands fisted his suit pants as she circled her hips against his hand.

"Still doubting my ability to make you come?" He kissed the side of her neck.

The sight of them in the mirror, his hand down the front of her underwear, a look of utter surrender on her face, was enough to make him blow. It was raw and intimate. More intimate than he was used to—usually there was a lot of "careful, don't ruin the lace" when he screwed women. They were practiced and perfect. Sensual, yes. But it felt like they restrained themselves so they still looked "pretty" while they had sex.

Darcy, on the other hand, had her mouth hanging open in a silent moan and her eyes squeezed shut. When she panted, a cute, little crease formed between her eyes—he wanted to kiss her there until the tension melted away. But there was only one way to take care of that now.

He circled her faster, thrumming her clit in time with the harried puffs of breath coming from her lips. Her words had turned to an incoherent babble, a breathless chant of pleasure that snaked through him and gripped him at the base of his cock.

"You're so close, Darcy." He tugged on her ear with his teeth. "Come hard for me, baby. I want you to be nice and wet for me."

"Reed," she gasped. "Oh God."

The tremors started in her thighs and moved up until her hips jerked against his hand. He wrapped his free hand around her waist, keeping her upright as the spasms took over her body. Her head fell forward and a rush of moisture coated his hand.

"Am I good enough?" He clucked his tongue as he buried his face into her hair. "Silly question."

"That was…" She sagged back against him. "I don't even know."

"It was a warm-up." He picked her up and carried her through the suite until they hit the bed. "Act one."

"Act one of…?" Her eyes fluttered. "I don't think I've got more than one in me."

"I'll be the judge of that." He set her down on the bed and dropped to his knees, his fingers unknotting the laces on her boots.

She lay back, propped on her elbows, and watched him. The crease was back between her brows, but this time it looked like something else. She was trying to figure him out.

"What?" He pulled off one boot and dropped it onto the floor with a *thunk* before he got to work on the other one.

"You're a confusing guy."

Reed raised a brow. "How's that? I'm in a hotel room with a gorgeous woman who's pretty much naked. Sounds exactly like my MO."

"Is this how you normally are with other women?" She tilted her head.

"How do you think I am with you?"

Color crawled up her neck. "I don't know… Gentle. Sweet."

"Gentle? Like I said, that was the warm-up." He nipped at the skin on the inside of her leg. "I'm partial to a little spanking. Maybe I'll tie you up as well."

She huffed. "When you're not being a smart-ass, you're actually a nice guy."

"Don't be fooled." He tugged off the other boot and rocked back on his heels. "It's all for show."

Chapter 14

"Just think of Reed McMahon as a human vibrator. He'll leave you panting, but he won't cuddle you after."

—*FormerlyMissBrown*

*D*arcy flopped back onto the bed and sighed at the silky duvet caressing her back. This was premium all the way. She moved her arms back and forth, creating "snow angels" in the fabric. Focusing on those things felt a hell of a lot easier than trying to figure out the mystery that was Reed McMahon.

Hot, cold, up, down. Was he a selfish prick or a victim of bad PR? How much of this was an act? If only Darcy's love of reading translated into being able to read this confounding man.

"What are you doing?" Reed hovered over her, one hand planted beside her hip and the other tugging her underwear down. He was still fully clothed and that made her nakedness feel even more extreme.

"Just basking in the post-orgasm glow."

"Don't get too comfy." He divested her of the Thursday panties and brought his lips down to her belly button. "We're going to get you back into pre-orgasm glow shortly."

"Isn't it your turn yet?" she asked.

Reed speared her with a hot, penetrating stare. It was the kind that all girls hoped to receive one day—the kind that made you feel like you were the only person in the world. Darcy swallowed, squirming beneath him.

"My turn?" He dragged the question out. "That your way of saying you want to do something to me?"

Yes. The word hissed in her mind, low and dark. Desire unfurled in her belly at the thought of unbuckling that expensive-looking belt at his waist and sliding those baby-soft pants down his muscular thighs. She could tell already he was going to be big. Thick. There was something about the idea of taking him in her mouth that made her tummy flutter—perhaps because her ex had only ever let her do it with the lights off.

"Darcy." His fingers came to her chin and she realized she'd been squeezing her eyes shut. "I can't give you what you want if you don't tell me."

"You've been doing a pretty good job so far," she said, running her tongue along her lower lip.

He brought his mouth to hers and pressed her into the bed, his thigh settling between her legs. Darcy wound her arms around his neck, her moans stifled by the thrust of Reed's tongue into her mouth. The man kissed like he was fighting for his life—it was heady. Intoxicating.

The cold metal of his belt dug into her stomach. "You need to be wearing far less clothing," she said, catching her breath between kisses. "I can't be the only one naked."

"I guess I got so caught up in you I forgot to undress myself." He propped himself up on both hands, his legs still between hers.

Darcy reached for his buckle. "I can help things along."

He watched her intently and she tried not to let her nerves show. She and Ben had been together so long that sex had become a routine, like doing the dishes or drying her hair. At the time, she'd thought that was normal—slipping into infrequent, lights-off, boring sex.

Not normal, just one of many red flags you didn't catch.

She gritted her teeth, forcing the shameful memories out of her mind. She had a sexy man here now. The past wasn't going to rob her of that. Yanking the belt, she focused on slowly unveiling Reed. This was her gift from all she'd gone through last year and she was going to unwrap him like a present.

The buckle made a *chinking* sound as it fell open and she pulled his shirt out. His stomach was flat against her palms, rippled with muscle, and the barest trail of hair tickled her fingertips. She worked at his buttons, popping them one by one, methodically and efficiently, through the holes until his chest was bared to her. Yep, he wasn't short on muscles, that was for damn sure.

"Sure you don't want me to help?" He stayed in position, balanced over her, his hair flopping down.

"Shh. I'm working." She came back to his waistband, unhooking the catch on his pants and then sliding his zipper down over the hard ridge of his erection. "Can't you see how hard I'm concentrating?"

A throaty chuckle vibrated through the air. "You *do* look like you're about to tackle a math equation."

"Yes. It's all a matter of numbers, isn't it?" Emboldened, she slipped her hand into his pants and rubbed the heel of her palm up and down his length. "Length times width."

"Is this how librarians talk dirty? I have been missing out." He grunted when she wrapped her fingers around him as best she could with his boxer briefs still on. "Does the solution add up?"

"I think you'll fit."

He brushed her hand away and crashed his mouth down to hers, grinding his pelvis between her legs. The edge of his open zipper dug into her thigh, but Darcy didn't care about the bite of metal on her skin. Nor did she care that he'd pinned her arms by her sides while he feasted on her neck, rubbing himself against her. Her focus had narrowed to a pinpoint—to the one single thing her body needed to continue existing.

"Reed," she gasped, her lips at his ear. "I'm done with the foreplay."

"I don't hear that too often." He pushed back and toed off his shoes before shucking his shirt and pants. "Getting impatient, are we?"

"Please." Her hands fluttered by her sides. The need burned inside her, like an out-of-control house fire. If she didn't tame it now, she'd be reduced to ashes. "I want you inside me so bad."

A satisfied smile played on Reed's lips. "How bad?"

"You want me to beg?" She narrowed her eyes.

Chuckling, he pushed his boxer briefs down. His cock bobbed

up against his stomach and Darcy's breathing grew shallow. But it was nothing compared to the hard jolt of arousal that shot through her when he wrapped his hand around himself.

"No need to beg. Your face is doing that for you." He ran his fist up and down, slow and steady. "Your eyes are all wide and those sexy lips are parted just so."

"Maybe you *do* affect me," she whispered.

He reached down and shoved his hand into the pocket of his suit pants, pulling out his wallet and flipping it open. "Never a doubt in my mind." He produced a condom and tore it open.

"Arrogant."

Darcy scooted to the edge of the bed, her eyes trained on his hands as he sheathed his cock. There was something utterly delicious about the way Reed handled himself. He didn't lack confidence in his body or in the way other people viewed it. He *knew* he was hotter than sin.

"I am." He stalked over to her, tilting her face up to his. "You'd do well to be a little more arrogant too."

"You'll have to teach me," she murmured as he scooped her up and sat with her in his lap. He yanked her into place, her knees digging into the bed on either side of his hips.

The position offered no cover—no blanket, no hiding under his broad chest. All she could do was bury her face into his neck. But she was open. Exposed.

"We should get the lights," she whispered.

"No way," he growled against her ear. "I want to watch every bit of this. I have voyeuristic tendencies, Darcy. I feast with my eyes."

His hands smoothed up and down her back. When he cupped her backside, firmly kneading her, she turned pliable beneath his fingertips. It was like he knew exactly what to do to refocus her brain on the here and now, instead of the doubt swirling like a sandstorm in her brain.

"Which one was your first?" he asked.

"Huh?" She blinked.

"Your tattoos." His fingertip traced the open book with the letters spilling out that sat right below her shoulder. "Which one was first?"

"The black cat and the moon." She pointed to her thigh. "I got it here because it would be easy to hide from my mother. But it turns out tattoos are a little addictive."

"And you stopped worrying about hiding things?"

"Kinda." She rocked back and forth in his lap, feeling the latex-covered head of his cock pushing up against her. "I guess I still hide some things."

"Like how much of a bombshell you are." He slipped a hand between them and brushed his thumb over her clit. Darcy's body tensed in response.

"I wasn't hiding that. Just in denial, I guess."

"Lucky I put a stop to it." His lips traced a line along her jaw. "Denial is the devil's foothold."

Who was this complicated man? Darcy searched Reed's face, but the flicker of seriousness had been replaced by a hungry, wolfish smirk. Distracted, Darcy almost missed that he'd moved his hand and was now curling two fingers inside her.

"Oh," she gasped. "That feels good."

"Rock against me." His free hand snaked around her waist and he held her tightly as her hips swirled to some natural, silent rhythm. "I want to make sure you're ready for me."

She'd never been so ready for anything in her life. All this buildup had made her positively combustible. "Yes, now. Ready."

"I'm sure there was a sentence in there somewhere." His white teeth flashed, but Darcy's attention was laser locked on Reed's hand moving between them.

He gripped the base of his cock and guided himself to her entrance, moving slow and deliberate. Drawing the final act out until the very last second. The man was a master of anticipation—he stretched time until she wasn't sure whether it had been minutes or hours since he'd started touching her.

"Sink down on me, baby." His hands bit into her hips as he helped her down.

There was a brief flash of discomfort as he pushed into her, her body scrambling to accommodate his size. Holy shit, he was even bigger than he looked. Gasping, she clamped her eyes shut and willed herself to relax.

"I'll go slow." He brushed the hair from her forehead and when she opened her eyes she found herself drowning in the endless warmth of his gaze.

This was why women fell for him. *This* exact moment. Fantasy had weaseled its way into reality, tempting her to believe, to want. To think that maybe she could be his type. The way he looked at her was *everything*.

"You still with me?" His thumb caught the edge of her mouth, opening her to a kiss as he rocked up into her.

"God, Reed." Sex had never been like this before. Sensual and a little dirty and filled with teasing and communication.

He flipped them around, her back landing on the soft covers. "Yes, some people do like to call me God."

She swatted him, but with all the endorphins rioting in her body, she couldn't be annoyed. In fact, his self-deprecating humor had charmed her. Or was that simply the way he plucked at her breasts as he thrust into her, creating a rhythm that was uniquely theirs? The muscles inside her sex fluttered, another orgasm building.

Reed hooked his arms under the backs of her legs and encouraged her to lock her feet behind his back. The slight change made him plunge deeper, harder.

"Holy shit." Her head lolled back. "I'm so close. I can't... I... Ugh..."

"Shh." He covered his mouth with hers. "Let it come."

His fingers tangled in her hair as he kissed her deeply and passionately, like it meant something. Then the feeling burst like a bubble on a needle, light fracturing behind her closed lids as she quaked in his arms. A second later, he followed her.

....

Reed pulled up in front of Gabriel's house, killing the engine on the car and sucking in a big breath before he pushed the door open. It was Tuesday evening, a whole day after he'd slept with Darcy. Vaguely, he wondered if she'd done her laundry yet. Perhaps he should send some panties to her house.

Do you even know her address? Uh, no. That's because you and her are not a thing. You're not dating her and that means no fucking panty deliveries.

His conscience could be such a little bitch sometimes. But it had a point. Yesterday, while fun, was a one-time thing. He and Darcy were working together, and the last thing he needed was for her to throw a wrench in the works. Especially now that he was going to use the fundraiser to hook Dave Bretton as a client.

The plan was perfect really, since no other publishing industry events would touch him at the moment. The guy's publicity opportunities had dried up, and Reed was going to leverage the hell out of it. Which meant keeping Darcy compliant with his plans.

Still, he couldn't regret what had happened last night. Seeing her blossom from the human version of Grumpy Cat into the sexy, little minx who'd cooed in his ear as she came was something he wouldn't soon forget. But keeping the memory fresh and acting on it were two different things. And Darcy needed to be put squarely back in the colleague box. The woman was far too dangerous—and too damn good at seeing through his shit—to be anything else.

He walked to the front door, the early-summer air warm on his skin. Golden light spilled out of the twin windows of Gabriel's house, inviting and cozy. A family home in the making. The kind Reed had wished for growing up.

He rapped his knuckles on the front door and smiled at the

sound of chaos inside. There was barking, someone shouting in Spanish, music. A second later, the door flung open and a woman launched herself into his arms. Her big belly prevented her from getting too close, however.

"Sofia darling." He leaned in to kiss her once on each cheek. "You're looking radiant."

"Suck-up!" Gabriel yelled from inside the house. The kitchen wasn't too far from the front door, and Reed chuckled at the sight of his friend waving a pair of tongs in the air like a madman.

"He's jealous because I'm so excited that you've come over." Sofia draped her arm around his shoulders and led him into the house. "It's been too long."

Reed had taken a while to get used to the affection Sofia doled out generously. It was like love seeped out of every one of her pores, and she was always hugging and kissing people, her vivacious laugh never silenced for long. She and Gabriel did everything with passion—cooking, fighting, making up.

For a guy like Reed, who'd grown up with a father who believed that sweeping emotions under the rug was the only way to deal, the overt PDA had been more than a little uncomfortable at first. But he'd grown to accept Sofia and Gabriel's way, and even looked forward to it from time to time.

"It has been a while," he agreed, crouching down to greet the baby of the family. Sofia's Golden Retriever, Benito—or Benny, as they'd taken to calling him—whined with excitement. "Oh boy, you've missed me, haven't you."

The dog slapped his paws over Reed's shoulders, toppling him.

The damn thing was the only creature possibly more affectionate than Sofia.

"Gabe, Benny is making out with Reed. This is really getting inappropriate." Her tinkling laughter disappeared as she swanned back into the kitchen and Gabriel appeared.

He was wearing a black tank top under an apron that read *I'm not yelling. I'm Hispanic* in bold, white print. "Hey, man." He slapped a hand down on Reed's shoulder. "Glad you could make it. Did the corporate drones let you off early?"

"I told them I had a meeting off-site." He disentangled himself from the dog and brushed off the gold hair from his jeans. "Not that anyone gives a shit. I'm a dead man walking."

"That bad, huh?" Gabriel frowned. "I really thought this Bad Bachelors stuff would die down."

"Yeah, you'd think so."

Only, the closer he looked, the more he wanted to kick himself for not acting sooner. He'd gone through every review on his profile and made a note of who he thought wrote it. So far, he'd only accounted for half the reviews. A further dozen were so vague that he'd probably have no chance of figuring out who wrote them.

Then there were the few that made alarm bells go off in his head. The ones that smacked of ulterior motive. He'd spoken with Bath and Weston's IT manager to determine if it was possible to see who'd been looking at the site at work. But apparently, he was only able to request that information for his direct reports, which meant he'd need to involve someone higher up in the food chain, and he was a little reluctant to draw more attention to the problem than was absolutely necessary.

"Can I grab a beer?" Reed said. "It's been a long fucking week."

"It's Tuesday." Gabriel shook his head. "If you're saying that already, beer's not going to cut it."

They walked into the dining area, and Gabriel grabbed a bottle of tequila from the bar against the far wall. Don Julio, his favorite. He had a collection of glasses stacked on a silver tray that were his pride and joy. They were heirlooms from his mother that he was already planning to pass down to the little boy who hadn't yet emerged from his wife's belly.

"This is the Reposado. It's good," he said, lining up two shot glasses alongside two tumblers. He poured the shots and handed one to Reed, holding his glass up. "*Salud!*"

"*Salud.*" The glasses clinked and Reed tipped the liquid down the back of his throat, humming at the smooth, warming sensation. He'd always thought tequila to be a college drink, something you got trashed on once and brought it back up so hard you never drank it again. But Gabriel had proven him wrong.

"Now the slow one." Gabriel poured two fingers into each tumbler and handed one over. "Enjoy."

There was yelling from the kitchen, Spanish words. Reed wasn't fluent by any means, but he knew the curse words. "What did she say?"

"Dinner's almost ready." Gabriel grinned.

Reed chuckled. "That's definitely *not* what she said."

Ten minutes later, they were seated at the table. Benny had curled up on the floor, his big, silky head resting next to Reed's sneaker. Sofia served the food from the center of the table, her dark, curly hair falling into her face. Her apron barely covered her belly, and she had some sauce splattered on her cheek. Gabriel grinned at her dotingly and wiped it away with his thumb, while she waved him away with a spoon.

They were the kind of couple who were so in love it could have been sickening if they didn't deserve one another so damn much.

"So, Reed. I hear you've been having a stressful time," Sofia said as she placed a plate in front of him.

"You're only supposed to tell her when I'm doing well," he said, shaking his head at Gabriel. "You're making me look bad."

Gabriel held up his hands. "For once, it ain't me who's making you look bad."

"How's your dad?" Sofia swatted at her husband as she took her seat. "Is he feeling okay after what happened?"

"Yeah, he's fine. Well…" He paused. "Not fine, exactly. But he's doing okay all things considered."

"Did you find out what happened?" Gabriel asked between shoveling the paella into his mouth. The guy ate like every meal was his last. Though Reed couldn't judge him—Sofia's cooking was incredible.

"All I know is that he fell and hit his head on the coffee table, but what caused him to fall is a little fuzzy." Reed skewered a shrimp on his fork. "Donna wasn't in the room and you know what Dad's like… getting information out of him is like trying to squeeze blood from a stone. But the doctor said he was dehydrated, more than normal."

Ever since his wife left seventeen years ago, Adam existed primarily on cigarettes and coffee, to the point that he'd lost the taste for food. These days, there were no more cigarettes, but he guzzled coffee like it was about to become a scarce resource. Donna was supposed to keep an eye on his fluid intake—of the non-caffeinated variety—but some days, even she couldn't get the old man to do what he was supposed to.

"Maybe he tripped or got the oxygen tank caught on a piece of furniture like last time." Reed shook his head. "I don't know."

"You think he's embarrassed to tell you what happened?" Sofia asked. "My *abuela* was like that. Stubborn like a mule."

"He's stubborn all right."

Gabriel snorted. "Like father, like son."

"What can I say? It's a family trait." Reed reached for his tequila and took a sip. He could already feel the alcohol working its magic on him, warming his muscles so they didn't feel as bunched. "But it makes it very hard to help him when he won't say what's wrong."

"And his breathing is still giving him issues?" Sofia frowned.

If only his dear old dad could see all that sympathy in her pretty, brown eyes—he'd want to smash something. They were two peas in a pod like that. Sympathy was for other people. *Weak* people. The McMahons were tough and independent. Other people's pity only made them work harder to keep their problems to themselves.

"The emphysema isn't going away." Reed found his throat closing around the words, making his voice sound choppy and rough. He cleared his throat. "We can manage it, but he'll be like that until…"

The silence was filled with the scrape of cutlery against plates. Reed knew his dad was never going to get better—that was a fact. But saying it aloud made it hard to breathe, as though his body were mimicking the pain and struggle his father slogged through every day. His fists clenched underneath the table.

"Have you ever thought about taking him to a therapist?" Sofia asked quietly. Gabriel shot her a look, but she waved him away.

"It's not in his head," Reed replied.

"Oh, I know that." She reached out to place her hand over his, the gentle touch stirring something painful in his chest. "But chronic pain can be very tough to deal with from a mental and emotional standpoint. Maybe talking to someone—"

"Sof," Gabriel warned.

"I'm just saying," she protested. "There's nothing wrong with getting help. He has a caregiver to help him with the physical stuff. Why not see a psychologist for the mental stuff?"

Reed had wondered on and off if his father's problems had grown outside the realm of the physical. Christ, he couldn't even bring himself to think about his dad having depression. But any discussions about talking to someone were met with hostility usually reserved for election time. If there was one thing his father hated more than politics, it was the idea that a doctor was going to mess with his head.

McMahons don't talk about their feelings with strangers… It's not the family way.

His father's words rang in his head. Hell, McMahons didn't talk about their feelings, period. Not the men anyway. They packed it all down and gritted their teeth, moving on without showing the world they were hurting.

And that's what Reed would have to do.

"He's fine." He patted Sofia's hand. "I promise."

Chapter 15

"I don't believe in regrets. Dating Reed taught me a lot of things, even if it took a while for the pain to subside. Now I know how to avoid men like him."

—*AnyaMark*

Reed eased himself into a booth, cringing as his quads protested the movement. Last night, after dinner with Sofia and Gabriel, he'd punished his body at the gym in the hopes it might quiet the worry. But no amount of physical activity seemed to get his head in the right space.

It was that damn woman.

He couldn't seem to get through a night without replaying what it was like to peel away the clothes from her skin. To kiss her deep and hard. To show her she didn't need to settle for some boring, middle-management type.

"Can I get you something to eat?"

He hadn't even realized the server had come to take his order. "Just coffee."

"How do you like it?" The server winked at him saucily, her bright-blue eyes and cherry-stained lips something that should have appealed. *Would* have appealed if he wasn't so damn occupied with a certain prickly librarian.

"Black," he said. "One sugar. And whatever my friend wants."

He gestured to Peter, who was ambling toward the table slow and steady. The man was good at his job, but he never seemed to move with any sense of urgency. Reed's mentor had told him once there was a fine line to how a man walked—too fast and people assumed you didn't have things under control. Too slow and people assumed you didn't care.

But Reed had found people who walked slowly toward a meeting were usually stalling because they had bad news.

"Coffee. Two creams and two sugars for me." Peter grunted as he slid into the booth. "And a bagel with cream cheese."

When the server had gone, Reed turned to Peter. "Okay, you said you needed a week to fully look into this. I've been exceptionally patient, but I'm hoping to hell you have something for me."

Peter wriggled his nose, causing his giant mustache to bob up and down. "Depends on your definition of *something*. The people behind Bad Bachelors have made an effort to cloak their identities. I had my tech guy look at the site and they're locked down tight. Whoever built it knew how to cover their tracks better than a bunch of Russian hackers."

Not surprising. Reed would have bet his last ten bucks he wasn't the only one after answers either. The folks at Bad Bachelors would be racking up enemies. Fast. But he wouldn't allow them to stay hidden if he could help it. If they wanted to expose him, then they could expect a taste of their own medicine.

"That's why I'm paying you to go digging," Reed said. "What have you got so far?"

Peter pulled out a small notebook from his satchel and flipped it open to a page with some scrawled notes. Old school. "I started with the company that created the app, Bad Bachelors Inc. It's referenced on their website and in several articles about the app. However, I can't find anything which corroborates that it's an actual company."

"So they're saying they're a company but they're not really?"

"Correct. However, the Bad Bachelors domain name was purchased by a company called Maximum Holdings. That's the company listed on the app stores as well. Apparently, they're based out of Delaware. It was set up last year and it *does* appear to be a real company. An LLC, to be exact."

They paused the conversation as the coffees were delivered along with Peter's bagel. "Delaware?" Reed asked, taking a sip of his drink. "I'd assumed they'd be based in New York, given the focus of their app."

He had a sinking feeling in his gut and Peter's knuckle cracking did little to ease it.

"Privacy laws in Delaware allow people to set up an LLC without disclosing the name of the owners, nor do they require the members or managers to be residents of the state." Peter shook his head. "There's a damn good reason why more than half of Fortune 500 companies are based there…on paper anyway."

"Shit," Reed muttered. "Surely they have to file tax forms or something. If they're making money, *someone* will know who they are."

"That's the thing." Peter scratched his head. "I can't see how they're making any money. The app is free to download, and there are no advertisements on it or their website. There are no paid memberships, subscriptions, or upgrades of any kind that I can see."

Reed blinked. It'd never occurred to him that Bad Bachelors wasn't being run as a business, one that would surely be lucrative at that. "Why would they possibly do it if they weren't making money?"

"Beats me." Peter took a bite out of his bagel, cream cheese clinging to his mustache as he chewed. "They would have costs to cover too. Hosting for the website and setting up the LLC. Not to mention the design of the app and website itself. Even if it was done in-house, it would have taken time."

"The whole premise of the app is to lift the lid on dating, right?" Reed rubbed at the back of his neck, his mind whirring. "Why would someone do that if money *wasn't* the object?"

"Personal vendetta?" Peter wiped his mouth with a napkin. "Someone got burned and now they're trying to make sure other people don't go through the same thing."

"There's nothing more powerful than the anger of a lover scorned." Reed should know; he'd faced it in his work on more than one occasion. Angry exes had tried to take down one or two of his clients before. It had only solidified his opinion that a relationship could really screw with one's life.

"I'm sure my ex-wife would agree with that." Peter chuckled. "She scratched my girlfriend's car up good after I started dating again. Took a key to it and carved her name in these big, jagged letters."

"Maybe this is the passive version of the car keying." A picture was starting to form—a motive, other than money, that would befit someone who'd had their heart broken. "Question is, am I the target? Or do I just represent what she hates?"

"You're assuming it's a woman," Peter said. "We don't know that."

"True," Reed said. "But my gut tells me it is."

If money was out of the equation, the only reason left was passion. Bad Bachelors was an attempt to lash out—revenge in the most basic sense. It was a new solution to an age-old agenda—ruin the reputation of the person that hurt you. Only now, with social media being a key pillar of reputation, it could be done en masse. Why hurt the *one* bastard when you could hurt them all?

"Keep digging," Reed said. "See if you can find someone in Delaware who knows how to bend the rules."

"It's gonna cost ya," Peter replied.

"It's already cost me."

Reed drained his coffee and slid out of the booth. As much as he wanted to untangle this mystery right here and now, he had bigger fish to fry. With Chrissy Stardust gone, he had a new whale in mind. One that would not only bring in more money for Bath and Weston—and therefore him—but one that would also get him in the good books with a certain tattooed librarian.

....

Darcy sat on her sister's bed, being forced to give her thoughts on things she knew nothing about. Like which of too seemingly identical black skirts went better with a tank top. She eyed the two options for longer than necessary, so at least she could give the illusion that she'd put some thought into her opinion rather than singing *eenie, meenie, miney, mo* in her head.

"That one." She pointed to skirt number two. "I like the… flippy bit."

"You mean the asymmetrical hemline?" Cynthia grinned and held it up in front of her.

"Is that what the kids are calling it these days?" Darcy picked at the white fibers poking out around the rip in her jeans. "You'll look gorgeous even if you wear a paper bag. Besides, it's just a baseball game."

"It's the day I introduce my big sister to my boyfriend." Cynthia spun around and threw skirt number one onto the bed. "It's a milestone."

Darcy had managed to stick to her internal promise of not telling her sister what to do, but she *had* been checking in more often. So she'd feigned interest when Cynthia had mentioned that he played baseball every Sunday with his friends and had managed to score an invite. Not that it would likely do much, but Darcy figured she might feel a little better about the guy if she met him.

Brad, ugh. What kind of name was that anyway?

At least this way she might be able to steal a moment with him to make it clear she wouldn't tolerate anyone screwing her little sister around. Discreetly, of course.

"You could have worn something a little less"—Cynthia wrinkled her nose—"emo teenage boy."

"What's wrong with my outfit?" She looked down at the vintage AC/DC tour T-shirt and ripped jeans. "How the hell is this emo? It's not like I'm wearing a My Chemical Romance T-shirt."

"It was a *phase*," Cynthia said with a huff and she shimmied out of her jeans.

Darcy tried not to look at Brad's name stamped onto her sister's thigh as she slipped the skirt over her legs. "A terrible phase. I had to do my homework next door while I listened to you wailing like a dying cat to that god-awful music."

"Oh, because that's better than listening to you and Mom screaming about your piercing?" Cynthia snorted. "You really thought she wouldn't notice. That woman makes the FBI look inept when it comes to sniffing things out."

"I knew she'd find out." Darcy shrugged. "I'd stopped caring by that point."

She remembered the argument plain as day. After weeks of switching her piercing out with a clear plastic spacer whenever she came home from school, she'd finally just left it in and counted down the minutes until her mother noticed and had a heart attack. One minute and thirty-four seconds. She'd timed it.

"How do I look?" Cynthia twirled on the spot, the edge of her black skirt kicking up just enough to show her slim, tanned thigh but not enough to flash her ink.

Darcy always blamed their differences on the fact that they were half sisters. They didn't look alike—Darcy's pale complexion and dark locks appeared harsh next to Cynthia's olive skin and soft, chestnut hair. They didn't sound alike or act alike. They had no hobbies in common. They didn't even share the same surname. And, until Cynthia had gone and gotten herself tattooed, they hadn't rebelled alike either.

"Perfect. As always," Darcy said. "But I'd grab a cardigan unless you want Genio to bitch about you going out with bare shoulders."

"It's eighty degrees out." Cynthia shot her a look but grabbed a lightweight chambray shirt and slipped it on over her white tank top.

"So where are we going?" Darcy pushed up from the bed and checked her own appearance in the mirror. Okay, so Cynthia had a point—she didn't exactly look like Little Miss Approachable. The spike through her left ear might have been a bit much. "I'm assuming you gave Mom some story to throw her off the scent."

"We're going to a gallery." Cynthia winked and slung her bag over one shoulder. "She was most impressed that I managed to get you to do something cultured."

"I work in a fucking library. I read classic novels. What more does she want?"

"Probably for you to stop swearing like a sailor." Cynthia reached for the hem of Darcy's T-shirt and knotted it so that the fabric pulled tight around her waist. "You have such a great body. I have no idea why you hide it away all the time."

She certainly hadn't been hiding it in Remi's dress when she met with Reed on Monday night. Memories washed over her—his hands in her hair, between her legs. His tongue working her into a frenzy. God, she'd been thinking about it all week.

"You okay, Sis? You look a little flushed." Cynthia pressed the back of her hand to Darcy's forehead the way their mother had done when they were kids.

"I'm fine. It's hot in here." She fanned herself. "Let's get iced coffee on the way."

"I like the way you think."

An hour later, Darcy and Cynthia headed across West 110th Street and into Central Park, beverages in hand. Darcy couldn't understand what would possess her sister to make the almost two-hour round trip from Bensonhurst to watch her boyfriend play beer league baseball.

"Isn't it a gorgeous day?" Cynthia sipped on her hazelnut iced latte, which was piled high with whipped cream and drizzled with syrup.

See, even your coffee isn't the same.

Darcy took a sip of her black cold brew. "Yeah. I probably should have brought sunscreen."

"Oh no, you might get a tan. How awful," Cynthia teased.

Darcy ignored the dig. "So, tell me about Brad. How did you meet?"

"Remember when I had that little, uh…incident with my car?" She spooned some whipped cream into her mouth.

"If by 'incident' you mean that time you backed into a tree, then yes."

Cynthia narrowed her eyes. "*Anyway*, I didn't want to tell Mom and Dad about it, so I couldn't go to the regular mechanic. I found a different place and he was the guy who took all my details."

"So he chatted you up while you were waiting?"

"Not exactly. I had to leave the car there because they were super busy and I got the impression they usually take care of fancier cars than mine. But Brad made sure I got their best guy to look at it." She beamed. "And he was finishing his shift, so he, uh…gave me a lift home."

"That's very personal service," she said carefully.

Men hitting on Cynthia wasn't unusual, the girl was a knock-out. Plus, she seemed to be unencumbered by the same soul-deep cynicism that affected Darcy. Lord knew people preferred Little Miss Sunshine and Rainbows, especially men.

"Well, I'm assuming they don't do that for everyone," Cynthia said.

"Just young, pretty women."

"Why do you have to make it sound sleazy like that? It was a sweet gesture."

"I'm only worrying about your safety, Cyn. Did you skip the childhood lesson about getting into cars with strangers?"

Her sister's icy silence was broken by the squeals of children as they drew closer to the Lasker pool. The pool—which turned into an ice rink in winter—was a hive of activity. Parents lined the edge, feet in the water, while their kids splashed and played. A lifeguard sat, ever vigilant, under a high-visibility orange umbrella.

"I know Mom and Dad think it's okay to keep treating me like a child," Cynthia said eventually. "But I don't expect it from you."

"I'm sorry." Darcy slung an arm around her sister's shoulders. "The older I get, the more I sound like her, you know. It's terrifying."

"You'd better put a stop to that now." A smile crept onto Cynthia's lips. "The world can't handle two of her. Could you imagine? Nagging would become the national pastime."

"Well, well, well." Darcy took a long sip of her iced coffee. "Who would have thought you'd be chewing off my ear talking ill of our precious mother?"

A look of guilt flashed over her face. "I know. But lately she's been driving me crazy. I feel so…stifled." She sighed. "Maybe it's time to move out."

"Not with Brad."

Cynthia huffed. "You can't help yourself, can you? No, not with Brad. With one of my friends. Melissa from work is looking to move after her lease is up. Might be nice to have freedom and privacy… and to not have to okay my every movement with her."

"I remember those days." They crossed a street and Darcy spotted the sports fields up ahead. "Which one are they playing on?"

Cynthia pulled out her phone and tapped at the screen. "North Meadow Baseball Field number five."

"No freaking idea which one that is."

Cynthia sucked on her straw. "Me either."

....

Reed dropped his sports bag onto the dirt. For once, he hadn't been looking forward to his weekly game and catch up with the guys. Which wasn't a good sign. Life had to be grim for a ball game and beers not to appeal.

But this week had been a royal mind-fuck. First off, Monday night with Darcy had thrown him for a loop and he *still* couldn't stop thinking about her a whole week later. Most unusual. Secondly, he'd tried—unsuccessfully—to schedule a meeting with Dave Bretton and his agent. The guy had blown him off twice and was dodging his calls. And with Donald Bath breathing down his neck, he needed to land this big fish. Fast.

"You look like you've aged a decade since dinner." Gabriel slapped his back. "Maybe it's time to invest in some of that anti-wrinkle shit girls use. I'm sure Sof can set you up."

Reed snorted. "How about I tell your pregnant wife that you think she's an expert on wrinkle cream and we'll see how that goes?"

"I'll deny it till they stick me in the ground."

Reed ferreted out a cap from his gym bag and then grabbed a water bottle. He should probably have been warming up, like the other guys already tossing the ball around, but he couldn't seem to get into the right mood.

"Who's pitching today?" Reed leaned back against the wire fencing that sectioned off the dugout from the field. "I'm happy to do it."

Brad, their star outfielder, snorted. "Yeah, 'cause you did such a great job last time. That dude ended up with a bruise on his chin for his engagement party."

The Smokin' Bases were a competitive lot, but clocking a batter in the chin was *not* encouraged.

"He walked." Reed tossed his head back and chugged his water. "And scored too, if memory serves me correctly."

"No one wants it in the face. Well, not in the field anyway." Brad laughed at his own joke and Gabriel shook his head.

"You're a dirty son of a bitch, you know that."

"Speaking of dirty," Brad said. "The chick I'm seeing is coming along today."

"The preteen who got your name tattooed on her leg?" Reed shook his head. "You're gonna have trouble with that one."

"Preteen," Brad scoffed. "Don't be such an asshole. She's twenty-two."

"Just legal." Reed looked his friend in the eye. "You serious about her?"

Brad shrugged and didn't respond. Reed knew it was none of his business, nor was he the person who should be lecturing *anyone* on relationships right now. Or ever. But encouraging a young woman to get your name tattooed on her…it was wrong. Unless you were dead serious that it was going to last. And Brad was the kind of guy who never seemed dead serious about anything.

"Maybe you should worry about your own problems, McMahon," Brad suggested. "Seems like you've got enough to keep you occupied."

Reed's hands twitched as resentment zipped through his veins. Having a lothario like Brad call him out was salt in the wound after a shitty couple of weeks. But they were nothing alike. Reed, while certainly not perfect, had been open about his desire to remain single. His jaw twitched.

"Why don't we just stick to playing ball, eh?" Gabriel said.

Brad wasn't worth his time, and if it wasn't for the fact that the guy was magic on the field, Reed would have convinced Gabriel to kick him out long ago. But the Smokin' Bases lived by one rule only when it came to the game: leave your issues at home.

Chapter 16

"I never met a guy who made me want him as much as Reed. There's something about him that inspires the chase. It's thrilling...and ultimately disappointing."

—*User212*

B y the way," Gabriel said as they walked onto the field, gloves in hand, "you're not pitching. Especially after that."

"Think I'll bean someone?"

Gabriel chuckled. "I *know* you will. And as team captain, I'm not stupid enough to put you in that spot when you're looking like a bull staring down a matador."

"We could find someone else for outfield," Reed said. He tipped his face up to the sky and let the summer warmth wash over him. If this wasn't enough to pull him out of his funk, then he was in deep shit.

"No way. The Pokémaster stays." Gabriel winked. "He really does catch 'em all."

If only Brad were as good at playing nice with the team as he was at catching fly balls. He glanced over to where he stood at the fence, his arms draped over it while he chatted with two women. The one with lighter hair giggled as she flipped it over her shoulder. That must be the "chick," as he'd so eloquently called her.

Reed stopped dead in his tracks as he looked at the woman standing next to Brad's girlfriend. Defensiveness seeped from her posture—she had her arms crossed over her chest and her head tilted to one side—but it was the all-black outfit and tattoos on one arm that had him frozen.

What the hell was Darcy doing here?

"Give me a minute," Reed said as he left Gabriel standing with a confused look on his face.

He marched over to the edge of the field, watching closely as Brad talked to the two women. Was his girlfriend a friend of Darcy's? A relative? They didn't look alike, at least from a distance. Though it was hard to compare two people who were dressed so differently. He looked at the girlfriend in her short skirt, preppy chambray shirt, and tiny handbag. Yep, nothing like Darcy.

"This must be your new girlfriend," he said as he slapped Brad on the back like they were old friends. "How about an introduction?"

Brad looked at him like he'd spoken in gibberish. "Reed, this is Cynthia and her sister, Darcy."

Sister, interesting.

"Reed?" Darcy blinked. "What a coincidence."

Cynthia extended her hand in perfect ladylike fashion and shot him a beaming smile. "It's so nice to meet Brad's friends. I've been hearing all about how well your team is doing."

"No thanks to this guy here." Brad jerked his thumb toward Reed. "Sometimes I'm not sure what team he's on. He managed to hit a batter last week."

"It slipped," Reed drawled, shooting Cynthia a smile. "We all make mistakes sometimes."

Darcy looked at him curiously. "Do we?"

Was she asking if their night together was a mistake?

"Only if you do something permanent," he said.

Darcy shoved her hands into her pockets. She appeared to have relaxed since he'd walked over, her concentrated scowl disappearing.

Don't take it as a compliment. She probably doesn't want to be doing this any more than Brad does.

His teammate looked awkward as hell. Obviously, the introduction to the big sister wasn't planned—at least not from Brad's perspective. Reed had to hold back a laugh. Darcy might be slender, but she looked like she'd take you down if necessary.

"How exactly do you two know each other?" Cynthia asked. "Don't tell me you're dating, that would be such a funny coincidence."

"No!" Reed and Darcy both said it at the same time, the force of their denial making Cynthia throw her hands up.

"Okay, okay. Geez." She laughed. "Sorry for asking."

"We're working together," Darcy clarified. Her cheeks had warmed to a delightful shade of pink, but she kept a straight face as she explained how he was "so generously" offering his services for free to help out with the library fundraiser. Which, according to Darcy, was because he loved books so much and felt very passionately about the relevance of libraries in today's society.

Give me a bucket.

Darcy shot him a smug look as Cynthia awwed. "That's so nice."

"He's a real stand-up guy," Darcy said. "He even told me he thinks more people should be reading books than using the internet. Especially where etiquette and manners are concerned."

Before he could retort, Gabriel was yelling at them to hurry up and take their places for the first inning. Cynthia had thrown her arms around Brad in what was apparently a good-luck kiss but looked a hell of a lot closer to a teenage make-out session.

"You going to kiss me good luck?" Reed said, leaning over the railing.

"Not a chance in hell, buddy." She grinned. "You'll have to get lucky all on your own."

"I've been doing that a bit too much this week."

She snorted. "You are so inappropriate."

"It's my specialty." He winked and she shook her head, her cheeks flaming even brighter. "And don't think I've already forgotten about that little quip. Etiquette books my ass. You'll pay for that."

"Bring it on, McMahon." She poked her tongue out and the silver ball glinted in the sunlight. Taunting him.

Cheeky. Little. Minx.

Gabriel yelled again and Reed dragged himself away, his mood buoyed for some stupid reason. It wasn't seeing Darcy. It was watching the inevitable crash and burn of Brad and Cynthia...at least, that's what he was going to keep telling himself.

....

Reed played one of the worst games of baseball in his life that afternoon. Not only did he fail to score a single run, but he also managed to miss the world's easiest out while playing third base.

"What the hell got into you today?" Brad said as the team traipsed off the field. "I was only joking before when I said I wasn't sure which side you were on. You didn't have to take it so literally."

Brad, of course, had played a perfect game and no doubt impressed the panties off Cynthia.

"I'm preoccupied." Reed slipped off his cleats and slammed his feet into his sneakers. He'd done so little that he'd barely even broken a sweat. "Plus I thought I'd make you look good in front of the girls."

"I don't need your help with that. Trust me." He laughed as he stripped off his T-shirt to change into a fresh one. "So I said I'd go with Cynthia and her sister to grab a drink somewhere. You should come since you're friends with Darcy and all."

"Friends is generous. We're colleagues."

Colleagues who happened to have incredible sex you can't stop thinking about...

"Aw, come on, man." Brad clamped a hand down on his shoulder. "You can't leave me to battle the awkward family meet and greet on my own."

"Actually, I can."

"But you know the sister, right? She looked like she wanted to claw my face off when Cyn introduced us." Brad's voice had morphed into a soul-grating whine. "But the second you came over, she was all smiles and rainbows. Can't you use your lady magic for good instead of evil, just this once?"

Lady magic? He refrained from telling Brad the first thing to do would be to lose the toddler voice. "You need a lesson in how to ask for a favor," Reed said dryly.

"I'm begging, man." He sighed. "I like this girl, okay? And I know I don't always make the best first impression."

"Or tenth," Gabriel muttered as he walked past to catch up with the other guys who were already heading off.

"So you *do* like her?" Reed glanced to where Darcy and Cynthia were standing. "I thought she was just 'a chick,' or did I hear that wrong?"

"I like her enough to not be blowing her off right now to avoid the big, bad sister."

Reed smiled. Darcy would *love* knowing he'd called her that. "Fine. But I'll be collecting a return favor when the time comes."

....

Darcy wondered what hellish kind of twilight zone she'd ended up in. She and her sister, along with Brad and Reed, were crowded around a small, round table in the middle of a noisy sports bar not far from Central Park. The Yankees were playing Toronto in an away game and losing. Badly. Which meant the crowd was not only noisy, but also angry.

"I don't know what's got into them this season." Brad chugged his beer. "They shouldn't be losing to the goddamn Canadians. It's an embarrassment."

"So what? The Mets won," Reed said, a smug smile on her face. "That's all that matters."

A collective groan rose from the crowd as the Blue Jays outfielder caught a fly ball and ended the inning.

"Well, the AL East *is* the most competitive division," Cynthia said. When Darcy raised a brow, she added, "Everyone knows that."

"Since when are you into sports?"

Cynthia was not the average sports-bar patron, let alone someone who knew which division was the most competitive. Even now, she looked out of place delicately pushing her salad—dressing on the side—around her plate.

"I've always liked sports," Cynthia said, shooting her a look.

Darcy tried not to roll her eyes as she gnawed on a chicken wing. As far as she was concerned, sports belonged with salads in that they could be classified as *stupid things she refused to partake in*. Having said that, it hadn't been a chore to watch Reed on the field. Not only because she was able to admire his athletic body without him noticing, but also for the fact that she now had something to tease him about.

"So were you just filling in today, Reed?" She reached for her beer.

"No, this is my regular team." He didn't ask her why she thought that, probably because he'd already guessed she was looking to needle him.

"Might not have looked it today, but Reed's played ball since he was tyke. Isn't that right?" Brad said cheerfully. "Weren't you getting scouted at one point? I'm sure Gabe told me that."

Something dark washed over Reed's face, hardening his expression. His lip twitched, as if some sharp response were trying to push its way out. "Yeah, when I was a kid. Obviously I never went pro."

Darcy blinked. "Wow, I didn't know that."

"That's because I don't talk about it."

The table fell silent and Darcy could have cut the tension with a knife. Cynthia stabbed at a lettuce leaf with her fork. "So, uh… Brad, why don't you tell Darcy about where you took me for our first date?"

Darcy immediately tuned out as Brad dug into a very detailed account of how much effort he went to get a reservation at some fancy Manhattan restaurant. As an introvert and hater of both parties *and* small talk, she knew exactly the right spots to nod and give an interested *mmm-hmm* to give the appearance of listening. But she let her eyes wander over to Reed.

He looked so different outside work. Not that she'd assumed he wore suits on the weekend or anything, but seeing him dressed in sweats and a T-shirt, his hair mussed from sitting under a baseball cap, was scarily appealing. This outfit couldn't hide the rock-hard muscles in his chest nor his washboard-flat stomach. Even the clingy sweats clued you in to what was underneath.

She reached for another chicken wing and bit into it. Maybe if she stuffed her face enough, she might be able to fill the void of dissatisfaction that'd been aching all week. But food wasn't a replacement for sex…especially when she'd been woken up to the possibilities of how good sex could be.

How intimate and personal.

It's not personal for him, you know that. He just knows how to make it seem *that way.*

"Isn't that romantic?" Cynthia sighed. "And to think I would never have met you if I hadn't crashed my car."

"It was more of a bump than a crash." Brad leaned over to her and brushed a strand of hair from her forehead before kissing her.

Darcy turned to Reed and made the motion of sticking her fingers down her throat. The return smile was quickly covered up when the lovebirds broke apart and he pretended to inspect something on the menu. Out of the corner of her eye, Darcy caught Brad's hand sneaking under the table. A second later, Cynthia declared she had to go to the restroom, and Brad coincidentally had to make a phone call.

Which left the anti-lovebirds alone.

"Well, this is awkward as fuck, isn't it?" Darcy said, taking a long gulp of her beer.

Reed's laugh boomed over the din of the sports bar. "Glad it's not just me."

"How'd you get roped into coming along?"

He turned in his chair and shot her a cheeky look. "Apparently, someone seemed a little overprotective at the first meeting. I was brought in for reinforcements."

"You?" She blinked incredulously.

"Why not me?" He planted an elbow on the table and leaned in closer.

The catch in Darcy's breath was swallowed by the crowd's raucous cheer. The Yankees must have finally done something right. "You're not exactly the poster boy for polite conversation."

"No, I guess I'm not."

Up close, she could see the stubble lining his jaw, making the angle look even sharper and more devastatingly sexy. He was always smoothly shaven when she saw him, but this must be one more thing that was different between Work Reed and Weekend Reed. Curiosity niggled at her—she wanted to know more about this man who played baseball with his mechanic friends and didn't shave. Who was Reed McMahon when he wasn't working so hard at being Reed McMahon?

"You do know I *can* behave like a decent human being, right?" he said.

"But you choose not to?" She cocked her head as though giving the conversation serious thought. "Or does your definition of 'decent behavior' vary from mine?"

"That depends. Do you think what we did Monday night was decent?"

It couldn't have been her imagination, but she swore the question rolled through her body flipping on every damn switch to every damn part of her. Especially the southern parts. It seemed fitting that a guy who was so good with his words was also so good with his mouth…and his hands.

And his—

"Cat got your tongue?" he drawled.

"It was adequate." If she were the spiritual type, she might have been concerned about all the lying Reed encouraged her to do. There was nothing "adequate" about Reed or his skills in the bedroom. "No complaints."

"Not exactly a rousing endorsement." His expression said he didn't buy her response one bit.

But she wasn't about to give Manhattan's most notorious womanizer the chance to reject her. She didn't expect anything from him, so she wasn't going to come across as some needy woman desperate for his love and affection…even if she might have been a teensy bit desperate for his body.

Maybe *desperate* was a bit much. During her relationship with Ben, she'd been starved for affection. So wanting a replay with Reed wasn't exactly unexpected or unnatural.

Very logical. Good work, brain.

"You seemed to think it was more than adequate when you were screaming my name over and over." His eyes raked over her, lingering for an extra few seconds on her mouth. "How did you put it? 'Oh, Reed. God, that feels so good. Harder.'"

Darcy looked around them to make sure no one heard him mimicking her sex talk. The last thing she wanted was a *When Harry Met Sally* reenactment. "You're too much," she said, reaching for her drink and chugging the rest of her beer. It'd gone warm and didn't have the cooling effect she'd hoped for.

"Thought I was adequate." He looked smug as all hell.

"What's the matter, Reed? Can't handle it when someone isn't falling over your feet to tell you how good you are?" She set her pint glass down with a loud *clink*. "You might be used to women who'll act the way you want them to, but that's not me. Sorry to disappoint you."

Reed opened his mouth and looked as though he was about to retort when his gaze suddenly flicked sideways. "Oh, hi, Cynthia. Brad."

Shit. How much of that interaction had her sister seen?

Darcy pulled back, realizing she'd been leaning into Reed, her knees almost touching his. The man had a gravitational pull that should have been limited to planets. And yet again, his taunting and teasing had sucked her into his vortex.

"Brad and I have decided to go and see a movie," Cynthia said. "I hope you don't mind that I'm ditching you, Sis? There's this silly comedy on and we both were planning to see it."

"Of course." Darcy waved her sister's concern away.

Truth was, the less time she had to sit here in the midst of this awkwardness, the better. She hadn't totally warmed up to Brad after meeting him—he seemed immature considering his age. And the longer she had to listen to him speak, the more likely she was to let her facade of the nonjudgmental big sister slip. Though, if what Reed had said was true, she hadn't been hiding her opinion too well after all.

As the waitress stopped by with the bill, Cynthia turned the full force of her angelic smile onto Reed. "I don't suppose you have a car, do you? Darcy and I caught the subway and I don't like the idea of her having to catch it all the way back on her own."

"Uh, since when?" Darcy didn't have a car, so the subway was her MO. She gestured to the front of the restaurant, where the glass door showed that the sun was still hovering above the horizon. "It's still light out."

But her dastardly sister didn't give a shit about safety—at least not in this particular situation. The falsely innocent expression on her face told Darcy she'd gone into matchmaking mode.

Oh, hell to the no.

"I'll be fine on my own," she said, holding up a hand to stop any further discussion. "I'm a big girl. I can ride the subway by myself."

"Nonsense." Reed pushed his chair back and tossed a few bills onto the table. "I'm parked on Eighty-Third and I'm heading back to my dad's place in Red Hook. It's no trouble."

"Sounds like you don't even need directions." Cynthia threw her arm around Darcy's shoulders and planted a kiss on her cheek. "He's really cute," she said in a not-so-subtle stage whisper.

Damn her. Was the whole family trying to marry her off?

Brad stuck his hand out and she shook it. "It was nice meeting you," she said.

To his credit, Brad looked relieved. "You too. You should come along more often. We're not used to having an audience."

"Sure." She nodded politely.

"The extra attention is good for most of us." He chuckled as he shook Reed's hand. "I'm sure you'll be fine next time, McMahon."

Reed grunted a response, but it wasn't audible over someone shouting at a screen a few feet away. The Yankees were down and the ninth inning was about to start.

"Come on." Reed pressed his hand into her lower back. "Let's get out of here before the crowd gets any messier."

"You don't want to stay for the end?" If he did, she could excuse herself to go and put some much-needed distance between them. A country's worth is what she needed to let her feminine parts calm down, but a borough would have to do. "It's fine. I really don't need a lift."

Cynthia and Brad were waiting for them to follow, his arm slung around her shoulders in a way that made Darcy's heart twinge. She may not have picked the guy as a good match for her sister, but he *did* seem to like her. And they'd already developed an easy connection she'd never managed to share with anyone.

That's because you don't open up to people. Hard to build a connection if you keep everything locked up inside.

But Darcy had spent her childhood keeping her emotions tucked away for fear of inciting an outburst—or further encouraging criticism—from her overly emotional mother. And when you'd done something like that for so damn long, it was a hard habit to break. The last year had made her wonder more and more if that's how Ben had managed to keep his secret for so long. Darcy didn't like questions about her feelings, so she tended not to ask them either.

"Let's go," Reed said. "We'll have you home in no time."

Chapter 17

"If there is one thing I've realized by dating men like Reed, it's that a guy who can't talk about his past is more damaged than I want to deal with. I'm not looking for a fixer-upper."

—*LadyGotham*

*W*hat do you know about Brad?" Darcy asked as they climbed into Reed's car. Which, surprisingly, was an older BMW X5. She'd expected something a little smaller. Sportier. "Should I be worried?"

Reed tossed his sports bag into the back seat and then took his place behind the wheel. The car rumbled to life at the turn of the key. "I know he plays baseball and he's a mechanic."

"That's it?" She looked at him incredulously. "How long have you been teammates? That's *all* you know?"

"Well, I do know something else." He placed his left hand

behind Darcy's headrest and looked over his shoulder as he backed the car out of the parking spot.

The action brought his face closer to hers and she found herself staring at him again. She had to stop that. Not that she could blame any woman for staring at Reed—the guy looked like he'd been created with every woman's fantasy in mind. The scent of yesterday's after-shave and something earthier, manlier, sent a tremor through her.

She sucked in a breath and turned to look out the windshield. "What's that?"

"That it's always a bad move to get involved in other people's relationships." He swung the car around using only one hand on the steering wheel.

Darcy huffed. "I'm looking out for my little sister, not trying to meddle."

"It's a fine line," he replied. "Honestly, there isn't much more to say. I don't know him that well."

"Do you like him?"

He let out a throaty chuckle. "That's a loaded question."

"No it's not. I'm asking for your opinion." She watched him closely as he pulled up next to the garage's ticket taker. "Though I'm taking your reluctance to answer the question as an answer itself."

"He's not a bad guy." Reed flicked his gaze over to Darcy. "Would I want him dating my sister? I don't know about that."

"You have a sister?" Her ears perked up at the possibility of learning more about Reed's personal life.

"No. I was speaking hypothetically."

Darcy leaned back against the plush leather seat and let the sun streaming in through the windshield soothe her as they exited the parking garage. "Do you know she got his name tattooed on her thigh?"

"I had heard that." He paused. "Not that you're one to judge about that kind of thing."

"Of course I can judge. You don't get people's names in permanent ink." She folded her arms across her chest. "Especially not some guy you've been seeing for five minutes. Hell, I wouldn't even get my own mother's name tattooed on me."

She regretted the words the second they left her mouth. Not because she didn't mean them—she absolutely did—but she feared they said just as much about her as they did about Marietta.

"What I mean is that tattoos should have a connection to you as an individual—whether it's a symbol that means something or because the artistry inspired you. The second you tie it to someone else…" She swallowed the rest of the sentence because it hurt too much. "Forget it."

"Who was it?"

His question felt like two hands wrapped around her throat, squeezing and squeezing until her lungs burned. "Who was what?"

He glanced at her as they stopped at a red light. "The person whose name you got tattooed."

"I've never had anyone's name inked on me because I know it's a bad idea." Okay, so that wasn't the whole truth. She chewed on the inside of her cheek.

"Someone talk you out of it?" he asked softly.

"Yeah. A friend." Something was blocking her throat, making

it hard to swallow. "He'd done a few of my pieces. But he refused to give me an appointment for that one."

She'd been so angry that she'd stormed out of his shop, cursing and swearing she'd never speak to him again. The plan had been for Ben's name to be her something blue on the wedding day. She'd even drawn the design herself—it was small, tasteful. Blue and black ink with scrolling letters that would live just below the crook of her elbow, because that's where he always tickled her. It'd been pure luck that all her favorite artists had been booked up for the month before the wedding and she'd refused to try out someone new for the sake of getting it done prior to the big day.

To Darcy's horror, tears pricked the backs of her eyes, barely giving her warning before the fat drops fell onto her cheeks. Oh God, she could *not* be crying in front of Reed Lady Killer McMahon. So. Freaking. Embarrassing.

"Whoever he is, he's a dick." Reed reached across the center console and grabbed her hand. "All men are. Don't take it personally."

She wasn't really angry at Ben. Not anymore. With time to think after all the drama had died down, she knew he had been dealing with demons of his own. And while he shouldn't have broken their promises by cheating on her, coming out to his religious family must have seemed impossible. From what she knew, Ben and Mark were still together. And although she'd continued to ignore his calls and attempts to make amends, she hoped he was happy. That *they* were happy.

But that didn't stop the shame that rolled through her whenever she thought about that day—shame that she'd been totally blind to who he really was, shame that she'd been in a relationship with someone who wasn't attracted to her. Shame that her own mother had tried to convince her to "marry him anyway" because she may not find someone else.

Like her mother had more confidence in her being able to live a lie than convince someone else she was worthwhile.

"I don't even know why I'm telling you this." She wiped the tears from her cheeks and steeled herself. Chances were, Reed would make some excuse to drop her off at the nearest subway station just to get himself out of this awkwardness. "It's personal stuff and I'm sure you're very bored."

His silence ripped through her chest. God, she was making a fool of herself. He probably thought she was one of those girls who acted like they were in a relationship because they'd had sex.

"Do you want to come with me to visit my dad?" he asked out of nowhere.

....

The question slipped through his lips before he had the chance to give it proper consideration. But Darcy had stirred something in his chest, a niggling sense of empathy that he hadn't experience in so long he wasn't quite sure what it was at first.

Must be phantom pains.

"I usually visit my dad on Sunday nights after the game to see how he's doing," he explained. "He's always nicer when I take a friend."

She smiled, her pale skin tinted pink around her eyes. He'd never been one to find crying attractive, but somehow her eyes looked even bigger and bluer. The vulnerability was a stark contrast to her all-black outfit and the spike in her ear.

"I'm not really dressed for dinner." She smoothed her hands down her stomach.

"There are no airs and graces in the McMahon household. No dress code either."

She nodded. "Okay." Her voice sounded lighter. Happier. "I'd love to."

By the time they arrived at his father's house, Darcy's mood had improved considerably. But Reed was spiraling into a black hole of confusion about why the hell he was breaking his primary rule about women—don't let them into your personal space.

He's already met her and you're right about him being nicer when you have a friend with you. This way you won't have to hear him bitch you out for trying to help him.

But that opened up a whole new can of worms. Friend? Since when?

He couldn't come up with a single thing to counter that thought. Hanging out with Darcy wasn't too far from hanging out with Gabriel—they ribbed one another and she wasn't trying to impress him, that was for damn sure. The major difference, of course, was the annoying fact that he was *still* attracted to her. Sleeping with her hadn't dulled the feeling like it usually did. If anything, he'd found himself increasingly occupied with thoughts of her.

"This is it." He pulled the car to a stop in front of his father's place and killed the engine.

The sun sat fat and low, resting on the horizon like an overweight cat—lazy and round.

"Did you grow up here?" She pushed the door open and stepped out.

"Yeah, no way my dad is going anywhere else unless a doctor orders him to." Reed snorted. "Probably not even then. He'd be happy to die here."

The comment, which had meant to be light, settled like a rock in his stomach. Since his dad's trip to the hospital, the old man hadn't been himself. Every time Reed called, his father made an excuse to hang up—the game was on, he was eating, he needed to go to the bathroom. The withdrawal worried Reed, because he hadn't been like that in years. Not since Reed's mother had left.

What had caused the spiral? If only it were possible to ask a question like that. But Reed knew the answer would be a sharp request for him to mind his own business—probably with a few expletives thrown in for good measure—and a swift change of topic. Like father, like son.

Reed locked the car and headed up the path to the front door, Darcy in tow. He climbed the stairs quickly and jabbed at the doorbell, which screeched into the quiet evening.

"Are you sure it's okay for me to be here?" Darcy asked. "I don't want to cut into your father-son time."

"Trust me, you're here as my buffer." He shot her a rueful look. "It's been a long week and I can't deal with him at full tilt tonight."

"Still problems with the Bad Bachelors thing?" She drew her bottom lip between her teeth, worrying it back and forth.

"Yeah, but other stuff too." There was a thump inside followed by a string of curse words and then the door flew open.

"I told you, Reed: you don't—" Adam stopped abruptly. "Now who is this?"

"Dad, you remember Darcy from the hospital," Reed said, pulling open the screen door and holding it for her. "We thought you might want some extra company tonight."

"It's nice to see you again, my dear." Adam McMahon was suddenly all smiles and fatherly charm. He stuck his hand out and gallantly helped her into the house.

"You too, Mr. McMahon."

"Please, call me Adam. You probably can't tell from looking at my son, but we didn't grow up with silver spoons in our mouths here."

"I'll try to be less fancy," Reed quipped, glancing down at his sweats and sneakers. "Good thing I left my gold-lined sweatpants at home."

Darcy laughed, her cheeks rosy pink. The splotchy patches and tears had gone away, leaving her looking like her usual self. But Reed couldn't shake the image of her quivering lip. He'd hated seeing her like that.

"How's your head?" she asked, her brows crinkled with concern. "Reed said you didn't have a concussion in the end."

"Not that they could tell. But who can trust those quacks?" Adam grunted.

"The millions who visit hospitals every year," Reed said under his breath. "Normal people."

Adam shot him a look but didn't engage. He motioned for them to head into the living room, and Reed let Darcy have the side of the couch without wayward springs. The place looked messier than usual—there were half-empty coffee cups on the table, a pile of newspapers teetering beside Adam's chair. A plate sat in the middle of his coffee table, which now had a new sheet of glass, and contained the remains of an apple that had turned a nasty shade of brown.

"Sorry about the mess," he said, moving to pick up the cups.

"It's all right, Dad. I got it." He bent down and inspected a spill on the table—dark liquid, probably coffee—which had dried into a tacky puddle. "When was the last time Donna came by?"

His father grunted. "She's been sick."

"That's right." He nodded. She'd called him a few days ago to let him know. "She said the agency was sending a replacement."

"You mean they sent some stranger."

Reed sighed. Perhaps he shouldn't have brought Darcy here tonight. It sounded as though he needed to have it out with his dad, to set him on the straight and narrow. Weariness wound its way through his body, making the cups and plates seem even heavier. He wasn't the kind of guy to let the world drag him down, but the last few weeks were starting to take a toll. His energy was flagging and he wanted to hole up in his apartment and pretend life was fine and dandy.

"I'll give you a hand." Darcy shot a winning smile in his father's direction. "How about I put some coffee on? Would you like a cup?"

Who *was* this girl? Darcy had never been like this before, at least not in his presence. But the second she laid a soft hand on his father's shoulder, the old man was about to melt like ice cream on a hot day.

"You don't have to do this," Reed said as they walked into the tight kitchen area. More dishes were piled up in the sink, and something smelled a bit funky. He checked the trash can and recoiled, tying a knot at the top of the liner to keep the smell in.

"What, make coffee?" She emptied out the remains of the pot into the sink and rinsed it clean. "I may not be a rocket scientist, but I am capable of basic hospitality."

"Should be us showing *you* hospitality," he grumbled. "That's how it works when you invite someone over."

Except here they were, standing in the beginnings of a pigsty. What the hell was going on with his father? Not that his place normally looked like *Better Homes and Gardens* by any means, but Adam McMahon was a proud man. He kept a tidy home as best he could. Reed made a mental note to check in with the agency about the replacement. Given his father's appetite had waned in recent months, this didn't look like only one or two days' worth of dishes.

"Reed." Darcy planted a hand on his arm, her blue eyes sincere. "Are you okay? You've been staring at that sink with a trash bag dangling from your hand like you're a statue or something."

"I'm fine." He turned and headed out of the house to dispose of the trash.

The sun had dipped farther, settling a hazy, purple light over the neighborhood. Two women walked along the path, crossing in front of his father's house in their matching black leggings. A small white dog trotted in front of them and they both waved when they caught sight of him.

He remembered this place from his childhood days, how rough it had been back then. Red Hook had been considered one of the worst neighborhoods in the entire country, the "crack capital" of the United States. Many of the families had struggled to make ends meet, and crime and violence were rife. But now it was becoming upscale. The houses were being bulldozed or renovated, sold for millions. Hell, they even had a Tesla showroom. If fancy electric sports cars weren't a sign of complete gentrification, then he didn't know what was.

All of which illustrated what an eyesore his father's house could become if he didn't do something about it soon.

With a sigh, he replaced the lid on the trash can and headed back up the stairs to the front door. Darcy's sweet voice floated out, her laughter cutting through all the dark muck in his head. He found her sitting next to his father, their hands wrapped around twin floral mugs as she chatted animatedly about her love of the classics.

His father smiled, enraptured. And, for the first time in a long time, Adam McMahon looked genuinely happy.

....

By the time she'd finished her coffee and poured another, Darcy's cheeks hurt from all the laughing. Reed's father was a delight— charmingly self-deprecating, inquisitive, and a smooth talker. Like his son.

It saddened her that she'd felt more at home and at ease with

Reed's father than she ever had in her own family home. At least here, she wasn't made to feel like an abject failure. Nobody was commenting on her appearance or her marital status. Adam seemed to genuinely enjoy her jokes and all the funny stories about her quirky library patrons. Reed had been quiet, but she felt his gaze on her constantly, burning holes into her ability to concentrate. Whenever she made eye contact, a frisson of anticipation shot through her.

"I guess I should take you home," Reed said, setting his mug on the coffee table.

His deep voice smoothed over her like a caress...like *his* caress. *I should take you home...* Such an innocent statement, and yet her mind was doing cartwheels and shimmying like she was about to get some. Not likely. From all accounts, Reed could only count to one where sex was concerned—one night, one encounter.

"Sure." She stood and reached for his cup, batting his hand away when he told her she didn't have to help clean up. But she was hardly going to leave it to Adam, who had trouble getting in and out of his chair without huffing and puffing.

In the kitchen, she caught snippets of two male voices—one rich and smooth, the other raspy and full of emotion. The words were a little hazy, but it sounded as though Reed was trying to convince Adam to do something. Darcy's eyes skated over the messy kitchen. She wasn't one to judge—hell, she let the dishes pile up on occasion—but Reed's expression told her that this wasn't normal. He'd looked so worried that her heart had squeezed for him.

She placed the mugs gingerly on the side of the sink, since they wouldn't fit in it. The voices rose in the lounge room and Reed's empathic "Jesus, Dad" cut right through her. Ugh, that sentiment was all too familiar. Nice as tonight had been, there was a big difference between how someone acted with a guest versus their own family. Hadn't Reed called her his buffer?

She bit down on her lip. It sounded like they needed a few more minutes together. Darcy hovered for a second, trying to figure out if there was anything she could do to help. But the small space was overwhelmed by dishes and she couldn't even see a dish towel. Reed poked his head in a few seconds later.

"We're leaving," he said gruffly. The easy smile that had been on his lips a few moments ago was gone, replaced by a stiff line. A crease had formed between his brows. She'd seen Reed wear many faces—teasing, confident, even angry. But this weariness was new. "If I don't get out of here soon, I might kill him."

"I feel like we should clean up for him." Her eyes flicked to the sink.

"Leave it. I've already put a reminder in my phone to call someone tomorrow." He raked a hand through his hair. "I need to speak with Donna anyway. One more night won't make a difference."

"Okay."

They said their goodbyes to Adam, who squeezed Darcy's shoulder and made her promise she would accompany Reed again. Talk about awkward. How was she supposed to tell the guy that her relationship with his son could be categorized as work with a side of smut?

One time only smut no less.

"Your dad's a real sweetheart," she said as they walked down the steps outside Adam McMahon's house.

"He can turn it on, that's for damn sure."

The sky had turned to an inky indigo and the temperature had dropped. It wasn't exactly cold, but Darcy's old T-shirt did nothing to stop the cool breeze brushing over her skin. She shivered. Without a word, Reed unlocked the car and reached into the back. He tossed his hoodie to her as she slid into the passenger seat.

"Thanks." A warm, fuzzy feeling settled deep in her belly as she inspected it. The fabric was an old and faded blue, but the orange New York Mets logo remained bright.

"You're supposed to wear it," he said as he got into the car and started the engine. "I know it's not your style, but you looked cold."

"Thought you had a 'lump of coal where your heart should be,'" she said, pulling the hoodie over her head. Goddamn it smelled good—cologne and soap, something fresh yet rich. A contradiction that was uniquely him.

"True, but I do have a nervous system. I understand the concept of feeling cold," he said dryly. "Now, give me your address."

Darcy grinned in the darkness, burrowing her chin into the soft, well-loved fabric as she spelled out her street name. "Why did you really bring me here tonight?"

"Told you, I needed a buffer." Streetlights danced over his face as they drove, enhancing the sharp angles of his cheekbone and jaw.

"And you didn't have a friend who could have helped you out with that?" Maybe she was poking the bear, but curiosity had sunk its claw in.

"I do. But my father was always better when there was a woman around—something about pride and being the center of attention."

He paused. "And, if it's not abundantly clear, I'm in short supply of female friends."

He looked like he was going to say something else, but the silence stretched on and he didn't elaborate.

"Is that because *all* women want to sleep with you?" she teased.

"I believe I said *most*."

Darcy laughed. "I wish I had an ounce of your confidence. Or is it a lack of modesty? I can't tell the difference."

Reed shrugged. "It's all just labels, isn't it? Such a human thing to do: we love putting people into tidy, little boxes."

Bitterness laced his tone, but Darcy couldn't blame him; she'd been the victim of labeling on more than one occasion—rebel, antisocial, ingrate, bad influence. Jilted bride. Reject.

She swallowed. "You think your dad does that to you?"

"Don't all parents?" A sharp laugh rang out in the car. "Or maybe that's just my fucked-up, dysfunctional family."

"Uh, I've talked about my mother before, right? She ain't exactly Carol Brady." She laughed. "Although now you've met the golden child you can probably see why I disappoint her. No boyfriend, no ambitions to be a housewife. I'm a blight on her record of mother-hood—it feels like that anyway."

"At least yours stuck around." The second the words were out of his mouth, his jaw clenched. She could practically hear him admonishing himself internally. He cleared his throat. "Seems I need a muzzle around you."

It struck Darcy that she and Reed were far more alike than she could ever have anticipated. Sure, the images they both presented to the world were vastly different. But they were still images—personas even. She hid behind her scowl and snarky retorts, whereas he used an expensive suit and tie. But on the inside, they were both a little damaged, a little isolated. They were far better at pushing people away than they were at keeping them close.

"How old were you when she left?" she asked, fully expecting him to clam up. He was well within his right to tell her to mind her own freaking business.

"Fifteen." His eyes were straight ahead, locked on the road as though it required every ounce of his concentration. But they were moving slowly, navigating back streets at an easy pace. "Same year I put my hand through a wall and ended any chances of chasing the majors."

No guesses required as to whether those two events were connected. So he'd lost his mother and his dream all in twelve months. That was a lot for anyone to handle, let alone a teenage boy.

"Do you still see her?"

He grunted. "No, she's long gone. Visits stopped after two years and birthday cards after five. Good riddance."

Darcy sensed there was more to it than that, but he already looked brittle. Pushing him further might backfire and then she'd lose whatever ground she'd managed to gain.

Since when are you trying to gain anything with him? You don't care about him. You're not friends.

But something about that didn't quite ring true. They weren't friends, not technically, and she probably viewed him more as a puzzle than someone whom she cared about. Yet there was something niggling in her chest. Like a tiny seed of emotion that'd been planted but not watered—it could die, or it could flourish with the right attention.

"I never knew my father," she said. "My mother wouldn't even tell me his name."

"Wouldn't or won't?"

She glanced out the window, resting her forehead against the glass. "Won't."

There'd been blazing arguments about it when Darcy was a teenager. Eventually, her mother had said that part of her moving on was fully letting go of the past (a.k.a. acting like it never happened). Apparently, her closure was more important than Darcy's.

"I wondered if I might get to meet him one day." She sighed. "All I know is that my mom got pregnant but she wasn't married, and my father didn't stick around. Her family told her the only way they'd support her—and me—was if she became involved in the church. That's where she met my stepfather."

"Cynthia is your half sister, then?" He made a little noise in the back of his throat. "I thought you looked quite different."

"Look different, act different, think different." All the resentment she worked so hard to repress came rearing up, stoked by Reed's words. "They love her more because my mom thinks she's the legitimate child and I'm just the nasty mistake that reminds her of the past."

"I'm sure that's not true."

"Hey, you wanted to play fucked-up family bingo. Don't be a sore loser."

The corner of his mouth lifted ever so slightly. For some reason, that made her feel good…and confused. And annoyed. So far her history of picking men to entangle herself with wasn't looking so good—Ben and Reed. Both wrong for her, both unattainable either physically or emotionally.

"Fucked-up family bingo." He bobbed his head. "I like that."

"You shouldn't. You're losing." She twisted in her seat so she could look at him more closely. "And I got plenty more where that came from."

"You don't want to try me, Darcy. I've only scratched the surface."

So had she. There was far more lurking beneath Reed's polished veneer than anyone would suspect. All they saw was the womanizing playboy who slept his way around the city, caring for nothing and nobody. But she saw something else: a man who was frightened of connecting. Who rolled in on himself so the spikes faced outward, scaring off anyone who might dare to get close.

"I think I *do* want to try you," she said. "I've got a bottle of gin and a pen so we can keep score."

"Are you asking me to come up to your apartment?"

Darcy hadn't even realized they were stopped in front of her walk-up. Reed's face was close in the dark, his breath whispering over her skin and seeping into her body. Remi was always out Sunday nights. They would have the place to themselves.

Think very carefully about what you're doing. This is premeditated, and the penalty for that is higher. You can't pass it off as lust.

She wanted him; oh *God* how she wanted him. But this wasn't about scratching an itch or trying to get anything out of her system. It was something else…something new.

"What if I am?" she whispered.

"I don't do the personal stuff." His hand slid along her jaw, his thumb brushing the corner of her lip. "So why do I feel like going up to your place is a good idea?"

"Maybe I'm tastier than the girls you usually date." Her breath hitched. "Or perhaps you went too long between meals."

His throaty chuckle sent a ripple of anticipation through her. "Let's go with the first one."

His lips brushed hers with a featherlight touch and she curled her hands into his T-shirt. Blood rushed in her ears, the roar drowning out the little voice telling her to stop. Slow down. Reconsider.

Why? So what if Reed was wrong for her? So what if her friends and her mother would be horrified? They had chemistry and, against the laws of logic, they had a burgeoning personal connection. Her hand skated up Reed's thigh and he moaned into her. Turns out something *else* was burgeoning too.

"Do you need to warn anyone up there?" he asked, his teeth scraping along her neck.

"That we're going to play bingo?"

"You know that's not all we'll be doing," he growled.

"Greedy." She let out a satisfied murmur as he sucked on her earlobe. "My roommate is out. She won't be back until later tomorrow."

"We could always head into the city. I can get us a room—"

"No." The word shot out of her before she could stop it.

Fun as the hotel room was, she wanted this time to be more personal. Maybe it was an extension of the satisfaction she got from knowing he was going against his policy to be with her. Or perhaps it was that she'd finally found someone who wasn't wishing she were someone else.

"We're already here and I really…want that drink."

Nice cover, idiot. He won't see through that at all.

"Me too." Reed bobbed his head, his fingers still tangling with her hair. "Let's go."

Chapter 18

"Reed has a lot of rules. No visits to his place or yours, no deep and meaningful talks, no promises. I don't think the word yes is in his vocabulary."

—AnneofGrenville

Reed sat at the two-seater, round table in the corner of the living room. The apartment's tiny kitchen was tucked away and didn't have enough room for seating. So Darcy had left him there to fix them both a drink. The clink of ice cubes hitting glass echoed into the main room.

The place was cramped but well utilized. A bright-blue sofa faced an exposed-brick wall where a TV sat atop a white unit. The couch was decorated with a brightly colored throw in purples, oranges, and yellows, which matched a collection of small yellow elephants that ran along the edge of one windowsill. A shelving unit without doors held an array of mismatched cups, plates, and glasses.

On first glance, it looked as though Darcy couldn't possibly live here—after all, the girl seemed allergic to color. But he could see hints of her personality in the sharply modern painting created only with shades of gray, and the funky, industrial-looking coffee table that had a smooth white top and legs made out of old pipes.

He got up to have a closer inspection of the table and noticed a white book sitting in the center. It had blended with the pristine surface of the painted wood. The white canvas cover looked professional, and a logo was embossed on one corner. Curious, he picked it up and a note fell out. The looping cursive was written in hot-pink ink.

Darcy—Sorry, I couldn't help but take a peek. The photos are perfect. You really do make a beautiful bride. Glad I could help you celebrate. Love, Remi

Bride? What the hell?

Shooting a glance toward the kitchen, he was glad Darcy was still making their drinks. He flipped the cover open and almost choked at a picture of her in a white wedding gown. Lace covered her arms and chest, a big, puffy skirt bloomed out from her small waist. She looked like a goddamn cupcake. But there was something off about the photo—a resolute sadness in her eyes that was like a knife to his chest.

The next page showed three photos of her in the same position, her eyes staring off into the distance. Behind her, the sun glowed. Light flares dotted the pictures, giving her an ethereal look. Her eyes were as bright as the sky.

Jesus. She's married? Was married?

"Does it get the McMahon seal of approval?" Darcy walked into the room holding two glasses of gin and tonic garnished with cucumber. Her eyes widened when her gaze snagged on the album. "What the hell are you doing?"

"It was sitting here. I didn't know…" He dropped the album onto the couch as though it was made of hot coals.

"Didn't know what?" Her jaw tightened as if she was grinding her back teeth.

"That you were married." He frowned. "Or are you married?"

"Do you really think you'd be here if I had a husband?" She glared at him. "I'm not sure what women you usually sleep with, but I'm not a cheater."

He ignored the dig. On this occasion, he deserved it. "So you're divorced."

She sighed, plunking the glasses down on the dining table before turning on her heel. A minute later she returned with a bottle of Hendricks. "I have a feeling I'm going to need a refill."

"Probably wise."

"Bring the album over." She waved a hand in the direction of the couch. "I guess if we're going to play, this is a good place to start."

He did as she asked and took a seat. "Well," he said, holding his glass up to hers. "Here's to fucked-up families."

"Maybe they continue to chip away at our resolve to succeed." She laughed. "Gosh, that was a bit dramatic, wasn't it?"

"A bit." He sipped his drink.

"So in answer to your question, no. I'm not divorced." She drained half of her G&T in one go and reached for the album. "I was about to get married."

She flipped through the album, a sad smile on her lips. When she found the page she wanted, she turned it around to show Reed. The picture brought an instant smile to his lips. Darcy stood, flanked by two women—one brunette, one blond. The wedding dress she'd worn on page one was no longer a pristine white, but instead was covered with splatters of green, pink, orange, and something murky-looking that was probably a combination of all three. The other women wore matching dresses in two different colors—pink and blue—and were also covered in paint. They looked like some kind of crazy, psychedelic warrior princesses.

Darcy's head was thrown back in laughter, her cheeks smudged with paint. The blond to her right was midshriek as the brunette hurled what appeared to be a water balloon at her.

"This is the best wedding photo I've ever seen," he said, laughing.

"They're called 'wreck the dress' photo shoots and they're popular with divorcées and jilted brides, apparently."

His chest clenched. "I'm guessing you're the latter then."

"Great deductive powers you've got there, Sherlock." She finished the rest of her G&T and refilled it—straight gin, no tonic this time.

"How long before the wedding?"

Her bravado wavered then, a ripple of sadness starting with a shimmer in her eyes and ending with the tiniest quiver of her lips. "The day before."

Ouch. "That's rough."

"I'm just glad I caught him... Well, I wasn't at the time but I am now." She sighed. "It would have been worse to go on living a lie. For both of us."

Oh, fuck. So not only had she lost her fiancée the day before her wedding, but she'd caught him in the act too? Brutal.

"But he's still with the guy now, so I guess I'm happy at least it meant something for him."

"Who was he?" Reed drained the rest of his drink in solidarity and refilled his glass.

"Our best man." She waved a hand in his face. "No sympathy, okay? But I told you I'd win fucked-up family bingo."

"I don't even know what to say." He shook his head. "I'm not often at a loss for words, I'll tell you that."

"Your turn." She flipped through the album, leaving it open between them so he could see the photos. He got the feeling this was an intensely private and painful moment for her, and yet here she was sharing it with him.

He wasn't worthy.

"Come on," she said. "You can't leave me hanging."

"Well, you know my ma left when I was fifteen, but that's not the whole story." He swallowed his gin and poured another. Screw it. He wasn't going to leave her tonight, so he could use the alcohol to numb his pain. And hers.

"Okay." Her bright-blue eyes were trained on him and he wondered if it might be possible to drown in those crystalline depths. He'd been attracted to her from the first time they'd met—but this was something else. She wasn't just attractive... She was beautiful. On the inside.

"Dad was really cut up when she left." His gut churned at the memory. It'd been years since he'd told anyone what happened—years since he'd allowed himself to remember. But it was like finding an old scar: it might look healed, but remembering the pain came far too easily. "It was like he was sad...but it was something else. He refused to talk to anyone about it. Then he took up smoking." Reed let out a long, slow breath. "My dad was the kind of guy who would bike to work every day. He'd go for runs, throw the ball around with me for hours. But after she left, he stopped caring about his health. He went from a guy who wouldn't have a piece of chocolate after dinner to a guy who smoked two packs of cigarettes a day."

"That's terrible."

"Two years ago, he started feeling short of breath. I'd been telling him to give up the smokes, but he wouldn't." He rolled the glass between his hands, his eyes on the half-melted ice cubes swishing in the dregs of his drink. "Then the coughing worsened. It was this god-awful hacking sound that shook the whole house."

"And that's when he found out he had emphysema?"

"Not for a few months. The stubborn bastard refused to go to the doctor." He set the glass down and swallowed, trying to force down the lump in his throat. "But the damage was done, whether he wanted to accept it or not. Stage two at the time. I threw out every last cigarette, but he was still mobile then. He could easily buy more. I think he wanted to kill himself with those damn things."

"Oh, Reed." She reached across the table and squeezed his hand.

His instinct was to shake the gesture off, to pack the memories back into that heavily guarded box and go back to denial. But her skin was soft, her touch like a soothing balm for his soul.

"He used to be this incredible man. Sure, he never had the best job. He was a school janitor, so we didn't have much money, but he used to *try*. He used to care about his life."

About my life.

These days it felt like Reed was the fly in his father's ointment—the constant thorn in his side that wouldn't let up with all the rules: *Don't smoke. Don't forget your appointments. Do what the caregiver says.*

"He might only have a few more years left." Reed didn't recognize his own voice—it was as cracked and peeling as the paint on his father's house. "And if I don't fix this shit storm at work...who the hell is going to hire a PR guy who can't manage his own public image?"

It wasn't the ruined reputation that frightened him. Reed had never cared much for other people's opinions in truth. But his job was the only thing that gave him purpose. He poured the money into his father's health and squirreled the rest away for when the day came that he might need it. Knowing he could take care of the man whom he'd admired for so long, who'd cared for him when his own mother had abandoned him, was the thing that got Reed out of bed in the morning.

"What are you going to do?"

Her hand was still on his, the genuine warmth and concern radiating through his skin until he felt the ice thawing in his veins. It'd been so long since he'd opened up to anyone—each year that passed made his heart grow harder, cementing his stubborn desires to go it alone. But now this quirky, unusual, sexy woman had slipped past his defenses and started to bust down the walls that protected him.

He needed to regain his composure, to get back into a situation where he felt control firmly in his grasp.

"Right now?" The mask slid back over his features as he turned her hand over in his, pressing his thumb to the pulse point at her wrist. "We're going to have another drink and then you're going to show me where the shower is."

Uncertainty flickered in those big, blue eyes. "Okay."

He reached for the bottle of Hendricks and refilled both glasses. The alcohol had loosened him up, enough that his muscles no longer felt bunched and tight. A hot shower would set him right again—no more of this emotional shit. He was done talking, done acting like words made an ounce of difference.

"By the time I get out of the shower, I want to find you naked on your bed with your hands between your legs."

That put a bit of color in her cheeks. "I guess conversation time is over."

"Yes." He knocked his drink back and pushed up from his chair. "The only words I want to hear out of your mouth for the rest of the night are all the ways I can make you feel good. Acceptable alternatives include 'yes,' 'oh God yes,' and 'fuck.'"

"Acceptable alternatives?" She grinned. "You know alliteration gets me hot and bothered."

She left the glasses on the table and motioned for him to follow her toward the bathroom. Focusing on that pert little ass beneath her jeans sent familiar lust coursing through him, hardened him.

Yes, this was exactly what he needed to concentrate on right now.

....

Darcy lay on her bed per Reed's instruction. The sound of rushing water from the bathroom that separated her bedroom from Remi's should have soothed her. Continuous sounds always had the effect of restoring her equilibrium. But tonight she was a bundle of nerves… and not because she was about to sleep with Reed for a second time.

The whole day had thrown her for a loop. Here was this guy who, by all accounts, was a waste of air. And yet he'd broken her heart in two with the story about his parents. While he'd kept the focus on them, she could see plain as day that he still hadn't gotten over the rejection. First he'd lost his mother, and now he was at risk of losing his father.

Guilt twisted in Darcy's gut. His story had made her realize that she took having her mother for granted. Sure, their relationship was the stuff Dr. Phil episodes were made of, but she knew her mother cared, even if she had an odd—and sometimes damaging—way of showing it.

The faucet squeaked and the sound of water ceased. She could see what Reed would look like, beads of moisture smattering his broad chest and muscular stomach. The urge to confirm whether her fantasy met reality surged through her, but she stayed on the bed. He'd told her to be here, laid out like a gift for him… Oh! And she was supposed to have her hands between her legs.

She flushed at the thought. It felt so…brazen. But that was Reed. When it came to sex, he was totally out in the open. He knew what he wanted, what felt good. There was no shame, but there was no vulnerability either. Not from him at least.

Stop thinking. You didn't bring him up here to have a full-blown psychoanalysis—this isn't therapy.

Yet being with Reed today had unlatched some compartment inside her. It'd opened up a part that had been dormant for as long as she could remember.

Closing her eyes, she allowed her head to loll back against her pillow as she slipped her hand down her stomach to the edge of her panties. Were they supposed to be on or off? He hadn't said.

At least this time he hadn't watched her undress—so she'd had the opportunity to slip out of her boring basics into something a little more occasion appropriate. Nothing fancy, because that wasn't her style, but this pair had a hint of lace at the edges—and not an incorrect day of the week in sight.

"If he wants them off, he can damn well take them off," she said to herself. Her fingers brushed the neat section of hair behind the soft cotton before dipping lower. She was already damp, her fingers sliding easily through her sex.

Even with her eyes closed, she could see the glow of her bedside lamp. Touching herself with the lights on felt like a new level of naughtiness. Knowing he could walk in any moment and see the pleasure scrunching up her face was the icing on top of the kinky cupcake.

"You're much better at following instructions than I thought you would be." His deep voice caused her thighs to clench, trapping her hand between them.

Darcy snapped her eyes open. "Only when it suits me."

He had one of her towels around his waist—soft, baby-blue fabric hung low on his hips, enhancing the sharp *V* of muscle at his waist. The hair on his head glistened darker from the water, almost black. He was so attractive it bordered on obscene. But all that traditional attractiveness was nothing compared to what she'd uncovered today—the softness behind all the quick wit and bravado.

"Please." He motioned for her to continue. "Don't stop on my account."

It was one thing to do it knowing she'd get caught, but it was quite another to keep the camera rolling after that. She was leaning on her Dutch courage, but she'd need more than a few standard drinks to take her to that level.

"How about I unwrap my present?" She crawled to the edge of the bed and reached out.

He stepped forward, hands by his sides as her fingertips brushed the knotted fabric at his waist. She smoothed her hand over it, tracing the hard ridge hiding beneath. How long had he been watching her lay there, pleasuring herself? Her sex pulsed. She still wasn't used to how out in the open sex was with Reed—nothing was furtive or blanketed in darkness.

"You waiting for a personal invitation?" he asked, brushing her hair over her shoulder.

"How would you word it exactly?" She looked up, flattening one palm to his abs and tracing the line of hair that extended down from his belly button.

"The honorable Reed McMahon requests the presence of one very naughty Darcy Greer for an evening of fun and frivolity." He grinned. "And cock."

"Fun, frivolity, *and* cock. How could I possibly say no to that?" She tugged on the towel until it opened, revealing him.

He was magnificent. Intimidatingly so.

"You thrill me, you know that?" He ran his hands through her hair, the firm touch against her scalp sending a shiver running down her spine. "You somehow manage to be totally innocent and yet insatiably sexy at the same time. You're an enigma."

The compliment spurred her on, and she wrapped her hand around his length. "Enigma, hmm. You should have gone with that instead of telling me I was interesting."

He chuckled. "So 'enigma' isn't a code word for anything?"

"Nope." She worked her hand up and down, her eyes turned up to watch the pleasure roll over his face.

He swore under his breath. "Glad I managed to find the right adjective. I should have known a librarian would be picky about words."

"I'm picky about everything." She climbed off the bed and dropped to her knees, one hand on his stomach to steady herself and using her other to pleasure him. When she gave him a squeeze, his hips jerked into her.

"That feels so good, Darcy."

"I want to…" She swallowed, unsure exactly how to voice her desires. Talking dirty wasn't her forte for sure, but stating her needs wasn't something she felt confident doing either. "Umm."

He caught her chin between his fingers and tipped her face up, his eyes blackened with arousal. "You can say anything you like here. There's no judgment."

Her eyes fluttered shut, because looking at him as she said the words that were swimming in her head seemed like too much. "I want to take you in my mouth."

"God yes." His voice was shredded and rough.

It was the most perfect sound in all the world. Hearing the effect she had on him was all she needed to keep moving, to push past the barrier of insecurity and indulge in the fantasy reel playing inside her head.

She opened her mouth and guided him to her lips. The velvety slide of his head along her tongue was exquisite, as was the sound of breath hissing out between his teeth. Not to mention the clean and fresh scent of him, where her citrus soap mingled with his earthy maleness. An incredible feeling of feminine power rushed through her. She'd never once thought that being on her knees could make her feel ten feet tall.

"Darcy." Her name was followed by a string of incoherent, half-formed words.

She ran her tongue up and down, working him with her hand.

Experimenting with what moves gave the best response—what caused his hips to jerk or his breath to catch. Toying with the stud in her tongue, she rubbed the metal ball over the head of his cock and he grunted. Oh yes, he liked that very much.

"Do it again." His grip tightened in her hair. "Whatever you did just then."

"Like this?" She nudged the piercing against the sensitive underside of his head, back and forth until his swore under his breath.

"Enough. Otherwise, I'm going to embarrass myself." He pulled back and looked her in the eyes. "You're too good at that."

She scooted back onto the bed and crooked her finger. "You can always even the score."

"And now you're giving orders." The crooked smile turned her into a puddle of female hormones. "Who are you and what have you done with my Darcy?"

His Darcy? Her breath stuck in her throat, but as he stalked forward, panther-like, she tried to act unaffected. Only a fool would believe she'd become his. Wasn't this why so many women were tearing him to shreds online? Because he made them believe it all meant something?

She shoved the wrenching fear aside. Darcy Greer was not one of those dumb girls who turned words into what she wanted them to be. She was sensible. Logical. Cynical enough to protect herself.

She was not his girl.

"I'm an alien," she teased, pulling back the covers.

His hands captured her. A strong arm wrapped around her

waist, hauling her beneath him. "Well, you *are* into monster smut. It makes sense."

Damn him. Why did he have to be so funny and charming… and sexy? Confident. Kind.

"Shh." She pressed her fingertip to his lips. If he said any more, she might not be able to keep the line drawn between them. "Enough talking."

"Yes, ma'am." He eased her back into the mattress and settled between her legs.

She was going to enjoy this, and her heart wasn't going to have a say.

Chapter 19

"I wasn't going to be one of those stupid girls who fell for the wrong guy. I had all my tools—a list of criteria, important questions, and had a healthy dose of realism. Then Reed came along and it turns out I am one of those stupid girls."

—YankeesNo1Fan

*D*arcy woke to the feeling of something scratching her cheek. Reed hovered over her, a sexier-than-sin grin on his face.

"Good morning, sunshine." His lips found the crook of her neck.

"Now that is a hell of a way to wake up." She yanked his face to hers and melted into his kiss. "I wasn't sure I'd see you this morning."

Something flickered in his dark eyes and his heavy brows lowered into a frown. "I would have let you know if I were leaving."

"Ah, yes, but you don't seem to understand what a heavy sleeper

I am. I can get woken up, have a full conversation with someone, and not remember a damn thing in the morning."

His expression softened. "So next time I want to pry some top-secret information from you, I should do it in the middle of the night?"

Next time. Her heart thumped unsteadily, logic and desire warring despite her intention to remain emotionally unattached. But his hands roamed her body, more curious than sexual, as though he wanted to understand her on a physical level. He inspected her sleeve, his finger tracing all the intricate, little designs that made up the piece.

"Never been with a tattooed woman before?" she asked.

"I've never been with anyone like you." He looked up, the warmth in his eyes quickly replaced by what she'd come to think of as Reed's "public" face. "Women who haven't grown out of their teenage rebellion phase are normally not my type."

She rolled her eyes. "And I don't like pretty boys who care too much about what other people think."

"Pretty boys," he said in mock outrage. "You're going to pay for that."

He slid under the sheets and buried his face against her bare stomach, rubbing back and forth so his whiskers tickled her.

"Stop it." She squirmed and laughed. But the sound of the kettle whistling froze her to the spot.

Reed poked his head out from under the sheet. "What's wrong?"

"Someone's home."

It was Monday. Pale rays of early-morning sun peeked through the curtains. Darcy glanced at the clock next to her bed: 5:30 a.m. Remi wasn't supposed to be home yet.

"It's nothing. Probably my roommate." She bit her lip. "She normally spends Sunday night at a friend's place because it's near her work."

Judging by the sounds coming from outside, Remi's 6:00 a.m. barre class must have been canceled. *Shit.* She'd been counting on that so there would be no interruptions or awkward run-ins with Reed. Just when Darcy thought it couldn't get any worse, she heard talking. Two voices. The other one sounded a hell of a lot like Annie.

Crappity crap crap crap!

"I should probably get going," Reed said, pressing her into the bed with a long, searching kiss. "I'm usually in the office by seven, and I can't very well turn up in my baseball gear."

"What *would* people say?" she teased in a quiet voice.

Would it be rude to ask him to leave via the fire escape? Probably. Of all days, why did Remi have to change her plans today? Ugh. Maybe she could ask them to cover their eyes while he left.

"Why do you look stressed out all of a sudden?" He tilted his head. "I thought those three orgasms I gave you last night would have sent you into a bliss coma."

"It was four, at my count." She tried to laugh, but the sound came out weird. "I, uh…didn't tell my roommate you were coming over."

"I won't walk to the bathroom naked then." He rolled off her and got out of bed.

His sculpted body drew her gaze and she sighed. The statue of

David had nothing on that ass. Reed's lack of modesty made Darcy smile—while she was reaching for the sheet, he was strutting around like he was Adam in the Garden of Eden.

She leaned over the edge of the bed and grabbed a fresh pair of panties from the bottom drawer in her nightstand. As Reed tugged on his underwear, Darcy's mouth dried. Why couldn't she haul him back into bed so they could screw like bunnies and forget about the real world?

"I should warn them." Still holding the sheet to her chest, she motioned for Reed to hand her the bra that had ended up on the floor beside his foot. "They don't know I'm seeing anyone."

Are you even seeing him? You haven't talked about what this means. He's made it clear he doesn't do relationships.

"Right." His expression was unreadable, his dark eyes concealing whatever reaction he might've had. But he didn't jump in to make it clear they *weren't* seeing each other.

You're not dating. *Get it through your thick skull.*

"I'm, uh…I'm going out there." She hopped out of bed and grabbed the robe hanging from a hook on the back of her door.

She caught a glimpse of herself in the antique mirror that hung on the wall just outside her bedroom and shook her head. Between the robe, the wildly rumpled hair, and the fuchsia flush in her cheeks, she looked the very definition of *up all night not sleeping.*

"Hey, you." Remi leaned against the back of the sofa, looking like she was still half-asleep, a mug of tea cupped between her hands. "Late night?"

"Anything you want to tell us?" Annie sat at the table wearing a pretty floral dress under a black cardigan, half a bagel in one hand. She, by comparison, looked totally awake.

"Aren't either of you working today?" Darcy pulled the belt of the robe tighter around her waist, stalling while she tried to figure out how to broach the situation.

"Annie's boss is forcing her to take the day off since she worked all weekend." Remi yawned and toyed with the tag dangling from her cup. "And she convinced me to swap classes so we could do brunch. We're going to that Aussie café, Bluestone Lane. I've got a hankering for an avo smash."

Annie laughed. "She needs to be with her people."

"You try moving countries and having to repeat yourself every time you order a glass of water," Remi grumbled. "Anyway, we thought you might want to come if you're not working early today."

"Uh, sure." She bounced on the spot. "I'm not going in until twelve."

A Cheshire cat–like smile spread across Annie's face, and she exchanged looks with Remi, who suddenly appeared more alert. "So, who'd you have over last night?"

"Just…a friend."

"A *male* friend?" Remi grinned.

"Deets. Now." Annie pointed to the free chair at the table.

"Well, the thing is…" Crap. Why was this so awkward? She shouldn't be ashamed for having a guy over. Her friends were only teasing, but they had no idea how confused Darcy was about the whole thing. "He's still here."

Two heads snapped in the direction of Darcy's room, where she'd pointedly closed the door so Reed got the hint not to come out until she was ready for him. The apartment was eerily quiet for a heartbeat, and when a soft thump came from Darcy's room, Remi giggled.

"Who is he?"

"He's no one." The minute she answered, a repulsive taste filled her mouth. Would Reed have heard her? "Like I said, just a friend. Can you please hide in the kitchen or something?" God, even asking made her feel like a loser.

"Oh, babe." Remi slung an arm around her shoulder. "There is *nothing* to be ashamed of. We're happy for you. I'm glad you're getting some."

"Please," she repeated, pressing her fingertips to her temples. "It's already awkward. I don't need any help in that department."

But as she watched the expression on both Remi and Annie's faces morph from intrigued to downright shocked, she knew shit was about to hit the fan. Sucking in a breath, she turned and saw Reed standing in her doorway, dressed in his baseball outfit from yesterday, his Mets hoodie slung over his shoulder. The dark shadow along his jaw gave him a dangerous edge. But what looked even more dangerous was the chilly expression on his face. His jaw was tight, his eyes looking right through her.

"I've got to run," he said, walking over to her and politely nodding at Remi and Annie. "Ladies."

Awkward alert. How long had he been standing there? Was she supposed to introduce him to her friends? Oh crap, why was this so hard?

"Uh, Reed, this is Annie and Remi."

"Nice to meet you both." He pierced her with a look, as though waiting for her to say something more, but Darcy's tongue felt heavy in her mouth. "I guess I'll see you around."

Oh God, it sounded terribly cliché. Or was it code for something else? Had last night not been as magical and explosive as she'd thought? What if he'd been dying to get out all night? Surely if he'd hated it, he would have left.

Her brain whirred. Something had changed in the time she'd come out of her bedroom—but was it because he'd heard her call him "no one"? Or maybe it was because Remi and Annie were gaping at him, their stance on his presence clear. The last thing she needed right now was their judgment.

Reed paused, as though waiting for a response, but Darcy couldn't get her brain to operate her mouth. When it was clear she wasn't going to say anything further, he headed for the door. His hand brushed lightly over her arm before he left. A moment later, the front door slammed shut and the air rushed out of Darcy's lungs.

What in the hell had just happened? Her mind had already stockpiled worst-case scenarios for her to stress over.

Super helpful, brain. I can always count on you.

This wasn't supposed to be complicated. When she'd started seeing Ben, everything had swum along without a hitch. There was no dancing around things, no concerns over feelings or whether it was okay to ask if you could see the person again. Shouldn't casual sex be *easier*?

"Reed McMahon, are seriously crazy?" Annie looked at her as though she'd sprouted a second head.

"So much for you minding your own business," Darcy grumbled.

"That explains why you were so awkward about us meeting him." Annie shook her head. "What the hell were you thinking sleeping with him?"

"I was thinking it's my decision, not yours." She folded her arms across her chest.

"We're not judging you." Remi shot Annie a stern look. "We don't want you to get hurt. You know he's not the guy who's looking to settle down."

"Maybe I'm not looking to settle down either."

Remi pulled Darcy into a hug. "Hey, if that's all it is, then I'll shut my mouth right now...and so will Annie."

Annie huffed. "I won't stand by and watch some sleazebag take advantage of my best friend."

"How do you know he's a sleazebag, huh?" Darcy shut her eyes. "Everything that people are saying about him is based off a few reviews."

"He's got at least sixty reviews now," Annie corrected. "Imagine how many women he's slept with. The man is a walking advertisement for venereal disease."

"How do you know he actually slept with all those women? Is it not possible he's turned a bunch of them down and writing a fake review is the best way to get revenge? Or maybe people started up multiple accounts? It happens. He probably doesn't even know them all." She shook her head. "Would you say the same thing about me if I slept with a lot of men? Would that make me a slut?"

Remi and Annie looked at her with saucer-like eyes, but the floodgates were open and there was no stopping her now.

"Don't you think this world would be a better place if we all stopped judging one another so much? God, I put up with this shit my whole life thanks to my family and I'm so fucking sick of it. Reed is the only person who's never expected me to be someone other than who I am."

Reed might be wrong for the long term—or even short term—but his reputation was out in the open. No way any skeletons could jump out of the closet and throw her off balance. But then she'd done the stupid thing and opened up to him...and he to her.

Remi tried to pat her arm and soothe the situation, but Darcy waved her off. "You two go to brunch. I'm not feeling so good all of a sudden."

Chapter 20

Marriage of convenience? Apparently, they're not just for romance novels.

Just when we thought the worst of the worst couldn't stoop any lower...in walks Reed McMahon. A fake marriage. Have you ever heard of something so ridiculous? Only the ultimate commitment-phobe would use what should be the best day in someone's life to close a business deal. Luckily for us, we managed to track down the lucky woman who dodged a bullet to get the inside scoop.

"I was one of those girls who'd always dreamed of being married," said Barbara Elizabeth Waverly. "I knew exactly what kind of dress I wanted to wear and how happy I would be to have my father walk me down the aisle."

If the name sounds familiar, it may be because you've heard of the jewelry store Waverly & Whittaker. Barbara's great-grandfather, Edward Waverly, cofounded the company back in 1911. They've long been known for their elaborate designs and prestigious customer base, most notably providing the jewels worn by socialite Miranda Tulley at her second and third weddings.

Needless to say, landing a client such as Waverly & Whittaker would certainly have been a career boost for an up-and-coming public relations whiz kid. That's exactly what Reed McMahon intended to do.

"Reed was good to me," Barbara said. "But it was clear that he intended our union to be for some other purpose. He assured me it had nothing to do with my family, although when you come from money like I do...you always suspect."

According to Barbara, Reed's list of demands for the wedding included an out-of-the-way location and absolutely no journalists or photographers. Why would a man who intended to marry the love of his life not want to capture it on film? Highly suspicious.

Barbara eventually called off the wedding, reporting to papers at the time that she and Reed had decided mutually that it wasn't right to proceed. "I'm with an incredible man now," she said. "We have the kind of love that fills up every cavity in your soul. It's all encompassing and totally real. I really do believe I'm meant to be with my fiancé. He's my best friend."

There you have it, ladies, a perfect lesson in why it's right to wait for the perfect man. Don't sell yourself short by accepting the first guy who comes along, unless he's exactly what you want in a partner. Be discerning, be informed, and understand that you are worthy of the perfect man.

> With love,
> Your Dating Information Warrior
> Helping the single women of New York since 2018

R eed, I am *so* sorry."

Barbara's tearful voice came through his work phone and struck like a tiny pickax into the side of his head. Thanks to the Google Alert he'd set up on his name so he could keep track of what people were saying—and possibly because he had masochistic tendencies—he'd seen the latest drivel on the Bad Bachelors site.

Barbara called before he'd even had the chance to pick up the phone. That was one thing he'd always liked about her; she was honest to a fault.

"Calm down, Barbie," he said, leaning back in his desk chair. "It's okay."

"No it's not. She totally twisted what I said and took everything out of context." She hiccupped. "I swear if I'd known what the article was really about I would have refused the interview."

He rubbed a hand over his face and sighed. When he'd first read the article—which had the most clickbait title ever—he'd been furious at her. But that hadn't lasted more than five seconds, because he knew that Barbara wasn't the spiteful type. And if you read the article closely, the most damaging statements came from the author, not Barbara. He could easily see how her quotes were used to say something other than what he was sure she'd intended.

Some days he wondered if he should have gone through with marrying her. She was a delightful person—bubbly and sweet. But there was one thing true about the article: he *had* intended the marriage to be fake. It was around the time that his father was diagnosed and Reed had lost his grip on reality. A wedding had seemed like the best gift he could possibly give the old man, since Adam had wanted to see his son married since forever.

Barbara had been a logical choice. They were friends, coworkers, and she was the closest he'd come to falling in love. Turns out falling into friendship wasn't quite enough for her in the end. But he'd never once held it against her.

"What did you think the interview was for?" he asked, trying to get her talking so she'd calm down.

"She said it was for a special on weddings for the Bad Bachelors site. Most of the questions were about Mark and everything we have planned for November, but none of that made it into the article. Of course."

"Ah, so it was a ruse to get you talking."

"And the bit about me thinking you wanted our wedding to be for some higher purpose…" She sniffled. "I was talking about your dad, not because I thought you wanted access to my family. And that was *after* the interview. I thought it was off the record."

"I believe you."

A few weeks ago, he might have flipped his shit about the article, but ever since he'd left Darcy's apartment on Monday morning, he was finding it hard to care about anything. Overhearing her call him "no one" had struck him right in the chest—not to mention the fact that she'd tried to convince her friends to leave so they wouldn't meet him. But it was his reaction that'd angered him more than anything else. He wasn't supposed to be *someone* to her...that was the whole point of casual sex.

And yet he'd walked out of there like she'd kicked his goddamn puppy. Idiot.

"Gosh, you'd think being their head writer, she would act with a little more integrity," Barbara huffed.

"Head writer?" Reed frowned. How could a company that didn't appear to make money afford a head writer?

In his experience, people running small businesses had to wear many hats. And if the owner of Bad Bachelors was focused on preserving anonymity enough to set up a company in Delaware just to protect her identity, who was to say that this "head writer" wasn't the owner as well?

"What did she say her name was?"

"Leanne something. You're not going to track her down, are you? Oh dear, what a mess this is." She sighed. "You know, Mark told me not to call you."

"I'm shocked," he said sarcastically.

Barbara's fiancé didn't quite understand their relationship. Reed wouldn't call her a close friend these days, but they kept in touch. She sent his father a Christmas card every year and called Reed occasionally to check in. The woman had a heart bigger than Texas and Mark worried Reed would one day attempt to steal her away. But the thing was, even back when they were engaged, his relationship with her had always been more platonic than sexual. They didn't have chemistry...unlike what he had with Darcy.

That's enough of that. You have bigger fish to fry.

"I'll forward the email from when she first contacted me," Barbara said, ignoring his dig.

"What did she look like?"

"She was about my height, brown hair. Fair skin. I think she had brown eyes...maybe?" She sighed. "I know that's not super helpful."

"Do you know *anything* else about this woman?" His spidey senses tingled the way they did whenever he was about to hook a client.

"Not much. She seemed nice." Pause. "We met at that little Italian coffee place on the corner of Fifth and Forty-Second, right across from the library. They knew her. One of the guys made a comment about how they'd missed her when she didn't show for her 'usual' on Tuesday afternoon."

"Refresh my memory. What's the name of that place?" He reached for a scrap of paper and scribbled the details down, making a note of the information about Tuesday afternoons. It wasn't much, but compared to an anonymous LLC, it might as well have been a gold mine.

"Just don't make a scene, okay? I don't want any of this causing more trouble than it already has."

"I promise, Barbie. I'll be as stealthy as a ninja." He tapped his pen on the edge of his desk. "Good luck with the wedding planning. Don't get too stressed out about this, okay?"

"Thanks for understanding."

"Anything for you."

He ended the call and turned his cell phone over in his hands, trying to figure out which action to take next. While he was used to being busy, it wasn't often he had *this* many balls in the air.

The second he'd gotten into the office that morning, he'd called Donna to find out what the hell had gone on with his father. A few quick calls had revealed that his father had paid the replacement not to show up again after the first day and to keep her mouth shut about it. Needless to say, he was livid and Donna was absolutely mortified. They'd turned it over to the agency, who'd assured him it would not happen again.

Reed rubbed a hand along his lower jaw. Then there was the issue of Dave Bretton and his massive ego. Apparently, Reed hadn't fawned over him enough earlier in the week and now the stubborn ass was refusing a second meeting. Bretton's agent had told Reed that he needed to act like a fan in order to win him over, which was ridiculous. You'd think the guy would care more about Reed's ability to boost his reputation rather him being able to list all the characters in his books.

But luckily for Reed, he knew someone who *was* a genuine fan.

....

Darcy stood in the kitchen of her apartment and looked despondently at the pot of bolognese sauce bubbling away in a large pot. No matter how many times she tried to re-create her grandmother's recipe, something always went wrong. The meat didn't break down properly or the tomato made it too acidic or the carrot made it too sweet. This time it wouldn't seem to thicken up the way she wanted it to.

Tonight, she was hosting the family dinner for this month. It was a week early, since the fundraiser was scheduled for late the following week, and Darcy would be up to her ears in final preparations. Genio had declined to come to Darcy's place, which was fine by her. But she hadn't missed that, for a guy who had no hobbies, he was always mysteriously busy whenever Darcy invited them over.

She'd even thought about suggesting they go out, rather than her cooking. But her mother always complained about the food. As far as Darcy was concerned, it was better to take a hit and be criticized than to suffer through the embarrassment of her mother trying to tell a professional chef how to do their job.

She stirred her wooden spoon through the sauce and fished out a mouthful for a taste test. Hmm, it needed more salt. Resting the spoon on the side of the pot, she was about to reach for the salt grinder when her phone buzzed.

Reed.

The name caught her off guard, and she fumbled with her cell, almost dropping it into the pot. "Shit." She brought the phone up to her ear. "Hello?"

"Have I called at a bad time?"

Her body immediately turned to mush at the sound of his whiskey-smooth voice. *Girl, this is a problem. You need to control those damn hormones.*

"No, it's fine. I'm just making dinner."

"Where's my invite?" he teased.

"Uh, my mother is going to be here. Trust me, the lack of invite is a blessing." She put the lid on the saucepot and moved into the living room. She caught a glimpse of herself in the mirror and noticed the streak of red across her cheek. "What's up?"

"I'm calling about work."

"Oh." She cringed at the disappointment in her tone. "Sure. What do you need?"

"I'd like you to attend a meeting with me. It appears I didn't adequately stroke Mr. Bretton's ego the first time around, and now he's refusing to meet with me again."

Darcy could practically hear him rolling his eyes on the other end of the line. "Wait. Let me get this straight—you want me to come to a meeting with Dave Bretton. *The* Dave Bretton."

"I would really appreciate it, Darcy. I know you like his books and it'll benefit the fundraiser if we can lock him in. I've been trying to get him on the hook for a week now, and given our tight timeline, I ideally would have had him booked already. Lucky for us, I don't think he'd in high demand after the BEA debacle."

"Are you freaking kidding me?" She jumped up and down on the spot. "Of *course* I'll come to that meeting. I already finished the book you gave me and it was so good. The series took this entire new twist and I can't even—"

"Excellent." The sound of his laughter warmed her insides. "It's tomorrow night. Short notice, I know."

"It's no problem."

Darcy sucked on her lower lip. She wanted to ask if everything was okay between them after his swift exit yesterday morning, but she wasn't sure how to do that without revealing that she was *still* thinking about it.

"Uh, so did you find out what was up with your dad?" The pause on the other end of the line stretched on, each millisecond stabbing her in the chest.

"Everything's fine," he said in a way that told her that not a single thing was fine. But obviously she wasn't someone he would confide in. "I have to go. I'll see you at the meeting."

"Sure. See you then." She ended the call and dropped her cell into the pocket of her apron.

At that moment, the front door swung open, and Remi swanned in with Cynthia and Marietta in tow. "Look who I found," Remi said.

"What's that smell?" Darcy's mother turned her nose up. "Is that…burning?"

"Shit." Darcy raced into the kitchen to check on her sauce. She waded the wooden spoon through it carefully and found it sticking to the bottom. Freaking perfect.

"You had the heat up too high." Her mother was behind her, clucking her tongue and shaking her head. "Low and slow, how many times have I told you? Low and slow."

The beginnings of a nasty headache throbbed behind Darcy's eyes. "Yes, Ma. I get it. I'm a shit cook. You *have* told me many times before."

"No need to be so sensitive," her mother huffed. "Well, I suppose we should just order pizza or something. It'll probably be greasy, but we can't possibly have burned sauce."

Darcy closed her eyes and drew in a long, slow breath, begging the heavens to give her strength not to snap and send her mother packing.

Her mind strayed to Reed and his father, and how she'd promised not to take her mother for granted…no matter how infuriating she was.

"What would you do?" She turned and handed her mother the wooden spoon. "Do you think we can salvage it?"

Puffing her chest out like a bird in mating season, her mother shuffled forward and inspected the sauce. "Well, you haven't mixed the burned bits through the rest of the sauce, which is good."

It wasn't quite a compliment, but Darcy would take whatever she could get. "Can we transfer the top part to another pot?"

Her mother dipped the spoon into the sauce and tasted the top portion. "It doesn't taste too burned. Let's put it in another pot and then add some more wine."

Darcy fetched another pot from the cabinet under the stove and they set to work on saving the sauce. Twenty minutes later, they sat around the coffee table—since their dining table couldn't fit them all—while they ate. Remi had decided to stay because she had no classes that night, and Darcy was grateful for reinforcements.

"So, Remi, have you been auditioning for any shows lately?" Cynthia swirled her fork into the spaghetti and collected a small mouthful. How the girl managed to eat spaghetti without ever flicking sauce all over herself was mind boggling. She had some kind of neatness voodoo that Darcy didn't share.

"I've been building up my profile at the barre studio," Remi replied, using a fork and spoon to twirl her pasta. Marietta pressed her lips together in judgment, but she didn't say anything. "I'm getting more hours there now, which is great. Makes paying rent a hell of a lot easier."

"But don't you miss the stage?" Cynthia sighed, a dreamy look on her face. "Wouldn't it be magnificent to stand there while people throw roses at your feet?"

Remi laughed, but her eyes were trained on her food. "Well, that doesn't happen at small shows and I'm out of practice. You never know. I might go back to it one day. At least I'm not having to work in a café and do the classes on the side to make ends meet."

"Good for you." Cynthia nodded. "Hard work always pays off. And how's everything going with you, Darcy? You're working on that fundraiser for the library, right?"

"Yeah. I'm having a meeting soon with our PR consultant and…" She paused dramatically. "Dave Bretton."

The three women looked at her blankly and Darcy rolled her eyes.

"Dave Bretton, the guy who writes only the most epic planet-hopping bounty hunter of all time. He's like the George R.R. Martin of science fiction." Still nothing. "You girls need to pick up a book once in a while."

"Hey." Remi swatted her. "I read a Sophie Kinsella book recently. I simply prefer my stories to be a little more grounded in reality."

"In any case, I'm meeting one of my favorite authors of all time. I'm pretty pumped."

She tried not to think about Reed. Because it was clear from his phone call that his mind was on business, not on her. Not to mention she'd tried to call twice after his awkward exit, but both times he hadn't picked up the phone.

After dinner was done, Darcy and Remi cleared everyone's dishes away. They had to wash them by hand, since there was no dishwasher in their apartment. The two of them had lived together for a few years now, so they had a routine down pat. Remi washed and Darcy dried.

"I take it the topic of your man candy is off-limits," Remi said as she turned the faucet on to fill the sink.

"Would you tell your mother about your sex life?" Darcy snorted. "Actually, your mom's cool. You probably would."

"I still have issues with her, don't worry about that." Bubbles floated up from the sink as she swished the dish soap around. "Being in a different hemisphere helps, but she still manages to bitch me out from across the globe."

"That's comforting. Sometimes I feel like every other girl out there is BFFs with their mothers and I'm still struggling to make her like me." She leaned against the counter and twisted the dish towel in her hands. "Some days I wish I could be more like Cynthia."

"And she wishes she could be more like you, trust me."

"No way."

Remi nodded sagely. "She looks up to you, Darcy. Why do you think she got that tattoo?"

"Because her boyfriend convinced her."

"Nope. She wants to be like you." She smiled. "Her face was all sparkly when I saw her downstairs. She loves spending time with you."

"And how did my mother look?"

Remi handed over a clean plate without making eye contact. "One family member at a time."

"That's what I thought." Darcy sighed. "She thinks I'm a loser."

"I'm sure she doesn't. She's…of a different mind-set. She wants you to settle down and get married."

"So do you and Annie by the sound of things."

They still hadn't talked about what'd happened Monday morning. After Darcy had all but ordered them out of the house, she'd been dodging Annie's calls and skulking around in her room when Remi was home. But that could only last so long; even introverts needed *some* human contact.

It hadn't helped that Annie had forwarded a link of the Bad Bachelors latest article on Reed. He'd been engaged before. Funny how he never mentioned that when she was pouring her heart out on Sunday night.

"We were surprised, that's all. I know Annie flipped out a bit, but she only wants you to be happy." Remi pulled off her yellow rubber gloves and gave Darcy a hug. "Every time she sees someone getting involved with a guy like that, she thinks about what happened with her ex. Her reaction was more about her own fears than it was about you. You know that."

"We've all got a habit of picking the wrong guys, don't we?" Darcy rested her head against Remi's shoulder. "You'd think if we were all meant to procreate and keep the human race going they wouldn't have made the whole dating thing so hard."

"I hear you." Remi gestured toward their stove. "Now hand me that pot. We're going to have to soak that thing for days to get the crust off the bottom."

Chapter 21

<To: leanne@badbachelors.com>

<From: barbara.waverly@waverlyandwhittaker.com>

Subject: Our "interview"

Dear Leanne,

I was appalled to read your article and "interview" with me last Wednesday. Your unethical approach to journalism has put me in a very difficult spot personally.

Despite all the things you've written about Reed (and implied that I said), I know him to be a kind and generous man. He has a big heart, and while he may not want to settle down, I know he's never been anything but honest with the women he dates. I don't know whether you've been rejected by him personally or you're out to get any man who doesn't fit your idea of what a good person should be, but I find you and your entire business to be repulsive.

You claim that you want to empower women to make better

decisions, and yet you're not above lying to get the results you want. That's a level of hypocrisy I cannot abide.

I withdraw permission to further use any material from our interview and request that you remove the article quoting me immediately. I have kept my lawyer abreast of this development. If you use my name on anything again, you'll be hearing from the Waverly & Whittaker legal team.

Sincerely,

Barbara Waverly

*O**h, Barbara.* Reed cringed at the email that had popped up on his phone while he was waiting for Darcy to show for their meeting. He knew his ex meant well, but he could only hope this didn't enrage whoever this Leanne person was and incite more vitriol against him.

Unfortunately, Reed didn't yet have the information required to hit Bad Bachelors where it hurt. He'd passed Barbara's information on to the PI who was going to stake out the place and do further digging. But so far, nothing had turned up.

First things first: make sure you have a job to go to tomorrow.

Donald Bath had been breathing down his neck with increasing frequency, which wouldn't have bothered Reed normally. He could handle the grumpy old codger. But when Edward Weston had come down on him about the loss of Chrissy Stardust and the subsequent lack of new clients, he knew time was running out. Which was exactly why this meeting with Dave Bretton needed to go according to plan.

If it didn't…he could very well be looking for another source of income. And given he was thinking about upping his father's care, that wasn't a good thing.

Darcy waved as she trotted down the street toward the entrance to his office building, where he'd asked her to meet him. "So, do I look 'appropriately dressed' for a lunch meeting?" she said with a roll of her eyes.

"I'm sorry I said anything. I didn't want you feeling uncomfortable wearing ripped jeans in a five-star restaurant." His gaze swept over the demure black blouse tucked into a black pencil skirt. "And yes, you look appropriate."

Appropriate didn't really do it justice. She looked hotter than sin. The blouse was sheer and gauzy, leaving a black camisole peeking through the thin fabric. As usual, Darcy wore flats, but they were simple, black, ballet-style shoes rather than her usual Docs or combat boots.

"You look better than appropriate," he added.

"Was that a genuine compliment from Mr. Grumpy Pants?" She pressed a hand to her chest in mock horror. "Now, where are you hiding the real Reed McMahon?"

He looked straight ahead as they walked toward Forty-Second Street. Keeping his eye on the prize was his motto for the day. Secure the client and his job. After that, he could worry about his annoying attraction to Darcy and the ongoing issues with both his father and Bad Bachelors.

Christ. He needed a vacation.

"No response, huh? Is that question not in your database?" She poked him.

"Are you implying I'm a cyborg?"

"It would explain your ability to detach."

His gaze flicked over her as they rounded a corner, dodging a group of men in suits who appeared to be returning from a boozy lunch. He slipped his hand around Darcy's shoulders and steered her out of the way of their leering glances.

"Is that because I didn't serenade you before I left your place last week?" The words came out with a little more sting than he'd intended. "Sorry, that's not my style."

"Not your type, not your style." She huffed. "Do you ever think about what the other person might want?"

Oh, he'd thought about it all right. It'd been two whole days and he couldn't seem to get the words *no one* to stop echoing in his head. And now she was going to give him a hard time for being detached?

"And what kind of reaction are you wanting or expecting from someone who is 'no one'?" He all but growled the words.

"So that's why you didn't return my calls?"

"I called yesterday."

"To arrange a meeting, Reed. That's not what I'm talking about."

This was why he didn't do relationships. What started off fun and sexy inevitably turned to sniping and taking not-so-subtle shots. That much he remembered about his mother and father from the early days. Then, when carefully worded digs were no longer effective, it turned to out-and-out verbal warfare.

He remembered sitting with his back pressed against the living room wall, listening to his mother and father fight. Back then he hadn't known what the word *whore* meant, but later on, the pieces fell into place. His mother had lots of boyfriends and that wasn't allowed when you were married.

"Then what *are* you talking about, Darcy? Because I don't remember us exchanging promise rings or any bullshit like that." He jammed his hands into the pockets of his suit pants. "And you certainly didn't act like I meant anything when you were trying to avoid me meeting your friends. So I really don't understand what's gotten you so pissy."

"You weren't supposed to hear that," she said, her voice softer.

That only made it worse, because it proved Darcy was like the other women he'd dated who said one thing and meant something else. For some unknown reason that realization made him want to stalk off in the other direction.

Why? You never wanted it to be anything serious and neither did she. So why are you both acting like fucking crybabies?

He couldn't deal with this right now. If he wanted drama in his life, then he'd go back to the office and have a chat with Donald Bath. He needed Darcy to play her role and help him hook Dave Bretton. Once the fundraiser was done, *they* would be done.

The thought didn't reassure him the way he'd hoped.

"For the record, it's not the reason I never called," he said as they approached the restaurant where they were meeting Dave and his agent. "I've had a shit storm of things to deal with and my mind has been preoccupied."

"Right." She didn't look at him, her blue eyes fixed on something farther down the street.

She wasn't going to buy his noncommittal explanation; that much was obvious. "Dad's been giving me grief. Turns out he paid the replacement caretaker to leave him alone and no one had checked in on him for days, but Donna didn't know."

"Oh." She tilted her head. "I'm so sorry."

"It's fine. I don't want to talk about it, but I got the impression you wouldn't be satisfied with my vague response."

A sheepish smile played on her lips. "That obvious, huh? I thought you were just saying that to shut me up."

"I was." He pressed his hand to her lower back. "Come on. We have an author's ego to stroke."

....

Darcy caught a glimpse of their reflection in a large mirror that hung in the restaurant's reception area. They could have been any high-powered couple—matching black outfits, him in a custom suit and blood-red tie, her in a blouse and minimal makeup.

They'd walked past the name of this place—Gabriel Kreuther—on the way in. So it was another one of those difficult-to-pronounce places, no doubt Michelin starred, for lunch.

When Reed had texted her the meeting details, he'd specifically pointed out that the dress code was "smart casual, no denim." Darcy had been tempted to text him back a picture of her giving the middle finger. Though his method had been subtler, the request wasn't any better than the comments her mother made about her appearance.

But now that they were in the restaurant, her resentment faded.

This place was fancy with a capital *F*. White linen; plush, patterned carpet that would look at home in Buckingham Palace; floral wallpaper; and a clientele that looked as though they would turn their nose up at anything that wasn't caviar infused. The whole place had an air of crazy, rich, old aunt about it.

She should have swung past her tattoo artist on the way over so he could write *I don't belong* in the center of her forehead.

But this was Reed's world. Well, the Reed she knew from *before* the baseball game. The Mets hoodie–wearing Reed was someone else. Someone who opened up about his past, who came to her house and gave her the most amazing orgasms she'd ever had in her life. That was the Reed she'd hoped she'd see today.

But she'd slapped that Reed in the face by calling him no one. She cringed.

The maître d' stopped in front of a table in the back corner, where two men were waiting. She recognized Dave Bretton instantly—she'd thought him attractive once, with all his wavy, dark hair and chiseled features. But next to Reed he looked like a poor imitation of the original piece of art. A cheap knockoff.

"It's an absolute pleasure, Mr. Bretton. Thanks for having me along to your meeting." She stuck out her hand. "I'm a huge fan."

Over the course of the next hour and a lot of weird food, including foie gras—she still wasn't certain from which animal it originated—she proceeded to watch Dave and Reed act like a couple of gorillas beating their chests for male superiority. No wonder the first meeting hadn't gone very well. Dave had an ego that filled the space around them like a noxious gas. He enjoyed talking about himself and diverting any thread of conversation away from business and back to his own life.

"The fundraiser is the perfect opportunity for you to start rebuilding your profile in the industry. We'll use it to replace the negative news articles with positive ones, and get people excited for the new book." Reed sipped his water. "The charity event will expose you to a lot of important people and, of course, we'll have press there."

"Reed, what you don't seem to understand is that I *am* the important people," Dave said.

Darcy's eyebrows rose in automatic disbelief, but she covered it by reaching for a napkin to dab her mouth. Oh boy. Reed's patience was starting to thin—the muscle in his jaw was ticking and there was a vein pulsing in his neck that made it look as though he was about to lose it.

"We're going to have our full library staff at the event," Darcy said, pressing her hand to his thigh under the table, silently asking for him to give her a shot. "I know they love your work as much as I do. It would be a tremendous honor to have someone of your caliber at our event. We'll be the envy of all the other libraries."

"Well," Dave said, shifting his gaze back to her. "I wouldn't want to disappoint the fans."

"Reed has done a great job creating a guest list of people that will really help our library to thrive with their generous donations," she added. "But you would be a *huge* draw. If there's any way you could help us by coming along, we would be forever in your debt."

"And we can parlay this event into a broader PR plan specifically designed to promote not only your successful works, but also you as an industry leader," Reed said. He squeezed Darcy's hand under the table.

"I think that sounds fantastic." Dave's agent, Mike something, nodded enthusiastically. "I know the publisher will be thrilled, and that's excellent timing as we're about to go into negotiations for a film deal."

"Really?" Darcy didn't have to feign excitement that time. "I've been hoping that they'd make the Martin Pollinger Chronicles into a movie for years. You'll be making the fans very happy."

"Fine." Dave threw his hands up in the air. "I'll do it. Can we quit with the business talk now? I want another drink."

"Darcy and I should head back to the office, but I'll send the waiter over to take your order." He pushed back his chair and stuck his hand out. "Of course, lunch is on me."

"Damn straight." Dave reluctantly grasped his hand.

"I'll have my assistant draft up a contract for you to sign and we'll get the event details to you both as soon as possible."

Darcy shook Dave's hand and tried not to squirm when he turned his wrist so that he could kiss her knuckles. She was grateful she'd already finished his book, because something told her she might not be able to pick up another one of his stories without feeling a little slimy.

"How did I do?" she asked as they walked through the restaurant.

"Brilliant. I don't know where all that gushing came from, but I'm not going to question it." He held the door for her as they exited.

"To be honest, I feel dirty." She frowned.

"Welcome to my world," he quipped.

"The sad thing is, I love his books. You really should read them. They're a lot of fun."

Reed looked past her. "I don't read fiction."

She blinked. "Like, at all?" What the hell was the point of living without books? That was *not* a world she wanted to be part of.

The afternoon had grown warm, and the further into summer they ventured, the stickier it was getting. Even Reed, who seemed perpetually cool despite the weather, shucked his jacket.

"I've got to head back and get a contract drafted to make Bretton an official client," he said, ignoring her question. "The event is mostly done, but I'll have my team confirm the last details. I would suggest you get the library staff to read at least one of his books each, because the last thing we need on the day is for him to get pissy."

"Duly noted." She bobbed her head. "But I was hoping we could talk."

About what? There's nothing to say. If you want closure on a one-night stand, you picked the wrong guy.

Reed's wary gaze swept over her. "Let's grab a drink tomorrow after work. We can talk then."

"Okay. Sure." She nodded.

"I'll come by the library when I'm finished with work." He touched her shoulder but the gesture felt stilted and uncertain.

"Any dress code this time?" she said, hoping she sounded as light and unaffected as she wanted to.

His lip quirked, but it didn't turn into a smile. "Just be you, Darcy."

....

The following day, Reed stared out the window of his thirty-sixth-floor office. When he was younger, he used to imagine he could cut the other buildings in half to see what was going on inside. The first time he'd even set foot into this office, it had been to vacuum the floors.

Not many people knew he'd started out as a janitor, just like his dad. And it wasn't something he liked to talk about either. Edward Weston had hired him out of pity after meeting him at a career fair held by Reed's high school. They'd been stuck together after the fair closed, Reed waiting for his detention to begin and Edward waiting for his driver.

What an odd pair they'd made. Edward had asked him what he wanted to do with his life and Reed, the smart-ass, had answered that he'd probably end up like his father—poor and alone.

Edward had offered him a job on the spot, with one condition: Reed had to stay in school. So he did. He stayed in school and cleaned the offices three days a week, trekking in and out of Manhattan on the subway. Eventually, Edward had offered him an upgrade, working as a mail boy and general office gofer. Then it was an internship. Junior consultant.

Now, Reed was a partner, and up until recent events had shattered his reputation, he had been known as one of the best in the industry. He pressed a palm to the window as though it might help him to reconcile the tattered heap that was his life right now. Sure, Dave Bretton's business would make up for some of the lost clients.

But he was still in the doghouse with Donald and the other partners. It felt like people didn't take him seriously anymore. He'd confronted Melissa about whether she'd used the site to post reviews about him and had been met with a smirk and a "no, of course not." But her face said it all, and if she'd done it, then who knows how many other people had used the same tactic to get at him?

He made the decision not to waste his time on people like Melissa. If there was one thing he'd learned in all his years of PR, it was that you could drown yourself in the small stuff. The petty stuff.

Bad Bachelors was the big problem here.

However, perhaps it was time that he shouldered some responsibility for his actions. He *did* sleep around a lot, and though he never cheated on anyone, he kept people at arm's length. He had probably been harsher than he should have simply because he wanted to make sure nobody got too close. It wasn't a way of life he'd wanted, but rather an act of preservation after watching his father fall apart and stay that way.

But Darcy has pushed passed all that.

She'd snuck in when he was worn down and desperate for someone to believe in him. Even the people he usually went to for advice—his father, Edward, and Gabriel—had acted like the issue with Bad Bachelors had been partly his doing. Yet Darcy, who'd started out pricklier than a porcupine, had warmed to him when he needed it most.

Or maybe it's that you're sick of acting like nothing affects you… and she does. She's so terrifying because you can see how it might be with her, how you might want to take that risk.

Was that possible? Could he take a risk and do the one thing he swore he would never do: allow someone to make him vulnerable?

He glanced at his watch. He was supposed to meet Darcy for drinks in forty minutes so they could talk. What the hell was he going to say?

I really like you, but I'm scared of people leaving me.

No fucking way. McMahon men swallowed their fears like pills; they didn't put them on display for the world to see.

"Reed?" His assistant's voice came through the intercom speaker on his desk phone. "I've got Donna for you. Can I put the call through?"

"Yes, of course." He snatched the receiver up when the light blinked. "Hello?"

"Hi, Reed. It's Donna." The tone of her voice put every nerve ending in Reed's body on high alert. Her usually calm and soothing voice was wire tight.

"What's wrong?" he barked.

"It's your dad." Her voice hitched and Reed's stomach plummeted. "You need to come to the hospital now."

"What the fuck happened this time?"

Kerrie poked her head in at the sound of his raised voice, her brows knitted with concern. Reed scrawled the words *Driver, Now* on a piece of paper and handed it to her.

"He… Oh God." Donna's voice broke. Damn it, was she crying? "He got into the pill cabinet and…"

"Christ." The room spun around Reed and he slumped back into his chair. "Is he…?"

"They've pumped his stomach and admitted him for observation. They have a special room." Her words were stilted, raw. "There's a window so people can watch him, to make sure he doesn't…"

Reed's stomach heaved and the phone clattered to his desk as he rushed to grab the trash can next to his foot. Donna's voice came through the line. "Reed? Reed, are you there?"

His stomach contracted violently, and his breathing was short and ragged. But the nausea subsided before he could bring anything up. Instead, he was left with his throat burning and raw from coughing. A hand landed on his shoulder, and he jumped. He hadn't even noticed Kerrie come back into his office.

She picked up the phone. "Donna, it's Kerrie. Give me the details and I'll get our driver to bring Reed over right away."

Reed braced his forearms against his thighs and lowered his head to his hands. The world was still uncertain beneath his feet, and when he eventually pushed up, he swayed.

"I'll come with you," Kerrie said.

"No." He shook her off. "I need you to cancel drinks. Darcy, the contact for my library client. Her number should be in my email somewhere."

There was no way he'd let anyone see him in this state. Because the second he saw his father, he was either going to scream the roof off the hospital or cry. Like a kid.

"I'm fine," he said, sucking in a breath and straightening his shoulders. It took a moment, but the swaying stopped and the panic was slowly smothered. "Please clear my day tomorrow and the day after, and inform Edward that I'll be taking a short leave of absence."

"Of course." Kerrie nodded. "If there's anything else I can do…"

"I'll check in tomorrow afternoon, so we can look at what else needs to be done." The words echoed in his head. It sounded like he'd decided to go away for the weekend, rather than going to visit his potentially suicidal father.

Good. That's exactly how you have to sound.

Chapter 22

"I think the term 'ghosting' was invented because of Reed McMahon. One minute everything is sexy and steamy; the next, you're wondering if it was all a dream."

—*Don'tCallMeBaby*

*D*arcy turned her phone over in her hands as she stood outside her mother's house in Bensonhurst. The call from Reed's assistant had thrown her for a loop and she found herself anxious and unsure of where to go. Remi and Annie were still at work.

But Darcy needed to take her mind off worrying about this man and his father when she had no right to do so. Her finger hovered above the doorbell. Would talking to her family make it better or worse? She never could tell.

She jabbed at the button and the bell chimed inside. A few seconds later, footsteps sounded and the door swung open.

"What a nice surprise." Her mother's face lit up for a second before faltering. "Is everything okay? Are you hurt?"

Wow. Had it been *that* long since she'd dropped by just because? "Hey, Ma. I'm fine. I was close by so I thought I'd see if you were home."

"Come in." She unlocked the screen door with a smile. "I've already finished dinner, but we have leftovers. I can make you a coffee too?"

"Coffee would be great." The house was quiet. Only the sound of the grandfather clock ticking away in the living room broke the silence. "Where is everyone?"

"Cynthia is at a work function and Genio has gone to visit Enzo and Maria."

"You didn't want to go with him?"

Marietta gave a cheeky smile. "Even old married women need time alone. Cynthia showed me how to record my shows, so now I don't miss out even if Genio wants to watch something else during the day."

Her mom was having a girl's night watching soap operas by herself. A quick glance into the living room confirmed that she'd eaten on the couch too, something Darcy never thought her mother would do.

"I don't want to interrupt if you're having some peace and quiet," Darcy said.

"Nonsense." Marietta patted her arm. "You never drop in anymore unless I tell you to come. I feel like I have to call it a family meal so you'll actually visit."

Normally the comment would have gotten under Darcy's skin, but her mother had a point. These days she only came by because of Cynthia, that's how much she'd let her relationship with her mother deteriorate.

"Come. I'll put the coffee on."

She followed her mother into the kitchen and leaned against the counter, trying to figure out where it had all gone wrong. The wedding. If Bridezillas were a thing, then what was the equivalent for the mother of the bride? Marietta had stuck her nose into everything from the dress choice to the catering to the floral arrangement to the guest list. She'd wanted a say in it all…and then, when it all went to hell, she'd done nothing but criticize.

"I made some biscotti this afternoon," Marietta said as she pulled the old-fashioned Bialetti coffeemaker from the cupboard. No matter how many times Darcy had offered to buy her parents a fancy espresso machine, they refused. "It has almonds and orange peel. I'll pack some up for you to take home. I'm sure Remi would enjoy them too."

"I'm sure she would."

She watched as her mother made the coffee—scooping the grounds into the filter, filling up the bottom chamber, and screwing the two components together. There was something ritualistic about it. Darcy remembered being a little girl and watching her mother repeat these exact steps over and over.

Marietta had been her world then, her perfect *mama*. Before Genio, before Cynthia. Before Darcy became the other child. Tears pricked the backs of her eyes.

"Hey." Marietta set the coffeemaker down on the stove. "What's wrong?"

"It's nothing." She blinked the tears away, but her eyes were already feeling raw and watery. "A friend got some bad news about a family member. I'm worried for them."

"Oh no." Marietta frowned. "I'll give you extra biscotti then. You can take them to your friend."

Typical Italian. Always thinking that food would solve the world's problems. "Thanks, Ma."

"It's no trouble. I'll make another batch for Genio tomorrow."

"I, uh…" The weight of all their differences suddenly fell heavily on her chest. Coming here had dredged up the past, and now she couldn't find the strength to push it back down. "I got rid of my wedding dress."

Bracing herself, she waited for the torrent of criticism. The verbal lashing. But her mother only sighed.

"I know."

Darcy blinked. "You do?"

"I saw the photographs." Her mother's mouth was downturned, but not in the way that usually accompanied a complaint about her appearance or single status. "The album. Cynthia and I were looking for the remote when we were at your apartment and I found it hidden under the newspapers."

"Oh." So her hiding spot hadn't been that well thought out after all.

"I wish you had told me." Marietta sighed. "Actually, I wish you had told me you didn't want to keep the dress, so we could have done something with it instead of ruining it with paint. It was such a beautiful dress."

She swallowed. "I hated it."

"Really? But you looked so beautiful. Like a princess."

"I'm not a princess, Ma." She shook her head. "Don't worry. I'm sure Cynthia will get married and you'll be able to dress her up like the perfect angel she is."

Her mother went back to the stove, turning away so Darcy couldn't see her expression. When the coffee was done, she poured the steaming, dark liquid into two cups and added a dash of milk to each.

"Do you think I'm harder on you than I am on Cynthia?" She carried the cups to the small, rickety table squashed into one corner of the kitchen and they both sat.

"Yeah, I do."

She cradled her coffee cup. "Maybe I am."

It'd been a long time since Darcy really looked at her mother. They only shared a few features—the small, heart-shaped face and vibrant-blue eyes. But everything else was different. Her mother had given more to Cynthia—soft brown hair, olive skin, pert nose, and small frame. Whereas Darcy assumed she got her near-black hair and porcelain complexion from her father...whoever he was.

"I worry that you don't see your own potential," Marietta said, working her way through the words slowly. "I worry that you sell yourself short because you don't think people will like you. It's why I saved the top of the cake."

She sipped her drink, trying to understand what her mother was saying. "That doesn't make sense."

"I wanted to remind you that even though it didn't work out that time, it doesn't mean it won't happen in the future. Time goes on, even when we don't want it to." She paused. "I didn't want you to give up on finding love because of one bad experience."

"Oh."

That's certainly not the message she'd taken from it. But, in fairness to her mother, Darcy had been hurting too much to ask her to clarify. The anniversary of getting jilted had hit her harder than she'd expected.

"I guess I'm tough on you because we're so alike. When I see you getting frustrated, it reminds me of how I felt and I get angry at myself that I couldn't save you from that heartbreak."

Darcy stared at her mother. Never before had Marietta spoken to her like this…but then again, Darcy had always eschewed any real conversations, convinced she would end up feeling like even more of a failure in her mother's eyes.

"When I eventually found Genio, I was glad I kept going. I had told myself that was it for me. In those days, being single with a baby was not a respectable thing. Good girls didn't get pregnant before marriage. I thought all men would see me as baggage." Her eyes became misty. "But I loved you so much I was determined to set a good example. I would find the right man and I would be a good mother to you, even if I had started out so badly."

"Because you got pregnant by accident?" She swallowed. "It happens. And, as much as I don't agree with it, I get why you never wanted to talk about him. But it would have been nice to know who he was."

Marietta looked down as though grappling with her own demons. "I never told you his name because I don't know his name."

Her mother's words hit her like a punch to the solar plexus. All this time, she'd led Darcy to believe he was an old boyfriend who broke things off after news of the pregnancy.

"What do you mean you didn't know his name?"

"I had a one-night stand. I know his first name was Peter, but I never knew his last name." She reached into a pocket and pulled out a linen handkerchief to dab her eyes. "I knew you wouldn't be able to track him down with a first name alone and I was too ashamed to tell you."

"Oh my God." She reached out and grabbed her mother's hand. "I had no idea."

"I thought to myself, 'How can I be a good mother when I can't even give her this one thing she wants so badly?'"

Darcy thought back to all the times she'd asked about her father. The requests had become more and more demanding through her teenage years, and all that time, she'd assumed the withholding of information came out of her mother's selfishness. But instead it was shame.

"I'm sorry," her mother said, squeezing her hand. "I have no idea where he is, if he's dead or alive. I don't know."

"Why didn't you tell me?" she asked.

"Probably for the same reason you weren't going to tell me about the dress." She sipped her coffee. "We fear judgment from the ones we love."

"And rejection," Darcy added.

"And you'll realize this one day if you have children of your own, but they all need different things from their mother." She smiled, her expression wistful as if recalling a happy memory. "Cynthia was such an easy baby. She hardly cried and she slept well from the beginning. You were...difficult."

"So not much has changed, huh?" Darcy toyed with her coffee cup.

"As you both grew up, I realized you were difficult because you needed to figure things out for yourself. You were curious. Cynthia needed a lot of guidance and feedback, but you were stifled by it." She offered up a wry smile. "Not that I am very good at keeping my opinion to myself. But Cynthia always made me feel like she needed me close by, but you were ready to escape and rebel the second I gave birth to you."

"Sounds like me." This time it didn't feel like a criticism though. Darcy and Cynthia were different people—inside and out. And that wasn't a bad thing.

"I never quite knew how to be there for you. Sometimes it feels like the harder I try, the worse I do. We get under each other's skin so easily."

Darcy smiled. "Yes, we do."

"I don't agree with everything you do. I never will." She looked pointedly at Darcy's tattoos. "But I don't love you any less for it."

"I needed to hear that." Darcy nodded her head. "The whole thing with Ben totally shattered my confidence. You're right, I *do* want to get married and have a family someday. But I'm scared of picking the wrong guy again."

"Do you know I hated Genio at first?" Her mother had a mischievous twinkle in her eye. "He asked me on a date and I told him I wouldn't date him even if he were the last man on earth."

"You did not!"

"I did." Her mother nodded. "He used to tease me all the time when we worked together at the church functions. I thought he was cocky and rude."

"Then why did you go out with him?" Darcy planted her elbows on the table and leaned forward, fascinated.

"Because he was cute. Then I found out that all that bravado was a cover and he was a sweet man." She laughed. "Not that anyone would know it, since he acts like such a grump all the time."

Sound like someone else you know?

"All my friends thought I was crazy to go out with him. They used to tell me he'd break my heart. But I knew different." She tapped a finger to her chest. "When we were alone, I saw who he really was…and I liked that person very much."

She couldn't help but think of Reed and the way he tried so damn hard to care for his father—and the way he'd made her feel when they'd slept together. He'd seen how scared and vulnerable she was and made her feel desired and beautiful instead.

And the truth was, she wanted to explore that more. She wanted to learn his soft spots and find the dents in his armor. She wanted to see who he was, stripped of all his self-protection.

"Thanks for telling me the truth." Darcy sipped her coffee and leaned back in her chair.

She wasn't sure how she felt knowing the door was closed forever on finding her father—save for possibilities with DNA testing, if that kind of thing was even an option. She had no idea. But at least now there wasn't this barrier between Darcy and her mother. They'd bridged some gap created by the stress of organizing a wedding and amplified by the events that had followed.

"I ran into Ben recently," Marietta said. "I wasn't sure whether you'd want to hear about it."

"He's called a few times." A few months ago, this conversation might have sent her running. But the past was finally starting to stay where it belonged—behind her. "I haven't taken his calls."

"He told me as much," she said.

Darcy sucked on her lower lip. "Where did you see him?"

"At the supermarket. He was shopping with Mark. They asked about you." She smiled. "He seemed happy. They both did."

Darcy nodded, waiting for any ill feelings to surface. But none came. "I'm glad he was finally able to be himself."

"They're getting married."

"Oh?" Nostalgia crashed over her like a wave. She remembered how handsome Ben looked in the tux he'd rented for their big day. He'd modeled it at her request the day before it'd all fallen to pieces. "Good for him."

"I know his parents were shocked, but it sounds like everything has worked out. It was a good thing that it happened before you went through with the wedding." She sucked in a breath. "I see that now."

"Yeah," Darcy echoed. "Me too."

....

Reed waited as his father lowered himself into his chair. Donna was still puttering around the house, and Adam had grumbled at her until he was near blue in the face, but she insisted on tidying up before she left. Although it did appear that her nerves were starting to fray if the look she shot Reed was anything to go on.

"I can do it," Reed said.

"It's fine. It's what you pay me for." She collected Adam's mostly untouched dinner from the dining table.

"I'm still here," Adam snapped. "You can include me in the conversation."

Reed shot her an apologetic look, but she waved his concern away. No doubt the poor woman dealt with this kind of stuff on a daily basis. He made a mental note to slip her some extra money next time.

Adam had been home for two days after being kept under observation for seventy-two hours, while they watched his vitals and had him speak with a psychiatrist. They'd referred him to a local mental health clinic, and he was supposed to be seeing them the following day, but Adam had got it in his head that he didn't need to go.

"Are we going to talk about this?" Reed asked after Donna had left. "You've been home two days now and you're acting like nothing happened."

"Nothing did happen." Adam's voice was steely.

"You overdosed on painkillers, Dad. That's not nothing." Reed gripped the edge of the sofa because all he wanted to do was slap some sense into the old man. "You nearly gave me a heart attack and poor Donna... Thank God she was here."

"It was a mistake." Adam rubbed a hand over his face. "I took a few pills and they didn't work, so I took a few more."

"What were you doing, swallowing them by the handful? They're not fucking breath mints."

"I couldn't remember how many I'd taken."

Reed hung his head. The doctors had told him that his father's blood alcohol content was well over the legal limit. Not that he would have been driving anywhere, but the combination of drink and pills wasn't a good one. Adam was adamant that it was all a mistake, muddled thinking caused by the booze. But what was he doing getting drunk anyway?

"You need to tell me what's going on, Dad." Reed swallowed the panicky feeling in his chest. "I can't help you if you keep it all locked up."

"And talking about my feelings like a crybaby is going to help?" he scoffed. "It's not how we McMahons do things."

That was the old Irish roots coming out. Men didn't talk about their feelings—they dealt with problems by drinking and fighting. Adam wasn't in a state to throw any punches, but the man had a barbed tongue that would cut to the bone if he wanted it to.

"Fine. If you don't want to talk to me, that's okay. I'll be taking you to see Dr. Preston tomorrow anyway." Reed cleared his throat. "But I'm going to talk now."

Reed figured the only way his father might get past his refusal to talk was if he took the first step. But where to start? They had years—decades—of shit to work through. Even when Reed's mother left, his father had only said, "She's gone and she ain't coming back," and that was that. Every time he'd tried to ask about it, Adam had changed the subject.

Ever wonder if that's why she left? How would you work through marital problems if the other person wasn't willing to talk through the issues?

It made him sick to his stomach to empathize with his mother, but now he was starting to see why their marriage might have gone south.

"What happened to that girl anyway?" Adam said.

"You're not changing the topic."

"That your way of saying you got bored?" His father coughed into his handkerchief. "What was wrong with this one? I thought she seemed nice. It's the first time you've brought someone around here."

"She's a friend."

Adam scoffed. "You don't have female friends."

"Says who?"

"The newspaper." He pointed to a stack in the middle of the coffee table that Donna had tried unsuccessfully to tidy up. Adam had refused to let her throw the old ones out, and the tower had become unwieldy.

"You know it's all bullshit. They write whatever will sell papers, doesn't matter if it's the truth." Damn it. His father was goading him into arguing again, steering him off topic so they didn't have to talk about the painful stuff. "Nice try on distracting me too."

Adam harrumphed. "You're a thorn in my side, you know that?"

"Someone has to be. Because as much as Donna cares, she's not family. *I* am." Reed swallowed the frustration clawing up his throat. "I'm worried about you."

"You should be more concerned with what's going on in your own life."

How was he supposed to say that everything in his life *was* about Adam? The job and the money it brought was what kept him going, knowing he could care for the man who'd raised him. The rest—friends and baseball—was simply an outlet. There wasn't anything else of significance.

"Family is what matters to me." Reed picked at the frayed edge of the couch cushion. Once everything was settled down with work, he'd buy a new sofa to replace this eyesore. "You always said we had to stick together because no one else would care about us."

Adam heaved in a big, rattling breath. Reed tried not to notice how skeletal he looked these days—his cheeks were hollowed out, darkness pressed through the thin skin under his eyes. If only he would eat a little more. Reed was counting on this Dr. Preston to help his father deal with whatever messed-up voice was telling him to give up, because nothing Reed said made a lick of difference.

"I think I've done you a disservice, Son." The words were spoken so quietly that Reed only just caught them.

"What do you mean?"

"I was so angry after your mother left, and I poured that anger into you for the next fifteen years." He sighed. "Instead of shielding you from my pain, I let you carry it around. I let it eat away at you."

"No you didn't."

"I did." His jaw clenched. "I was too weak to move on with my life and I…poisoned you."

"Dad, stop."

Reed pushed up and went to his father. But he wasn't sure what to do—they didn't hug; they didn't comfort with physical touch. Yet the desire to connect with his father felt like the most important thing that he could do right now. With uncertainty, he placed a hand on his father's shoulder. A safe start. When Adam didn't shrug him off, Reed gave him a tentative squeeze.

"You didn't poison me."

"Didn't I?" Adam raised a bushy, gray brow. "So you enjoy changing women like you change your underwear?"

"I don't have time for a relationship."

"Bullshit," he spat. "You don't want to put yourself out there because you're worried you'll end up like me. *I* did that to you."

"She did it!" Reed couldn't hold back the angry swirl of emotion that tracked through his body, making his hands shake and his head pound. "She said she loved us and then she left and never looked back. What sane person would choose to go through that?"

He hadn't realized he'd shouted the words until he felt the scratch in the back of his throat. God, he needed to get a fucking grip. He'd barely slept a wink the last week, trekking to and from work and the hospital, forgoing solid meals and a real bed to spend as much time with his father as he could. But it was catching up with him. He needed to face-plant into his duvet and stay there for a few days.

"You blame her for how I am." It wasn't a question.

"You started smoking because of her when you'd never touched a goddamn cigarette in your life." Reed folded his arms across his chest. "It's not exactly a leap."

"I picked up the cigarette, I put it in my mouth, and I lit it."

The creases in his father's face deepened. "And then I did it again and again and again. It's *my* fault."

"But if she hadn't left—"

"Son." Adam looked up, the sadness in his eyes wrenching a hole in Reed's chest. "I have to take responsibility. I should have done it a long time ago. Your mother left because I wasn't a good husband."

The voices in his head wanted to protest *But she promised!* However, Reed knew it was pointless. His father seemed hell-bent on shouldering the burden.

"Now," Adam said. "If we can wrap up this Dr. Phil bullshit, I'd appreciate it. I'm going to take a nap." He made the slow ascent from his chair and Reed stepped out of the way, knowing better than to help. "Donna put some leftover pasta in the fridge if you want to eat."

"I'm not hungry."

Adam grunted. "Funny how it's okay for you to say that."

Reed bit his tongue and watched his father shuffle from the room. He had no idea what to make of Adam's confession. True, the old man was tougher than an overcooked steak and twice as gristly. But whatever happened about till death do us part? Half his colleagues at work were divorced and shelling out alimony to wives who probably never had any intention of sticking around. As for Gabriel...well, he was one of the lucky few. An anomaly in marriage-land.

His father could try to take the blame as much as he liked, but Reed knew the truth: people were out for number one.

But his mind flicked to Darcy. She'd been calling him all week, and every time her name flashed up on his phone, regret stabbed him in the gut. He should never have let her get so close. All the red flags were there—bringing her to see his dad, going to her house. The stupid "double date" with her sister.

Not to mention he'd sent himself into a tailspin over her denial that he was anyone important. The words *no one* were branded into his brain as a reminder of why he needed to protect himself.

Adam was right—there was no way Reed would let himself end up in pieces like his father.

Chapter 23

"It took me a long time to learn this, but sometimes you just have to accept that people can't be fixed."

—*HappilyMarried*

*D*arcy had been in a holding pattern ever since her meeting with Reed last Wednesday. Her thought process was running circles faster than a puppy chasing its tail. She'd reach for her phone, chicken out, reach for it again, call Reed, avoid leaving a voicemail, and then convince herself that was the last time she'd call…until she reached for her phone again.

Pathetic.

By Monday afternoon she couldn't take it anymore. So she'd done what any normal girl would do—liquored up and gone to deal with the problem in person. Like any good person with Italian heritage, she'd also brought food. Specifically, another batch of biscotti from her mother. Homemade food was homemade food, right? Shouldn't matter who'd made it.

She'd even wrapped the parcel up in red ribbon and put a tag on it with Reed's father's name. Hopefully the gesture would come across as thoughtful, rather than desperate, but Darcy was a little out of her depth. Not to mention the rum she'd downed at the bar around the corner from his office had gone to her head more than expected.

It's Dutch courage. You need it… How else would you be able to convince yourself to line up for potential humiliation?

She stood in front of Reed's office building, bouncing from one combat boot to the other. For a moment, back home, she'd wavered on whether to borrow a dress and those stupidly expensive flats from Remi. But then she wouldn't have been much better than the girl who'd bought a blouse for her honeymoon thinking it's what a wife should wear. Reed could take her as she was.

"Come on," she said to herself. "It's now or never."

If she walked away from this, it might take her another year to work up the courage to try again. Putting herself out there had required a lot of mental to-ing and fro-ing, as well as a little help from Captain Morgan. She swallowed past the lump in her throat.

Why are you even here? He's ignoring you for a reason.

The gremlin in her head liked to say destructive things like that. It had a whole arsenal of criticism stockpiled, but she was over listening to that crap. Since finally laying it all out with her mother, she'd done some serious thinking.

She'd even called Ben to congratulate him on his engagement.

The conversation had been awkward as hell, but she'd needed the closure. And Ben had said something that'd stuck with her: *There were no signs for you to see because I spent every hour of my day trying to hide them.*

It'd eased the burden a bit, allowed her to lift some of the blame from her shoulders. Not that it meant much in the grand scheme of things—she'd still fallen for the wrong guy, and she might still make mistakes in the future. But what she realized now was that there was no way to safeguard against that, aside from committing to being alone…and she didn't want to do that. She wanted love—the kind that Ben and Mark had. The kind that her mother and Genio had. The kind she now realized was blossoming between Cynthia and Brad, despite her initial impressions.

She not only wanted it—she *deserved* it. And she was strong enough to take a chance on Reed. Strong enough to face potential rejection, because she knew now that it was better to try and fail than to settle.

Squaring her shoulders, she walked toward the huge, gold-trimmed building and stepped through the turnstile. By the time she made it up to the thirty-sixth floor, her heart was pounding. She had no idea what she was going to say to him, because every time she tried to devise a script, her brain would scramble.

"Can I help you?" It was the same receptionist she'd seen on her last visit to the Bath and Weston offices.

"I'm here to see Reed McMahon, but I don't have an appointment."

"Let me check if he's available." She picked up the phone and spoke with someone whom Darcy assumed was Reed's assistant. An eternity passed before she returned the phone to the receiver. "He's going to come out and meet you. Take a seat in conference room D. He'll meet you there."

The receptionist directed Darcy down a small corridor. There were four rooms in total, all with glass walls and identical white tables and white leather chairs. Each room had a matching clear vase with white flowers and a modern-looking black-and-white print on the wall. The sameness unsettled Darcy—she wanted to find a can of paint and fling it across the pristine room. It couldn't have been further from her library, with its scribbled rainbow drawings and glitter masterpieces.

She walked into the room and sat in one of the chairs, her head feeling a little fuzzy from the alcohol. Maybe she should have stopped at two. She tapped her fingers against the tabletop in time with the seconds ticking away on the clock on the wall in front of her. It was bland and white and silver, just like everything else in this damn office.

Bouncing restlessly in the chair, her eyes darted to the corridor every few seconds. What was taking him so long? Perhaps he was working on a speech to let her down gently? Or what if he'd decided he was over her and had picked up someone else?

"Darcy."

Hearing her name in Reed's smooth baritone was like a jolt of electricity to her body. Warmth rippled through her as she looked up, taking in his arresting form in all its magazine-worthy glory. He seemed even more attractive now, because she knew what he looked like out of his three-piece suit and smiling instead of frowning. Wait, why was he frowning?

"I thought we had everything ready for Friday." He came into the room but didn't sit. Shadows curved under his eyes and his mouth was a grim line. He looked utterly exhausted.

"I, uh... No, everything's fine with the fundraiser." All the warm, fuzzy feelings from the alcohol evaporated into thin air. Now she was exposed to the chill in Reed's stare, unprotected and vulnerable. "I've been trying to call you."

He closed the door behind him with a click that sounded far too ominous for an inanimate object. "It's been a busy week."

"How's your dad?"

His Adam's apple bobbed, but the rest of his face remained impassive. A mask. "He's going through a rough time, but I'm getting him the help he needs."

She could read between the lines, and it damn near broke her heart. When his assistant had called to cancel their drinks, she'd only said it was a family emergency. But Reed's tone was far more telling. For all his faults, he loved his father like nothing else.

"I brought him something." She gestured to the parcel wrapped in butcher's paper and tied with ribbon. "They're homemade Italian biscuits. Confession, I didn't make them. My mother did. But they're *very* good."

"You shouldn't have."

Normally when people said that, it was meant as an offering of thanks. But, for some reason, it sounded like she should take it at face value. He was still standing, leaving a good few feet between them. Brows creased. Hands clasped in front of him. The absence of their usual spark settled in the pit of Darcy's stomach like a stone.

"I wanted to," she said, pushing the parcel toward the empty seat on the other side of the table. He nodded. The muscles in his jaw twitched. "Can you sit? You're making me nervous."

He hesitated for a moment but pulled out the seat across from Darcy and dropped down into it. He'd popped the button on his suit jacket, exposing the tailored vest underneath. She'd never been one for a guy in a suit, but *damn* he managed to have this sexy, aristocrat vibe going on, and it was doing all kinds of good things to her libido.

She waited for him to tease her about staring, but his facial muscles were rigid. "So…uh…" She swallowed down the nervous flutter in her stomach. "We were supposed to talk last week. I understand why you had to cancel, of course, but I was hoping we'd be able to reschedule."

"I don't have the time, Darcy." He raked a hand through his dark hair as though she was trying his patience. "I'm sorry. But things are tense here, even with me signing Dave Bretton. I'm dealing with a lot of backlash over the Bad Bachelors articles, and frankly, I'm about one wrong look away from telling all of them to go fuck themselves."

She cringed. Obviously she hadn't picked the best day to drop in for a chat. "I understand. It's just…I get the impression you're avoiding me and I wanted to make sure that wasn't the case."

He stared at her blankly. "Like I said, I've been busy."

"I get that." She gripped the edge of her seat, her knuckles turning as white as the walls around her. This wasn't going how she'd planned. "But it would have taken five seconds to send a text back to say, 'Hey, I'm busy. I'll call you when I can.'"

"Because I owe you something?"

The words made her reel as if he'd slapped her across the face. "I'm not saying you owe me anything, but it would have been nice—"

"You're saying *exactly* that."

"Well, when you canceled on drinks and then didn't answer my calls, I thought something might've happened to..." She shook her head. "I was worried."

Darcy's nervous system had gone into meltdown mode. Her heartbeat was accelerated, her cheeks overheated. And all this when she wasn't quite sure what she'd hoped to gain by coming here.

Bullshit. You know exactly *what you wanted to gain.*

This whole weekend had been a total joke. She'd been like a zombie, ambling around the library aimlessly, shelving books in the wrong spot and forgetting people's names. All because there was this sense of unfinished business with Reed.

"I appreciate your concern, but I have everything under control."

"I know we never discussed where this was going," she said. "But you don't have to shut me out like I'm a stranger."

"I don't understand what you want from me," he said. "We're not in a relationship and our work is on track. We're not even friends."

"You're right. I guess I would have known that you were engaged once if that were the case." The words popped out of her mouth and she regretted them instantly.

Way to tell him that you're still reading up on him like some obsessive internet stalker.

....

"Let me guess: you read the article about Barbara," he said, rolling his eyes. "You and everyone else in this goddamn city. Christ, why can't people mind their own business?"

Even mentioning that wretched site had him wanting to breathe fire. But thankfully, progress had been made in that area. His PI, Peter, had been frequenting the coffee shop where Barbara had met the interviewer, Leanne. Armed with Barbara's description, he'd managed to track the woman down. Turns out for all the secrecy behind Bad Bachelors, this particular woman was a creature of habit.

Each Wednesday and Friday, she'd arrive with her laptop sometime around 10:00 a.m. and order an Americano, work for an hour, and then purchase a sandwich to go before leaving. Peter hadn't made contact. *That* moment of glory was going to be saved for Reed. If it hadn't been for his father's hospitalization last week, he would already have confronted Leanne. But now he had to wait till Wednesday.

"You know I defended you to my friends when they told me I was crazy for sleeping with you," she said. Now two pink splotches colored her cheeks and her arms had folded tight across the front of her Mother of Dragons T-shirt. "I said you were so much more than what Bad Bachelors claimed."

The words rooted him to the spot. On one level, it was validation, proof that someone could see the real him. That he could *allow* someone to see the real him. But that was exactly the problem—with Darcy, he had let down his guard. He didn't feel the need to give her the facade he showed everyone else. Which was exactly why her declaration that he was no one had cut him straight to the bone.

He could see it now, Darcy facing judgment from her friends about being with him. She'd been...embarrassed.

"Was that before or after you said I was nothing?" He let the sarcasm give his words a razor-sharp edge.

"How is that different from what you do?" She was on the defense now, her hackles raised. He hadn't played into her sweet, little hands like she'd thought he would.

Damn it, he was hurt. And that pissed him the hell off, because he was supposed to be better than that. It was his own fucking fault for being tempted by the sympathy she'd shown him and his father that day at the hospital. He'd gotten a taste for it, let himself crave more than was safe.

Already, she was throwing things back in his face. If he let himself fall for her, how long would it be before he was in his father's shoes—broken and hopeless?

"How is it different from what I do?" He curled his hands around the edge of his chair to stop himself from slamming a palm against the desk. "Do you mean when I introduced you to my father? When I let you into the one part of my life that I keep to myself?"

Emotion flashed across her face like a bolt of lightning. He'd said too much.

"No, you're just quick to listen to a bunch of anonymous women on a website." He let out a bitter laugh. "Not all of them are even real reviews. I don't screw so many people that I forget them."

"I never said—"

"You implied." He leaned back in his chair and watched the kaleidoscope of realization shift over her face. "How easy would it be for them to hop online, create a fake account, and pretend to be some jaded woman? My job has been hanging on by a thread and there are people waiting for me to fall."

"Reed, I'm sorry—"

"No." He held up a hand, his whole body pulsing with frustration. "Thanks for proving you're like everyone else."

She pushed up out of her seat and planted her hands on the table. "I came here to tell you I want to be with you."

The words sucked the life out of the meeting room. He didn't know she'd shouted the words until two of his colleagues gaped at them from the other side of the glass wall. When they caught the end of his glare, they hurried on, heads bowed. No doubt headed straight for the office kitchen to pass on the gossip.

"I mean…" Darcy shook her head. Clearly the confession wasn't planned. "I just… You're right. I judged you and I'm sorry. I was worried about my friends meeting you and passing judgment because they *do* believe what people are saying."

"I'm glad you've found it in yourself to be honest," he drawled.

"You're not going to give me an inch, are you?" She clucked her tongue and the little silver ball flashed in the light.

His brain was trying to do too many things at once—namely, processing that she wanted to be with him (whatever the hell that actually meant), and fortifying the walls he'd put in place long ago to protect himself from this very situation.

The only way he'd be able to put a stop to this once and for all would be to make sure she stayed away. Frustrated and worn out as he was, he didn't want to hurt Darcy. In fact, the only thing he *did* want was to bundle her up in his arms and kiss her until they'd smoothed over all the mistakes and missteps and hurtful words.

But his life was already in the toilet, and he couldn't afford *anything* that might throw him off track. It was taking every ounce of his willpower to keep coming into work and making small talk with the assholes he knew were talking shit behind his back. But he was doing it for his dad.

"Darcy, I have nothing to give you. Not an inch, not an apology, not an excuse."

Her large blue eyes blinked at him, blinding him with her determined sincerity. For once, she didn't have a mouthful of comebacks and snark…which made him feel even worse.

"I feel like we have something. I'm not experienced at the whole casual hook-up thing…but that night you came to my house wasn't just sex." Her perfect, pouty mouth pressed into a tight line. "We talked about some really painful, personal stuff. You trusted me with that. And I trusted you."

"I thought I could win fucked-up family bingo." He shrugged.

"Okay, Mr. Smart Guy. So that's normal, is it? You sleep with a girl and tell her all about your life?"

Hell no. It was the furthest thing from normal. He'd told Darcy more even than Barbie Waverly, who was a true friend. Ice dripped down the length of his spine. It terrified him how much Darcy could cut through his bullshit. In mere weeks, she knew him better than anyone else.

You were too busy not taking her seriously to see how much she'd gotten under your skin. She crept into your life via the side door when you were fortifying the front.

"You're right, I don't." He stood, hating himself more with every breath. "But I'm not looking for a relationship. And even if I were, I wouldn't be looking for it with someone like you."

The blue of her irises looked even more vibrant as tears glimmered, threatening to spill. "What do you mean, someone like me?"

"This whole 'fancy pants' fundraiser thing—that's my world. Gala dinners, media, and reporters. Places like that restaurant where we had lunch with Dave Bretton." The words burned on the way out like cheap liquor. Her expression was totally unfiltered, the hurt pouring from her like he'd cut her open. "When I settle down, I need someone who fits in with that scene."

She dropped her head, her eyes skating down over her kitschy T-shirt and denim cutoffs. To him, she looked like a million bucks—far better than any polished society girl in a ball gown. Christ, why did she have to keep pushing his boundaries? He was already hurting, frustrated. He was using that to push her away—and what had she done? She'd been honest with him and taken the sting out of his anger.

Reed felt like the biggest asshole on the face of the earth, but this was the only way he knew how to protect himself. To ensure she didn't try again when his willpower was weak. Because the second he'd woken up in her bed, her smile lighting him up, he could see himself bending to this woman—he could see himself falling hard and fast until he ended up bachelor roadkill on the Manhattan sidewalk.

Given what had happened next, he was right to be concerned. She would ruin him like his mother had ruined his father, and he would allow her to do it.

"I see." She bobbed her head, her gaze stuck on the floor as she wrapped her arms around her waist. "I'm not well dressed or pretty enough to be anything real to you. Good to know."

She turned and walked from the room while every fiber of his being screamed at him to go after her. To throw himself at her feet and beg forgiveness. But it was better this way...no matter how much it felt like a colossal mistake.

Chapter 24

Dear Darcy,

I want you to understand why I did what I did.

A good part of my job is rewriting someone's mistakes. I can turn even the most vile human into someone you might consider having a drink with. It's a skill, one I used to be proud of. Something I almost never do, however, is issue an actual apology. It implies ownership of an error and means taking responsibility, two things I'm not very good at.

~~I behaved poorly. Reprehensibly.~~ I really fucked up.

I wish I could take back every word I said because I intentionally hurt you and each day that kills me a little more. How I feel about you frightens me.

You were right. It wasn't just casual sex.

I don't know how to make it better.

*R*eed stuffed the piece of paper, with what was probably the world's most pathetic apology on it, into his pocket. Darcy was a librarian, for crying out loud. A bookworm. She'd probably read love letters from the Shakespearean period that made his attempt look like something a first grader had vomited up.

It'd been two days since she came to his office and there hadn't been a peep since. He suspected she hadn't breathed a word of it either, since Brad had mentioned that Cynthia wanted to get the four of them together after the game on Sunday.

He wasn't sure if that made him feel better or worse.

His phone buzzed. A text from Peter Law: She's here, give me a few minutes. Reed drained the rest of his Americano and forced himself not to turn and look. He was about to meet Leanne of Bad Bachelors...not that she knew it yet. After Peter had figured out who she was and what her schedule looked like, they'd devised a plan.

Peter was going to pose as a source—a colleague of Reed's ready to spill the beans—and set up a meeting using a temporary Bath and Weston email address. Reed was going to be lying in wait, ready to hijack the meeting. Luckily for him, Leanne had suggested her usual café, which was full of business folk, so he blended right in at the bar.

His phone buzzed again: Back corner. Now.

He looked up and caught the back of Peter's stocky frame and shaggy, gray hair. Leanne was hidden, her back to the corner, which would no doubt seem like the perfect, intimate spot for an interview.

Throwing a few dollars onto the counter to cover a tip, he slid off the stool and headed toward the back of the seating area. He was at their table before she even looked up, but the second his eyes met hers, he realized something was wrong. For starters, he *knew* this woman, and her name wasn't Leanne.

The round pixie face of Darcy's best friend, Annie, stared back at him. "Well, well." Her pert, little nose turned up, but a deeper emotion flashed in her eyes as she swung her head between Peter and Reed. Fear. "Here to threaten me, Mr. McMahon?"

"It's Reed." He stood at the edge of the table, casting a shadow over her. "Since you seem to know me so well, there's no need for such formality. Although I take it your name isn't actually Leanne?"

"Legally it is. But everyone calls me Annie." To her credit, she didn't try to run from the confrontation. In fact, she seemed to relish it. Her dark eyes glinted as she turned her gaze to Peter. "I suppose this was all a ruse. Clever. I didn't see it coming."

Peter pushed up and shuffled out of the tight space. He planted a heavy hand on Reed's shoulder. "Good luck."

Reed dropped down into the seat opposite Annie, but a hard lump of ice had settled at the base of his spine. Any petty pleasure he might have taken from this meeting had dissolved the second he saw her face. It was hard to think of this woman as some cartoon villainess now that she was a real person—not to mention someone connected to Darcy.

He propped one ankle on the opposite knee and let the silence drag out for a few extra heartbeats. Annie shifted in her chair, but she didn't attempt to leave. The woman was prepared for a fight. "Are we going to dance around it, or are you going to admit you're not just a writer for Bad Bachelors?" he asked.

She cocked her head. "What makes you say that?"

"I've done some digging. I know Bad Bachelors isn't deriving an income, at least not through any obvious means." He cocked his head, studying her. "So I doubt you have money to pay staff."

"Then you'll also know Bad Bachelors was set up to maintain the privacy of the people who run it. It could be anyone." Her voice was cool and calm.

"But it's not anyone, is it? It's you."

She lifted a suit-clad shoulder in a delicate shrug. "Rumors are funny like that: lots of people like to take a guess, but no one really knows."

He ground his back teeth together. "Yes, I am aware of that."

"Did you come here to waste my time playing a guessing game, Reed?" She reached for the latte in front of her. "Because, believe it or not, I have a day job to get back to."

He leaned back in his chair while his mind whirred, desperately searching for a solution. The plan had been simple—meet this mysterious Leanne and threaten to expose her as the owner of Bad Bachelors. Because, after trawling the site, he'd collected dozens of names of other men who'd be very interested in knowing the identity of the person behind the blasted site making their lives miserable.

But now his plan was anything but simple.

"You're friends with Darcy." He blurted the words out because the rest of the script had flown out the window the second he'd laid eyes on her.

What does it matter? You and Darcy are done.

But every time he said it to himself, his body rebelled, as if physically incapable of processing the thought. No matter how hard he tried, saying her name still caused his heart to thump and the feeling hadn't lessened since their conversation. But he was out of his depth now, beyond the precedent set by any previous dating debacles.

He wasn't supposed to regret calling this off.

"I am. Did she tell you we've known each other since we were kids?" She might have been able to keep her expression neutral, but her eyes betrayed her. They were hard. Judging. "We grew up together. She's practically family."

"So I guess you trusted her enough to tell her that you run Bad Bachelors, then?"

"No, I haven't told her." Her eyes searched his face as if waiting for a reaction. But he didn't give her one. "What do you want, Reed?"

"You've caused trouble for a lot of people."

"And by 'caused trouble' you mean I've given women a platform to help one another and be informed." Annie sipped her coffee. "Yes, I have."

"Please," he scoffed. "Half the reviews on your damn site aren't worth the pixels they're displayed on. I know some of my reviews have nothing to do with my dating habits."

"I work very hard to weed out fake reviews," she said indignantly. "I've designed an algorithm that specifically targets bogus accounts. I know it's not perfect—"

"So you *know* they're not all real." His jaw ticked.

"I take the steps any online business would to ensure quality data," she stammered. "But if you have enough enemies willing to make fake accounts, that's more of a reflection on you than it is on my business model."

"Why are you targeting me?"

"I'm not. I don't know you." Annie sucked on the inside of her cheek, her gaze roaming him for a second. "But I know your type."

"So I was simply the lucky guy who rose to the top of the shit heap?"

"Something like that." Her lips twisted. "But the fact that you hurt my friend didn't help."

Ah, so that's when it had become personal.

"Who do you think she came to in tears after her little visit to your office on Monday? She was a wreck, Reed." Annie's smug expression shifted to unadulterated animosity. "It took me hours to console her. How *dare* you treat her like that."

Letting her leave his office had been one of the hardest things he'd ever done in his life. Her tearful expression had been a recurring image, haunting him nightly. He tried to tell himself it was a small pain now to avoid a larger pain later, but the more he repeated his mantra, the less impact it had.

"I deserve that." He nodded. "But you've made my life hell, Annie. You don't *know* me. You don't know how hard I work, what I do for the people I care about."

Guilt flashed across her face. "It's not about how you treat the people you care about. It's about how you treat everyone else."

"It's not really about how *I* treat anyone though, is it?"

She'd admitted it herself—she wasn't targeting him until the morning he'd walked out of Darcy's bedroom. But Bad Bachelors had been talking about him for weeks before that.

"Why did you create the app?" he asked.

"Because I wanted women to know who they were getting into bed with." She swallowed. Annie might have had a good poker face, but Reed could still detect the slight waver in her voice, the way she white-knuckled her coffee cup.

This was a woman who'd been hurt. Badly.

"It's hard to find someone who doesn't say whatever's necessary to get what they want," she added. "As I'm sure you're aware. You've made a career out of twisting the facts after all."

"I never twisted anything with Darcy. I was up front with her from day one." Up front, yes. But he'd still shut her out the second things got complicated.

"You *hurt* her." Annie frowned. "She really liked you, Reed. Against my advice and everyone else's, she thought there was something worth pursuing."

He could tell Annie was torn. It was obvious that Darcy *was* very important to her and that she was pissed at him for how he'd treated her. Rightfully so. But if she really had built an algorithm to fish out fake profiles, then perhaps her intentions with the app weren't to bring people down. Maybe she really did want the truth.

And *that* was something he could appeal to.

"And you thought it would help Darcy to create a fake interview with my ex-fiancée?"

She looked down into her coffee. "That wasn't one of my finest moments, I'll admit. And I've removed the interview and apologized to Barbara."

He bit back the urge to ask when *his* apology would be forthcoming. "Thank you," he said. "She was really stressed about it."

"So what, you've come here to change my mind about Bad Bachelors?" She looked at him warily. "I'm not going to shut it down."

"Look, you said before you wanted to create something to help women be informed. I get that. But this thing has taken on a life of its own." He curled his hands over the edge of his knees. "Don't you see how this kind of thing is ripe for abuse? An algorithm can only do so much. I *know* that I haven't slept with all the women who've put a review on my profile. That isn't giving people the truth."

"It's better than nothing," she said earnestly. "Do you have any idea what it's like to pin your hopes on someone only to find out they've been going behind your back?"

"I do." He nodded. "Not in a romantic sense, but I know what it's like to love someone and have them walk out on you without warning."

She drew her bottom lip between her teeth and worried it back and forth. For a moment he thought she might cave, that perhaps his appeal had hit its mark.

"I can't, Reed. I'm sorry." She shook her head. "This whole thing is too important to take down. I see comments on the app every day of women thanking me for giving them a fighting chance to protect their hearts. I can't let that go."

"Originally I came here to tell you to take down my profile and all the articles about me." He raked a hand through his hair. "I was going to threaten to release your identity to the public. People are very interested to know who's behind Bad Bachelors."

She stared at him, eyes wide. "You wouldn't."

He *wanted* to. God, how he wanted to. But doing that would be the final nail in the coffin of him ever having a chance with Darcy.

You sent her away. You ended it. This should be the perfect solution to make sure it stays ended.

But the truth was, he didn't know if he could go on like this. The night after their chat, he'd gone home and drowned his sorrows in a bottle of tequila Gabriel would *not* have endorsed. It'd burned a fiery path down the back of his throat on the first shot. But each subsequent glass had made it easier, and eventually, he'd stopped feeling anything at all. Since then, food had lost its taste and he hadn't left the office before midnight to avoid being home alone. Correction—to avoid a pathetic drive past her house to see if she was okay.

If he turned on Annie now, he wouldn't have a hope in hell of getting her back.

Why the hell would she take you back? You have nothing to offer her—there's no white picket fence, no big, soppy declaration of love.

Love. It was something he'd feared like a monster under his bed. Ever present. Waiting for the moment to strike. In his mind, love equaled vulnerability, which equaled pain. Abandonment. Hopelessness.

"If you ever *really* cared about Darcy, you wouldn't do that." Annie's nostrils flared, panic glimmering in her eyes.

"I *do* care about her. Present tense." There it was, cards on the table. She'd won; he'd lost. "I care about her very much."

He was about to pass up the one possible solution to his problem—without being able to expose Annie, he had nothing. No way of erasing the reviews, no way of getting anything else but Bad Bachelors to come up when people searched for his name. No way to redeem himself with his clients.

She folded her arms across her chest. "Then how could you have said what you did?"

He wanted a hole to open up under his feet and suck him down into the bowels of hell. It was all he deserved for the way he'd behaved. His father's situation wasn't an excuse. The stress with his job wasn't an excuse. Through it all, she'd been a source of light. The bright spot in his week.

And he'd thrown it back in her face by telling her that she wasn't good enough. *Asshole.*

"I can't justify it." He raked a hand through his hair. "She got too close and I got scared. I lashed out, simple as that."

If only it were as simple to reverse. That night after, he'd gone to visit his dad and had screwed up further by spilling the whole stupid incident to the old man. Adam had chewed him out in a way he hadn't experienced since he was a teenager.

It dawned on Reed at some point around three o'clock in the morning that ending things with Darcy had been a unique experience. With her, he'd had to lie about how he felt to break things off. Usually, the truth about his disinterest did the work for him.

"Well done, you've admitted to acting like a man-child. So what?"

"I want to make it up to her." He dug his hand into the pocket of his suit pants and pulled out the crumpled piece of paper. "I sat there"—he pointed to the stools along the edge of the café's countertop—"and wrote this before I had any idea you were connected. I can't control what you believe, but I swear I regret hurting her more than I regret any of the other stupid things I've done in my life."

He waited for the pain and embarrassment to rise up, for some recognition of the risk he'd taken in baring himself to someone who had the power to use it against him. But it didn't come. In fact, the imaginary weight around his neck lightened, allowing him to drag more air into his lungs than he'd been able to in days.

Annie took the paper from him, her expression hesitant. As she scanned the letter, her lips quirked. "This is terrible. You know that, right?"

"I'm aware it's not Pulitzer-worthy," he ground out. "But it's honest."

She stared at him for a long moment, the pause stretching out until he felt compelled to break the silence. But when he opened his mouth, she held up a hand. "You came here to threaten me today. Are you still planning on going through with that?"

He pictured Darcy's sweet face, her sharp, blue-eyed gaze, and that snarky, perfect mouth.

"No," he said. If there was any chance at all Darcy might forgive him, he wasn't going to ruin it by feeding her friend to the wolves... no matter how much satisfaction it would give him personally. He would have to fix things at work the old-fashioned way—by putting his head down and hoping his work would speak for itself. "I'm not."

"I'm still not going to help you," she said. "I won't take your profile down or the articles. They bring in huge traffic for my site."

"Fine." He stood and grabbed the letter from her hands, shoving it into his pocket. "Don't remove anything. But I *am* going to apologize to Darcy, and if by some small miracle she decides to give me a second chance, you'd better not interfere. I'm sure you're going to tell her Bad Bachelors is your site at some point in the future."

Annie's lips tightened. "Of course I'm going to tell her…in the future."

"Do the right thing," he said. "And so will I."

....

Darcy walked the length of the table displaying the silent auction lots. Reed had outdone himself. They'd secured the garden pavilion at the Bryant Park Grill, right next to the New York Public Library, which was fitting. The outdoor area had been decorated with fairy lights that mimicked the glow of the city towering around them. It was glamorous but cozy. There was an air of romance about it with the majestic, old building behind them and Bryant Park stretched out in front.

Of course, it was still bigger than *Ben-Hur* and packed to the brim with important-looking people in expensive-looking outfits. At one point, Remi and Annie—who'd come along for moral support—had declared they were going to sit on the floor and "shoe watch" for the rest of the night. But there was an intimacy here that made her realize that, despite his faults, Reed was *very* good at his job.

There was a dessert table set up with small cakes in the shape of books, all iced in different colors with classic titles piped in precision frosting text. They'd covered all the big names—Hardy, Poe, Twain, Tolkien, Shelley. But they paled in insignificance to the centerpieces on each table, which were small stacks of color-coordinated books flanked by vases of flowers and tea-light candles in matching hues. Each place setting had personalized nameplates with a famous literary quote, including one that made her throat clench.

In the end, we all become stories.

As much as she'd wanted to hate how he'd turned her small idea into something big and fancy, she had to admit it was breathtaking. The menu they'd selected together had been perfect—delicious and impressive, without being hard to eat. And she'd heard nothing but praise from her branch manager, who appeared to be having the time of her life.

The lots for the auction were lined up along a table covered in a white cloth, with a piece of paper sitting in front of each one. They had a few beautiful pieces of jewelry from local artists, vouchers to a fancy hair salon, and tickets to a Broadway show. Plus, Reed had convinced Dave Bretton to auction off a personalized critique for any budding writers in the room, as well as a few advanced copies of his next book with the opportunity to have Dave sign them at the end of the night.

He must have leaned on the agent as well, because there was a basket of goodies from Dave's publisher that included some more sought-after advanced releases. Darcy wouldn't mind getting her hands on that particular lot, though she doubted her wallet could compete with anyone else's in the room. But she jotted her name and a paltry dollar amount down on the bidding sheet anyway.

"Got your eye on something?" Reed's voice startled her and she jumped.

"Way to sneak up on the guests, creep-o."

Damn it. So far she'd managed to avoid him all night, slipping between clusters of people whenever her radar picked him up. Remi had run interference on a few occasions, but now her wing-ladies were nowhere to be seen.

Just freaking perfect.

The last thing she needed was to have a meltdown in front of a crowd. And, if the last week was anything to go on, she'd lost her ability to keep the waterworks under control along with any budding hope that perhaps falling for Reed wasn't the biggest, stupidest mistake of her life.

Yeah, she fell for him. Hard. The one guy in the city who could only be counted on to walk away. The one guy who was so bad, his Bad Bachelors profile practically said *You* will *get hurt*. If that wasn't proof she had a death wish for her heart…

"Can't you even look at me?" he said.

He was standing close, the shadow of his nearness causing her to both recoil and gravitate toward him. Her mind screamed at her to run, but her heart—her stupid, stupid heart—tugged her closer. This was the limbo created by her poor judgment.

"What do you want, Reed?" She turned to him, determined to prove she was the bigger person. That she'd moved on.

God, why did he have to look so damn good in a tuxedo? His hair was mussed just so, his bow tie perfectly knotted at the base of his neck. Her hands itched to smooth over the silky lapels on his jacket, to graze the mother of pearl buttons that formed a line down his chest.

"This is your event, I wanted to make sure you're happy with how it turned out." His dark eyes simmered with things unspoken.

"This is *your* event." She waved her hand, gesturing at the room around them. "Can't you tell? I don't really fit this scene, do I?"

Hurling his words back at him should have been more satisfying. But the tightness in his jaw and the bob of his Adam's apple only made her want to cry—and maybe scream until her throat was raw.

"Darcy." He reached out to touch her, but she flinched and pulled away. "I know you hate me right now, but I want to apologize. Can we talk after this is all over?"

"You've talked enough." Her voice betrayed her by wobbling, the threat of tears evident in her high, uneven pitch.

"Please."

If she didn't know him any better, she might have said he looked sincere. His dark, heavy brows were crinkled above worried eyes. His full lips were downturned, his jaw muscles tight and twitching.

"I need to set things right." He rocked back on his heels. "It's been eating me alive, how we ended things."

She wanted to correct him, because *he'd* ended things. "It's hard to end something that hasn't started."

"You said this wasn't just sex." He stepped forward, and she pressed back against the auction table. "That we had something more."

"Consider it a moment of delusion and the product of reading too many Jane Austen novels." She swallowed, her breath stuttering in her throat. "I was mistaken."

"No, you weren't." He placed his hand on her bare arm, but she brushed it away. "*I* was an idiot. A frightened, cowardly idiot."

"We were both idiots." The table pressed into her butt, and she curled her hands around the soft, linen-covered edge, squeezing until her fingers ached. She needed to remember the pain he'd caused her. "I knew you were bad news, yet I didn't listen to that little voice."

"What little voice?"

"The one in the back of my head that told me you'd chew me up and spit me out." Her throat closed around the words. "I knew you'd hurt me, yet I walked straight into the flames without any protection."

He squeezed his eyes shut. "Darcy, I'm sorry."

"Save it." Her eyes flicked to the front of the room, where her boss had stepped up to a small podium at the front of the room. "I think it's your time to shine."

Chapter 25

Thank you all for coming. On behalf of the Hawthorne Public Library, I'd like to extend our deepest gratitude for your attendance at this event. Your generosity is going to affect real change for the local community, meaning that kids in the area will have access to important after-school programs, and a wider variety of learning technologies and skill-development initiatives.

When I took on the task of organizing this fundraiser, I was ignorant about the importance of libraries and the people who work in them. Naively, I assumed that the internet had made them redundant. But I was proven wrong by an incredibly special librarian who, upon first meeting me, told me I was in need of a book on etiquette and manners. Truer words have never been spoken...

D arcy braced her hands around the edge of the sink, her breath coming in great gasping lungfuls. The reflection in front of her was a sorry state—red-rimmed eyes, smudged mascara, a deep furrow in the center of her forehead. Hardly glamorous enough to be in the restroom of such a place, let alone rubbing elbows with New York's rich and philanthropic.

"Are you okay?" Annie and Remi stood on either side of her, Annie rubbing soothing circles on her back.

"It's this dress," Darcy lied. "It's too tight."

The slinky, beaded slip clung to her waist, but it was far from the reason for her hiding in the restroom.

"So it had nothing to do with Reed's speech?" Remi said.

Goddamn Reed. The second her boss had called him forward to make a speech, she should have run. But no, she had to torture herself by watching the whole room swoon at his feet while he told some bullshit story about how organizing this fundraiser had changed him. Made him a better man.

Why did he have to drag her into it?

He hadn't spilled the beans about their nonrelationship, but he *had* talked about how she'd impacted his life and shown him what community and support was all about. Then he'd deftly linked it back to the library's values before handing it off to Dave Bretton who'd, thankfully, remained sober enough to deliver a speech that had the audience in peals of laughter. Not that Darcy had stayed. As soon as Reed had made a move to leave the podium, she'd hightailed it to the ladies' restroom. Remi and Annie had burst in a second later.

"Why would his speech affect me?" She willed her heart to start beating at its normal rate, instead of trying to punch its way out of her chest. "He's saying whatever will make people fork over their money."

"I don't think that's true," Remi said. "He seemed sincere."

"The man doesn't have a sincere bone in his body," Darcy retorted. But instead of sounding tough and strong, her lower lip trembled, and she had to fight the urge to throw a fist at her reflection.

Why do you always pick the wrong men?

"You should talk to him," Annie said, almost as if she begrudged giving the advice. "Hear what he has to say."

"I was under the impression you thought he was the spawn of Satan." Darcy looked up, pressing a hand over her stomach to try to soothe the churning there.

"Maybe there's more to him than meets the eye," she said cryptically.

"I doubt it. I think Bad Bachelors hit the nail on the head, and I was too stupid to listen to what they had to say." She glanced at her reflection again and cringed. "I look like something the cat dragged in."

"No you don't." Remi pulled a cotton swab out of her tiny evening bag and swiped it under Darcy's eyes to clean up her mascara. "You look like an accomplished woman who made her library thirty thousand dollars."

Darcy blinked. "Really?"

"You ran out of the room before they announced that bit." Annie gave her arm a squeeze. "And that was just from the ticket prices and Dave Bretton's personal donation."

"He donated money as well?"

"Apparently, Reed twisted his arm," Remi said with a smile. "By the time they close the silent auction, it could be fifty thousand or more."

It was a great outcome, money the library desperately needed, and she'd get to tell Lily they could have her creative writing program back. She should be over the moon.

"It was all Reed," Darcy said, shaking her head. "I wanted to have some Podunk-style thing in the library itself. Probably would have scraped in five hundred bucks at most."

Okay, so he was good at his job. So what? The guy was still a commitment-phobic jerk.

Yes, you hate him so much. So why did you run out of that room like some drama llama?

She didn't want to see Reed being humble and kind, because that would only make it harder. As it was, each night since she'd fled his office had been increasingly painful. Her body craved his, which was bad enough. But her stupid, stupid heart craved him as well.

"Talk to him," Remi said. "At least get some closure."

"I've got all the closure I need." She sucked in a breath. "It's over."

She splashed some water on her face, despite Remi's protest reminding her that her mascara was not waterproof, and then waited patiently while her friend cleaned up her makeup once more. The night would be coming to a close soon, and Darcy couldn't leave before the final event because explaining that to her boss would be harder than trying to avoid Reed for another hour.

The silent auction bid sheets had been gathered up, and the emcee was going through each lot and announcing the winners. Darcy remained off to the side of the room, her back pressed against the wall while her eyes darted around, ensuring Reed didn't sneak up on her again.

Her boss was mercifully busy at the station where guests were writing checks for their winning bids, schmoozing and making important connections and doing all the things Darcy sucked at. Reed shook hands with a silver-haired man who looked vaguely familiar.

"Lot number thirteen, a one-of-a-kind earring and ring set by New York designer Rose Lawson..." The emcee paused. "Congratulations, Mrs. M. Sartori."

There was a small cheer from a woman who had so many rings on her fingers that Darcy was surprised she could raise her hands.

"Lot number fourteen, a basket of exciting advanced reader copies from Gravity Books, including the much-anticipated next installment in the Melbourne Dark Magic series..."

Darcy's ears pricked up. Whoever had beat her paltry fifty-dollar bid would be very happy.

"Congratulations to our event organizer, Reed McMahon."

Darcy snorted. Figures—something else she wanted was snatched out of her grasp by the man himself. She wandered into the crowd, noticing it had thinned out significantly in the last five minutes or so. She hadn't worn a watch and the clutch she'd borrowed didn't even fit her phone. It only had room for "essentials," and apparently, that meant lipstick, not communication devices.

"Congratulations, Darcy." Her boss, Hannah, appeared in front of her. "This was an incredible success. So much so that we're thinking we may do it annually. Although perhaps on a smaller scale, since we won't always have the luxury of a free PR consultant."

"I'm glad it's gone well." The words sounded stiff. Out of the corner of her eye, she could see Reed approaching. Shit. How could she get away discreetly?

"It's gone more than well, my dear." Hannah winked. "This silent auction has been an even bigger moneymaker than the ticket sales."

"Fantastic," she whispered. Reed was closing in, parting the crowd as he strode forward, eyes locked on her.

"Ms. Fratelli." He nodded at Hannah. "I hope you don't mind, but I'd like to steal Darcy away if that's all right."

So polite. Darcy wanted to roll her eyes at his smooth, panty-melting tone.

"Of course." Hannah waved him on with a slightly starstruck smile. "The emcee said we're done with the announcements and the restaurant manager has assured me we can let people linger for a while longer. But the work is done, so if you two want to head off, feel free."

"Shall we?" Reed held his arm out.

"No, we shall not," Darcy said once Hannah was out of earshot. "Besides, don't you have a prize to collect?"

"It's being delivered."

"Of course. Wouldn't want to dirty that perfect tuxedo by making you carry something." She made a noise of disbelief in the back of her throat. "God forbid."

"Thanks, it is a nice tux, isn't it?" He smirked.

"Won't you just go away?" She made a shooing motion and looked around for Annie and Remi. "I don't want to speak to you."

"Can I at least give you a lift home?" he said. "I've got a driver, and it'll be much more pleasant than a cab."

"I doubt that," she said. "I'm going home with my friends anyway."

"Annie and Remi have already left."

Her mouth hung open. "Excuse me? What do you mean they already left?"

"I bribed them." He was totally unabashed. "I really want to speak to you, and I'm worried if we part ways tonight, I won't have the opportunity again."

"So you paid my friends off?" She shut her eyes and pressed her fingertips to her temple. "What the hell?"

A few heads snapped in their direction, and she realized she'd yelled at him. Damn it, could she not control herself around him?

"Please. I only want five minutes. Once it's done, if you want to go home on your own, I will get the driver to take you. No questions asked."

She oscillated from wanting to slap him to wanting to throw her arms around him. When she'd confronted Ben, there hadn't been so much as a protest from his lips about it being over.

"Please," he repeated, his hands finding hers. "I don't like to beg, but I will absolutely do it if it's necessary."

She pursed her lips, forcing her brain to stay in charge of her body because her heart wanted to melt like Frosty on a summer day.

"So beg."

He dropped down to one knee right there in front of every-one, a blasted smirk on his face, before she yanked him back up to standing.

"Jesus, Reed," she hissed, dragging him toward the function

room's exit. "It looked like you were about to propose. Are you trying to start rumors?"

"You told me to beg."

They headed into a pocket of space between the function room and the restaurant, which was semiprivate thanks to a few large potted plants. People came in and out, but no one noticed them.

"You have thirty seconds and then I'm leaving," she said. "If you try to follow me, I swear to God I will kick you in your—"

Reed cleared his throat, interrupting her as an elderly lady walked past, her eyes wide as she placed a hand over her mouth. "Mind the company, Darcy."

"Sorry," her voice dripped with sarcasm. "You see I'm so used to living on a pig farm that I talk like that all the time. You can't expect me to know the rules of your *elite* society."

"I deserved that." He bobbed his head. "You have every right to hate me."

"I don't hate you, because that would require me to have feelings for you," she lied. "And I don't."

If only that were true.

Unfortunately, she hadn't listened to her head. Instead, she'd fallen so hard for Reed McMahon that her entire body lit up whenever she laid eyes on him. And even after all that'd happened, she wanted nothing more than to melt into a puddle at his feet…just like she'd promised herself she wouldn't.

He can't mean anything to you because you don't mean anything to him.

....

Reed waited for the sting of Darcy's words to pierce his skin. But looking at her—her electric eyes bloodshot and watery, her chest rising and falling with shaky breath—he knew it wasn't true. She'd tried to tell him that afternoon in his office the one thing he wasn't ready to hear.

She cared about him as much as he cared about her.

They had this strange bond, built when neither of them was looking. On paper, they should have nothing in common. Yet when he was with her, he lost the sharp edges and rough exterior that normally drove people away. He lost the lens of cynicism that he'd looked through since his mom left.

With Darcy, he was a better man—the man he realized he wanted to be.

"Okay." He nodded, his mind racing for how best to handle this situation. But that was the thing with Darcy—she didn't respond well to being handled. "I still want to apologize for what I said. It was cruel and dishonest."

"It wasn't dishonest." She tucked a strand of dark hair behind her ear. "You're right. I don't belong with a guy like you. I won't be a yes-woman whose only goal is to look pretty."

"That's not what I want."

"You're welcome to waste your next fifteen seconds telling me how you were wrong and how you really want to get in my pants again," she scoffed. "But I'm not buying it."

"Fine. How about I use that time to tell you why I hate libraries?"

Curiosity skittered over her face, but then she blinked and her mask was back in place. "Fourteen seconds…thirteen seconds."

"My mother was a librarian. She used to read to me every single night before bed." The memory of his mother sitting on his bed, her red hair brushing his cheek as she read in her melodic voice, blew a hole in his chest.

"Twelve seconds," Darcy said, but her voice was less sure. Less prickly.

"When she left, I failed English because I refused to read the books they assigned us. I got through the rest of high school by purely reading nonfiction or CliffsNotes, because it was the only type of book that didn't remind me of her." He sucked in a breath. "I hadn't set foot in a library again until the day I came to see you for our first meeting."

"Then why did you want to help us?"

"My assistant's grandson loves your library. They go all the time and she came to me for help. At the start, it was purely because of wanting to help her." He swallowed against the lump in his throat.

"No wonder you seemed so cranky about it."

"But being there with you made me think about libraries differently. Hell, you made me think about *everything* differently."

She wrapped her arms around herself. "You've really never read a novel since you were fifteen?"

"Not a single one."

"And yet you bid on a basketful of books tonight." She shook her head. "What the hell?"

"They'll turn up at your apartment tomorrow morning."

She tried to maintain the annoyed look on her face, but her eyes softened. "You bought it for me?"

"Cost me a pretty penny too. Someone kept trying to outbid me." He huffed. "Too bad for him I was not going to let anyone else have that basket after I saw your name on the bid sheet."

"You can't buy me, Reed. Not even with books." Her hands dropped to her sides and she fiddled with her dress.

God, she looked gorgeous. The floor-length slip was black with a floral pattern created out of reflective beads that glimmered like stars. A tight, black jacket covered her arms and back, the little points at the end of each sleeve giving her a subtle Victorian Goth look.

But the thing that really got to him was the raw vulnerability in her face. The hope.

It wasn't what usually drew him. If anything, that kind of expression on anyone else would have sent him running for the hills because it smacked of expectation. But that was the only thing he'd realized this past week; he *wanted* her to expect things from him. And, more importantly, he wanted to deliver on everything she asked for.

"I never let people get close to me because I'm afraid I'll do something to drive them away," he said. "For a long time I feared being abandoned. But I learned recently it was more a fear of being the *reason* for someone leaving."

"You think you're responsible for your mother leaving?" she asked.

"No, that was her and Dad." He cleared his throat to try and loosen the tightness strangling his words. "But I made her stay away because I refused to take her calls. And whenever she did talk to me, I hurled all my anger at her."

"You were a kid," she said softly.

"I was. But I'm not now." He sighed. "Just as my father is an adult making his own decisions, but I've been blaming my mother all this time."

"Why are you telling me this?"

"Because I lied to you when you came to see me. You're exactly the type of person I want in my life." He plowed on, hoping she'd at least give him the chance to finish what he wanted to say. Because he needed her to know he regretted it more with each day that passed. "I pushed you away because I was terrified if I didn't do it now, then I'd do it in the future when it would hurt more."

She shook her head. "You're just saying that…"

"It's true. And what scares me more is how much you know me. I've shown you more of my life than any other person I've ever met."

Her eyes were wide, full of emotion. "Why?"

"You're the one person in the world who makes me think it *is* okay to let someone in." God, he was bumbling his way through this. Every day at work, he crafted these perfect messages, and now he couldn't seem to get one sentence out without being terrified he was going to blow it with her. But he couldn't feel embarrassed, because he meant it from the very depths of his soul. "I've buried myself in work because I could count on it. But I'm tired of living this shitty, half-assed existence where I come home to an empty house and keep everything bottled up. I'm a zombie, for crying out loud, and I'm fucking tired of it."

It wasn't until he heard the echo that he realized he sounded like a wounded animal fighting for its last breath. But that's how it felt with her—she was his last hope for something more. For something good.

"What if you wake up one day and decide I'm not right for your life?"

He reached out and this time she didn't back away. When his palms smoothed over her shoulders, a ripple ran through her body and he tugged her to him. "That won't happen."

"How do you know?"

"Because it'll be *our* life." He rested his forehead against hers. "You and me, starting from scratch. Baggage and all."

"Okay," she whispered, a smile dancing on her lips. "You might need to send a trailer. I've got a lot of baggage to bring with me."

"I'll help you carry it." His lips grazed hers. "Bring all your books too. I've got some catching up to do."

"I have the perfect one." She grinned, and the sight of that uninhibited smile warmed him from the inside out. "It's a history of manners and etiquette."

"I'll read anything you want." He lowered his head to hers and captured her mouth with a kiss that held the weight of his hope. "I have a good feeling about this, Darcy."

"Me too." Her teeth dented her lower lip in a smile that was so sexy and sweet he thought very seriously about hiding them both behind one of the potted plants so they could take it further. "I think I could love you, Reed McMahon."

"I think I could love you too."

Epilogue

Three months later

The Higher You Climb, the Harder You Fall

The team at Bad Bachelors isn't above admitting when we're wrong. Self-awareness is hot, right?

Former number one on our Bad Bachelors list, Reed McMahon, might be one of the rare cases when it takes the right woman to tame the bad boy. The man himself was spotted carrying a telltale little blue bag earlier this week, and our sources have confirmed that he's popped the question to girlfriend Darcy Greer.

Both parties declined to comment when our head writer reached out to them. But we wish them the best of luck on their pending nuptials, which are rumored to be happening rather quickly.

On that success story, we wanted to take a moment to reiterate our policy with you all. It has come to our attention that some of the reviews on this site haven't come from legitimate sources. Now, while we understand that a lot of passion comes up when talking about the dating jungle, we ask that you please only report on your actual experiences.

With love,

Your Dating Information Warrior

Helping the single women of New York

since 2018

*D*arcy shook her head, snapped her laptop shut, and placed it on the coffee table. "Can you believe this article? Of course I freaking declined to comment. Goddamn Annie."

"I'm glad she told you," Reed said, pulling her back against his chest. "Though I'm guessing you've been sworn to secrecy."

"She wanted me to sign a nondisclosure agreement." Darcy snorted. She snuggled back against him, relishing the soft groan when her butt rubbed between his legs. "I said I would if that's what she really wants, but she knows she can trust me."

Reed nipped at her neck. "You are very trustworthy."

"I wish she would have agreed to tell Remi as well. I hate keeping her out of the loop. But she said the more people who know, the bigger the risk her identity will get out." Her voice was solemn. "I guess people do crazy things when they've been hurt."

She turned in his lap, looking up into his thoughtful, dark eyes and running her hand along the scratchy stubble coating his jaw.

The last three months had been an interesting time. Reed had met with the other partners at Bath and Weston not long after the library fundraiser, and they'd made the mutual decision that it was time for him to try something different. So he'd accepted an opportunity to speak to communication studies students at Pace University on reputation and the media. To his complete surprise, he'd absolutely loved it—the students' enthusiasm and energy had given him back an excitement for his work. So when a part-time lecturing position became available, he'd jumped on it.

Darcy stifled a smile. Her big, bad, suited bachelor had turned out to be a wonderful teacher, and the students were rubbing off on him too. These days, he seemed less cynical about the world. He'd even turn up at her library when he had an afternoon off just to say hello.

When he'd popped the question a week ago, it'd been a surprise. They were still so early in their relationship. But a yes had burst forth from her mouth without hesitation. It was a testament to how right it felt. How right they felt.

She glanced at the ring sparkling on her left hand as she cupped his face.

"Getting distracted by the shiny rock again?" He chuckled and pressed a kiss into her palm. "I would never have taken you to be someone who fawned over a diamond."

"You bring out some strange things in me, Reed."

It was true. She was a different woman these days—her relationship with her family was improved and she was more confident in herself. She'd even taken to wearing the occasional color now that she didn't mind standing out. Remi was most impressed.

"And you in me." He grinned. "Dad keeps telling me I'm like a new man."

Adam McMahon still had his good days and his bad, but his regular sessions with Dr. Preston appeared to be working. Slowly. There hadn't been a single hospital incident in three months. *And* Adam was already talking about how they could manage getting him a more portable oxygen tank so he could be at the wedding when they eventually organized it.

But Reed had wanted to show how committed he was—that this time he wasn't going to walk away. The wedding itself could wait until they knew exactly how they wanted it to go. But the ring was a symbol that he was ready to go all-in.

"You are a new man. A new *literate* man."

"Speaking of which, you're encroaching on my reading time," he said. A worn copy of *Around the World in Eighty Days* was tucked between him and the back of the couch. It was a gift from his father, a family heirloom that was now in their possession.

"Since when do you take books over women?" she said, poking out her tongue.

"Woman," he corrected with a grin. "Singular. And I only want one more chapter. I've just gotten to the good stuff."

"One more chapter," she scoffed, pushing him back against the couch so she could straddle him. "Famous last words."

Acknowledgments

First and foremost, I need to thank my agent, Jill Marsal, who stuck by me as we worked and reworked the premise for this series. Thanks for pushing me to dig deeper and be more creative, and for all the encouraging words along the way.

Huge thanks must go to Cat Clyne, Dominique Raccah, and the Sourcebooks team for giving Bad Bachelors a wonderful home, and for getting so excited about this project. Thank you also to Stephany Daniel, Heather Hall, Laura Costello, Dawn Adams, and everyone else who had a hand in helping to bring this book out into the world.

My writer friends for keeping me sane in this crazy, unique career path, so my eternal thanks must go to Lauren, Denise, Taryn, Jennifer, Mary, Shana, the Nifty Nine, and the Toronto Romance Writers.

Thanks to my incredible friends who continue to share their "stranger than fiction" stories with me, knowing that I *will* use them in a book at some point. Huge thanks to Shiloh, Madura, Myrna,

Tammy, Karen, Lou, Jill, and Luke for helping to make Canada feel like home. And to my family in Australia: thank you for never letting me feel like I'm *that* far away.

And to my husband, Justin: I know I say this constantly, but it will never, ever lose its meaning—I would not be here without you. Thank you for the high-fives, for the tough love, for brushing away the tears, for growing better and older with me. You are the reason I write about love.

About the Author

Stefanie London is the *USA Today* bestselling author of contemporary romances with humor, heat, and heart.

Growing up, Stefanie came from a family of women who loved to read. Originally from Australia, she now lives in Toronto with her very own hero and is currently in the process of doing her best to travel the world. She frequently indulges in her passions for good coffee, lipstick, romance novels, and zombie movies.

Stefanie loves to hear from readers. You can find her at stefanie-london.com.

THE TOURIST ATTRACTION

He had a strict "no tourists" policy...
until she broke all of his rules

When Graham Barnett named his diner The Tourist Trap, he meant it as a joke. Now he's stuck slinging reindeer dogs to an endless parade of resort visitors who couldn't interest him less. Not even the sweet, enthusiastic tourist in the corner who blushes every time he looks her way...

Two weeks in Alaska isn't just the top item on Zoey Caldwell's bucket list. It's the whole bucket. One look at the mountain town of Moose Springs and she's smitten. But when an act of kindness brings Zoey into Graham's world, she may just find there's more to the grumpy local than meets the eye...and more to love in Moose Springs than just the Alaskan wilderness.

"Fresh, fun, and romantic."

—SARAH MORGAN, *USA Today* bestselling author

For more info about Sourcebooks's books and authors, visit:

sourcebooks.com

THE KISSING GAME

She's one kiss away from finding Mr. Right in
this fun, sizzling romance from Marie Harte

Rena Jackson is ready. She's worked her
tail off to open up her own hair salon, and
she's almost ready to quit her job at the
dive bar. Rena's also a diehard romantic,
and she's had her eye on bar regular Axel
Heller for a while. He's got that tall, brood-
ing, and handsome thing going big-time.
Problem is, he's got that buttoned-up
Germanic ice man thing going as well.
With Valentine's Day just around the corner, Rena's about ready to give
up on Axel and find her own Mr. Right.

At six foot six, Axel knows he intimidates most people. He's
been crushing on the gorgeous waitress for months. But the muscled
mechanic is no romantic, and his heart is buried so deep, he has no idea
how to show Rena what he feels. He knows he's way out of his depth
and she's slipping away. So, he makes one crazy, desperate play...

"Marie Harte at her best! *The Whole
Package* delivered everything I love!"

—DONNA GRANT, *New York Times* bestselling author

For more info about Sourcebooks's books and authors, visit:
sourcebooks.com

THE BAD BACHELORS DON'T END WITH REED!

Find out who else has made the list of eligible—and notorious—bachelors in this smart, funny series from *USA Today* bestselling author Stefanie London

BAD REPUTATION

Wes Evans, son of Broadway royalty, just wants to achieve something without riding his family's coattails. Too bad the whole world is talking about his sex life after the notorious Bad Bachelors app dubs him "The Anaconda." But when he sees a talented ballet dancer, he knows she is exactly what he needs to make his show a success.

BAD INFLUENCE

Annie Maxwell had her whole life figured out...until her fiancé left her when his career took off. If that wasn't bad enough, every society blog posted pictures of him escorting a woman wearing her engagement ring. To help the women of New York avoid guys like her ex, Annie created the Bad Bachelors app. But try as she might, Annie just can't forget him...

> "Completely original, witty, and sexy.
> My #1 romance read of the year!"
> JENNIFER BLACKWOOD, *USA Today*
> bestselling author, for *Bad Bachelor*

For more info about Sourcebooks's books and authors, visit:
sourcebooks.com